STING

SANDRA BROWN

HODDER &
STOUGHTON

First published in the United States of America in 2016
by Grand Central Publishing
A division of Hachette Book Group, Inc.

First published in Great Britain in 2016 Hodder & Stoughton
An Hachette UK company

1

A CIP catalogue record for this title is
available from the British Library

Trade Paperback ISBN 978 1 444 79152 5
eBook ISBN 978 1 444 79151 8

Printed and bound by Clays Ltd, St Ives plc

Hodder & Stoughton policy is to use papers
that are natural, renewable and recyclable products and made
from wood grown in sustainable forests. The logging and
manufacturing processes are expected to conform to the
environmental regulations of the country of origin.

Hodder & Stoughton Ltd
Carmelite House
50 Victoria Embankment
London EC4Y 0DZ

www.hodder.co.uk

STING

Prologue

———◅◉▻———

Exactly twenty-two minutes before Mickey Bolden met his maker, he tossed a handful of popcorn into his mouth and said, "A woman walks into a bar."

Shaw Kinnard, hunched forward on the bar stool next to Mickey's and, staring into his drink with every indication of boredom, gave the shot glass of tequila a couple of idle turns. "Yeah? And?"

"And nothing."

"That's the joke?"

"No joke, and not a damn thing about this is funny."

As though he'd been popped with a rubber band, Shaw's boredom vanished. His head snapped around to look at Mickey.

The man's eyes were no larger than raisins and half shuttered by pillows of fat, but Shaw was able to follow their tracking movement from one side of the beer joint to the other. Tempted as he was to take a look for himself, he stayed on his partner's bloated face. In dread of the answer, he asked, "Any woman in particular?"

"Particularly, our woman."

"She's *here*?"

"As I live and breathe." Mickey dusted popcorn salt off his hands. "Currently at one o'clock over your right shoulder, claiming a stool where the bar crooks, so don't turn around, 'cause she's facing this way."

Mickey's grin suggested that the two of them were engaged in easy conversation, when, in fact, Jordie Bennett's unexpected arrival came as a jolt.

"Well this sure as hell screws the pooch," Shaw muttered. "She alone?"

"Came in that way." One of Mickey's puffy eyes closed in a wink. "But the night is young." His smirk only made him uglier, if that was possible.

Shaw lowered his gaze back to his glass of Patrón Silver. "You think she's made us?"

"Naw. How could she?"

"Then what the hell is she doing here?"

Mickey shrugged. "Maybe the lady's thirsty."

"She gets thirsty the day we hit town?"

"Stranger things have happened."

"Strange things make me nervous."

"'Cause you don't have the experience I do," Mickey said.

With unconcealed scorn, Shaw gave the other man a once-over, thinking that in this instance, *experience* amounted to a stupid and dangerous complacency. "I'm not exactly a rookie at this," he said.

"Then you should know to keep your cool if the plan develops a kink."

"A kink? This is a sheepshank."

"Maybe. But until we know better, I'm gonna look at it as a wild coincidence and not jump to conclusions that are probably wrong. Shit happens. Best-laid plans get shot to hell. Sometimes you just gotta go with the flow and improvise."

"Yeah? Well what if the flow floats you into an ocean of sewage?"

"Relax, bro," Mickey drawled. "Everything's okay. She's giving the place a survey, casual like, not like she's looking for anybody in particular. Her baby blues skipped right past me, didn't light."

Shaw snorted as he raised his glass to his mouth. "Because you're butt ugly."

"Hey, there's plenty of ladies that like me."

"If you say so." Shaw tossed back the remainder of his tequila. As he returned the empty glass to the bar, he glanced toward the subject of their interest, who was presently thanking the bartender for the glass of white wine he was setting down in front of her.

She was his and Mickey's reason for being here. *Here* being the boondocks of south central Louisiana. Not *here*, a local watering hole, built of rusty, corrugated metal, unstably situated on the muddy banks of a sluggish bayou. If the establishment had a name, Shaw didn't know it. BAR was spelled out in red neon letters that hissed and crackled as they flashed above the door outside.

Inside, the place was smoky and reeking with the ripe odors of its rough, blue-collar clientele. Zydeco music blasted from the jukebox, which looked like it had ridden out twenty or so hurricanes that were dress rehearsals for Katrina.

He and Mickey blended reasonably well into the joint's general seediness, but this wasn't the kind of place one would expect to see Jordan Elaine Bennett, known to family and friends as Jordie. Yet here she was. Drinking white wine, for godsake. Like that didn't make her conspicuous in a place where the beer was bottled and hard liquor was poured neat.

Mickey scooped another handful of popcorn from the plastic bowl and shoved it into his mouth. Talking around the charred kernels, he asked, "You're thinking her being here is something besides coincidence?"

"Hell I know," Shaw muttered. "Doesn't feel right, is all." He bobbed his head in thanks to the bartender, who wordlessly offered to pour him a refill of tequila then, with accurate presumption, uncapped another long neck for Mickey.

As he took a pull from the fresh bottle of beer, he squinted down the length of it toward the far end of the bar, where it formed an ell. He swallowed, belched lager fumes, said around the burp, "Could be she's just cruising."

Shaw cocked his eyebrow in doubt. "For a man, you mean?"

"Well, why not?"

"She's not the type."

Mickey chuckled and nudged Shaw's arm with his elbow. "They're *all* the type."

"The voice of experience speaks again?"

Mickey gave a sage nod. "Hard to get? Total female bullshit, designed to make us work for it."

Shaw considered Mickey's editorial, then picked up his tequila and shot it. Decisively he set the empty glass on the bar and slid off the stool, making sure as he stood up that his shirttail covered the grip of the pistol holstered on his belt.

Mickey choked on his beer. "Where're you—"

"To test your theory, fat man."

"You can't...she—"

Shaw left Mickey sputtering.

As he ambled along the row of bar stools, he was sized up by drinkers of both sexes. Women regarded him with either speculation or flat-out invitation. Disinterested, he didn't engage, not even with a smile. Men gave him hard, cold, challenging stares, which he returned harder, colder, and more challenging. All looked away before he did.

Shaw had that way about him.

No one had yet worked up enough courage to occupy the vacant bar stool next to Jordie Bennett's. Locals probably understood that she was off-limits to riffraff. In her opinion Shaw must've qualified as such because, as he got closer, he caught her eye, but briefly, before she directed the referred-to baby blues back down to her glass of wine. No change in facial expression, no shift in body language, not a flutter of a single long eyelash.

Unapproachable was Jordie Bennett.

With that face, that body, she could afford to be selective. No two ways about it, she could make just about any man's mouth water.

Which kinda sucked.

Since Shaw had been hired to kill her.

Chapter 1

———◉———

Three days earlier, Shaw had been sunning himself beside a sapphire-blue swimming pool, watching two topless girls cavort in the shallow end, catching a buzz from a tall, pastel drink from which a hibiscus blossom sprouted, enjoying the hedonistic lifestyle that could be bought with new money in Old Mexico.

He was a guest in a villa that sat on a cliff overlooking the Gulf. The white stucco structure sprawled atop a jungle-draped hillside that tumbled down onto the sandy shore. The palatial property belonged to the man Shaw would execute later that night.

However, that afternoon as he'd watched the girls play and sipped the tropical cocktail, he didn't know that yet.

After the swimming party, guests had been given time to retreat to their rooms and change into their casual chic before reconvening for an extended cocktail hour, followed by a four-course dinner served by a deferential, all-male staff who wore white cotton gloves on their hands and carried black pistols belted around their crisply starched uniforms. For dessert each guest was offered his choice of sweet confection, after-dinner cordial, controlled substance, and senorita.

While making his selections, Shaw's cell phone vibrated. He excused himself to take the call and left the terrace for one of the open-air rooms that accessed it. The study was opulently furnished. Too opulently. It attested to the owner's youthful flamboyance and poor judgment.

Shaw answered his phone with a laconic "Yeah?"

A gravelly voice said, "You know who this is?"

Mickey Bolden.

Shaw had spent months trying to win enough trust to be granted an interview with the hit man. Bolden finally agreed to a meeting with Shaw, during which both were watchful and wary...of their surroundings, surely, but mostly of each other. In carefully coded language, Shaw had provided Mickey with his résumé and the extent of his experience in their unique field of endeavor.

Something, maybe his subtlety and disinclination to boast, had convinced Mickey that Shaw was competent. At the conclusion of their coffee date, Mickey said he would be in touch should the need for Shaw's services ever arise. That had been six months ago. Shaw had almost given up hope of hearing from him.

"You still want a job?"

Shaw glanced out onto the terrace where the dessert course had deteriorated into a full-fledged orgy. "One-man show?"

"You partner with me."

"Must be a special gig."

"You want it or not?"

"What's the split?"

"Fifty-fifty."

You couldn't get more fair than that. "When do you need me?"

"Thursday."

That had been Tuesday evening, leaving Shaw very little time to wrap up his job there and get to New Orleans by the appointed time.

He'd had a hundred more questions for Mickey Bolden, but, the opportunity being too good to pass up, and figuring he would get the details of the contract soon enough, he'd put his curiosity on hold and told the man that he could count on him.

It had required some deft maneuvering and tortuous travel, but he'd finished his business in Mexico that night and managed to reach Louisiana with time to spare. He and Mickey had rendezvoused yesterday and then had driven together to the township of Tobias this morning.

They'd spent the day reconnoitering and developing a strategy for how best to go about killing Jordan Elaine Bennett, owner of Extravaganza, a much-sought-after event planning business in New Orleans. She was sister to and only living relative of Joshua Raymond Bennett, a much-sought-after crook.

He and Mickey had followed Jordie Bennett around town as she ran mundane errands. At a little after six p.m. this evening she'd returned home. They'd waited three hours, but she didn't reappear. Believing their target had settled in to spend a quiet Friday night at home, he and Mickey had gone to a local diner for dinner. Over tough steaks and greasy fries, Mickey outlined a plan of attack.

Shaw had expressed surprise when Mickey had identified their target the day before. Now he questioned the expediency of the hit. "Why tomorrow?"

"Why not?"

"Seems rushed. I figured we'd watch her for a few more days, get a better feel for her routine, then pick the best place and time."

"Panella picked our time," Mickey said as he sawed into his T-bone. "And the customer is always right. He wants it done tomorrow, we do it tomorrow."

"He's under a deadline?"

"Looks like."

Following dinner, they'd decided to wash down the bad food with a drink before making the hour drive back to New Orleans. This bar had been recommended by the diner's busboy, whose standards obviously weren't very high.

However, it had suited their purposes, because in no-name places like this everyone kept his head down.

Jordie Bennett sure as hell did. As Shaw continued walking along the bar toward her, she was concentrating hard on her glass of wine as though waiting for it to ferment some more. When he reached the end of the bar, he didn't break stride, but walking right past her, he caught a whiff of expensive perfume. A spicy scent. Something exotic and elusive that would make a man want to conduct a sniffing search for its source along all sixty-six inches of her.

He didn't stop till he reached the listing Wurlitzer against the wall. Standing in the multicolored glow of its bubbling tubes, he propped his forearm on the arced top. The stance put his body at a slight angle so that while he flipped through the song selection cards pretending interest, he could use his peripheral vision to keep an eye on Jordie.

She took a sip of wine with lips straight out of a dirty dream, then lowered the glass to the bar and left her hand resting there. Long slender fingers. No rings. Nail polish so pale Shaw wondered why she'd bothered to spend an hour in the salon that afternoon. Her wristwatch was a basic tank style with a no-nonsense brown alligator strap, more practical than pretty, but you could probably buy a good used car with what she'd paid for it.

A satin bra strap showed in the sleeveless armhole of her simple white top, and, with the slightest motion of her head, it was brushed by long strands of mahogany-colored hair that looked even more satiny. Her sandals were high-heeled and her jeans tight. Perched on the bar stool, her ass looked real sweet.

He wasn't the only man in the place to have noticed. A guy, younger than her by at least a decade, younger than Shaw by twice that, was being egged on by his pool-playing buddies. Fueled by whiskey and goaded by guffaws, he sauntered over to the empty stool beside hers.

"You mind?"

Her small red handbag, no larger than a letter envelope, was lying on the bar, a silver chain snaking from it. She scooted it closer to her, granting the yokel permission to claim the stool.

Maybe Mickey was right, and she was cruising. But she hadn't looked at the would-be Romeo with either recognition or encouragement, and Shaw wouldn't place odds on him succeeding at anything except to annoy her.

Shaw looked toward Mickey to see if he'd observed that she now had company. He had. His porcine face had turned red and sweaty. He was talking on his cell phone. Shaw didn't have to wonder who was on the other end of that call. No doubt Mickey was consulting with their retainer about how they should proceed now that Ms. Bennett's surprise appearance had thrown a wrench into the plan.

Shaw returned his attention to the progression of the romance. As expected, Jordie Bennett was replying to the guy's slurred come-ons with increasing impatience. He was young and drunk and out to prove his appeal to the fairer sex, but couldn't he see that he was way out of his league? Not that Shaw faulted the fool for taking a stab at it. Shag her, have bragging rights for life.

Coming from his blind side, a hand landed heavily on Shaw's shoulder. Automatically he reached toward his pistol.

"Relax," Mickey growled, "it's me." He pointed to the song list. "They got any Merle Haggard?"

Shaw flipped back through a few of the song menu cards. "Who were you talking to on the phone?"

"Who you think?"

"What did he say?"

"Dropped a load of F bombs, then said this dive was getting crowded and we should split. Like now." He subtly tilted his head toward the scene being acted out behind him. The drunk was leaning toward Jordie Bennett at such a steep angle, he was barely maintaining his balance on the bar stool. "What're they doing now? What about him? You see anything that should have us worried?"

Shaw watched the couple for several moments longer, then shook his head. "He only wants in her pants."

"You sure?"

"I'm sure."

"Okay. Let's go." Mickey turned away from the jukebox and led the way to the exit.

Shaw fell into step behind him. He resisted the temptation to take one last look at Jordie Bennett.

As soon as he and Mickey cleared the door, he sucked in a deep breath to try and ease the tension between his shoulder blades and to clear his head of bar fug.

But the outside air was hot and humid, only a little fresher than that inside the bar. His shoulders remained tense as he followed Mickey to their car. They'd left it at the far edge of the parking lot, which was only a fan-shaped patch of crushed oyster shells in front of the tavern.

Mickey wedged himself into the passenger seat. As subordinate partner on this job, it fell to Shaw to drive. Which was okay by him. He hated riding shotgun. If and when a situation went tits-up, he liked having control of the vehicle.

He put the key in the ignition, but Mickey said, "Hold on. We're not going anywhere yet."

Shaw's heart bumped. "Why not?"

"We're doing it here."

Shaw just looked at him, then, "You joking?"

"No. Panella said there's no time like the present."

"Hell, there isn't," Shaw hissed, gesturing back toward the bar. "We were seen in there."

"Which is another reason why Panella said to go ahead."

"That doesn't makes sense."

"Makes perfect sense."

"Only if you want to get caught. Speaking for myself, I don't."

"So then don't get caught." Mickey grunted with the effort of extracting his pistol from the holster lodged between the folds of his belly. "Panella advises against it, too."

"Easy for him to say. It's not his ass that's exposed, is it?"

Mickey gave him a sidelong glance. "First time out and you're going soft on me."

"Not soft, old man. Sensible. I don't see why the fucking hurry."

"I explained that."

"Yeah, but tomorrow would be soon enough."

"Not anymore. Panella has changed his mind. Small town like this, where everybody knows everybody? Word gets around quick that there's two 'strangers' in town."

"Okay. So we wait to do it till she goes back to New Orleans."

"That could be days. She doesn't go into the city on a regular basis. Works out of her house here a lot. Anyhow, it's not our decision to make. Panella says get her done, especially now that we happened to be caught under the same roof as the target."

Shaw understood the reasoning, but he still didn't like it. Not at all.

Mickey kept talking. "Like you, Panella is scared that maybe her showing up here tonight isn't a coincidence."

"That's what I *said*, but I was only mouthing off. Her coming here has gotta be a fluke. There's no way she could know about us."

"Well, whatever, Panella said to do it now, so..." For punctuation, Mickey used the slide of his 9mm to chamber a bullet.

Shaw realized two things: His vote didn't count, and further argument was pointless. "Shit." He pulled his pistol from its holster and glanced back toward the door with the crackling neon sign above it. "So how do you want to do it?"

"We wait here till she comes out. If the redneck asshole leaves with her, you pop him. I'll take care of her."

"If she comes out alone?"

"I'll do the honors," Mickey said as he worked his hands into latex gloves. He passed a pair to Shaw. "You take her purse. Panella says to make it look like a robbery gone bad. A random crime."

"With no connection to either him or her brother."

"With no connection to anything."

Shaw scoffed. "Like anybody will believe that."

Mickey chuckled. "Not your problem who believes what. You'll be far and away, enjoying your half of two hundred grand."

"That'll buy a nice boat."

"That'll buy nice pussy."

"Your mind's in the gutter, Mickey."

He chuckled again. "Where it feels right at home."

Noticing motion from the corner of his eye, Shaw took another look through the rear window. "Here she comes."

"By herself?"

Shaw waited to answer until the door had closed behind Jordie Bennett and no one followed her out. "Yep."

Since the building didn't have any exterior lighting, the parking lot was almost in complete darkness. A pale, slender moon was obscured by the moss-bearded branches of an oak that extended across three-quarters of the lot. There were no approaching headlights from either direction of the narrow state road.

Seizing the opportunity, Mickey opened his car door and got out, moving with more alacrity than Shaw would have thought him capable of. The fat man was jazzed. Mickey Bolden relished his line of work.

But so did Shaw. The tequila shots hadn't given him near the rush that straight-up adrenaline did now.

Being as light-footed as possible, they followed Jordie Bennett as she wended her way through the parking lot. It was jammed with dented pickup trucks and salt-water-corroded heaps. Her recent model sedan was a shiny, sleek standout. She used a key fob to unlock the driver's door.

Shaw captured another drift of that seductive fragrance as she suddenly did an about-face.

Apparently his and Mickey's footfalls on the crushed shells hadn't been as light as they'd thought. Or maybe animal instinct had alerted her to mortal danger. In any case, when she saw them rushing toward her, her lips parted on a quick inhale, her eyes went wide with alarm.

As Mickey swiftly closed the distance between them, his right hand snapped up from his side with precision and deadly purpose.

The sound suppressor on the pistol muffled the shot, but in the surrounding stillness, the spitting noise seemed as loud to Shaw's ears as a fire alarm.

Mickey dropped like a sack of cement, his ravaged head hemorrhaging a red tide over the crushed shells.

Jordie Bennett watched in horror as a stream of blood funneled toward her sandals. Then she looked up at Shaw, who still held his pistol shoulder high and extended toward her. He said, "My half just doubled."

Chapter 2

———◈———

FBI Special Agent Joe Wiley was just about to sit down to a meal of pork pot roast when his cell phone rang.

His wife, Marsha, frowned. She'd had to warm up the dish for him, because he'd come home too late to eat with her and the kids. But she knew better than to object when he said, "Sorry, hon, I need to take it," and clicked on his phone. "Is this important, Hick? I'm sitting down to eat."

"Hate to interrupt," Agent Greg Hickam said, sounding earnest. "But, yes, it's important. Knew you'd want to hear it ASAP."

Giving Marsha an apologetic look, Joe stepped into the utility room. "Okay, I'm listening."

"A few hours ago, Mickey Bolden was found dead in Terrebonne Parish, outside a backwater beer joint about a fifteen-minute drive from Tobias."

And just like that, a hot meal was no longer in Joe's immediate future.

He dragged his hand down his face, over his mouth, past his chin. "I don't suppose there could be more than one Mickey Bolden."

"Probably, but this is the one we know and love. Loved."

"Clarify 'found dead.' I'm guessing he didn't pass peacefully in his sleep."

"Hollow tip fired into the back of his head. Blew most of his face off."

"Then how do they know it's him?"

"Driver's license in his wallet was phony, but the ME finger-printed the corpse. The local authorities got all excited when they saw he was linked to the Billy Panella case and, as requested, contacted the nearest FBI office."

"Lucky us." Joe glanced around the door frame into the kitchen, where Marsha was seated across the dining table from his empty place setting, looking perturbed as she sipped from a glass of iced tea. Into the phone, he said, "Bolden buys it near Tobias on Friday night, only three days after—"

"Tuesday. There's got to be a correlation."

"Are you certain or are you guessing?" Joe asked.

"Damn near certain. Jordie Bennett was on the premises when Bolden was killed."

"Say again?"

"Jordie Bennett—"

"Never mind. I heard you the first time. Holy shit. Wait, you said, *was*?"

"She and Mickey Bolden were in the bar at the same time."

"Together?"

"No. But they left within minutes of each other, she a few after him. But, here's the clincher—her Lexus is still in the parking lot. Mickey was about three feet away from it when he was popped."

"By her?"

"Unlikely."

"Why?"

"If she killed him, why would her car still be there?"

Joe didn't have a clue. "I'm missing pieces. Fill me in."

"A guy in the bar was schmoozing Ms. Bennett. She asked him nicely to get lost and, when he didn't, she told him to go to hell, grabbed her purse, stalked out, and hasn't been seen or heard from since."

"Jesus. Please tell me that I'm not hearing this."

"Sorry, but you are," Hick said. "She's unaccounted for."

"I thought we had local guys surveilling her since Tuesday."

"Guy. One. Well, two sheriff's deputies who've been rotating shifts. The night shift officer logged her leaving her house at nine thirty-two. In no apparent hurry, she led him through town. But once out in the boonies, she hit the gas pedal and managed to shake him."

"And goes to a beer joint?"

"Where she was last seen. Nobody at her house or place of business. Both locked up tight. Nothing disturbed in either. Security alarms still set. Sheriff's office fears foul play—"

"No shit."

"—and already have a BOLO out for her and the guy."

"The schmoozer followed her from the bar?"

"Not that guy, the other guy."

"What other guy?"

"Mickey's friend."

"Mickey had a friend?"

"Inconceivable, I know. But the two came in together, had a couple of drinks, looked simpatico. No cross words, no bad vibes. Nothing like that. They didn't engage anyone else in conversation and left together. But if the guy shot Mickey's face off, I guess they weren't that close of friends." Hick paused and took a breath. "That's where we are, and that's why I interrupted your supper. Tell Marsha I'm sorry."

"Has the scene been secured?"

The agent snuffled. "The homicide detective who notified me works out of the Tobias branch of the parish's sheriff's office. He sounds sharp enough. He arrived shortly after the first responders, but even at that, was too late. Told me that as soon as the body was discovered, the tavern's clientele scattered like roaches when the lights flipped on. Said that probably a dozen or more had warrants out for them. Parole violators. Bail jumpers. Nickel-bag dope dealers. It's that kind of place. He and other deputies have corralled a few lingerers. Not many. And those few are reluctant to talk to the authorities."

"Goes against their grain."

"There's that, but also they're grumbling about being detained on account of Josh Bennett. I was told that when one spoke his name, he spat on the floor."

"I don't suppose that either he or Billy Panella has been sighted."

"Except by proxy."

"Bennett's sister Jordie."

"And Mickey Bolden. We know that he was Panella's go-to person for wet work."

"Known but never proved," Joe said.

Imagining uncooperative witnesses and a crime scene contaminated to the point of uselessness, Joe sighed and ran his hand over his thinning hair. "Ask that SO detective to detain the witnesses till we can have a crack at them. I don't care how loud they bellyache. Get the chopper gassed up. I'll meet you at the heliport."

"What time?"

"I'm leaving now. Dispatch our own crime scene crew."

"Did that before I called you. They'll probably beat us there."

"Good. See you in a few."

Joe clicked off and reentered the kitchen. Her lips set in resignation, Marsha was assembling a ham and cheese sandwich. He slid on his shoulder holster and lifted his jacket off the hook by the back door. "It's the Panella-Bennett case, or I'd stay long enough to eat. Roast sure smells good. Is that rosemary?"

Ungently, she slapped the Saran-wrapped sandwich into his hand. "I hate you flying around in the dark in that damn helicopter."

"I know, but—"

"How old is it anyway?"

"Old, but reliable." He kissed her mouth, but got only a semipucker in return. "Tell the kids I'm sorry I missed them. I'll check in."

"I may not answer," she said. "I'm gonna watch *Top Gun*."

He paused on his way through the door. "That's my favorite movie."

"I know. And I'm gonna double-butter the popcorn and do some serious harm to a bottle of wine." She smiled with malicious gaiety. "Have fun!"

He walked back to her, leaned in, and whispered, "Know my favorite part of that movie?" He put his hand on her breast and squeezed. "When Maverick and the chick get it on."

She shoved him away. "Go!" She said it sternly, but she was smiling.

———◆———

When Shaw felt he'd covered enough distance for it to be safe to stop, he pulled off the highway onto a rutted track that led into a dense thicket. He cut the engine and turned off the headlights. For what he needed to do, he would use the flashlight on his phone, which was new. Only he had the number.

He shone the flashlight over the seat to check on Jordie Bennett. Best as he could tell, she was still out cold and hadn't moved since he'd placed her in the backseat. But she wouldn't be unconscious forever, and he had to prepare for that inevitability.

He got out, retrieved what he needed from the trunk, then opened the backseat door and placed his phone on the floorboard to provide him light.

She was as limp as a dishrag, making it easy for him to reposition her arms and legs. Once, she murmured something unintelligible, and he suspended what he was doing until he was certain that she wasn't about to wake up. The longer she was out, the better for him.

Better for her, too.

But she didn't come around, so, moving quickly, he removed her sandals, cursing the dainty buckles on the straps, then efficiently secured her feet and hands. He was backing out of the door, when he paused to brush a strand of hair off her cheek. That was when he noticed the blood spatters on her face.

"Shit." She would freak. He debated, then decided that taking a couple extra minutes wouldn't matter.

When he'd finished everything he needed to do, he gently closed the backseat door and the trunk and got back into the driver's seat. Her and Mickey's cell phones were lying in the passenger seat where he'd tossed them as he made his getaway from the bar.

He started with hers and was relieved to see that it was getting a cell signal. He accessed the log of recent calls and scrolled through it rapidly, scanning the calls she'd made or received throughout the day today and for the past several days. All the names were listed in her Contacts. Nothing was noteworthy.

Nothing except the last call she'd received.

It had come in a few minutes after nine o'clock that evening. Nearby area code. A number with no name attached. She'd called it back twice. Shaw considered, then called it himself. It rang several times but went unanswered. He clicked off.

Turning his head, he thoughtfully watched her sleeping form for several moments. Then he shut her phone down, removed the battery from it, and placed both in the glove compartment.

He picked up Mickey's phone, accessed the Recent calls and knew the Caller Unknown belonged to Panella. He would be standing by, waiting to hear "Mission accomplished" from Mickey.

"Too bad, asshole," Shaw whispered. "You're dealing with me now." He removed the battery from Mickey's phone, and locked it in the glove box along with Jordie's. Now feeling the pressure of time, he started the car.

As he pulled onto the dark and deserted highway, he thought back over the evening. It hadn't gone as he'd thought it would, but had actually turned out far better than anticipated. He'd come away with the primo prize. She lay unconscious in his backseat.

Chapter 3

———◆———

"Lord have mercy," Hick sighed when they alighted from the sheriff's office patrol car and surveyed the crime scene. "Bad as I expected."

The chopper that transported him and Joe had set down in a field which, in early fall, served as a regional fairgrounds. A deputy shuttled them from there to the site of Mickey Bolden's murder.

Portable lights had been brought in. The ugly tavern was lit up brighter than the Las Vegas strip. The men in uniform who were milling about cast eerie shadows that stretched into the surrounding forest before being absorbed by it.

"Worse," Joe said in response to Hick's summation of the situation. The two of them ducked beneath the yellow band that was intended to keep people off the parking lot but had been largely ignored. However, most of the trespassers were giving wide berth to the Lexus. He and Hick made a beeline for it.

An efficient young agent named Holstrom, one of the crime scene investigators from their New Orleans office, was consulting with a man whose natty seersucker suit and elfin countenance didn't fit here in deep bayou country, where no one had the courage to identify all the hunks of meat in the gumbo, and the mere notion of gun control laws was knee-slapping hilarious.

Joe and Hick exchanged subdued greetings with their colleague who introduced the small man he'd been talking to as Dr. Something-or-Other, the parish medical examiner. All were wearing gloves, so they didn't shake hands, which was just as well because they would have had to reach across the gulf of chunky, congealing blood between them.

Going straight to business, the ME said, "He's already at the morgue, but when he was identified they called me back out here to talk to y'all. I've got pictures of what he looked like when I arrived."

He tapped his iPad screen and held it up so they could see. He flipped through several photos of Mickey Bolden's sizable corpse taken from various angles and distances. None were pretty. Joe almost felt sorry for the lawless bastard.

Hick, a devout Catholic, breathed a prayer and crossed himself.

Joe, who was also Catholic but less devout, said, "No need to ask cause of death."

"He never felt it," the ME said with more dispassion than Joe would have expected from a man with such a benevolent face.

Joe pointed to one of the photos on the iPad, specifically to the pistol lying within inches of Mickey's outstretched hand. "Who retrieved his weapon?"

"First responders determined that it hadn't been recently fired," Holstrom said, "but they left it for the homicide detective from the SO to collect."

"Good." Joe also noticed in the photographs that Mickey's hands were gloved. He asked about those.

"He wore them to the morgue," the ME said. "I bagged them. A deputy picked them up, so the sheriff's office has them, too. Chain of possession has been recorded."

"Thanks. We'll want the autopsy report as soon as—"

"I know, I know. You fellas never say, 'No rush, Doc. Whenever you can get to it will be just fine.'"

He might look like a leprechaun, but he had the disposition of a rattlesnake. Joe decided he didn't like him. Surveying the immediate area, he noticed a pair of markers that had been left in the gravel. "What was there?"

"Ms. Bennett's purse and key fob," Holstrom replied. "The detective retrieved them."

Joe looked wider afield, searching for heel skid marks that would indicate that a scuffle had taken place or that someone— Jordie Bennett—had been dragged away. But there was nothing like that. "No signs of a struggle?"

"What you see is what we've got. We're searching," Holstrom added. He pointed out a team member who was several yards away, crouched down studying the loose surface of the parking lot. "But the manager, who also tends bar, estimated that when this went down there were fifteen to twenty vehicles in the lot."

Hick, who noted that only five remained, said, "Must've been quite an exodus."

Holstrom nodded. "We've got dozens of crisscrossed tire tracks, only a few shoe imprints." He raised his hands at his sides.

"No one saw a car leaving?" Hick asked.

Holstrom shook his head. "No one's come forward yet. Someone still might, though."

Joe said, "Yeah, and it might snow anytime now." He pinched the fabric of his damp shirt and pulled it away from his sweating torso. Addressing Holstrom again, he asked, "Security cameras?"

The younger agent smiled without humor. "The plumbing system is as sophisticated as this place gets. And that 'system' is a toilet around back that doesn't have a lid, but does have a hand-lettered sign warning that it flushes only on occasion."

"So that's a no to security cameras," Joe deadpanned.

"No to security, period. Unless you count the two sawed-off shotguns kept loaded behind the bar."

"Probably the most effective system," Hick remarked.

Joe pointed to a nasty-looking puddle a few feet away from the front grille of the car. "Is that vomit?"

"To be specific, a semidigested cheeseburger, chili fries, and lots of whiskey," the ME reported.

"Who was the precious owner?" Hick asked.

"According to one of the first responders, the young man who found the body puked his guts up," Holstrom said. "Here, then three times inside. Fortunately they keep a bucket handy for just that purpose."

"Where's he now?" Joe asked.

"Still in there. Being made to cool his heels till you arrived."

"Am I done here?" the ME asked.

Joe thanked him and then, mostly out of spite, reminded him that the autopsy report was an important factor to their investigation. Huffing complaints, the pathologist stamped away.

Joe turned to Holstrom. "Nice guy." Then, "Under the heading of 'What the fuck happened?' do you have anything useful to tell us?"

Holstrom absently scratched a spot on his cheek that looked like a fresh mosquito bite. "Not much, I'm afraid. The car is registered to Jordan Bennett. It was found unlocked, but all the doors were closed when first responders arrived. A deputy is going to dust it for prints, but, honestly, I don't think she ever got in it after exiting the bar."

Joe said, "So she left with whoever popped Mickey?" Since neither of the other two agents replied or offered a differing hypothesis, he said, "Okay then, did she leave with this unsub voluntarily or under duress?"

Agent Holstrom looked over at Hick, who shrugged.

"That makes it unanimous," Joe said, "because I don't know,

either." He started walking toward the bar's entrance, saying over his shoulder to Holstrom, "Notify me immediately if you find anything."

"Sure thing."

"What's the name of the detective you talked to?" Joe asked Hick as he pulled open the door into the bar.

"Cliff Morrow."

Morrow was in his midthirties, with nothing distinguishing about him except for his attire. He had on a baseball cap, team t-shirt, coaching shorts, and dusty sneakers. Joe and Hick removed their latex gloves and shook hands with him. As they did, he explained his appearance. "I coach my daughter's softball team. We were celebrating our win tonight at a pizza place when the call came in. I didn't take time to change."

He seemed competent and more than willing, perhaps even relieved, to share the investigation with them. "People around here harbor a lot of ill will against Josh Bennett," he said. "Homegrown boy."

"Gone bad," Hick said.

"They'd forgive that," the detective said. "But the way a lot of folks see it, he's a turncoat."

"Much worse than a crook," Joe said.

Morrow gave a sheepish grin. "To some minds it is."

"What about to your mind?" Hick asked him.

"I'm a peace officer. Josh Bennett broke the law."

It was a matter-of-fact answer that Joe was glad to hear. "So, despite Bennett's local ties, we have your full cooperation?"

"Absolutely, sir. You have the support of the entire Terrebonne Parish SO. The sheriff said to tell you so. He's already chewed that deputy's ass for letting Ms. Bennett elude him. He's green. Been a deputy three whole weeks. He didn't even know why she was being surveilled. In fact, no one's been told why you requested surveillance on her."

Joe pretended not to hear the implied question mark. Maybe

he should have shared the reason for the surveillance with the sheriff and impressed on him its seriousness. Perhaps if he had, a more seasoned officer would have been assigned that responsibility. But it was too late now, the damage was done, and he didn't have time to waste on second-guessing himself.

He said, "Bring me up to speed, Detective Morrow."

"As soon as I and my partner got here, we separated them for questioning." He referred to a handful of disreputable-looking men and women scattered around the bar.

Assessing their sullen expressions individually and collectively, Joe said, "Let me guess. Nobody knows diddly-squat."

Morrow grinned. "Basically. But so far there've been no red flags to make me think otherwise. My partner is interviewing the bartender in the back room, but initial questioning indicates that he was an innocent bystander like the rest. More observant, maybe. And he's the only one who interacted with Bolden and his companion."

"No one has IDed the companion yet?"

"None of the locals claim to have seen him before tonight."

"Of course not," Joe said. "We'd never be lucky enough to get the name and address of the prime suspect. Where's Bolden's pistol?"

Morrow motioned them over to the bar. The pistol had been bagged and labeled. "The tool of his trade," Joe remarked as he studied the pistol with the sound suppressor still attached.

"He didn't fire it tonight," Morrow said. "Full cartridge except for the bullet in the chamber."

Joe picked up the evidence bag containing a small red purse. There was nothing special about it except that it looked expensive. He hoped Marsha never got a hankering to have one like it.

Also on the bar, separately bagged, were the key fob to Jordie Bennett's car, a tube of lip gloss called Gossamer Wings, a credit card, a twenty-dollar bill, and a Louisiana driver's license.

"The lady was traveling light," Morrow said, as Joe and Hick studied the items individually.

Conspicuously absent was a cell phone, and Hick remarked on it.

"I picked up on that, too," Morrow said. "The clasp of her purse was open when it was found. I'm guessing he took her phone from it."

"But left the twenty and her credit card," Hick said.

"This wasn't about stealing," Joe said around a sigh. "It's about who she is, who she knows, and *what* she knows." He turned to Morrow. "Did you grow up here in Tobias?"

"Since I was eight."

"How well do you know the Bennetts?"

"To speak to and ask after each other's health. Like that. Josh was in my class, but we didn't hang out together. Jordie was a couple grades ahead of us."

"Any sibling rivalry between them?" Joe asked.

"Nothing cutthroat. Not that I'm aware of, anyway. Both were smart and made good grades. She ran with the popular crowd."

"Josh didn't?"

"He was several levels down from popular and didn't really run with anybody. He was a geek, and I don't mean that unkindly. Into video games and such."

"She was social, he was brainy. Fair to say?"

Morrow considered Hick's question and nodded. "Fair to say. But, as brothers and sisters go, they were close."

Joe perked up. "Oh?"

"You know what happened to Josh when he was little?"

Both Joe and Hickam nodded.

"Well, I guess because of that, Jordie was always protective of him." When he paused, Joe motioned for him to continue. "Her senior year, she was with this guy, a superjock. A meathead, but, you know, coveted. One day after classes, Jordie was sitting with this guy in his car out on the school parking lot.

"Rumor had it that they were quarreling. In any case, Josh rode up on his scooter. Not a Harley, nothing with that kind of muscle. He and the meathead exchanged words through the driver's window, and Josh, whether accidentally or on purpose—accounts varied—bumped the fender of the meathead's car with his front tire.

"Didn't even make a dent, but the guy was pissed. He got out of his car and threatened to tear Josh's head off. He was yelling, trying to shove Josh off his scooter, calling him every name in the book. Josh didn't—or couldn't—counterattack.

"But Jordie did. She flew out of the car and got right in this jock's face. Now he probably outweighed her by a hundred pounds or more, but she had him backing down in no time flat. Then she climbed onto the back of Josh's scooter and off they went. That was the end of her romance with the meathead. She dumped him and to my knowledge never spoke to him again."

Joe mulled over the story, then gave Morrow a long look, gauging his trustworthiness. "You wondered why surveillance on Jordie Bennett was requested earlier this week? Well, here's why."

The detective's intelligent eyes registered the significance of what Joe told him. He whistled softly. "You—the FBI, I mean—have kept a lid on it."

"We have," Joe said. "And it does not—and I mean does *not*—go public until the Bureau is ready for it to."

"Because of what Billy Panella might do if he gets wind of it."

Hick nodded. "Exactly. What has us worried is that the news has already reached Panella, wherever in the world he's holed up. Or else why was Mickey Bolden here tonight? He was Panella's hired gun."

"It doesn't sadden me in the slightest that Mickey is no longer a worry," Joe said. "But there's this other guy, who apparently isn't the least bit gun-shy. He remains unknown and at large."

"And Jordie Bennett went missing at the same time." Grasping the gravity of the situation, Morrow removed his baseball cap and wiped his forehead with the back of his hand. "We didn't obtain her cell phone number until about ten minutes ago. This is Friday night. Everybody's out. But we finally reached her office manager. She gave us Ms. Bennett's number and we've been calling it."

"Let me guess," Hick said. "Nothing."

"Not even voice mail."

"Our unsub would be smart enough to take the battery out so it couldn't be tracked," Joe said. "Did you find a phone on Mickey?"

"Negative," Morrow said.

"No doubt he lifted that, too." Joe put his hands on his hips and swore softly. "This unidentified companion of Mickey's is beginning to worry me."

Chapter 4

⟶━◆━⟵

The otherwise innocuous sound had the impact of a gunshot. Jordie froze.

When the first click was followed immediately by another, she realized what they signified.

From the driver's seat, he had flipped a switch that released the child safety lock on the backseat door, then flipped it again to relock it, and, by doing so, mocked her futile attempt to get the door open.

About an hour earlier, she had been roused from unconsciousness by a dull ache on the side of her head. A self-preservation instinct had cautioned her not to let on that she'd come awake. Up till now, she'd thought she'd played possum well enough to fool him into believing that she was still out. Apparently she hadn't been as convincing as she'd thought.

She was the fool, not he.

After waking up and assessing her situation as best she could without opening her eyes, she'd determined that she was lying on the backseat of a traveling vehicle with her hands and feet bound.

Moving incrementally and as silently as possible, she'd discovered that if she extended her legs just so, she could reach the backseat door with her bare feet. With increasing frustration and muscle strain, she had been covertly trying to lift the lever with her toes, all the while thinking that her abductor was oblivious.

Knowing now that he was on to her, and more than likely had been all along, despair, fear, and anger coalesced into a moan.

After coming to, and as soon as some of the residual muzziness had cleared from her head, she'd realized that this wasn't her car. Her cheek was resting on cloth upholstery. The familiar texture and smell of her car's leather seats would have provided her with a small measure of security, but, as it was, this car was as unknown to her as the driver, their whereabouts, and their destination.

No longer needing to pretend to be unconscious, she opened her eyes and blinked them into focus. She had only the dashboard's glow for illumination. No city lights shone through the backseat window. There were no lighted signposts or overpasses indicating that they were on a major highway, no headlight beams coming from the opposite direction. She could see nothing beyond the window glass except black sky and a sprinkling of stars.

Which was as good a view as any to let her try and block the mental images of the overweight man aiming a pistol at her forehead, then of his facial features disintegrating, his hard fall to the ground, his blood spreading toward her feet as rapidly and darkly as spilled ink.

She remembered staring into a pistol at point-blank range and hearing the second man say, *My half just doubled.*

Upon waking, her first thought had been amazement that she was still alive.

Rather than shoot her, the tall one must have knocked her unconscious, perhaps with the sound suppressor on his pistol, and abducted her from the scene of the brutal murder that she had witnessed him commit. Leaving her now to wonder why he hadn't also killed her. Wouldn't that have been more practical and expedient than kidnapping? So why had he kept her alive?

Speculation on his motives brought on a surge of panic and, because stealth was no longer necessary, she began struggling to free her hands. They were restrained at the small of her back by something thin but incredibly strong that bit into her flesh. Her efforts to get loose grew more frantic.

"Cut it out."

The unexpected command from the driver's seat startled her, and for a moment she lay perfectly still. Then she said, "Go to the devil," and renewed her tug-of-war to work her hands free.

But after five minutes, she was bathed in sweat, which the car's AC rapidly turned to ice water. She conceded that no matter how strenuously she worked at it, the struggle was futile and would result only in exhaustion and raw, bleeding wrists. She forced herself to lie back on the seat, took several deep breaths through her mouth, and willfully tamped down her panic.

Thinking more calmly, she tried to isolate a single advantage that she could exploit, and soon realized that whatever was binding her feet was softer and more giving than the hand restraint.

Lifting her head, she looked down the length of her body and was forced to swallow rising gorge when she saw the dark spatters on her white top.

Dried blood. The dead man's blood.

She shuddered but didn't allow herself to think about how he'd died. If she did, fear of meeting the same fate would paralyze her mentally and physically.

Steeling herself to look beyond the grotesque stains on her clothing, she saw that a camouflage print bandana had been knotted around her ankles. She began grinding her feet together, trying to stretch the cotton cloth and create enough give in it so that she could possibly free her feet, and then—

Then what?

The backseat door would still be locked and inescapable.

She could kick her abductor in the back of his head. A well-placed, surprise kick might stun him for a precious few seconds.

And cause him to crash the car.

Or provoke him into killing her sooner rather than later.

Perhaps she could distract him somehow. If she made a noise, maybe pretended to choke, or did something that would force him to stop the car, and then if he opened the backseat door to check on her, she might stand a chance of getting out and running if—

There were a dismal number of *ifs*, and none of the options held much promise of success. But, dammit, she wouldn't just lie here to be dealt with when he felt like it. She wouldn't make it as easy for him as his previous victim had. She wouldn't be dispatched without giving him a fight.

However, she also knew on an instinctual level that this man wouldn't be easily tricked or overtaken physically.

When she'd left the bar, the parking lot had been dark and, she'd thought, deserted. Rushing footsteps over gravel had alerted her to the approach of her two attackers. In the nanosecond between her spinning around and the pistol being fired, she'd recognized both from having seen them in the bar just a few minutes before: the heavyset man who hadn't made any kind of memorable impression on her; and *him*, who had.

As he'd walked past where she sat at the bar, they'd made brief eye contact. She remembered his above-average height, an unhurried but somehow predatory stride, a severe face, and eyes sharp enough to cut diamonds. She'd had a visceral reaction to that incisive gaze and had quickly looked away from it.

She should have heeded that intuitive warning of danger, but at the time, she had mistaken it for another type of reaction, another kind of danger.

Any sudden movement of her head caused the throbbing to

sharpen, so now she gingerly angled it in order to get a clearer view of him. Above the driver's-seat headrest, she could see a swirl of hair on the crown of his head. She remembered it being long and untidy. It looked darker in the blue ambient light of the dashboard than it had beneath the amber, smoke-fogged fixtures inside the bar.

Visible through the space between the two front seats was a portion of his right arm, sleeved in blue chambray. She recalled that the shirt had pearl snap buttons. The cuffs were rolled back almost to his elbows.

He hadn't impressed her as being particularly muscle-bound, not a body builder type, but evidently he was strong enough to carry her to his car, because she certainly hadn't made it here under her own power.

Reluctantly, she admitted how difficult it would be, if not impossible, for her to physically overcome him.

No, in order to survive, she must somehow outwit him, and in order to do that, she couldn't operate in a vacuum. She needed information, and he was her only resource.

She cleared her throat. "Congratulations. You have me. Who are you?"

For all the response she got, he could have been deaf.

"Do you have a destination in mind, or are we just putting distance between us and the scene of the crime?"

He remained silent, registering no reaction whatsoever.

"How long was I out?"

Nothing.

"Hours?"

When he still didn't respond, she said, "Actually, it doesn't matter. The police will have quickly deduced that you murdered that man in cold blood and kidnapped me."

Stone silence.

"By now, they'll have launched a full-scale search. Kidnapping is a federal crime. So not only the local authorities but the

FBI will be in on the manhunt, and they won't give up until they find me. And they *will*."

"I give them three days."

Since he hadn't responded to anything else, she was momentarily taken aback to hear his voice again and even more alarmed when she realized that he had gradually braked. As the car slowed, he steered it into a right turn.

Once they were off the highway, the view through the car window changed. Their headlights danced crazily across overlapping treetops that obscured the view of open sky. For fifty yards or so, rocks knocked against the undercarriage as the car jounced over deep potholes.

"Three days minimum," he said. "By that time, I'll be back in Mexico, sipping cerveza and shopping fishing boats."

"What about me?"

He stopped the car, shifted it into Park, and turned to address her through the space between the seats. "You won't be going to Mexico."

That blunt declaration caused another surge of gorge in her throat.

He cut the engine, switched off the headlights, and got out. The dome light came on when he opened the driver's door. Jordie blinked against the sudden glare that shone directly down on her.

He opened the back door and ducked his head inside. Again she felt the bite of his razor-sharp eyes. The overhead light cast harsh shadows on his face, emphasizing prominent cheekbones and unsmiling lips.

Without saying anything, he closed his fingers around her left ankle. At his touch, she yanked her knees up, freeing her feet from his grasp, and then tried to drive them into his face. He jerked his head back just in time. Her heel barely clipped his chin.

She tried again. He stayed just out of reach. On her third at-

tempt, his hand shot out, grabbed her ankle, and roughly pulled
her feet against his chest, where he kept them in place with one
hand while, with the other, he picked one of her sandals from off
the floorboard and worked her foot into it. He secured the tiny
buckle with the same detachment with which he'd fired a pistol
into the back of his cohort's head.

"You're going to kill me, aren't you?"

That cold gaze lifted to meet hers. "Not inside the car."

When both her sandals were on, he backed out of the door
and shut it. He went around to the other side and opened the
door behind her head. Reaching in, he cupped her underarms
and hauled her out.

As soon as he set her on her feet, he turned her to face him.
"Don't try any more dumb stunts like trying to kick me."

"Go to hell."

As though she hadn't spoken, he said, "I'm curious. If you *had*
gotten that door open with your toes, what were you going to
do? Try to worm your way through it without me noticing? Was
that your plan?"

She didn't honor him with a reply, only glared up at him.

"And say you had cleared the door, what then, Jordie?"

Her knees nearly buckled when he spoke her name.

Of course, if he had taken her purse when he kidnapped her,
he would have read her name on her driver's license and credit
card. Right?

Wrong. Because both bore her full legal name, not the familiar nickname Jordie.

He knew her.

Most despairing, however, was that it came as no real surprise
that he'd called her by name. When she saw the grim pair strid-
ing toward her on the parking lot, she'd realized instantly what
their purpose was and who had sent them.

The only thing she didn't know was *Why now?*

"You didn't think it through too well," he said, continuing on that thread. "We were going over seventy miles an hour. If you'd opened that door, it would have sounded like a wind tunnel.

"And say you had managed to wiggle out, you'd have landed on the pavement like those bugs on the windshield." He gestured toward it. "*Splat*! I'd have had to stop and scrape you up, which would have been time-consuming and messy as hell."

"Why bother to stop and scrape me up?"

He replied without a blink. "Because in order to collect my money I have to produce your body."

Chapter 5

—◆—

Well, she'd asked, hadn't she?

And he'd told her, answering the question without hesitation or inflection, without even a taunting lilt. More frightening than a voice scratchy with menace was one entirely devoid of emotion. It was characteristic of the cold-blooded way he'd shot the other man.

She swallowed with difficulty. "Who was he? The man you killed."

"Mickey Bolden. Killer for hire."

"He was hired to kill me?"

He just looked at her.

"Now you'll do it alone."

His expression didn't change.

"Who hired you?"

As expected, he didn't answer. Not that he needed to.

She said, "I suppose I should be flattered that I merited two hit men. Did you and Mr. Bolden often work in tandem?"

"First time."

She looked at him with surprise.

He gave a shrug of complete indifference. "His retirement was overdue. He'd gotten comfortable in the job. Sloppy. For instance, when you walked into the bar, he told me to relax and go with the flow. Said your showing up there tonight was just a coincidence."

She saw the bait for what it was and said nothing.

"But see, I had a problem with that coincidence theory."

She didn't ask the nature of his problem, but he told her anyway.

"For one thing, that joint out in the sticks isn't exactly your kind of place."

His tone was a shade judgmental, reverse snobbery, which put her on the defensive. "You have no idea what my kind of place is."

"Well, there you're wrong, Jordie. I did my homework. I know a lot about you."

The probable truth of that statement disturbed her greatly, but she held her silence and her ground, keeping her gaze as direct on him as his was on her.

"Even without doing the homework, I'd know that a woman like you doesn't socialize in bars that cater to trailer trash. I also had a problem with your boyfriend."

"Boyfriend? Jackson?"

"Last name Terrell. Mickey told me all about him. Said he dropped you like a hot potato at the first sign of trouble. Cut and run like a regular heel. That true?"

She remained stubbornly silent.

"Doesn't matter," he said. "I wasn't talking about him anyway. I was talking about the guy who joined you at the bar tonight."

She sputtered a short laugh of disbelief. "That jerk? He was a total stranger."

"He was all over you."

"Not by invitation."

He tilted his head. "You two didn't set a time and place to meet?"

She opened her mouth to speak, then thought better of it, clammed up, and didn't tell him anything.

He raised an eyebrow. "You were about to say?"

"I was about to say *fuck you*." She didn't stop there, either, but gushed a stream of invectives. He withstood the tirade without blinking, but when she began repeating herself, he pressed his index finger lengthwise against the center of her lips.

"Stop it."

She stopped, as she had stopped struggling against the hand restraint when he'd told her to, more because of the chilling voice in which he'd issued the order than because of the order itself.

Her lips held his attention for several moments. Perhaps he was watching them turn white from the pressure he applied. Then gradually he withdrew his finger and his eyes moved back up to hers. "You've got some mouth on you, Jordie Bennett."

Again, it was the manner in which he spoke as much as the words themselves that caused a shakeup of her insides. She didn't think he was referring strictly to her language, and the implication of that paralyzed her. By the time she remembered to breathe again, he was crouched in front of her, loosening the bandana from around her ankles.

The instant the knots came undone, she was off like a shot.

She got all of three feet from him before he hooked his arm around her waist and jerked her to a sudden halt, then spun her around to face him. He was furious. "Don't think you can outsmart, outtalk, or outrun me. You can't. Try and you'll only make yourself miserable."

"You're worried about my *comfort?*"

"I'm not being paid to torture you."

"Just to kill me."

"That's the job description."

She gulped in a harsh breath. "Then why didn't you do it on the parking lot when you shot your buddy? Why drag it out, why this . . . this . . . *torture*? Why am I still alive?"

He lowered his face closer to hers. "Because your skin is worth a hell of a lot more than Mickey settled for, and I haven't negotiated my deal yet."

Like everything he said, his words were candid and to the point. At least now she understood why she was still breathing.

He gave her a little shove that put space between them. "Besides, I gotta take a leak."

He grasped her elbow and propelled her slightly ahead of him along the uneven gravel track which was pressed upon from both sides by dense woods. Beyond the dim glow provided by the car's interior light, the surrounding darkness was impenetrable. She picked up the stench of stagnant water, sensed life-forms watching them from nests overhead and from hidey-holes in the underbrush, and felt the ghostly brush of insect wings against her arms and face.

Paralyzing fear encroached on her again, as did the teeming darkness. The darkness she could do nothing about, but she must keep the self-defeating fear at bay. Information, she reminded herself. Without information, she had no hope of escape.

"Your half doubled when you killed your partner."

"If you remember me saying that, I must not have hit you very hard."

"With your pistol?"

"It was a tap."

"Hard enough to knock me out."

"Your eyes rolled back, your knees gave out. I caught you on my shoulder as you slumped forward. Had to juggle you so I could get your and Mickey's phones. But I managed to come away with both of them."

While she tucked away the knowledge that he had her phone, he was saying, "I carried you to the car."

"Where you tied me up."

"No, I drove five or six miles before stopping to do that. When I stretched you out in the backseat, you groaned a couple of times but didn't wake up. I used a bottle of water to wash off your face. That didn't bring you around, either."

She glanced down at her stained top. Her face would have been similarly spattered with...She didn't want to think about the matter he had washed off her. Nor did she want to think about him washing her, touching her, handling her.

They were getting farther away from the car and the weak circle of light it provided. The ground had turned spongy. The heels of her sandals sank into it with each step, making walking difficult. Whenever she stumbled, his hand tightened around her elbow to help her regain her balance, but he never let go and continued to prod her forward.

Perhaps he'd only said that about negotiating a deal to put her at ease, to get her to cooperate, go peacefully, so he wouldn't have to exert himself overly much to finish the job.

Keeping her voice as steady as possible, she said, "You'll be caught, you know."

"Not anytime soon. They don't know what I'm driving."

"They'll get a description of the car from someone who saw you leave the parking lot."

"No one did. I made sure of it. I went a full mile before turning on the headlights, and, anyway, I didn't meet a single other vehicle on that backwoods road. When I stopped to tie you up, I also changed the license plates. That precaution was well worth the few minutes it took. I switched them from Louisiana to, uh, Arkansas, I think. Or was it Tennessee?"

"If you had states to choose from, you went prepared."

"Credit goes to Mickey. Before we set out for Tobias he stashed a collection of extra plates in the trunk."

"That doesn't sound like someone who'd grown sloppy."

"His ego was more bloated than his belly. Thought he couldn't be caught. That kind of arrogance is a recipe for disaster. He drew attention to himself, made himself memorable. If you're a hit man, those are bad habits."

"Won't executing him draw attention to you and make you memorable?"

He actually chuckled. "No doubt."

"That doesn't concern you?"

"No."

"It should."

"It doesn't. Here." Suddenly, he steered her off the uneven track and into tall weeds.

Her heart clutched. Despite her vituperative outburst of only a few minutes earlier, she was now in the grip of mortal fear and couldn't hold back a whimper. Was he raising his pistol? Would she hear the click when he pulled the trigger? Would she experience pain? Or just... nothingness? *Please God.*

She would appeal to God for her life. She would *not* beg *him* to spare it.

When they drew even with a stout hardwood, he began unbuttoning the fly of his jeans with his free hand. She looked up at him, unable to conceal her dismay.

"What?" This time, there was a taunting quality to his voice which matched the tilt of one corner of his mouth. "I told you I had to take a leak. Wha'd you think?"

"You know what I thought, you son of a bitch."

Her anger seemed to amuse him. He made a derisive sound and turned slightly toward the tree. "Unless you want an eyeful, better close them."

She did and didn't reopen them until he said, "Okay, it's safe to look."

He had buttoned up but was now digging into the front pocket of his jeans. Her heart tripped when he withdrew a knife.

It was small, but a flick of his fingers released a wicked-looking blade. "Turn around." She hesitated, causing him to frown. "You want your hands freed or not?"

She was still mistrustful, but the promise of having her hands loosed was too enticing to resist. She turned her back to him and wanted to weep with relief when the knife snapped through the plastic grip. As she came around, she shook feeling back into her hands. "Thank you."

He slid the knife into his pocket. "You can go behind the tree."

Realizing now why he had unbound her hands, she shook her head. "Absolutely not."

"Scared of snakes? Bugs? Or are you just bashful? Too lady-like? What?"

"I'm not going."

"I know you have to. You drank that wine."

In truth, she'd been uncomfortable since she'd regained consciousness.

He waited for a ten count, and when she still hadn't moved, he said, "I don't want you peeing in the car."

"I won't."

"That's right, you won't. Because you're doing it here, and you're doing it now."

She shook her head again.

"We don't have time for this, Jordie, so here's the deal. You can step behind the tree or stay here, and I'll watch. You can undo your jeans and pull them down, or I'll do the honors. Doesn't matter to me either way, although choice number two has its appeal, because then I'll know something I've been wondering since I saw you atop that bar stool, and that's whether or not there's anything under that denim except you. I could find out anyway, but my mama raised me better, so I'll let you decide, and you've got exactly two seconds to make up your mind. One."

The indignity of relieving herself was preferable to wetting herself. And if he was worried about her doing it in the car, he didn't plan on killing her right away.

"Two."

The longer she stayed alive, the greater her chances of escaping or being rescued.

His knuckles pressed against her navel as he slid his fingers into her waistband to undo the top button.

She gasped. "All right."

He withdrew his hand with less expedience than he'd shoved it in. She turned around and took a couple of steps away from him before he caught the hem of her shirttail and pulled her back.

"I trust you have better sense than to try and run," he said. "Look around. What's out there? Total darkness, swamp, marsh, sword grass, gators, razorbacks, wild dogs, panthers, water mocassins, insects, all sorts of critters that bite and suck blood."

She yanked her shirttail free. "I might stand a chance of surviving all that. Do I have any chance of surviving *you*?"

He looked down at her, his eyes uncompromising, not a glimmer of warmth or compassion, nothing that gave her hope. After several seconds, he hitched his chin toward the other side of the tree. "Hurry up."

For all the reasons he'd cited, she realized the foolhardiness of trying to escape. If she managed to outrun him long enough to reach the main road, he could easily chase her down in the car before someone else came along. If she eluded him in the darkness of this swamp, without water, direction, or any means of protecting herself, she had little chance of surviving before she could find help or help could find her.

With haste and as little thought as possible, she did what was necessary. When she came out from behind the tree, he clasped her wrist and slipped another plastic cuff around it. "Please," she whispered.

For several seconds, he stared at the ugly red marks the restraint had left on her skin, then looked into her eyes. "Tell me about the boyfriend."

"Oh, for godsake!"

"He have a name?"

"I'm sure he does, but I don't know it."

His eyes narrowed. "Save the cute and sassy for somebody who'll appreciate them. Doesn't cut it with me. Now, I'll ask you again, *what's his name?*"

"I don't know. I swear. If he told me, I don't remember."

"Why were you meeting him there tonight?"

"I wasn't!" With defiance, she returned his doubtful stare, but she was the first to relent. She lowered her gaze and addressed one of the pearl snaps on his shirt, saying quietly, "I've told you the truth. He was a stranger who came over and offered to buy me a drink. I told him no thank you."

"You said more than three words to him. What else did you two talk about?"

"Mostly about how I wish he would go away and leave me the hell alone."

"You didn't set up a meeting with him?"

"How many times do I have to say it?"

"Till I believe you."

"I didn't set up a meeting with him."

Suddenly, he reached around her, planted his right hand on her bottom, and jerked her forward and up against him. Before she could react to that, he worked his left hand into the right rear pocket of her jeans and removed something from it. As suddenly as he'd hauled her against him, he pushed her away. He looked at the scrap of paper he had fished from her pocket, cursed, then dangled it inches from her nose.

"Mickey asked me if that guy was up to something. I told

him no, that he was a drunk who only wanted to get in your pants. But I knew better. I saw him slip you this. Now," he said softly, but with menace, "rethink telling me that he was a stranger, Jordie. Because lying to me could be hazardous to your health."

Chapter 6

Joe Wiley asked Deputy Morrow to point out to him the young man who had hit on Jordie Bennett, followed her from the bar, and discovered Mickey Bolden's body.

The detective nodded past the pool tables toward the far wall. Only a foot of space separated the ceiling from three blacked-out windows. Beneath them was a row of booths, only one of which was occupied. "We put him there all by his lonesome."

Joe and Hick made their way over. Between two, lumpy red vinyl benches was a table scored with countless names and initials, as well as sentiments of love and hate. Some looked recently carved, others like they'd been there for decades.

The agents slid into the booth opposite a man in his early twenties. He had long, stringy hair. Except for it and his threadbare goatee, he bore a striking resemblance to the gray skull on the front of his faded black t-shirt.

He glowered at Hick with a redneck's resentment toward a black man so obviously superior in every respect. He snorted contempt. "You the preacher, the groom, or the corpse?"

Hick, who was always smartly dressed, smiled pleasantly at the snide reference to his dark suit, white shirt, and necktie.

Joe asked, "What's your name?"

He slid his surly gaze toward Joe. "Who wants to know?"

Joe just looked at him for several seconds, then reached for his ID wallet, flipped it open, and extended it across the greasy tabletop.

The young man's reaction was immediate. "You gotta be fuckin' kidding. You're *feds*? I didn't do anything."

"Doesn't look that way from where I and Agent Hickam are sitting. You harassed a woman—"

"I didn't harass—"

"You followed her out when she left, which amounts to stalking."

"My friends dared—"

"A guy winds up with his brains on the ground, and you say you found him like that." Joe let that dire description of his predicament resonate, then said, "If I were you? I'd lose the attitude and stop pissing me off."

He squirmed, he swallowed, he picked at the red eye socket of the skull on his shirt, and finally he mumbled his name— Royce Sherman.

Hick tapped it into his iPad and started a search to see if Royce Sherman had a police record.

Joe asked, "You live around here, Royce?"

He named a nearby town, not Tobias.

"What brought you over here tonight?"

"Met up with some buddies to shoot pool, have a coupla drinks, hang out."

"Did you know Jordan Bennett before tonight?"

"Never saw her before she walked in. Still don't know her."

"But you recognized her name."

"No. Didn't know it till he told me." He motioned toward Morrow.

"Witnesses told Deputy Morrow that you came on to Ms. Bennett pretty strong. That true?"

"No." Some of the attitude had edged back in. He sank deeper into his seat. "I went over and asked could I buy her a drink. That's it," he declared, stabbing the top of the table with the tip of his index finger.

"Of all the women in the bar, you picked her to hit on. How come?"

He gave a short laugh. "Are you yanking my chain?"

Joe's expression didn't change. "Am I yanking his chain, Agent Hickam?"

"I don't believe you are, sir."

Their somber tones collapsed the young man's leer. He shifted on the bench again. "If you saw her, you wouldn't have to ask how come. She's hot."

"I have seen her. In fact, I and Agent Hickam have spent a lot of time with the lady."

Royce Sherman's bloodshot eyes sawed back and forth between them. "Seriously?"

"In the line of duty."

"Wha'd she do?"

"Are you familiar with a fugitive named Billy Panella?"

"A fugitive? Like, from justice?"

"Heard of him?"

"No."

"Joshua Bennett?"

"Her kin?"

"Her brother."

"Don't know him, neither."

Joe didn't think he was bright enough to be lying that well. "According to witnesses, Ms. Bennett didn't welcome your attention and declined your offer of a drink."

"Said she had a drink, thank you, and asked me to adios."

"But you didn't adios. You persisted."

"No law against making friendly conversation, is there? I . . ." Stalling, he shot a glance at Hick, who was watching him, waiting for an answer. "I . . . you know, I—"

"—persisted," Joe repeated. "You harassed her."

"I never laid a hand on her!"

"But you didn't take no for an answer."

He slumped, sighed, looked at them sourly. "Okay, I offered again, and when she said no again, I told her she looked lonely to me. She said she wasn't, and, anyway, it was none of my business if she was lonely or not. And then I asked if she was expecting somebody else to join her."

Joe leaned forward. "What did she say to that?"

"Nothin'."

"She didn't answer?"

He shook his head. "Just turned a cold shoulder."

"What did you derive from that?"

"Derive?"

"How'd you take that? Like maybe she *was* expecting someone?"

"I dunno." He gave them a stupid grin. "I wasn't thinking too clear."

Joe kept at it for a few more minutes, but it became apparent that the young man hadn't been thinking clearly at all, that he'd had more than a "coupla drinks" with his pals. He saw a pretty lady and was goaded into approaching her with nothing more in mind than the prospect of getting lucky.

"Witnesses overheard her tell you to go to hell."

"Turns out she wasn't a friendly sort a'tall. Truth is, she was a snotty bitch. Who needs that? Actually, I'm glad she turned me down."

Not believing that for a second, Joe looked at Hick, who snickered. He didn't believe it, either. Going back to the young man, Joe asked, "How long between when she stormed out and you followed?"

"My friends were giving me shit for being shut down, so five minutes, maybe."

Hick, referring to notes Morrow had taken, whispered to Joe, "His friends said it was more like ten minutes."

Joe asked, "How'd you know where her car was parked?"

"Didn't. I was just stumbling around out there in the dark, looking to see if I could catch up with her before she drove off."

"Did you?"

His stringy hair flapped against his cheeks as he firmly shook his head. "Swear to God. Never saw her again. Didn't come upon anything except the...the...you know, the body." He swallowed so thickly that Hick asked if he needed the vomit bucket again. "No. I'm okay."

"Did you touch anything?"

"Out there you mean? Hell no. Well, maybe the fender of the car. I think I propped my hand on it while I was bent over yakkin'."

"You didn't notice any headlights, or a vehicle leaving the parking lot?" Hick asked.

Another head shake. "Too busy puking."

Joe asked, "Had you noticed Mickey Bolden in the bar?"

"That the dead guy?" After a nod of confirmation, he said, "Yeah. Right before he left, he went over to the jukebox and was talking to the other guy."

"What did the other guy look like?"

He raised his bony shoulders in a shrug. "Like a guy."

"Young, old, short, tall, black, white?"

"White. On the tall side. Older than me. Younger than you." Then he looked at Hick. "Maybe 'bout your age."

"Any tattoos, distinguishing clothing, facial hair?"

"Couldn't tell you. I was eyeballing that gal's rack, not lookin' at some dude."

Joe looked over at Hickam, who looked back, his wry expression saying, *Nowhere to take that.*

Joe noted the jukebox's proximity to the ell of the bar where he'd been told Jordie Bennett was sitting. He went back to the young man. "While standing there at the jukebox, did those two show any interest in Ms. Bennett?"

"Not that I saw. But, like I said, I wasn't paying them no mind, and I was pretty wasted."

Morrow approached and asked if he could have a word with Hickam. He left the booth so they could confer in private.

Royce Sherman sat back against the vinyl, rubbed his eye sockets, and whined, "Can I go now?"

"You got somewhere else to be?" Joe asked.

"I'm gonna catch hell from my old lady for not coming home when I said I would."

"You're married?"

"No, but you'd think so the way she stays on my ass. The first cop that questioned me took my phone, so I can't even call her."

Hick slid back into the booth. "Mr. Sherman, you have a problem."

He regarded Hick sullenly. "Whut?"

Rather than addressing him, Hick turned to Joe. "A witness says he saw Mr. Sherman placing something in Ms. Bennett's pocket."

Joe leaned against the back of the booth, folded his arms over his middle, and fixed an accusing frown on the young man, who'd suddenly grown nervous.

"Oh. That. Yeah. See..." He ran his tongue over his lips. He cracked his knuckles. "I forgot about that."

Joe said, "He must think we're stupid, Agent Hickam."

"Guess so."

"I swear!" he squeaked. "I forgot."

"You told me you didn't know her."

"I didn't. Don't!"

"That you hadn't laid a hand on her."

"I didn't, except for...for that."

"What did you pass her?"

"My digits."

"Your what?"

"My phone number. B-before I went over to her, I tore off a piece of my cheeseburger wrapper and wrote my phone number on it. I poked it down into the pocket of her jeans."

"What did she do?"

"Told me to get my hand off her ass. Not in those words, but I—"

"You have a gun?"

"Whut?"

"I'm not stuttering, Royce. Answer the question."

It was clear that he contemplated lying, but then nodded with reluctance. "A deer rifle out in my truck, 'less it's been stole while I've been in here for so damn long."

"Handgun?"

Again, he conducted a brief mental debate before saying under his breath, "Two."

"Where are they?"

"One in my truck under the driver's seat. The other's home with my old lady. She keeps it on the nightstand when I'm out at night. You can call and ask her."

"Oh, count on us doing that, Royce. It will take time to get a search warrant for your truck. However, you can waive the warrant."

It took him a moment to process that, then from the front pocket of his dirty jeans, he produced a set of keys and slid them across to Joe. "Knock yourselves out. I got nothin' to hide."

"Like your priors, you mean?" Hick said.

Royce swore under his breath, then copped an attitude and defended himself in a mutter. "Everybody shoplifts something in their lifetime."

"You served thirty days for that. A hundred and twenty days for vandalizing a tire store."

"The asshole fired me for no good reason."

"I've heard enough." Joe nudged Hick. Hick got out of the booth and Joe followed. But as Royce Sherman started to leave, Joe said, "You stay put. While we're checking out your firearms, you're going to sit here and try to remember everything else you've conveniently forgotten to tell us about your encounter with Jordie Bennett."

They left him protesting and claiming that his rights were being violated. Joe didn't think he was a conspirator or anything close to one, but, as he rejoined Deputy Morrow, he handed him Royce Sherman's set of keys and filled him in.

"I have no reason to think we'll uncover the murder weapon, but in addition to the search of his truck, have someone confirm that one of his handguns is at home with his 'old lady.' Also, make certain the officers questioning his friends ask about whatever it was that he slipped into Jordie Bennett's rear pocket."

Morrow assured him that both issues would be handled and left to see to it.

"Okay," Joe said to Hick, "next up, the bartender."

The man behind the bar was a barrel-chested giant with a bushy black beard that blended into his hair, which he wore in a braided ponytail extending almost to his waist. He was dressed in an army-green wifebeater, which left his arms bare to show off their sleeves of elaborate tattoos.

If Joe owned a bar in the backwoods that served a rough-and-tumble clientele, he would want this guy in charge.

He offered him and Hick coffee, and they accepted. After declining cream and sugar, Joe began the interview by asking him if Jordie Bennett was a regular customer.

He laughed, flashing remarkably straight, white teeth. "No. Her showing up here tonight made history. She walked in, my jaw dropped. That's why I noticed the time. Ten p.m. on the dot."

Joe and Hick looked at each other, thinking, *Like she was meeting someone.*

Joe went back to the bearded man. "She'd never been here, but you recognized her."

"Soon as she cleared the door. She and her brother are the closest thing we have to celebrities in this town. People who didn't know them already sure as hell did after that Billy Panella mess. Y'all haven't treed him yet?"

"Working on it," Joe said tightly.

"Find the money?"

Joe ignored that. "The shooting victim, had he ever been in here before last night?"

"Not that I recall, and I have a talent for remembering faces. Especially faces like his. Ugly son of a bitch."

"Uglier now," Hick murmured.

"Yeah," the bartender said with a small sound of regret. "When the kid came running in here, yelling and puking, I went outside to see what was what." His beard only partially concealed his grimace. "I'd seen the like in Iraq. Only good thing about going out that way is that you never know it. This poor bastard turned his back to the wrong guy, I guess. When they came in, I knew right off that both were carrying, but I never would've—"

"How'd you know they were carrying?" Joe asked.

"I have a talent for that, too," he said without false modesty. "I spot someone packing, I keep an eye on him. Or her. But those two didn't seem to be looking for trouble."

"Ms. Bennett, was she packing?"

"No. Purse was too small and her clothes fit her too good." He flashed a man-to-man smile, which Joe was hard-pressed not to return.

"Tell me about the other guy."

He squinted one eye. "Better looking than his pal, for sure. In fact, they didn't strike me as two who'd be friends. They were as different from each other as daylight from dark."

"How so?"

"Every way. The fat guy seemed more easygoing. Looked you in the eye when talking to you. He drank beer and went through a bowl of popcorn. The other one never touched it. He drank two shots of tequila. Oh, sorry about the glass."

They'd learned from Morrow that the bartender had washed it as soon as his customer had emptied it, so there was little hope of lifting prints from it for identification. The beer bottles Mickey Bolden had drunk from had gone into a barrel with other trash, but they hadn't been needed to ID him.

"What else about the two?" Joe asked.

"The fat guy talked a lot more. The other one didn't say much at all. Avoided eye contact. Never caught him smiling. Looked like a man with a lot on his mind."

"Taciturn," Joe said.

"If that means 'Do not mess with me,' then yeah. Wore the warning like a sign around his neck."

Hick asked, "Did you notice any reaction from them when Ms. Bennett came in?"

"I really couldn't say because my attention was on her. I re-member serving them another round after her arrival, though. The beer drinker seemed to be in no particular hurry to finish. But the other made quick work of his tequila, then went over to the jukebox."

He told them that Mickey had made a phone call, and when he concluded it, he paid their tab with cash and joined his buddy at the jukebox. Soon after that, they left together.

"Neither said anything to Ms. Bennett?" Joe asked.

"No. And I'm certain of that, because by then the kid had moved in and was hassling her. I was on the verge of telling him to back off when she up and left."

"How long behind the two men did she leave?"

"Minutes after. Five, maybe."

Joe rubbed his eyes, which were gritty from lack of sleep and stinging from the lingering tobacco fog in the bar. "Okay, the taciturn one, can you give us a more detailed physical description?" He began by asking his height, wanting to know if the bartender's recollection corresponded with Royce Sherman's "on the tall side."

"Six three at least. Lean, but ripped. More wide receiver than running back. Y'all Saints fans?"

Joe nodded, asking, "His approximate age?"

"Hmm, mid- to late thirties. A face that severe, it's hard to tell."

"Hair?"

"Brownish. Longish. Not as long as mine."

Joe noted the length of the man's braid and smiled. "That'd be hard for any man to beat."

"His came to his collar in back."

"Facial hair?"

He stroked his luxuriant beard. "No. I would've noticed."

"Tattoos, scars, piercings? Anything like that?"

"No tattoos. None visible, anyway." He extended his arms. "I would have noticed ink. He did have a scar, though. Here," he said, touching the side of his chin.

Joe's heart skipped.

Hick stopped pecking on his iPad screen and raised his head.

Joe cleared his throat. "You sure?"

"About the scar? Yeah," the bartender replied. "I noticed because it cut through his scruff. Oh, does that count as facial hair? He'd gone two, maybe three days without shaving."

"Describe the scar."

"Well, as I was facing him, it was..." He used Joe's chin as a means of remembering correctly. "On the left side. Sort of curved, like the letter *C*, only backward," he said, drawing one in the air inches from Joe's face.

Without taking his eyes off the bartender, Joe asked Hick, "Got a picture handy?"

Joe's heart had resumed beating and now thudded with

dread as Hick went through the necessary steps to open his photos file. He brought up a mug shot, zoomed it into a close-up, and turned the screen toward the bartender, who happily exclaimed, "That's the guy. No question." Then, gauging their expressions, his white smile wavered. "Not good?"

Joe turned away and reached for his cell phone, saying to Hick over his shoulder, "I gotta alert the office."

Hick was left to answer the bartender's question. "No. Not good. Especially for Jordie Bennett."

Chapter 7

———◆———

"Well?" Shaw demanded.

"What is that?"

Holding the scrap of food wrapper by both ends directly in front of Jordie Bennett's face, he stretched it taut so she could better see what had been scrawled on it. "A phone number. Local area code."

"That was in my pocket?" She looked from the strip of paper into his eyes. "I don't know anything about it."

He unsnapped the breast pocket of his shirt and stuffed the paper inside. "Right. And the jerk in the bar was also a total stranger."

"He was."

"You didn't cry foul when this stranger started rubbing your ass."

"I didn't want to make a scene."

"You made a scene when you walked into that place."

"I told him to take his hand off me or else. I didn't know he was slipping something into my pocket."

"Convenient, that he had the number already written

down. Like he knew you'd be there and planned on sneaking it to you."

"I'm telling you, I don't know anything about it."

"Next you'll be telling me that you're a regular customer, that you go there every night for your glass of white wine." When she didn't immediately respond, he tilted his head. "Well? Had you ever darkened the door of that place before tonight? Had you ever even driven past it?"

She said nothing.

"Thought so." He closed his hand around her elbow and nudged her forward. "But you went there tonight and let that jackass fondle you."

"Exactly. He was a jackass. Why would I want his phone number?"

He drew up short and faced her. "I never said it was *his*."

Her breath caught. They stared at each other for a ponderous few moments, then she blinked several times and said, "Who else's would it be?"

He leaned in and whispered, "You tell me, Jordie."

She held his gaze but wasn't quailed by it. In fact, her eyes narrowed. "How did you and your partner know I would be in that bar tonight?"

Shaw eased himself back. "We didn't. Truth is, it shocked the hell out of us when you came in. I had my heart set on a triple-X pay-per-view in the motel followed by a good night's sleep. Then there you were. Scrub plan A. We need a plan B.

"So I mosey over to assess the situation. In the meantime, Mickey makes a phone call, and comes back with, 'Get her done.' 'Here? Now?' I ask. 'Here, now,' he says. I had no choice except to go along. To a point."

He let all that sink in. "But don't mistakenly think that by putting a bullet through his fat brain that I was saving your skin. I was saving mine. Because as Mickey and I were closing in on you, it occurred to me that when he left that parking lot, there were going to be two bodies on the ground, and that one of them was going to be mine."

He shuffled forward a few inches, crowding in on her again. "So, Jordie, you see why it's important for me to know what you were doing in that place tonight, at that particular time, because to me it looks like a setup."

Her lips parted, but whatever she'd intended to say remained unspoken. Finally she said, "I wasn't part of any setup involving you. I don't even know your name."

"Shaw Kinnard. Pleased to meet you. Why were you in that bar?"

"Impulse."

"Bullshit."

"I stopped in to have a drink."

"At a place where you wouldn't ordinarily be caught dead. No pun intended. Who sent you there?"

"No one."

"Someone."

She took a deep breath and shook back her hair. "Okay, I'll play along. What were you being set up for?"

"To take the fall for killing you. Mickey even told me to grab your purse, make it look like a robbery gone south so the hit couldn't be linked to anybody else."

"That would have required some elaborate staging. He couldn't have—"

"He could. He has. He was a pro, well known to cops but never prosecuted. One of his means of consistently getting off clean was to blame the dead dude."

She absorbed that, then said, "I don't know anything about him, or his reputation, or a setup. You're just being paranoid."

"You're goddamn right I am." He stated that in a low, tight voice that left the words vibrating between them. "Now. For the last time. Who sent you there tonight?"

Her gaze dropped to his shirt pocket where he'd stashed the slip of paper with the telephone number on it, then she turned her head away from him. "Nobody. I don't know what you're talking about."

"You're lying through your teeth. But I'm not going to waste any more time trying to get the truth out of you here." He took her elbow again and propelled her toward the car.

She seemed relieved to be off the hook, at least for the present, and went more or less docilely. But when they reached the car and he pulled her hands together, she resisted.

"Please don't. It hurts."

"That's your fault. Stop pulling against it." He turned her back to him, but, before clipping on the cuff, he said, "But just to show you that I can be a nice guy…" He padded her wrists by wrapping them with another bandana before fastening the restraint.

She didn't thank him or acknowledge the gesture. Instead she jerked herself away from his touch as he handed her into the backseat. She sat staring straight ahead while he removed her sandals and tied her ankles with the original bandana.

That done, he opened the trunk and worked a bottle of drinking water out of a pack. He returned to the open door of the backseat, uncapped the water bottle, and extended it toward her mouth. "It's not cold, but it's wet."

"I'm fine."

"You'll dehydrate."

"The sooner I die, the sooner you can collect your money."

"That's just it. Dying of thirst takes too long."

He nudged her lips with the rim of the bottle and when she still refused to drink, he said, "It's a painful way to check out, but suit yourself." He tilted the bottle to his mouth and drained it, then used the back of his hand to wipe a dribble off his chin. He caught her looking at his scar. "What?"

"Nothing."

"I fell off my bike when I was a kid."

The drop-dead look she gave him said she knew he was lying. The scar was too recent to have been caused by a childhood mishap.

"Does your head hurt?" he asked.

"No."

He slid two fingers through her hair at the side of her head and explored her scalp. When he located a small bump, she winced. "Why lie about it? I have some Advil."

"No thank you."

"Look, I told you that torture wasn't part of this gig. So take the damn—"

"No. Thank. You."

"Fine."

He moved to the trunk, tossed the empty water bottle into it, closed it, then returned to her. "Lie down."

"I'll sit."

"You'll be more comfortable lying down than sitting up with your hands behind you."

She turned her head aside, clearly spurning his suggestion.

"I'm not giving you a choice this time, Jordie. Either lie down, or I'll tie your feet to the door handle and make it impossible for you to sit up."

"Go to hell."

"Been already."

He was about to force the issue of her lying down when he hesitated. Instead, he placed the tip of his index finger in the center of her forehead and traced her stubborn profile down the length of her nose, past her mouth, and over her chin before letting his hand fall away. "Have to say, I admire your sass. You could be bawling and begging."

"I'll never beg you for my life."

"Bet you do."

"You'll be disappointed."

He let a few seconds elapse, then said, "Maybe you won't. Bawling and begging are more your brother's style. He caves quick, doesn't he?"

Her head snapped around and she shot him a glare.

He huffed a laugh. "Well, that sure as hell struck a nerve." Grinning with satisfaction, he motioned for her to lie down. "Don't make me tie you down."

The look she gave him would have blistered paint, but she lay down on her side. He shut the door, got into the driver's seat, put the car in reverse, and backed out of the pockmarked side road and onto the highway.

Nothing more was said, but he could feel her anger smoldering. Eventually it cooled, and when he glanced between the seats a half hour later, he saw that she'd gone to sleep. Either that, or she had gotten better at playing possum.

Letting her go behind the tree to relieve herself hadn't been a chivalrous nod to her modesty. It had been a test, and she had passed.

He knew perfectly well that the redneck with the skull on his shirt had been nothing more to her than a nuisance. If he'd been a player of any significance, she would have memorized the phone number he slipped her and then disposed of the evidence, probably before she left the bar, but if not then, then surely while she was out of sight behind the tree. If she'd known about the scrap of paper in her seat pocket, it wouldn't have still been there when she rejoined him.

But he'd reasoned that if he made an issue of it, hammered her with questions about that guy and his phone number, he would eventually break her and learn why she'd gone to that bar tonight. Because he knew damn well that it wasn't happenstance.

As the sun was coming up, he pulled off the two-lane highway onto another side road that was almost as rough as the first. Leaving the car to idle, he got out and opened the trunk.

He took what he needed from it and by the time he opened the backseat door, she was struggling to sit up. He reached in to help her, but she recoiled, saying "I can manage."

"Maybe, but it's my time you're wasting."

He placed a hand on her shoulder and levered her upright. She looked at him resentfully but then noticed the bandana he was shaking out of its folded square. "How many of those do you have?"

"They come twelve to a pack."

"What's this one for?"

He placed his foot on the door frame and used his raised knee as a platform on which to fold the bandana into a triangle, then to fold the center point forward several times until he'd formed a strip about three inches wide. "Blindfold."

"What?"

"Blind—"

"You're going to blindfold me? Why?"

He gave her a stupid-question look.

"So I can't see when you shoot me?" Her voice went thin with panic. Just a trace, but discernible.

"Turn your head," he said.

"No."

"You're not gonna face a firing squad, Jordie. I just don't want you to see where we're going."

"I have no idea where we *are* much less where we're going. Not even the direction—"

"Turn your head."

"I can't see anything when I'm lying down. That's why you insisted on it, right? So I couldn't see road signs? The only thing I can see through the window is the sky."

"Which was fine when it was dark. But now it's getting light."

"I won't be able to see anything."

"Not if you're blindfolded. Now turn your head so I can tie this on."

"You'll have to force me."

"Is that what you want?"

She didn't move.

"Goddammit," he said under his breath. "It's been a long night. I'm tired of this crap."

"I'm tired of *you*," she said, her voice cracking. "Why don't you just get it over with. Panella wouldn't know when—" She broke off when she realized she had blurted out the name.

It hovered there, a sound wave momentarily trapped between them. Moving slowly, Shaw bent down to bring them eye to eye. "Ooops." He said it softly but with enough emphasis for her to feel his puff of breath against her face. "Earlier you asked who'd hired Mickey and me to kill you. Why'd you play dumb when you knew it was Billy Panella?"

When she didn't answer, he pinched her chin between his thumb and forefinger and tipped her head back so she had to look at him directly. "Do you know where he is, Jordie?"

"How would I know?"

"Fucking good question."

"No one knows. He vanished. No one's seen or heard from him—"

"Mickey did."

That momentarily stymied her. Then she said, "Well, I certainly haven't. I'd be the last person he would contact."

"You're completely in the dark about where he is?"

"Completely."

"Then why was he willing to pay two hundred grand to put you on ice?"

"You can ask him that when you renegotiate your deal. But if he thinks I know anything about *anything*, he's wasting his money to have me killed."

"What about your brother Josh? Does he know Panella's whereabouts?"

Her blue eyes were turbulent with anger, frustration, possibly fear, a catalog of strong emotions, but she didn't verbalize any of them, perhaps fearing that she would make another slip.

He goaded her with a cold grin. "Cat got your tongue?"

"Not at all. I can articulate *Go to hell*."

They stared at each other for several moments, then he said, "Interesting." She didn't ask him what was interesting, but he continued as though she had. "Yesterday morning as Mickey and I were leaving the city, he pointed out a billboard on the freeway."

Her face remained impassive.

"The thing couldn't be missed. 'Extravaganza' was spelled out in glittering capital letters, a sparkly firework exploding behind the letter *E*. And across the bottom of the sign was your name."

He gave her time to comment. She didn't.

"Now, your brother being an outlaw and all—"

"Josh hasn't confessed to or been convicted of a crime."

"—you'd think that you, his big sister, would want to keep a low profile. Maybe move someplace where you weren't so well known, even change your name to avoid any connection to him." He lowered his voice almost to a whisper. "But you didn't do that, Jordie. You put your name up on a billboard for all the world to see."

"Does this have a point?"

"Either—and here's where it gets interesting—"

"About time."

"—either," he stressed, "that billboard is a declaration that you're your own woman, separate and apart from Josh and his misdeeds..."

"Or?"

"...or, it's your way of giving everybody the finger. Let 'em think what they want to about your baby brother. You're not ashamed of him. You'll remain loyal, steadfast, and true, no matter what." He waited a beat. "Are you distancing yourself from Josh, or announcing that he'll always have your love and support, that you'll be at the ready to lend assistance if ever he needs you? Which is it, Jordie?"

"What difference does it make to you?"

"It doesn't," he said. "But obviously it does to Billy Panella."

Chapter 8

————◉————

Joe Wiley walked into his office, dropped a Subway sack on top of a pile of paperwork on his desk, and, without unnecessary preamble said, "I thought he was in Mexico."

"He was," Hick said.

"On the payroll of a drug kingpin."

"He was."

This was the first chance they'd had to talk freely about Shaw Kinnard.

As soon as Joe had notified his office of Kinnard's apparent involvement in the execution-style slaying of Mickey Bolden, he had wrapped up as swiftly and as neatly as possible in Tobias, relinquishing that aspect of the case to Deputy Sheriff Morrow so he and Hick could concentrate their efforts on the search for Shaw Kinnard and Jordie Bennett.

Sensing their urgency to get going, Morrow had brought them up to speed on what had transpired while they were interviewing the bartender. Royce Sherman's only crime beyond general stupidity appeared to be possession of unregistered firearms and carrying without a concealed handgun license. Nothing

72

substantive was obtained from any of the other witnesses, so they'd been allowed to go.

No further physical evidence had been recovered from the parking lot or surrounding area, but the FBI crime scene crew along with that of the sheriff's office were still searching.

Fingerprints had been lifted from Jordie Bennett's car. Hers were on record with U.S. Customs and Border Patrol because of her Global Entry status. If any prints other than hers were found in or on her car, Morrow would notify the agents immediately.

He offered to drive them to the field where the chopper was waiting, but at Joe's request they stopped first at Morrow's office to retrieve what was left of the bullet that the ME had removed from Mickey Bolden's head. Joe wanted the bureau to conduct the ballistics tests, although they would be academic. He knew who had put Mickey permanently out of business.

Standing in the downwash of the chopper blades, Morrow snapped a salute and promised that he would stay on top of the murder investigation and notify them first of any developments. As they lifted off, Joe felt they were leaving the mop-up to a good man.

Noise had prevented him and Hick from talking on the short flight back to New Orleans. Since each had left his car at the heliport, they'd split up there. Joe had offered to stop on the way to the office and pick up a couple of sandwiches.

Now, Hick took one from the sack, unwrapped it, discovered meatballs smothered in melted mozzarella, and passed it to Joe, who said, "Don't worry. Your Veggie Delite is in there." He took a bite of meatball and spoke around it. "To live in New Orleans and be a vegetarian—"

"'—is a waste.' So you've said. About ten thousand times."

"It's worse than a waste. It's a sin. Ask your priest. He'll back me up." He used a napkin to blot marinara from the corner of his mouth. "So Kinnard's no longer down Mexico way."

"Our guys went into overdrive. This is what they've got so far." Hick took a sip of sweet iced tea, reached for a folder, and flipped it open. "He made a notable exit." He turned the folder around so Joe could see the top photo in a stack. It showed the bodies of two men inside a late-model Mercedes, both bloody and indisputably dead.

"The car, as you see it here, was left two blocks from state police headquarters, which was as close as the concertina wire barricade around the compound would allow."

"The police must've appreciated that consideration."

"Not so much." Hick tipped his head toward the photo. "The guy in the uniform? Was the jefe."

"Of the state police?" When Hick nodded, Joe folded the wrapper around the remains of his sandwich and pushed it aside, predicting he was probably going to have raging heartburn.

"But don't cry over him," Hick said. "He was as corrupt as they come, playing both sides of the drug wars and taking graft from everybody."

Joe looked at the photo again. "Who's body number two?"

Hick slid the top photo aside to reveal the one beneath it. A name had been printed across the bottom in red marker. "Thirty-two-year-old American, originally from Phoenix, middle-class upbringing, son of two college professors. Started dealing in junior high school."

"The beginning of an illustrious career?"

Hick nodded. "Big-time operator in the guns and drugs markets. The late state police chief moonlighted as his senior bodyguard, but he employed an army of them, and they were needed. In addition to bloodthirsty enemies, he had a price on his head, wanted by an alphabet soup of federal agencies, including us, ATF, DEA. The list goes on."

Joe studied the picture taken with a telephoto lens of a baby-faced young man sitting in what appeared to be a nightclub booth with a cigarette dangling from his insolent smile. "He looks like a frat boy."

Hick smiled. "Basically, that was his mentality. An undercover DEA agent reports that he was running afoul of his allies south of the border, making them nervous by living too high off the hog and calling attention to himself. Big hacienda. Flashy cars. Wild parties. He was hosting one such wingding when Kinnard struck."

"When did this happen?"

"Tuesday night."

Joe grimaced. "This Tuesday? *Our* Tuesday."

"Yep."

"Can't be a coincidence."

"Nope. Kinnard was a houseguest at the guy's villa. One of the playgirls hired for the evening told the authorities that Kinnard, the frat boy, and the bodyguard left the party together in the Mercedes, Kinnard driving."

"He shoots them in the car, abandons it with the bodies inside and sure to be found, then what?"

"It's anybody's guess," Hick said. "Nobody knows how he got out of the area or where and how he crossed the border. He arrived in New Orleans midday Thursday on a flight from Dallas / Fort Worth. He grabbed a meal at an airport Chili's before boarding."

"How'd he get to Dallas?"

"We've got guys working backward from there, but so far, they haven't found a trail. All that's known is that he called a taxi to take him to the airport from a local motel, where he spent one night. We have him on numerous security cameras at DFW." Hick shuffled through photos, pointing out Shaw Kinnard in blurry shots of the busy, crowded airport. "Outside our airport, he hailed a taxi and had it drop him at the Doubletree. But he didn't check in."

"He walked through and went out another door."

"Not before waving to the security camera," Hick said sourly. "He exited the side-street door, strolled off down the sidewalk, and that was the last anyone saw of him until he showed up at that bar with Mickey Bolden."

Joe belched behind his fist. "What ID did he use when he went through DFW's security?"

"Georgia driver's license. Breezed through. He checked a bag. His weapons must've been in it."

Joe grumbled, "Don't count on it."

He stuffed his trash into the carryout sack, then stood up and made a circuit of the small room, giving Hick time to wolf down his sandwich. Joe resumed by asking, "Anything out of Mississippi?"

Mickey Bolden had kept an apartment in Biloxi. Basic shelter. Nothing fancy by any stretch. It was paid for by what he earned as a maître d' at a restaurant in one of the shabbier casino hotels. He reported his gratuities to the IRS, as any solid citizen would, and paid his income taxes and bills on time.

His hobby, for which he seemed to have a passion, was far more lucrative than the restaurant job. Unfortunately the Bureau hadn't yet discovered where he banked the fees he earned by snuffing people, which was one reason they were never able to make a case against him that a prosecutor felt would hold up in court.

"Last Wednesday, Bolden told his employer that he needed to take a few days off," Hick said.

"Which he did periodically."

"And nobody ever asked why."

"Probably because everybody knew why," Joe remarked.

"Probably. Anyway, he hasn't been seen around his Biloxi apartment since Thursday evening. But the car registered to him is still in the parking lot."

"Rental?"

"None leased in his name."

Joe hadn't expected there to be. Mickey would have had someone under the radar who supplied him with a vehicle when he went to a job.

"I did hear from Morrow," Hicks said, "but don't get excited. Deputies canvassed Jordie Bennett's neighborhood. One lady noticed an unfamiliar car parked at the end of the street yesterday. In a nutshell, all she remembers is that it was dark in color and had four wheels."

Joe chuffed.

"There might have been two men inside. She couldn't say with any degree of certainty."

Law enforcement agencies in Louisiana and surrounding states were on the lookout for Shaw Kinnard and Jordie Bennett, but they didn't even know what kind of vehicle to be looking for or in which direction Kinnard was headed. So far no sightings had been reported even by the crazies who routinely reported they'd seen Elvis and Osama bin Laden.

"Agents have been interviewing Ms. Bennett's employees and friends with whom she keeps in touch," Hick said. "All went hysterical when told of her disappearance and probable abduction. None were helpful, but they sing the same chorus. It must have to do with her brother and Billy Panella."

"Tell me something I don't know," Joe groused. "Anybody contact Jackson Terrell?"

"He was reached by phone at a ritzy wellness spa in Colorado. Woke him up, and he wasn't alone."

"New girlfriend?"

"New wife. They got married several months ago."

"Guess we weren't invited."

"Guess not."

"But he's not mooning over his breakup with Jordie Bennett."

"Apparently not. Can't speak for her, though."

Joe thought about it and came to the conclusion that they

had zilch. No leads, false or otherwise, to follow up. They might just as well be in a damn black hole, a situation infuriatingly similar to the last time Shaw Kinnard was their suspect.

As though Hick was reading his mind, he asked, "What was he doing with Mickey Bolden?"

"Mickey was a link to Billy Panella and thirty million dollars, give or take a few mil." Thoughtfully, he pulled on his lower lip. "Only a guess, but Kinnard probably approached Bolden a while back and laid some groundwork. In the hope of getting to Panella and all that dough, he established a quasi partnership with his trusted hit man."

"He offered his services."

"I'm only guessing," Joe reminded him.

"It feels right, though," Hick said. "He let Bolden know that he was available for down-and-dirty jobs, then sat back and waited for a call."

"Which he received on Tuesday."

"So he sewed up his business in Mexico and hightailed it here." After a beat, Hick asked, "Do you think he knew who the hit was?"

"He probably assumed it was Josh Bennett."

"At what point do you think he learned it was his sister instead?"

Joe rubbed his forehead with worry. "I don't know." He pushed his fingers through his hair, noticed that it was greasy, and realized how badly he needed a shower. Even Hick was looking less than bandbox fresh.

"Let's take a couple of hours." Joe picked up the folder with the gruesome photos and tucked it under his arm. "I need to touch base with my family. I think we're supposed to go to a carnival at the kids' school this evening."

"How will Marsha take you missing it?"

"She'll be pissed, but she'll forgive me. Eventually. How's your love life? Still in that 'promising relationship'?"

"Yes. It's still promising."

"Oh yeah? When will you be taking it to the next level?"

"No time soon."

"How come?"

"Because of all my other promising relationships."

Joe rolled his eyes and motioned Hick toward the door, but he hung back. "One thing I failed to mention earlier. The hired party girl who talked to the authorities in Mexico?"

Joe nodded.

"She was with the three men when they left the party."

"Explain."

Hick told him that after the bodies of the two victims were discovered near police headquarters, the young woman was rounded up from the villa along with all the other guests. He pointed to the folder under Joe's arm. "She cooperated in exchange for anonymity, so you won't find her name or photo in there. But she's the one who IDed Shaw Kinnard.

"She told the investigators that just as the party was getting into full swing, Kinnard approached Frat Boy and confided that there was a guy he needed to meet, someone from a rival cartel who wanted to switch teams. To demonstrate his sincerity, this guy was willing to tell everything he knew about the rival's operation, but it had to be right then before the rival caught on and silenced him for good.

"Our frat boy was reluctant to leave the sex, drugs, and rock and roll, but Kinnard impressed on him that this guy could decide that the life expectancy of a traitor was short and chicken out. They had to move on it or say bye-bye to a golden opportunity. So Frat Boy grudgingly went with Kinnard, and, at Kinnard's suggestion, took only one bodyguard so the soon-to-be-traitor wouldn't get spooked."

"The frat boy chose his top guard, the chief of the state police."

"Actually Kinnard made the selection," Hick said wryly. "We

know all this because the frat boy was all over the party girl during this discussion, and she heard everything. When the time came to leave, the frat boy insisted that she go along to 'keep him company.' Her words.

"They piled into the Mercedes. Kinnard behind the wheel. Just beyond the villa's security gate, he stopped the car and ordered the girl to get out. Frat Boy objected, but Kinnard told him his hard-on should be for this guy who was going to supply them with valuable information, not for a chick when chicks could be had for a dime a dozen. The jefe agreed with Kinnard. Kinnard got out, opened the backseat door for her, and told her to scram." Hick stopped to take a breath.

Leading him, Joe said, "Okay."

"Why'd he do that? Why not just kill the girl, too? Which would have been quicker and neater." He shrugged. "Maybe he has a soft spot for the ladies."

Joe thought about it for a moment, then, grumbling again, said, "Don't count on that, either."

Chapter 9

As the car slowed and then rolled to a stop, Jordie pressed her spine against the back of the seat and used it as leverage to sit up. If he didn't like it, too damn bad. "Where are we?"

Her best guess was that it had been close to an hour since he'd stopped to blindfold her. It seemed that they'd been driving in circles, but without her sense of sight, she could have easily become disoriented.

Without saying a word, he opened the driver's door and got out.

"Where are you going?"

Her question went unanswered, but she could tell by his footfalls that he was walking away from the car, treading cautiously. What was he doing? What was he about to do?

Seized by panic, she struggled to free her hands and feet. To no avail, of course, but she had to do something or she would go mad with anxiety.

She jumped in fright when the trunk popped open, which he must have unlatched remotely using the key fob. As she heard him returning to the car, she asked, "What are you doing?"

"Checking things out."

"Please take the blindfold off."

"I'm busy."

He walked away again and, a few seconds later, the silence was broken by the noisy clanking of metal against metal, followed by a scraping sound and a squeal that sounded like rusty hinges.

He came back to the car and replaced whatever he'd taken from the trunk. It landed with a heavy thud. A tire tool of some sort? He didn't bother closing the lid of the trunk before getting back into the driver's seat and engaging the gears.

"What was that racket? What were you doing?"

The car rolled forward slowly, its tires crunching over gravel. She knew the moment they entered some sort of enclosure. Even with the blindfold on, she could tell they were no longer in sunlight, and the air quality changed, becoming musty and dank, smelling faintly of motor oil and mice.

He stopped the car, turned off the engine, and got out. He was gone for a minute or more, but she could hear him moving around, then he returned to the car and opened the backseat door. When he touched her cheek, she flinched.

"Easy," he said.

"What are you doing?"

"Trying to turn your head."

"What for?"

"I thought you wanted the blindfold off."

She hesitated then turned her head away from him. He untied the bandana and caught it as it fell away from her eyes. As she blinked him into focus, he was tucking the corner of the bandana into the front pocket of his jeans.

Neither spoke as he squatted in the wedge of the open door and reached in to unknot the bandana around her ankles. As he straightened up, he looked into her face but didn't say anything. He motioned her out of the car. It was awkward to do with her hands bound behind her back, but he made no move to help her, probably because she had rebuffed his previous attempts.

Once on her feet beside the car, she made a slow pivot to get her bearings. When she came back around to him, she said, "The view isn't worth the long drive it took to get here."

"Still mouthy." He stepped behind her and snipped off the plastic cuff, then unwound the bandana he'd used to pad her wrists.

As she massaged feeling back into them, she asked, "What is this place?"

"Looks to be some kind of multipurpose garage. Today, it's a hideout."

The corrugated tin roof had seen better days. The walls were constructed of wood, unpainted and weathered. Daylight squeezed in between the vertical slats and shone like tiny spotlights through the knotholes.

For the most part, the cavernous space was empty, but a large oil stain in the center of the concrete floor indicated that at one time it had housed a piece of machinery or a vehicle of some sort. A stack of bald tires occupied one corner. Some fishing gear including a net hung from pegs nailed into one wall. There was also a bow, the string attached at only one end. She didn't see any arrows. An outboard motor lay on its side against one wall. The end of one of its rusty blades had broken off, and the engine casing was covered with grit and cobwebs.

When her gaze came back to Shaw Kinnard, he was inserting a battery into the back of a cell phone. Her heart spiked with optimism. "Is that mine?"

"Mickey's."

"Where's mine?"

"Wouldn't you like to know," he said. "I hid it, but not in the same place that I hid its battery or the car keys." He spread his arms. "You're welcome to search all you want. You won't find them, and even if you did they wouldn't do you any good." He raised his shirttail to reveal that his pistol, without the sound suppressor, was still holstered on his belt. He watched the phone's screen, waiting for it to boot up.

"The police can trace cell phones," she said.

"Yes, but this has a disposable SIM card. Brand-new. Mickey put it in yesterday morning before we left New Orleans for Tobias. He's called only one person on it, and only one person has called him."

She didn't have to guess who. "Are you going to call him now?"

"No. I'm gonna let him call me."

"What if he doesn't?"

"He already has. Five times." He turned the phone to where she could see the call log. Caller Unknown had in fact called several times. "He'll call." He slid the phone into his breast pocket, where he had secured the slip of paper with the phone number on it.

"That moron with the skull on his shirt can verify that everything I told you was the truth, that he was only trying to pick me up and that I didn't know he was sneaking me his number. You can call him using Mickey's phone."

"Bad idea."

"Why?"

"Because by now the police will have questioned everybody who was in the bar at the time of the killing, including him. *Especially* him, since the two of you were so chummy. His phone was probably confiscated during questioning. So if I call the number he wrote down for you, and it *does* turn out to be his, a cop will be on the other end."

"But with a disposable number—"

"The police have their ways and means. I'm not taking any chances." He frowned ruefully. "Sorry. You probably had your heart set on me making a mistake. I don't make mistakes."

His sympathetic, patronizing tone infuriated her. "You'll make one."

He looked even more regretful over her self-delusion.

"You have to sleep at some point."

"That's true." He grabbed her hand and towed her toward the door of the enclosure, which he'd left standing open after driving the car through. "You need to see this."

The door was wide, like a barn door. A broken padlock dangled from a loose hook, which accounted for the loud clanging; he'd taken a tire iron to it. The oversized hinges were corroded with rust.

He pulled her through the opening to the outside. "Take a good look at the middle of nowhere."

Her heart sank, because the landscape beyond the derelict structure couldn't be more accurately described—and it looked exactly the same as the swampy landscape they'd left hours before. He must have been driving in circles all night, not only since he'd blindfolded her, but from the time he'd stuffed her into the car and left the beer joint on the banks of the bayou.

The narrow gravel road on which they'd arrived bridged a ditch at least twenty yards across. It was filled with water so opaque and ominously still that its depth was impossible to gauge. On the far side of the ditch, the road disappeared into a grove of cypresses and hardwoods that blotted out the daylight, creating a deep twilight beneath branches draped with forlorn-looking clusters of Spanish moss.

"And behind us..."

He pulled her along to the corner of the building, which she saw backed up to a body of water similar in viscosity to that in the ditch. It wound through stands of trees and around spits of land, creating a seemingly endless labyrinth of channels extending all the way to the horizon in every direction.

"You see what you're up against if you try to escape? That

water is a virtual science project. I don't recommend taking a dip."

When he hitched his chin in the direction of the swamp, her eyes were drawn to the C-shaped scar, which was even more evident now that his scruff was hours older. Associating that scar with his arrogance, his dominance, she channeled her anger toward it. Then she looked him in the eye and said with defiance, "I'll think of something."

He merely shrugged, turned his back on her, and headed for the door. "I'm hungry."

His dismissal of any threat she might pose made her feel hopeless as nothing else had. She was no longer bound hand and foot, but he wasn't concerned that she would attempt an escape. The likelihood of her succeeding was nil, and if she died while attempting it, he would collect his fee from Panella, and probably be glad that he hadn't had to expend another bullet.

When he reached the doorway he stopped and, looking back at her, tipped his head toward the opening. She remained where she was. He stood there waiting. No impatient tapping of his toe. No gestures of exasperation. Just *waiting*. A man supremely confident of her obliging him.

His attitude rankled, but staging a rebellion now would get her nowhere. It would only cost her energy she needed to conserve. However, she'd be damned before he saw her cowed. Acting as though it was her idea, she walked toward the door, then past him and through it. He pushed it closed behind them.

"Can't you leave it open and let in some fresh air?"

"No."

"It's stifling in here. And it stinks."

"Then hold your nose. The door stays shut." He moved to the trunk of the car and took out a handled grocery sack, then brought it over to her and held it open for her inspection. "Mickey did the shopping, so I can't vouch for the choices. Take your pick." He jiggled the sack.

Inside it were a variety of single-serve canned goods. "I'm not hungry," she said.

He bent his head low so he could inventory the selection. "Sardines. Beanie wienies. Chili mac. Ravioli. Tomato soup."

"I'm not hungry."

"And a box of plastic spoons."

"*I'm not hungry.*" She turned her head to glare at him. Which was a mistake. Because it brought her face so close to his they were almost touching.

His flinty eyes sparked, then dropped their focus to her parted lips. "You sure?"

His whisper had the texture of fine-grade sandpaper. She felt it like a stroke low on her belly, and, for a heartbeat—much too long—every nerve ending sizzled with awareness of him. He was body heat, and tensile strength, raw masculinity and leashed power, and her breathy reaction to all that panicked her.

She averted her head and stepped away. "Yes, I'm sure," she said, her voice husky and lacking the forceful positivity she wished it had. Wished she *felt*.

He remained as he was for a five count, then shook a plastic spoon from the box of picnic utensils, took a can of food from the sack, and replaced it in the trunk.

He carried the items over to an empty wooden crate, up-ended it, and sat down. Wincing, he reached beneath the hem of his shirt, pulled the pistol from the holster, and set it beside him on the crate. Then he peeled back the lid on the can and dug in. Hunched over, he spooned the food into his mouth with an aggressive efficiency meant to satisfy an appetite, not to savor, or even to taste.

Jordie backed up to the hood of the car and sat down on it. From that safe distance, she watched him. After a full minute had elapsed, she said into the silence, "Why haven't you killed me?"

"Told you."

"I don't believe you'll do it."

Keeping his head down, he froze with the spoon halfway to his mouth and held it there for a beat before he completed the motion and took the bite. "Believe it."

"I don't."

"Look, just because we nearly lip-locked—"

"No way in hell."

He briefly looked up. "Whatever. You're my bread and butter. Worth two hundred grand at least, and I think there's much more to be had."

"So why haven't you called Panella?"

"If I contact him first, I lose bargaining power. He's got to be worried over why he hasn't heard from Mickey and why Mickey hasn't answered his calls. I'm letting him stew."

"How much are you going to ask him for?"

"None of your business."

"My life isn't any of my business?"

"Not the price tag on it. That's between Panella and me." He watched her for a second or two, then said, "You've known all along it was him."

"Yes."

"Why'd you let on otherwise?"

"I was in denial."

"Dangerous place, denial." He resumed eating.

"I don't suppose he told Mickey where he is."

He snorted at the absurdity of that. "No, but he doesn't know where I am, either. Or, more to the point, where you are. His butt will stay chapped until he gets confirmation that you're dead."

Her thoughts were shifting and reshaping as rapidly as storm clouds, making coherency difficult. But she latched onto one word. "*Confirmation?* You no longer have to produce my body?"

"Never did. How could I deliver your body to him when I

don't know where he is, and he's not about to divulge it? I only told you that to keep you . . . cooperative."

"Terrified."

"Then it worked."

Her cheeks turned hot with anger and embarrassment over being so gullible, but she wanted to keep this conversation going. The more she learned, the better armed she would be. She just needed to brush up on her lie-detecting skills, because he was an accomplished liar.

But assuming he was being at least partially truthful, she asked, "What kind of confirmation will he require?"

"I'll know when I ask him."

"You've had twelve hours or more to negotiate a new deal with him. In the meantime, you're stuck with mouthy me here in these swell surroundings." She pointed out a rip in the tin roof that looked like it had been made with an old-fashioned can opener. "Aren't you anxious to get to Mexico and that cerveza? What's holding you back?"

He scooped the last of the food from the can, dropped the spoon into it, and set it on the floor. He pulled the bandana from his pocket and wiped his mouth and hands, then stretched his legs out in front of him, folded his arms over his midriff, and crossed his ankles.

She noticed that the soles of his cowboy boots had seen a lot of wear. They'd been lived in. Like his face.

"You love your brother?"

The unexpected question snapped her gaze back up to his. "Why do you ask?"

"Just answer me."

"Of course I love him. He's my brother."

"He's a double-crossing chickenshit."

Reacting as though he'd slapped her, she retorted, "What do you know about Josh, about anything?"

"Even a guy like me watches TV every now and again."

"Triple-X pay-per-view."

"Sometimes I catch the news. What I didn't know about the Panella case, Mickey filled in yesterday while we were trailing you."

"Trailing me?"

"We followed you around town. Waited while you got your manicure. Parked down the street from your house."

"Spying on me."

"Not so much spying as plotting how we were gonna...you know."

"You were formulating plan A. What *was* plan A?"

"Doesn't matter. It got scrubbed. Back to your brother— what was life like when you two were kids?"

"Why do you care?"

"Stop answering every question with a question."

"Then stop asking me questions."

"You don't like my questions?"

"I don't like your prying. Or is delving into the background of your victims part of your MO?"

"My MO?" That amused him. "I guess you watch some TV, too."

He came as close to smiling as she'd seen, but it didn't soften his mouth or any other feature. If anything, it emphasized the harsh angularity of his face.

Nor did the semismile last. It faded as he tilted his head to one side and studied her, then said, "I've had an idea. But before I advance it, I want to know why the subject of your brother makes you twitchy and defensive."

"It doesn't."

He merely looked at her with an unflinching, I-know-better gaze.

After an interminable length of time, she relented, ran her hand around the back of her neck, stretched it, released a long sigh. "There was nothing extraordinary about our family life.

We were typical. Middle class. There was Mom, Dad, me the big sister, Josh the younger brother."

"Did you watch out for him?"

"More or less. Like older siblings do."

"Which was it? More or less?"

"If I must pick, I'd say more."

"Why?"

She caught herself shifting her weight—twitching—and stopped. "Every family has a unique dynamic."

"Those are words that don't mean shit."

"In our family they meant that I, as the older child, had an implied responsibility to protect my younger brother." Actually her responsibility to safeguard Josh had been more than implied. Daily she'd been reminded of it, if not with a verbal admonishment then with sighs of disappointment or looks of reproof which were equally, if not even more, effective.

"To protect him from what?"

"Normal, everyday childhood hazards."

"Hmm."

With impatience, she added, "Like stepping on a rusty nail. Tripping down the stairs. Running with scissors."

"Tiresome and thankless job for a kid," he said, to which she didn't respond. "Did your protective tendencies carry over into adulthood?"

"No. We both grew up."

"Josh grew up to be a thief. What did your mom and dad think about that?"

"What did yours think about what you became?" she fired back.

"Actually my dad was tickled. I followed in his footsteps and had big shoes to fill. In our line of work, he was famous."

"Oh. Then your upbringing was anything but typical."

He shrugged. "It was commonplace to me. I was a kid, didn't know any other kind of family life."

She thought about that, then remembered his earlier reference to his mother. "Your mama taught you better than to molest a woman, but she was okay with the profession you chose?"

"No, she died wishing I'd taken another career path."

"She's deceased?"

"Both of them. Dad shot her, then put the forty-five to his own head and pulled the trigger."

She couldn't contain her shock. By contrast, his features remained unmoved and inscrutable.

Was he trying to stun her with cruel candor? Was he even telling the truth? There was no way of knowing. She reasoned that he could lie with nonchalance but could also reveal a terrible truth with matching indifference.

"Was Josh always a tattletale?" he asked.

"I don't want to talk about this anymore," she said. "Especially not about Josh."

"Well, see, you should open up to me about him."

"Why would I do that?"

"Because, Jordie, your little brother just might save you and your saucy ass."

Ignoring the remark, she pounced on the substance of what he'd said. "How?"

"At some point during our long, overnight drive—"

"You were going in circles the entire time, weren't you?"

"Do you want to hear this or not?"

Subdued by his sharp tone, she fell silent and gave a small nod.

"Here's where your life does become your business. Because somewhere between midnight and dawn, it occurred to me that you might be more valuable alive than dead."

Her heart rate ticked up. She glanced at the pistol, which remained set aside on top of the crate. "You're not going to kill me after all?"

"Depends. All you gotta do to prevent it is tell me where your brother is."

Her flare of optimism flamed out. Slumping, she raised her arms to her sides and gave a dry laugh. "I don't have any idea where Josh is."

"Jordie," he said, speaking softly, "what did I tell you about lying to me?"

"That's the truth! When Josh turned informant, he was placed in protective custody. Even I don't know where. I'm not allowed any contact with him. He's being guarded around the clock by federal marshals."

"Not anymore he's not."

Her stomach swooped. "What?"

"Your baby brother Josh eluded his guards and—" he made a whooshing sound and accompanied it with a hand gesture like an airplane taking off "—flew the coop."

The words and what they signified were so outlandish that at first she couldn't make sense of them. When the full meaning of what he'd said finally sank in, she was robbed of oxygen. Those scattered thoughts she'd tried to corral moments ago were swept away completely. "You're lying."

Slowly he shook his head.

She sucked in a breath. "Josh..."

"Skipped."

"He left the government's protection?"

"Sneaked away last Tuesday morning from wherever the feds had him sequestered."

While she was still trying to assimilate this information, he stood and started walking toward her in a measured tread. "What I think? Panella doesn't have the thirty million he and your brother stole. Worse for him, he doesn't know where it's stashed. Josh does.

"And now nobody, not the feds, *nobody* is protecting Josh from Billy Panella." Having reached the hood of the car where she sat, he placed his hands flat on either side of her hips and leaned over her. "Except you."

Chapter 10

━━◆━━

From the moment Josh Bennett determined that his best option was to make a deal with the federal government, he'd begun preparing for the day he would renege on it.

He'd been whisked to the safe house with only the clothes on his back and a small duffel bag containing a few personal items. The bag and its contents had been searched, but not that thoroughly. Special Agent Joe Wiley and company had been concerned about his secreting objects with which he could do himself in. Finding none, his duffel was returned to him with a few trinkets undiscovered.

More important than they, however, was the wealth of information he took with him inside his brain. Little did his jailers— that was not how they were referred to, but that was what they were—realize how many dozens of passwords, account numbers, credit card numbers, and such were committed to the hard drive of his memory.

Over the past six months, he could have outfoxed his guards and fled at any time, but he'd bided his time until a routine had been established, monitoring had loosened up, and the hubbub surrounding his turning FBI informant had died down.

Not that he'd been lax for that half year. He'd used the time to gradually alter his appearance. Pleading dry eye, he'd exchanged his contacts for eyeglasses. Pleading a loss of appetite for food as well as for life in general, he'd dropped the soft twenty pounds that had collected around his middle while he was cooking Panella's books.

Always before he'd been clean shaven, but he'd let his personal hygiene routine slip and shaved only every few days. His stubble grew in an unexpected ginger color, so even close acquaintances, and they were few in number, would recognize him unshaven and bespeckled.

He'd prepared well, and last Tuesday morning, he'd made good his plan.

He'd removed his ankle monitor, which was supposed to be impossible, but wasn't. Wearing two day's growth of reddish whiskers, and taking only a backpack full of things he'd pilfered over time, he'd slipped out of the second-story bedroom window and made it to the nearest highway on foot.

For the most part, the people of Tennessee, Mississippi, and Louisiana were friendly sorts. In a time when whack jobs would settle unfounded grudges with a grand-scale slaughter of strangers, Josh had counted on the milk of human kindness to help him escape and evade recapture.

Sure enough, in no time at all, he had hitched a ride with an old-timer in a pickup truck who was taking his pack of hunting dogs home after a month of training in Georgia. Every once in a while the hounds bayed from their kennels in the pickup bed, and Josh learned much more about blueticks than he ever wanted to know.

He and the dog owner parted company in Greenwood, Mississippi, where Josh went into a filling station men's room and applied a temporary tattoo to his neck. He put on sunglasses and a dirty, worn baseball cap that he'd swiped from a charity box while out shopping one day with his guards. So disguised, he walked to the center of town and joined the barely controlled chaos in a busy, crowded unemployment office.

He spent the remainder of the day filling out endless forms with information he made up as he went along. He was shuffled from one long line to another like dozens of other people being assisted by impatient and uncaring bureaucrats. It was an excellent hiding place.

When the office closed for the day, Josh tossed his stack of forms into the nearest trash can and used another men's room to wash off the tattoo and shave his whiskers down to a five o'clock shadow. He walked a few blocks to a motel, where he checked in under a false name and using a credit card that he'd successfully smuggled in his duffel when taken from New Orleans.

He'd spent most of Tuesday evening flipping through the channels on the TV. There was no mention of his escape on any of the news sources. He figured the U.S. Marshals Service didn't want to publicize their screwup. Law enforcement agencies would have been alerted to be on the lookout for him, but he hoped now, more so than ever, that he would blend into the woodwork.

It shouldn't be that difficult. He never courted attention. Indeed, he'd spent most of his life shunning it, avoiding it at all costs. He was so practiced at making himself invisible, he should easily slip through the cracks of everyday life.

Even so, he decided he'd rather be cautious than caught, so he opted to stay put and spend two more nights in that motel before moving on.

Friday morning, he dressed in his unemployed-burnout getup, but omitted the tattoo and liberally applied grease to his hair, so that what showed under the ball cap looked much darker than it actually was. He hitched a ride with a long-haul trucker who preached to him about the devil's cunning pitfalls, how to spot them, how to avoid entrapment.

Josh laughed up his sleeve, thinking, *If only you knew.*

After declining to be baptized but promising to think about it, he'd gotten out at the intersection of two state highways near the Mississippi-Louisiana state line and doubled back on foot to an Army Navy store he had noticed when they passed. He made a purchase, then walked to a nearby motor court and checked in.

It was there that his complacency had shifted to apprehension.

He no longer felt like laughing up his sleeve, and instead had restlessly paced the small room, waiting for something to happen but afraid of what might. He started at every sound. With the approach of every pair of headlights, he held his breath until they passed.

As the night wore on, his paranoia escalated, and he began to fear that he hadn't been as invisible as he'd thought. Had he outsmarted no one? Were people that he'd encountered along the way remembering him and providing a description to police? Were the authorities even now within closing distance of him?

Awful scenarios of arrest, trial, and imprisonment, all spotlighted in the media, spun round and round in his head. The room began to feel like a jail cell.

Now, in a state of high anxiety, he packed his few belongings and put on the khakis he'd purchased at the Army Navy store. He pulled the cap low over his brow. As he left the motor court, he tried to keep from looking over his shoulder, but the impulse was hard to resist.

It was well before dawn, but truckers were on the highway even at this hour. Only two passed him before one stopped and invited him to hop in. Almost immediately Josh regretted doing so. He wanted only peace and quiet in which to think, but the driver was gregarious and launched into lurid accounts of his wild—and what Josh suspected were fictitious—encounters with countless women.

Josh tuned him out, and brooded, and tried not to scream at him to shut up.

He had to hang on only long enough to get where he was going. He just needed to get there! Once he saw that everything was all right, *he* would be all right.

After crossing into eastern Louisiana, he asked to be let out at a wide spot in the road. He'd waited until the truck was out of sight, then walked along the rural highway to a convenience store. He needed a few basic provisions—no more than he could comfortably carry in the backpack—to tide him over until he implemented phase two of his getaway.

He did his shopping hurriedly and carried the items to the counter. Aware of the security cameras, he kept his head down so the bill of his cap would help hide his face.

The cashier gave him a friendly smile. "That everything, hon?"

"Yes, thanks."

"How about a coffee to go?"

"I'm fine."

Suddenly his focus was drawn from her blue eyeshadow to the television on the counter behind her. Specifically, to his sister Jordie's face on the television on the counter.

Jordan Bennett was superimposed across the bottom of the screen with a red tagline: *FEARED KIDNAPPED*.

Instantly Josh broke a sweat. His knees almost gave way. "Changed my mind," he said to the clerk and took a lottery ticket from the stack near the register. "Add this to my total."

He concentrated on keeping his hand from shaking as he used the ballpoint pen with the fuzzy tip to mark his numbers while covertly keeping one eye on the morning news being broadcast from a New Orleans station.

Jordie's photograph was replaced by video of a crime scene

demarcated by yellow tape. The super at the bottom switched to: *Live Coverage from Terrebonne Parish.* Josh recognized Jordie's Lexus in the background behind the reporter, who was standing just outside the flimsy barricade.

Another customer entered the store and greeted the cashier with familiarity. Josh kept his head down, meticulously coloring in spaces on the lottery ticket while following the action on the TV screen.

"You hear about this?" the customer asked the cashier. Out of the corner of his eye, Josh saw him gesture toward the television. "Turn it up."

Josh pretended to be oblivious, but he hinged on every word. *Homicide. Apparent abduction. Detectives.* The reporter's inflections underscored descriptive words until it was all Josh could do to keep from screaming.

The reporter wrapped up by saying, "At this point authorities are left with more questions than answers about this brutal murder. However, our news team has learned that there is a person of interest." A mug shot filled the screen. "Shaw Kinnard accompanied the victim into the bar and left with him. It's believed he may be responsible not only for the slaying but also for Ms. Bennett's disappearance. He's to be considered armed and dangerous. Notify the nearest law enforcement agency if you have any information. A spokesperson from Ms. Bennett's Extravaganza office has expressed concern—"

The cashier used the remote to lower the volume, even as her customer remarked, "Bet you anything that Billy Panella is behind this. Getting his payback on Josh Bennett."

The cashier nodded. "If that lady's found a'tall, it'll be when somebody fishes her body out of a swamp."

The man lumbered toward the dairy case, saying as he went, "Meanwhile that brother of hers got off scot-free. If she comes to harm, they ought to put that sumbitch in chains and lock him in a fuckin' dungeon."

Josh's ears began humming noisily. He could barely control his breathing. Jordie had been *kidnapped*?

"Those the winners?"

Every muscle in his body contracted when he realized the cashier was addressing him. Josh gave her a tight smile as he passed her the lottery ticket. "One can hope."

She registered his lottery numbers and totaled his purchases. He paid in cash, and it seemed to take her an eternity to sack up his purchases. When she was done, Josh thanked her and headed for the door.

"Have a nice day," she called to him as he left.

He beat the hell out of there and walked along the shoulder of the highway until he saw a path angling off into the trees. He followed it for at least a hundred yards, and when he reached a clearing, he dropped his sacks, worked off his backpack, and collapsed onto the ropy root system of a gigantic live oak. Whipping off his eyeglasses, he pressed his forehead against his bent knees and breathed in and out through his mouth in heavy gusts.

Words from the newscast jumped out at him like spooks in a haunted house.

...brutal...

...Mickey Bolden, a suspect in numerous unsolved homicides...

...armed and dangerous...

...Ms. Bennett's brother, Joshua Bennett, was accused of...

...Billy Panella and Joshua Bennett allegedly...

...turned informant for federal prosecutors...

This was terrible news. Terrible!

The buzzsaw in his ears grew louder, accompanied by the fast pulsing of his heart against his eardrums. His nose dripped snot. He was clammy and claustrophobic. He felt lightheaded and sick to his stomach. The skin across his back drew up into the familiar, tight, unforgiving ache.

Jordie *kidnapped*? That couldn't be right. It just *couldn't*. The

TV people had got it wrong. He wouldn't believe it until he heard it from Jordie herself.

Frantically he unzipped his backpack and withdrew the cell phone he'd taken from one of his guards within the first week of his confinement. For weeks after, he'd overheard the marshal bitching to his cohorts about losing it. Josh had replaced its SIM card with a new and untraceable one that he'd sneaked into the safe house in the lining of his duffel bag.

Once he found the phone, he couldn't immediately lay his hands on the battery that went with it. Growing increasingly desperate, he dumped the contents of the backpack onto the ground, then rifled through the clothing and various items, scattering them like a cyclone until he found the phone's battery. With clumsy fingers, gasping for breath, and blinking sweat out of his eyes, he managed to insert it and, as soon as he had a signal, began punching in Jordie's cell number.

But then his mind screamed, *Are you crazy?*

He stopped his frenzied motions and took a moment to think.

Whether or not Jordie was dead by now, she wouldn't be answering her phone.

But someone else might. Her kidnapper, maybe. Possibly the police. Whoever answered would want to know who was calling her. What would he say? "This is her brother. The one who double-crossed both the ruthless Billy Panella and the federal government? The one who became a fugitive last Tuesday. Maybe you've heard of me?"

Thinking more rationally now, he leaned back against the stout tree trunk, closed his eyes, and forced himself to take deep, even breaths. Several minutes passed. His pores stopped leaking sweat. His heart rate slowed. His nose stopped dripping and his nausea subsided.

He got a grip.

He opened his eyes, found his eyeglasses amid the strewn articles on the ground, and put them on. As though they were fitted with magic lenses, he began to view the situation from a whole new prospective—that of Billy Panella.

Because, even while working hand in glove with the man and hating him to his very marrow, he'd also come to admire the power Panella wielded. No one's knees shook when the name Josh Bennett was mentioned, but so much as breathe *Billy Panella* and grown men were said to wet their pants. Josh envied that quality.

Whenever something unexpected happened, he'd seen Panella's legendary temper erupt. But he'd also watched him quickly regain a cool head and deal with the problem. Never had panic or fear sidetracked him from achieving his objective.

Josh resolved not to be overtaken by them, either.

With hands now steady, he removed the battery from the phone and replaced both in the backpack. He wouldn't call Jordie. Even if by some miracle he was able to talk to her, what could he say?

Panella had threatened to go after her first if Josh ever betrayed him. Hadn't Josh dutifully passed along that warning to her?

Yes. Innumerable times.

She should have listened and been more careful. Whatever her fate, she had no one to blame but herself.

He must think only of what was best for him.

Chapter 11

Jordie angled away from Shaw, but there was no escaping his mesmerizing stare.

When she realized she was breathing through her mouth, she pressed her lips closed, but her respiration remained unsteady as she processed this distressing turn of events.

What could Josh be thinking?

He had cut a great deal, far better than she'd dared hope he would get. He'd driven a hard bargain, and the U.S. prosecutor had ultimately granted him full immunity in exchange for testifying against Billy Panella. Yet unbelievably her brother had squandered—

It *was* unbelievable, wasn't it?

Her gaze narrowed on her abductor, who was still leaning over her, applying pressure without even touching her. "You're a murdering, lying bastard. Why should I take your word for anything?"

"This isn't a lie."

"No? Tell me something that'll convince me it's the truth."

"Your heart is still beating."

He stated it without pause or contemplation. A simple fact. If Josh weren't a factor, she would be dead. This man would have killed her long before now.

He said, "The instant you're dead, your value tanks. Alive, you're a bargaining chip."

"With Panella."

"And your brother."

She scoffed at that. "Get over the notion that Josh has the money. Or even that he knows where it is. If he did, he would have surrendered it when he—"

"—bartered his soul by turning snitch?"

"*Saved* his soul by doing the right thing."

"Saved his soul, my ass. Everything Saint Josh has done has been self-serving. But now he's in a real pickle. He's reneged on his deal with the feds. And, as if that wasn't bad enough, he's made laughingstocks of them for being taken in.

"If they catch him, they'll throw the book at him. He'll spend the rest of his life in federal prison. But he had better hope they catch him before Panella does. Because he'll tear out your brother's forked tongue, rip open his belly, throw him into the Gulf, and ring the dinner bell. Either way, Josh is sunk. Unless I get to him first."

She feared his predictions about her brother's future weren't far off the mark. "If you reach him first, what then?"

"I convince him it's in his best interest to give me a share of all that filthy lucre. He does that, we all go home happy. Well, not *home*. But you get the gist of it."

"That's your idea?"

"Damn good one, you ask me."

She pressed her fingers to her forehead and rubbed the space between her eyebrows. "It's a lousy idea, Mr. Kinnard. Based entirely on erroneous speculation. Josh doesn't have the money, any money. And, say he did, say his pockets are stuffed with it, he could be anywhere in the country. How do you intend to track him down?"

"I won't have to. He'll come to me. Because I have you." He shot her a crocodile's grin. "Sooner or later he'll hear about your abduction."

"He'll assume I'm dead."

"Probably. Until you let him know otherwise."

"How am I supposed to do that?"

"The same way you've been communicating with him all along."

She actually laughed. "I haven't had contact with my brother since he was taken into custody. Zero," she said, forming an O with her fingers. "That was one of the conditions of the pact he made with the government."

He just stared at her, unblinking, unmoving.

"All right, believe what you want," she said. "The fact doesn't change. I don't know where Josh has been sequestered for the past six months, and I don't know how to reach him. Period. End of discussion."

"Like hell it is. We're *discussing* the little brother who you protected from slippery stairs and rusty nails. You're telling me that he hasn't come crying to you since Tuesday when he ran afoul of big bad Uncle Sam?"

"It's the truth."

"You didn't know he'd escaped?"

"No! Not until you told me."

He bent down closer. "Even if I believed that he hasn't contacted you in the past four days, *which I don't*, the FBI would have jumped on you like a duck on a June bug. Like Billy Panella did. Want Josh Bennett and can't find him? Easy. Stay on his sister, his next of kin, the first and only person he would scurry to when in trouble."

"The FBI didn't notify me of his escape."

He stared her down as though trying to intimidate the truth

out of her, which made her nervous, because she wasn't an adept liar. Not that she was lying, exactly.

True, no government agency had officially informed her of Josh's disappearance. But the authorities might very well have been keeping an eye on her to see if he would show up on her doorstep.

Last night, as she left her house for the bar, she'd noticed headlights in her rearview mirror. They had remained the same distance from her as she drove through town. It might have been perfectly harmless. But she'd been just paranoid enough to deliberately outdistance the other car when she reached the back roads.

She wasn't about to share that with Shaw Kinnard, however.

Instead, she kept her expression as impassive as she could, and he finally relented, straightening up, giving her space. She came to a full sitting position and for the first time in minutes, was able take a deep, even breath.

"You're wrong about Josh and the stolen money," she said. "Billy Panella absconded with it. Everybody knows that. He moved it somewhere out of the country."

"Then flew off to enjoy a happy rendezvous with his millions?"

"Doesn't that seem logical?"

"Perfectly. So answer me this," he said. "If Panella is jacking off onto piles of money, why's he so upset over Josh's vanishing act?"

"I don't know. Maybe he...he..." She came up empty.

"Hmm? What was that?" He gave her another moment to contribute something, and when she didn't, he said, "Mickey told me Panella wanted to kill you in order to send Josh a message. He hasn't forgiven or forgotten that your brother turned on him. I'm talking mafia-fashion revenge, Jordie. Panella's mindset is 'Rat me out, I slaughter your family, preferably while you watch.'"

She didn't need a lesson on Panella's methodology. She was well educated on it.

Josh had been working at a small investment firm when Panella sought him out and made him an offer. It was an unlikely pairing: Panella with his tailored suits and the glibness of a snake oil salesman, and her shy, self-conscious, socially awkward brother. But Panella needed Josh's genius mind, and it hadn't taken much to woo him with flattery and promises of wealth. However, no sooner had Panella reeled him in than he established what Jordie considered an unhealthy working relationship. It angered and sickened her to see how Panella maintained control of her brother by preying on his weaknesses and insecurities, sometimes in ways that bordered on sadistic.

Also concerning were the rumors of Panella's involvement in other enterprises in addition to the one he shared with Josh. She had begged Josh to see Billy Panella for what he was. At best, a manipulating bully. At worst, a shifty, possibly criminal, operator who couldn't be trusted. As he was wont to do, Josh had taken a stubborn stance and turned a deaf ear to her pleas, citing jealousy as her reason for disliking his boss.

It was almost a relief to her when the house of cards that Josh and Panella had built finally collapsed. But it did so on Josh's head. His participation in their crimes was unquestionable, so when the FBI gave him a chance to turn informant, she had pressured him to take the deal.

Panella had several reasons to resent her, but knowing that Josh wouldn't have capitulated without her encouragement made her his sworn enemy, and based on the rumors circulating around him, Panella didn't treat his enemies kindly.

For weeks after Josh was taken away and Panella presumably had left the country, she'd been wary and cautious of her surroundings, afraid that Panella would decide to get vengeance on her and, by extension, on Josh. Josh had even alluded to that possibility when he was trying to worm his way out of striking a deal with the FBI.

"He'll kill you, too," he'd wailed. "He's told me he would."

But as time passed and nothing happened, she'd relaxed her vigilance. Not until she saw Mickey Bolden and Shaw Kinnard approaching her last night did she realize that Josh hadn't been merely theatric. His warning had been sincere.

Trying to hide her apprehension from her kidnapper, she said, "Panella has had six months to get revenge. Why now?"

Shaw replied in a quiet voice, "You know why, Jordie. Panella made his move when Josh made his. Maybe he knows your brother better than you do. Maybe he figured all along that Josh was playing the feds. He's been sitting back waiting, and when Josh did exactly what Panella anticipated, he put into action the plan he'd had all along."

"To kill me?"

"Figuring that killing you would be the harshest punishment to inflict on Josh for his betrayal. Also, if you're dead, you can't tell the feebs everything you know."

"What *I* know?" she exclaimed. "I don't know anything."

"Panella must think you do."

"Well, he's wrong."

"According to Mickey, after Panella went missing, you were grilled pretty good."

She nodded, remembering those arduous sessions. "The FBI questioned me extensively over the course of several weeks. I couldn't tell them anything, because I didn't know anything."

"Did they believe you?"

"Of course."

He made a skeptical sound. "Why 'of course'? Was it your honest face? Or did you bedazzle them by pulling a Sharon Stone in the interrogation room?"

Outraged, she surged to her feet.

"Sit down." He placed his hand in the center of her chest and pushed her back onto the hood.

She encircled his wrist and pried his hand off her. "I told the FBI the truth and they believed me."

"Maybe. But Panella must be of the mind that you told them something, even accidentally, that jeopardizes his clean getaway."

"I didn't."

"You make him nervous, Jordie. Why else would he have contracted hit men to have you permanently silenced? Panella had retained Mickey to get rid of pests plenty of times, and for milder offenses than talking to the feds about him."

"Well, you saw to it that Mickey is no longer a threat to me, didn't you?"

"Panella's got others. And he's not above doing the deed himself. In fact, he'd enjoy it. Eye for an eye?" He chuffed. "Panella's starter kit."

Contrary to her own thoughts of moments earlier, she said, "Those are rumors. Exaggerations. Spun by people who wanted to claim a closer acquaintance with him when he became a celebrated fugitive."

"Rumors, huh? So what does that make Mickey and me? Figments of the imagination?" He didn't wait for an answer. "I sought Mickey Bolden out because even hit men talk, and the word going 'round our circle was that Panella paid well. If you think his only crime was stealing the life savings of hardworking folk, you're deluding yourself."

Josh had made vague allusions to Panella's "powers of persuasion," but he'd never given her specifics, and she hadn't asked for them because she hadn't wanted her suspicions of Panella's sinister side confirmed. She didn't want to acknowledge them now to Shaw Kinnard, who was painting a frightening picture to suit his own purposes.

She said, "All I know about Panella's business is what everyone does. He stole thirty million dollars and disappeared with it."

"He hasn't quite disappeared," he said. "Mickey was on the phone with him as recently as last night."

"He could have been talking to him from anywhere in the world. Switzerland. Kathmandu. South America."

"Could have." Two vertical furrows appeared between his brows. "But if Panella was in South America with thirty million at his disposal, he would be lounging on a beach, getting blown by dusky girls in thong bikinis, and the furthest thing from his mind would be the sister of his moneyman who turned snitch.

"If Panella had access to the money, he would have severed all ties with the good ol' U.S. of A. and everybody in it. Instead, the man's obsessed. He didn't want you leaving that bar alive, and I predict he'll go apeshit when I inform that you ain't dead. Now why would he care so much?

"He's also paranoid as hell," he continued. "Mickey said he uses one of those voice synthesizer things to garble his speech. If he was in Switzerland or Kathmandu, why's he bothering to disguise his voice? See where I'm going with this, Jordie? If he was languishing somewhere, using hundred-dollar bills to light his cigars, he wouldn't give a flying fuck that Josh had gone aground. Instead, Josh's flight last Tuesday made him angry and antsy and mean."

She tried not to reveal how uneasy she became over the thought of Panella being angry, antsy, and mean. It didn't bode well for her or Josh. "How did he even find out that Josh had escaped? There's been nothing on the news about it."

"You can bet the FBI are good and pissed off that their star witness welshed on the deal, but they're not gonna go on TV and broadcast that they let a bean counter slip through their fingers."

"Then how did Panella hear about it?"

"I asked Mickey that. He claimed not to know, and maybe he

didn't. I'm guessing that Panella has moles in law enforcement. He had to have had help getting away. Fake IDs. Private aircraft. He could spread around a lot of graft with thirty mil."

"You said he didn't have it."

"Not the jackpot, but he would have kept a million or two handy to cover expenses."

"Like your retainer."

"Yeah, like that. Two hundred grand, minimum." He placed his hands over his knees and bent at the waist to bring them to eye level. "But you don't have to worry about me icing you if you'll tell me where your brother is."

"We're back to that?"

"Where is he, Jordie?"

"How much clearer can I make it? I. Don't. Know."

"Do yourself a favor. Don't hold out on me."

"I'm not."

"Four days and Josh hasn't made contact with you in some way, shape, or form?"

"No."

"Message in a bottle, smoke signal, disappearing ink?"

She didn't honor that with a response.

Moving in closer, he whispered, "Why were you in that bar?"

Her heart lurched. He hadn't let go of that, damn him. Not trusting herself to speak calmly, she didn't say anything.

He flashed a wicked grin. "You went there expecting to find Josh, didn't you?"

She turned her head aside. He followed with his, and when she turned away again, he trapped her face between his hands. "Did Mickey and I spoil a touching family reunion?"

She closed her eyes so she couldn't see the ruthless determination in his. Also to prevent him from reading any giveaways in hers.

"Where is your brother, Jordie?"

She rolled her lips inward, refusing to answer.

"Be smart and tell me. Panella will pay me to kill you. Josh will pay me *not* to."

"You'll kill me regardless."

"I won't. Cross my heart."

His mocking tone angered her. She gripped his wrists, digging her nails into the skin on the undersides.

"Stop that! I don't want to hurt you."

"I want to hurt *you*."

"It hurts like hell."

"Then let me go!"

"I will as soon as you tell me where to find your brother."

"I can't," she said, straining the words through clenched teeth. "I don't know."

"Last chance. I won't ask again. Tell me, or you leave me no choice but to follow through with Panella. 'Cause I put a lot of time and effort into getting this job. It's boosted me to the top of the pay grade. No way in hell am I walking away empty-handed."

She opened her eyes to gauge his resolve, and what she saw chilled her. She figured she had just as well call his bluff. "Then I guess you'll just have to kill me."

They stared into each other's eyes—each as unyielding as the other—until the cell phone inside his shirt pocket rang.

Chapter 12

—◎—

Joe entered his house through the kitchen door, slid the folder he'd brought from the office onto the table, then tiredly removed his wrinkled jacket and hung it on the designated hook adjacent to the door. He placed his shoulder holster on top of the hutch out of the kids' reach.

"Anybody home?" He opened the fridge and decided on orange juice.

Marsha caught him drinking straight from the carton. "The kids know better than to do that."

"They know better than to get caught." He drained the carton and set it on the counter beside a large pumpkin. "What's that?"

"It's called a pumpkin."

Joe shot her a look.

"For the carnival. I have to draw a face on it." She held up the black marker she'd brought with her into the kitchen.

"Where are the kids?"

"Upstairs. Molly is in the tub. Henry is dressed and ready. He's in his room playing a video game."

"They okay?"

"They had a knock-down, drag-out this morning over whose turn it was to empty the dishwasher."

"Who won?"

"I did."

Joe smiled as he pulled a chair from beneath the dining table and dropped into it. "How was *Top Gun*?"

"Goose dies every time."

"The wine?"

"Maybe I should have splurged on an eight-dollar bottle."

"Anything's drinkable with popcorn."

"I skipped the double butter. I'm getting fat."

He reached for her and pulled her onto his lap. Running his hand over her hip, he said, "Your curves are womanly."

"Even my mom jeans are getting tight."

"I love 'em tight. Let's have sex."

"The kids could walk in on us, and I have to draw that pumpkin face."

"It'll take sixty seconds."

"The pumpkin or the sex?"

He laughed. "Tired as I am, I may need more than sixty seconds."

Kidding aside, she touched his face with concern. "You look exhausted. What's going on?"

"Josh Bennett got tired of the taxpayers' hospitality and pulled a disappearing act." Taking advantage of her speechlessness, he said, "Don't announce that over the speakers at the carnival. We haven't gone public with it yet. I was hoping to catch him before we had to."

"How in the world did he get away?"

"He didn't come down for breakfast. Marshals went to check. Room was empty, bed still made."

"I thought he had one of those ankle monitors."

"Clever little shit got it off. They found it in the bathroom.

That was Tuesday. Then last night..." He filled her in on everything that had occurred since Hick's initial call.

"He and I agreed to take a short break, then we've got to jump back in. Now that Josh Bennett's sister is missing, and the whole mess resurrected, I may have to change my mind about announcing his escape. In any case, I won't be going to the carnival. Sorry."

"It's okay." She stroked his head. She knew better than anyone how badly the Billy Panella case had eaten at him.

Over a three-year period, Panella had craftily enticed the clients of his investment firm to put their money into phony stocks, municipal bonds, pharmaceuticals to cure cancer, energy exploration that was ecofriendly, resorts and exclusive retirement communities, even shrimp and catfish farms—none of which existed.

With Josh Bennett's wizardry with numbers and money-juggling skills, Panella had committed fraud to the tune of thirty million dollars and change. He had made everything work for a while, paying occasional dividends with the promise of big payoffs to come.

They never did. Dividends got smaller, while growing larger were the number of client complaints filed with the FTC, SEC, et cetera, until a fat file landed in Joe's division and he initiated a full-fledged but covert investigation of the Panella Investments Group.

After months of study, he and Hick determined that Josh Bennett was the weak link in the partnership. They approached him, told him that his and Panella's scam was screwed, and offered to reduce the charges he faced in exchange for evidence and testimony against Panella.

Josh Bennett held out for full immunity, and, after a lot of legal ping-ponging, the federal prosecutor agreed to his terms. That didn't make Joe happy, but Panella was the much bigger fish. It was alleged that he had fingers in a lot of dirty pies, but with the information Bennett provided, Joe's division was the first to build a rock-solid case against him. À la Al Capone's conviction for tax evasion, they could put an end to Panella's unsavory criminal career and various illegal hobbies.

But apparently Panella hadn't been as oblivious to Bennett's betrayal as he'd pretended. Behind firewalls that Josh Bennett had helped him design, he'd managed to move bundles of money without even his genius partner in crime being aware of it.

By the time Bennett discovered that accounts were being methodically emptied, it was too late. Joe and Hick carried a federal warrant for Panella's arrest to his mansion on St. Charles Avenue only to find the place in disarray. Panella had cleared out in a hurry.

Upon hearing that Panella was at large, Josh Bennett lapsed into a suicidal depression. "I had just as well slit my own throat," he said when Joe broke the bad news.

The hell of it was, his doom-and-gloom prediction was well-founded. Rumors of Panella's violent temper and vengeful bent had circulated throughout the law enforcement community. No direct connection was ever drawn between him and Mickey Bolden, but Joe figured Panella was behind several missing persons cases and grisly homicides for which the hit man was suspected but never indicted. Authorities could never make an allegation stick.

The threat Panella posed to Josh Bennett, Backstabber, was real enough. The same day Panella went missing, the Bureau wasted no time hustling their informant out of Dodge. By nightfall Bennett had been relocated to a safe house in Tennessee and placed under tight guard.

Obviously not tight enough.

Joe said, "For the six months and eight days he's been up there, marshals have described him as sulky and morose, and scared of his own shadow, convinced that Panella would track him down and have him killed."

"I thought Panella had fled the country with the cash."

"That's the consensus. But even if it's true, he's got a long reach, and Josh Bennett knows that better than anyone. He's the accountant who paid Mickey Bolden for services rendered. Which leads one to wonder why he would pop out from cover and put his life at risk."

"Panic?"

"Possibly. According to the men guarding him, he's been growing squirrelier by the day. Went mental when they let in a guy to work on the house's AC. Josh was convinced he was an assassin sent by Panella."

"Has he had a psychological evaluation?"

"Several. IQ off the charts. But paranoid as hell and—"

"—squirrelly."

"Yeah. For someone so smart, he's done something really stupid. By taking off like this, he's cooked his own goose. Certainly with us. But also with Panella. Soon as he got wind of Bennett's escape, Panella wasted no time hiring hit men to go after Bennett's sister."

"Why her?"

"To send Josh a message. *Run, you traitorous son of a bitch. I'll kill your sister instead.*"

Marsha mulled that over. "I know you and Hick questioned her. Did you ever suspect her of being involved in their scam?"

"Not really. But..." He raised a shoulder. "Females make good crooks."

"We're wily, Wiley."

He smiled and gave her mouth a quick kiss. "Good one."

"This Mickey Bolden was killed by his own partner?"

"A badass. One Shaw Kinnard. No previous links to Mickey, but he was temporarily affiliated with an outfit here in New Orleans that dealt in guns and drugs, with a sideline in money laundering, which is how Hick and I became familiar with his name.

"Never got a chance to interrogate him, though. There was a nothing-to-sneeze-at body count chalked up to him in the DA's office. But the limp-dick prosecutor declined to indict. Lack of evidence, he said."

"Kinnard was let go?"

"Yep. Walked off into the sunset. But a few months ago, he showed up on the radar of the Bureau's El Paso office. Prime suspect in a homicide. He evaded capture by slipping into Mexico, and nobody down there has been able to collar him, because he was reputedly inside the fortress of a drug kingpin."

He glanced at the folder lying on the table. He didn't open it to the gruesome photos, but he told Marsha about the call girl who'd left a house party with the three men, two of which had turned up dead. "One was Kinnard's host, the other the chief of the state police."

"Good Lord."

"The guy was a cockroach. Both victims were. But Kinnard exterminated them in cold blood. That alone took gumption." He told her about his leaving the bodies within walking distance of police headquarters and about the wave he'd given a security camera in the New Orleans hotel. "Like he doesn't care if we know he's back in town. Pisses us off," he grumbled.

"And he kidnapped Josh Bennett's sister?"

"Well, he's gone and she's gone. Can't be good."

"You don't suppose they're in cahoots?"

He laughed. "Her with this character? No way. She's classy. Uptown. He's just the opposite."

"People have said that about you and me."

He bent his head and rubbed his nose in the open collar of her blouse. "I've said it myself." He kissed her neck, then pulled away. "We have to assume that Jordie Bennett is in danger of her life. If he hasn't killed her already."

"If he was going to kill her, why didn't he do it along with Mickey Bolden?"

"I'm afraid to venture a guess. Because he spared the call girl in Mexico from assassination, Hick thinks he may have a soft spot for the ladies."

"What do you think?"

Joe called to mind the face in Shaw Kinnard's mug shot, the rigidity of the features, the unfeeling gaze looking directly into the camera. "I don't think this guy has a soft spot for anything or anybody. Including himself."

For moments after the cell phone rang, Shaw and Jordie were held in suspended animation. He moved first, opening the flap on his breast pocket and taking out the ringing cell phone while she watched with wide-eyed apprehension.

He put it on speaker and answered. "How's it hanging, Panella?"

"What the fuck? Who's this? Where's Mickey? Why are you answering his phone?"

"I can think of only one reason."

Shaw had noticed Jordie's shudder upon hearing Panella's electronic voice. Maybe he did want to avoid a voiceprint, but Shaw figured he also used the device because he knew it sounded creepy and added to his mystique. Right now, however, he was silent except for the rasp of his breathing.

Then, "You're Mickey's second?"

"That's right."

"Where's Mickey?"

"Due to unforeseen circumstances, he had to stay behind."

"What does that mean?"

"I think you can figure it out."

"You motherfucker."

"That's not my name."

"He's dead?"

"Compliments of me. I also took Jordie Bennett," Shaw said. "Not her corpse. *Her.* Which means that if you still want her killed, you gotta deal with me."

Panella let loose a spate of profanities and threats which came through loud and clear despite the garbled voice. "You think you're awfully smart, don't you?"

"Well, I outsmarted Mickey. That wasn't my gray matter left to shovel up."

"I discouraged your participation."

"Really? So it was Mickey's idea to set me up to take the fall for her hit?"

Panella said nothing to that.

"I'm willing to overlook it," Shaw said, "but because my feelings were hurt, I'm going to need a bit more compensation than Mickey settled for."

"How do I know you even have Jordie?"

"Come on, Panella, let's cut this crap. You knew who you were talking to when I answered this phone. You already knew Mickey was dead. By now the story of last night's events will have been well covered by the media."

"Not where I am."

Shaw didn't believe that, but he let it pass. "Call the Terrebonne Parish Sheriff's Office. They'll verify that Jordie was snatched. Homicide detectives will have gotten a description of me, and I've probably been identified as Shaw Kinnard."

"Well, my contract wasn't with *Shaw Kinnard.* So I'm under no obligation to honor it. If in fact you did take Jordie, deal with her any way you like. I don't have to pay you a goddamn penny."

"That occurred to me, too. But here are some possible consequences of that decision. One, I use her phone to notify the nearest FBI office that she's alive. A little worse for wear, maybe, but very much alive."

He paused, but Panella said nothing. Shaw had his attention.

"I leave the phone on so they can track the signal straight to her. By the time they get here, I'll be long gone, but they'll be glad to see her. Tickled to have her back in the fold. She was their clubhouse sweetheart for weeks, you know. Cooperative. Chatty. Who knows, maybe this traumatic experience will have jostled loose a memory about you and her brother that slipped her mind the first go-round of questioning."

"I didn't tell them anything!" she shouted.

Shaw clicked off the speaker and pressed the phone against his chest. "Shut up," he hissed. "You fuck this up, I won't be happy."

"Like I care."

"You should. I'm your only chance at life, darlin'."

She tilted her chin up mutinously, but when she didn't speak again, he put the phone to his ear. "There, you see? I have her. But her welcome is wearing thin, which makes option two damned tempting."

"What's option two?" Panella asked.

"I walk away from this whole friggin' mess. You won't know if she's alive and in the bosom of the FBI, or buried where you'll never find her."

"If you walk away, you get nothing for your trouble."

"True. But neither do you. And here's why that would be consequential. First you lose sleep, wondering what happened with Jordie."

"I don't care that much."

"Bullshit, you don't. Because without his sister as a pawn, Josh will make good on his escape and retrieve the money. Because you ain't got it."

"You say."

"I say because, if you did, none of this would matter to you. We wouldn't be having this conversation."

Panella didn't respond.

"If Josh gets away," Shaw continued, "he'll collect the money and live to a ripe old age in a distant land, enjoying the grand lifestyle that you envisioned for yourself. If he's recaptured, he'll be locked behind bars forever with the key thrown away, and the money will molder till doomsday because he'll never tell you where it is. Either way, you wind up with only your dick in your hand."

He let all that sink in, then said, "Better choice, Panella. Agree to my current asking price. Jordie dies. Josh surfaces. You gain another opportunity to get your revenge on him, plus a shot at finding where he hid your money."

The only sound coming through the phone now was heavy breathing amplified by the electrolarynx. He was thinking it over. Finally he said, "I warned Josh that if he ever screwed me over, I'd kill him, but not before killing his sister first. That rat needs reminding that I always make good on my promises. Jordie coming through this alive is not an option."

Shaw's gut clenched. It was difficult, but he held her gaze as he said, "Understood."

"Okay then," Panella said. "Get at it and call me when it's done."

"We haven't come to terms yet."

"Five hundred thousand."

"Two million. Have a nice day."

After Shaw clicked off, he continued looking at Jordie for a beat or two, then turned away from her and concentrated on removing the battery from Mickey's phone. He put the phone in one front pocket of his jeans, the battery in the other.

Jordie moved around to stand facing him. "Two million dollars?"

"You think it's too much or not enough?"

"He still wants you to kill me?"

He sidestepped her and walked around the car to the trunk

and took out a bottle of water. He twisted off the top, poured half the bottle over his face, then drank the rest.

She knocked the empty plastic bottle out of his hand. "Answer me."

He looked down at the bottle that had landed and rolled, coming to a stop against the toe of his right boot. Then he raised his gaze back to hers. He wanted to strangle her, and at that moment he would have happily done it for nothing.

He went to the backseat door of the car, which was still standing open. "Get in. Lie down."

"Why?"

"Get in and lie down."

"Or what?"

He stormed back to her, grabbed her hand, and dragged her toward the open door.

She tried to wrest her hand free. "You said you didn't want to hurt me."

"I won't. Believe me, when I pop you, you won't feel it."

When they reached the door, she kicked it shut, which made him even more furious. They wrestled, although it was never any real contest. He easily backed her against the car door, her hands sandwiched between it and her butt. He held her there by pressing his body flush with hers.

"You had better hope Panella says no to my terms."

"You're not going to kill me or you would have already."

"For two million dollars—"

"Not for any amount," she retorted. "I don't think you will."

"You *know* I will. You've seen me in action. Mickey? Not my first. Not even my first this week." Her eyes widened fractionally. "Oh, yeah, Jordie. Tuesday night, I left two dead in Mexico before beating it to New Orleans. So don't delude yourself."

She swallowed. Blue eyes that had been throwing daggers moments ago now filled with misgiving. He felt her literally going softer against him as her resistance ebbed.

To impress upon her his point, he squeezed her shoulders tighter. "I did Mickey without a blink. The two in Mexico? A snap. Didn't even stop to think about it."

"You've stopped to think about me."

"Not really."

"Then what's stopping you?"

He stared into her defiant eyes, then lowered his gaze to her shoulder where her bra strap had slipped from the armhole of her top onto her upper arm. He slid two fingers beneath the strap, the backs of his fingers brushing her skin. It was warm and as smooth as the satin strip he rubbed between his fingers and thumb.

When he slid the strap up and replaced it inside her top, he didn't immediately pull his fingers from underneath it, but kept them there and ran them back and forth across her shoulder, once, twice, watching as his knuckles slid along her skin, the softest of it being that patch in front where arm and chest were adjoined.

His hand stilled there, then he pulled his fingers from under the satin and lowered his hand. His eyes moved to hers and held before he abruptly stepped back and turned away, saying roughly, "You'd be my first woman."

Chapter 13

You'd be my first woman.

He spoke in a rumble that was barely audible, but if he'd shouted the words, they would have had no less effect. They caused a catch in her breath and a little flutter of optimism around her heart. For one or two seconds, she let herself hope that her gender would be a deterrent, a deal breaker between him and Panella.

But that ray of hope was extinguished by his glower. Actually he seemed angrier now than before, possibly at himself for revealing his human side.

He took another bottle of water from the car trunk and twisted off the cap. "Drink this, or I swear I'll pour it down your throat."

He thrust the bottle at her in such a way that she either had to catch it against her chest or let it drop, and she didn't dare. Not after he'd looked ready to kill her on the spot when she'd knocked the empty bottle out of his hand and onto the floor.

She drank.

When she finished, he took her empty and tossed it into the trunk, then walked over to the crate and retrieved the pistol, shoving it into its holster. When he came back to her, he reached for her hand. She snatched it away, but he reached for it again and this time held on. He pulled her toward the door. "Where are we going?"

"Bathroom." He pushed open the door just wide enough to walk through, then stood aside and hitched his head.

She looked outside. "In broad daylight?"

"There's nobody to see you."

"I'll wait till it gets dark."

"I've got to sleep. I don't want to be woken up for you to take a bathroom break."

"I won't bother you."

He appeared to mentally count to ten, then said, "There's another option for me, you know. I could call Panella back, say to hell with all of you. I tell him where we are, then tie you up and split. What will he do? Dispatch a replacement who'd probably do you for fifty grand. Even less than Mickey settled for. Which should give you an idea of the caliber of guy who'll show up. I can almost promise he won't be nearly as nice or restrained as me."

He gave her time to think it over, then added, "You have two minutes of privacy before I come out looking for you."

She went outside. Two minutes was more than adequate time. She finished in half that, then ran toward the far side of the building, thinking that perhaps there was a reason why he hadn't shown it to her earlier. But as she rounded the corner, she was disheartened to find that the view from that side was as dismal as the other. If anything, the reeds behind the building looked taller and spikier, the water from which they protruded even more opaque and viscous.

She made it back to the door just as he emerged. Noticing that her face was shiny with perspiration, he guessed the reason.

"Go exploring? I could have told you there isn't a boat to go with that busted outboard. I already looked."

Smart-ass. She stepped around him and went back into the building. He followed, and when he reached for her hand, about to put another clip cuff on her wrists, she asked, "Is that really necessary?"

He just gave her a sardonic look.

"A tightly tied bandana would work just as well."

"Not even near." He turned her around.

"Can you at least leave them in front?"

"Not while I'm asleep."

"What could I do with my hands tied?"

"I'm not sure, but I don't want to be surprised. Don't move from this spot." He went outside.

She didn't move but she did conduct a visual search of the place. He'd hidden her phone. The phone battery. The car keys. *Where, where, where?*

When he came back inside, he was still buttoning up his fly. "Get in the backseat and lie down."

"I'll swelter inside that car."

"You want me to take your clothes off?" At the look she gave him, he snickered. "I didn't think so. Go lie down."

"When are you going to call Panella back?"

"After he's had time to think it over. Or, you could tell me how to contact Josh and we could be done here."

"I can't."

"Then get in the car."

"If you wait too long, Panella may—"

"Stop stalling. I'm tired."

Unprepared to engage in another wrestling match, this time with her hands tied behind her, she went to the car, got in, and lay down on her right side. "My arm goes to sleep in this position."

"When it does, roll over."

"I'll chatter, sing, keep you awake."

"I'll put a gag in your mouth."

He went to the trunk and rummaged among the things in it. She listened to the clank of license plates, the thump of the tire iron, the rattle of empty plastic bottles and sacks of canned goods, trying to think of ways in which one or the other could be used to debilitate him, at least long enough for her to get off a 911 call.

The tire iron would be ideal, but even though he left the trunk open, what good was having access to its contents with her hands bound behind her?

When he came back into her range of vision through the open backseat door, he was carrying a folded bright blue tarpaulin, which he dropped to the floor. He turned to her and, as though he'd been following the track of her thoughts, addressed the helplessness she felt.

"I'll leave your feet free. There's not much you could do without the use of your hands. I guess you could try running to the main road before I chased you down, but whatever you tried, you'd fail."

"If I'm going to die anyway, I had just as well try to escape."

"I admire that fighting spirit, Jordie. Truly I do. The thing is, I don't wake up in a cheerful mood on the best of days. If you woke me up trying some doomed-to-fail stunt, I'd be so pissed off I'd likely tie your feet together, gag you, shut the car doors, and then it really would be sweltering in there. Or I could always put you in the trunk."

As he turned away, she said under her breath, "You're not all that nice."

He came back around. "What was that?"

"Nothing."

He gave her a hard look, then his eyes tracked down the length of her body and all the way back up, pausing in places that grew warm under his scrutiny. "I'm not all that restrained, either."

He always had the last word, disallowing her to enjoy even a small triumph. Resentfully she watched him unfold the tarp. "I suppose you use that to wrap bloody bodies in."

"It comes in handy." He spread the tarp over the grimy floor a few yards away from the car, then popped open the first two snaps on his shirt and pulled it over his head.

She quickly looked away to avoid the sight of his bare chest.

"Jordie." He came to stand just beyond the open backseat door. "Jordie."

Feeling foolish and cowardly, she jerked her head back toward him. *"What?"*

"Pistol." He touched the holster at his hip. "Cell phone." He patted his right jeans pocket. "Cell phone battery." He patted his left jeans pocket. "You might manage to get one away from me, but not all three."

His hands remained flat against his pockets, bracketing the frayed fly of his jeans, which she was relieved to see he'd finished buttoning. The waistband was low and loose, curled slightly forward away from his torso where skin and hair were sweat-damp.

Cowardly or not, she turned her head aside again and closed her eyes. She heard the worn soles of his boots scrape against the concrete as he stepped away, the rustle of the tarp, sounds of him settling. Then an encompassing, almost palpable quiet descended. The next sound she heard was the even breathing of someone who'd fallen instantly but soundly asleep.

He slept like a baby, while she was still trying to attach a definition to the way he'd touched her when he replaced her bra strap. She didn't want to think of it as a caress, but that was what it had been. The most disquieting thing about it, the aspect of it that had stopped her breath, had been his absorption, his fixation on the textures of her.

Compelled by curiosity and a confounding restlessness, she raised her head so she could see him through the open car door.

He lay on his back, his shirt bunched beneath his head. One hand lay at his side. The other, the one that had handled the satin strap with such delicacy, maintained a loose clasp on the pistol grip.

But despite the rhythmic expansion and recession of his rib cage, she didn't trust that he lay in the boneless lassitude of deep slumber. Any stimuli would bring him bolt upright, eyes slashing like sabers, muscles instantly reactive.

She laid her head back down and settled more comfortably onto the seat. If she lay still and quiet and allowed him to sleep, it might buy her more time. If she provoked him, he might follow through on his threat to shut the car doors, or stuff her in the trunk, or decide that for two million dollars he could live with the guilt of having killed his first woman.

Chances were good that he would reach that conclusion anyway. Even if he had to settle for less, he would squeeze as much as he could from Panella and finish the job.

The job contracted by Panella but prompted by Josh.

Why had her brother done this stupid, stupid thing? Where was he? Had he paused to consider the tragic chain of events this irresponsible act would incite? When he fled the safe house, had it been a spontaneous decision spurred by desperation? Or had he meticulously planned it?

Of course he'd planned it, she told herself. He wouldn't have left anything to chance.

As always, thoughts of her brother were conflicting, suspending her between loyalty and resentment, anxiety and agitation. She worried for his safety and wanted to know that he was unharmed. But she also wanted to shake him senseless for continuing to cause so many people, herself included, untold distress and unhappiness. He'd stolen hard-gained funds from hundreds of people, but to her knowledge he'd never expressed remorse or compassion for his victims. In fact, on one occasion he'd disparaged them for being gullible and greedy, saying that if not for avarice, they wouldn't have been eager to sink their life savings into investments so transparently bogus.

No, it hadn't been Josh's conscience that had compelled him to turn informant, but rather a fear of harsher punishment if he didn't.

Even Shaw had recognized that everything Josh had done had been self-serving, but only she knew the extent of her brother's selfishness. She hadn't been bankrupted by his larcenous scheme with Panella, but she'd been the first and longest-standing victim of Josh's manipulation.

When he'd acknowledged his alleged crimes to her, she had lent moral support. But in a private moment, when Josh, with hand-wringing indecision, asked her advice on what he should do, she'd told him without hesitation, *Take your punishment like a man.*

That being not what he wanted to hear, he'd predictably turned the tables and made her the villain for not taking his side, for not doing enough, for not fiercely denying any wrongdoing on his part.

True to form, he harkened back to the accident that had ordained their relationship. It was Josh's excuse for any shortcoming, his season pass to cover any transgression, his free ticket for unlimited self-absorption.

Those fateful moments in 1992 had charted a course from which she and her brother had never deviated. Through childhood, adolescence, and into adulthood, it had kept her tethered to him as securely as a ship is to an anchor.

She had remained Josh's custodian until that day when he was escorted away by federal marshals. They weren't playground bullies against which she could defend him. Josh wasn't a child anymore. He was a man, and therefore accountable.

As she'd hugged him good-bye, she'd whispered in his ear, *This is it, Josh. I'm done.*

She had meant it, too. He'd wheedled his way out of facing

felony charges and had been granted a second chance that was more than fair. It was up to him what he did with it.

And he'd blown it.

So, yet again, she was suffering the consequences of his bad judgment and self-interest. Wherever he was, was he aware of what had happened to her last night? Would he care? If she didn't survive this, would he ever acknowledge, even to himself, that she had died because of his unrelenting selfishness?

Shaw— Had she thought of him as Shaw?

He wouldn't kill her. Would he? Surely not. Not after touching her that way.

She breathed deeply, as though inhaling an anesthetic. Her hairline grew damp. Her cheeks burned. A rivulet of sweat trickled through the valley between her breasts. Drowsily she realized that they felt heavy and full and achy, and, had her hands been free, she might have pressed them.

Surrendering to the drowsiness that the stifling heat induced, and lulled by the rhythm of Shaw's breathing, she closed her eyes.

Chapter 14

Disappointingly the noon newscasts didn't yield any leads on the murder-kidnapping in Terrebonne Parish.

They did, however, motivate an Orleans Parish prosecutor to pay a visit to the FBI division office. His name was Xavier Dupaw, and the only thing loftier than his name was his ego.

He strutted into Joe's office, announcing, "I was at lunch and caught the noon news. Looks like Shaw Kinnard is at it again."

Joe Wiley, feeling downright hostile toward the ADA for declining to indict Kinnard when he was in custody, offered nothing by way of a greeting.

Hick was only slightly more cordial. "Funny how that works, Dupaw. You let killers go, they kill somebody else."

Dupaw took umbrage. "My hands were tied. The police had nothing on him."

"They were still digging."

"Meanwhile an innocent man was languishing in jail."

"He wasn't—"

"Innocent until proven guilty," the prosecutor said. "Ring a bell?"

Joe wanted to ring his bell, all right. The prosecutor shied away from a case if there was the remotest possibility of losing it.

"Do you have any solid leads on the Bolden murder and the Bennett woman's disappearance?"

Hick glanced at Joe, who remained silent and sullen. Speaking for both of them, Hick said, "We have a crime scene unit assisting, but the Terrebone Parish SO is investigating Bolden's murder."

Dupaw frowned. "Do the personnel out there have the chops for it?"

"As murders go, it was straightforward," Hick said. "Kinnard came up behind Bolden and shot him in the back of the head."

"Yes, but the victim's association with Billy Panella make it bigger than a straightforward murder. Do a bunch of country bumpkins have the know-how to—"

"The country bumpkins have *balls*," said Joe, who had kept his cool for as long as he could. "When they catch Kinnard they'll charge him for murder and won't give a fuck how long he languishes in jail."

Xavier Dupaw puffed himself up with righteous indignation and stalked out.

Joe stood, pushing back so hard off his rolling chair that it hit the wall behind his desk. Each minute that ticked by without something happening was making him crazy, because every minute that ticked by reduced the odds of Jordie Bennett being found alive.

If she didn't make it, Joe would forever blame himself for not notifying her of her brother's escape from the safe house as soon as they'd discovered him gone. Joe had mistrusted her just enough to withhold the information, then watch her to see if Josh would seek her out for help and, if he did, to see what action she would take: Shelter him, or surrender him to the authorities.

He might never know, and that was gnawing at him.

He and Hick had reviewed witness statements taken in the

bar until they could recite them from memory. Deputy Morrow's only lead—a woman who called the sheriff's office and swore she saw Jordie Bennett being fed into a tree shredder—turned out to be the fabrication of a schizophrenic who'd gone off her meds. Her family apologized profusely, but investigators couldn't recover the time it had taken to ascertain that it was a false alarm from a head case.

Now, feeling claustrophobic, Joe headed for the door. "I'm gonna go to the bathroom. Call Tennessee again. See if they've turned up something."

Hick looked prepared to argue, but he reached for the desk phone. When Joe returned, Hick was hanging up in apparent disgust.

"Five minutes of conversation boiled down to two words: still nothing."

Joe hadn't expected there to be a breakthrough, but he shared Hick's disappointment and chagrin. Josh Bennett had been missing for four days, and the only traces of him discovered so far were the ankle monitor and a set of sneaker prints leading from the safe house through a greenbelt about two miles deep that eventually fronted the access ramp of the east–west interstate, where it was assumed he had hitched a ride.

Frustrated, Joe returned to his desk chair and pinched the bridge of his nose till it hurt. "Where *is* that sniveling little shit?"

"He's littler than when we last saw him."

Joe lowered his hand from his face and shook his head in bewilderment. "What gets me is that nobody became suspicious when Bennett began making these cosmetic changes."

"The dry eye was diagnosed by an ophthalmologist," Hick reminded him. "He was even prescribed drops for it."

"All right, but the drastic weight loss? I shed twenty pounds, Marsha might or might not notice if I'm standing in front of her buck naked. On Bennett's frame you'd notice that kind of drop."

"Not if he dropped it over a six-month time period."

"I guess," Joe sighed. "The bottom line, though? He played them like a freakin' fiddle."

"Played all of us, Joe," Hick said grimly.

Joe's scowl conceded that.

As the afternoon wore on, they decided to use the local evening newscasts to go public with Joshua Bennett's fugitive status.

Joe called in the office's media liaison. "Notify the local stations. Tell them in advance that I won't be answering any questions. I'll only read aloud a statement, so make it good."

The agent said jokingly, "What am I supposed to say? Accountant at large? Armed with a deadly calculator?"

Joe didn't think it was funny. "Say he's wanted for questioning into his sister's suspected kidnapping and Mickey Bolden's murder."

Hick looked at Joe askance. "He is? Since when?"

"Since I said so," Joe retorted. "And it's one hundred percent true. If Bennett hadn't taken a hike, Panella wouldn't have sent his favorite hit man and an accomplice after his sister. Mickey wouldn't be dead, and she wouldn't be missing. Last night would have been just another night of pool for Skull Head and his cronies, Deputy Morrow could have stayed to finish his victory pizza party, I'd have copped a feel off Marsha during 'Take My Breath Away,' and you'd have test-driven one of your promising relationships."

By now he was boiling over. "That nerd has eluded law enforcement agencies for four days. Maybe the public can do our job better and find him for us. So I don't care if we label him a goddamn ax murderer or the sniper who actually shot Kennedy, I want Josh Bennett's altered-state image on TV by five o'clock."

The other agent scuttled out to write the official statement.

A few hours later, Joe and Hick watched the first edition newscasts while eating another carryout meal off the desk. While Joe was reading the statement, the stations showed file footage from their coverage of the Panella-Bennett case and placed a photograph of Josh taken at the time side by side with an artist's sketch of how he'd looked when last seen in Tennessee.

"Well, let's see if that shakes something loose," Hick said as he muted the audio. "Wish you'd consulted me on your wardrobe, though."

Marsha called to tell him she'd seen him and asked when he was coming home. He told her not to expect him any time soon. He could wait for a development at home just as well as here, but while uniformed officers were out beating the bushes and dragging the bayous, he felt he should be on duty, too.

He paced while Hick essentially ran their trot lines.

"Call Morrow back."

"Joe, I talked to him an hour ago. He promised to call if anything . . ." He stopped arguing when the phone rang. He answered and identified himself. "That's us."

He listened for a moment, then sprang from his chair and motioned Joe out of his. "We'll call you from our car for directions." Promptly Hick hung up. Joe was already out the door. Hick followed.

They were moving down the hall at a fast clip when Joe worked up enough spit to ask, "Ms. Bennett?"

"Her brother."

"Dead?"

"Alive."

By the time they reached the elevator, Hick had explained that a man who lived in a small town near the Mississippi state line had called his parish's SO after watching the evening news. He reported having seen Josh Bennett in a convenience store earlier in the day.

"This isn't another schizo, is it?" Joe asked, and he impatiently jabbed the Down button repeatedly.

"Deputies followed up with the store's cashier. She didn't see the news, but they showed her the drawing of Bennett. She confirmed."

"Hot damn!"

"The chopper?" Hick was already tapping the number into his cell phone.

While Hick made the arrangements, Joe was thinking about Josh Bennett, and as soon as Hick ended his call, he expressed his puzzlement out loud. "He was smart enough to escape, but dumb enough to come back here?"

"This is where Ms. Bennett is, and she's Josh's security blanket. He also knows that this is the one place on the planet where Billy Panella ain't."

"Yeah, but..."

"What?" Hick asked as they walked in long strides through the parking garage toward Hick's car.

Joe pulled open the passenger door. "If last night taught us nothing else, it taught us how long Panella's reach is. Kinnard is out there somewhere. Doesn't Josh realize the threat he poses? The little turd needs to surrender."

"I doubt he will, Joe. He knows we'll lock him away forever."

"Yeah. But we wouldn't gut him."

"Mr. Panella? Is this a convenient time for us to speak?"

"A convenient time would have been two hours ago when I called you."

"I'm sorry I wasn't available. How can I serve you?"

The banker was Asian, but he had cultivated his British accent so that it was as silky as Devonshire cream. It inspired confidence and trust. The amplified distortion of Panella's voice didn't shock him. This was the manner in which their business had been conducted for years, and he understood the necessity for Panella's extreme caution. Nor was he put off by his customer's rudeness, which he'd also come to expect. Men who used offshore banks to hide sizable amounts of money in numbered accounts rarely wasted valuable time on polite conversation.

"I want to confirm the current balance in my account."

The banker excused himself and returned shortly to quote an amount. "To the penny," Panella said.

The banker smiled to himself. Amounts rounded off to the nearest dollar had never been satisfactory to this customer. Mr. Billy Panella tested the bank's accuracy frequently.

"I also wanted to alert you that I'll soon be making a sizable withdrawal."

"I hope the bank isn't losing your business."

"Not so long as you do what I tell you, when I tell you."

"You have my guarantee."

"I'll be requesting a wire transfer, and it could be on short notice."

"I'm happy to facilitate. This institution specializes in time-sensitive matters."

"Which I've always appreciated."

"The transfer made earlier this week was to your satisfaction?"

"You did what you were supposed to. Unfortunately others didn't."

"I regret to hear that."

"That's why this additional transfer is necessary, and there can't be any hang-ups. Understand? I want the money to be ready when I need it."

"Of course. American dollars, Mr. Panella?"

"Yes."

"Very good. And the amount?" The banker waited, poised, and when nothing was forthcoming, he prompted gently, "Mr. Panella?"

"Two fuckin' million."

Chapter 15

At first Jordie was too drugged by sleep to bother to identify the racket that had awakened her. She lay with her eyes closed, her brain muzzy from dreamless sleep and sultry heat. Subconsciously she was reluctant to wake up, so she fought it. However, the sound was persistent, and it eventually shook her awake and into full awareness.

A helicopter!

She struggled to sit up, cursing the awkwardness caused by her hands being restrained. She wormed her way out the open backseat door and stood. When she put her weight on her right foot, it tingled painfully and was virtually useless. Shifting most of her weight to her left foot, she ran in a lurching gait toward the door.

Shaw was silhouetted in the opening, looking up at the sky but from inside the building where he couldn't be seen. He heard her coming and turned in time to halt her before she cleared the door.

She screamed as loud as she could.

"Save your breath, Jordie. You won't be heard."

She knew it was futile, but she continued to scream anyway, mostly out of frustration as she kicked at his shins, at anything she could reach. When she aimed her knee at his crotch, he pulled back just in time, his body going concave. But she'd come perilously close, and he realized it.

Grabbing a handful of her top's fabric, he thrust her away from him and held her at arm's length, while using his other hand to pull the door shut. The clatter of the approaching helicopter became louder. The tin roof vibrated and rattled as it passed directly above them. Then the noise began to fade, as did Jordie's short-lived hope of rescue.

Eventually Shaw released his grip on her blouse, pushed open the door, and looked out. "They had better get where they're going soon. Storm's moving in."

She was surprised to discover that she'd slept away most of the afternoon. The sun was low in the west and blocked by a thick layer of clouds that had ushered in higher humidity. Now the shelter didn't feel so much like a convection oven as a steam bath.

They watched the retreating helicopter until it disappeared. He dusted his hands. "So much for that. Nothing to get you all excited."

His smugness outraged her and, giving no thought to the consequences, she launched herself at him. She resumed kicking, but rather than backing away from her, this time he drew her up against him and placed his feet between hers, making her efforts ineffectual.

The lethargy that had claimed her earlier was replaced by manic determination. She channeled every bit of strength she possessed into inflicting pain, or, at the very least discomfort, anything to upset his damned complacency. She twisted and squirmed, blind with fury, demented by rage, heedless of everything.

Until she realized that she was fighting only herself. He had stopped resisting.

He still held her, his hands splayed and firm on her hips, but the way they were securing her against him wasn't combative.

She fell still and tilted her face up to look into his.

"Now *I'm* excited."

There was an underlying, primitive thrum in his voice, and an insistent and unmistakable pressure against her open thighs where her body involuntarily responded with a purl of sensation.

Mortified, she stumbled back, and, to her surprise, his hands fell away and he let her go. But that only underscored that it was always his choice, that despite her tantrum, he maintained control.

She had no control, not even over her own body. Her breathing was hectic. She knew her face was flushed. His flint-colored eyes moved from her blushing cheeks to her breasts and in an attempt to explain their noticeable physical reaction, she said, "I'm angry. That's all."

"Yeah? Remind me to keep you angry."

Smarting, she said, "Look, I'm sick of your manhandling and your lewd innuendos. This isn't some kind of…"

When she failed to come up with an appropriate word, he arched an eyebrow. "Some kind of…what?"

"Don't flatter yourself, Mr. Kinnard. And make no mistake. If I get a chance to kill you, I will."

He watched her for a moment. "Noted."

He made to go around her, but then stopped suddenly and cupped her chin in his palm, forcing her head back. He ran his thumb across her lower lip. "Make no mistake. If I decide to turn this into something of that kind, Jordie, I won't use innuendos. I'll tell you straight out that I'm gonna fuck you."

Josh stared into the flickering television, which was the only light he allowed himself this evening.

Two images of him flashed onto the screen. Even he was shocked by the difference in his appearance from what it had been six months ago.

Jordie had gotten all the advantageous genes, even the good looks. His had never been anything to brag about, but he really looked pathetic in the drawing they were showing on TV. It was only a sketch done by a police artist, but...still.

No wonder the security on him had become lax. Who would've predicted that a scrawny dork who looked like him could pull a big one like this over on some of Uncle Sam's best?

He had. He should be taking a bow, toasting himself for the outstanding achievement.

Instead, as with the night before in the drab room of the motor court, after seeing the two faces of Joshua Bennett side by side on the evening news, his self-congratulatory state and self-confidence took a nosedive.

He directed his thoughts away from the artist's rendering and focused on what was being said about him. The anchorman rehashed the story Josh had seen in the convenience store during the noon hour about what had taken place last night in a bar outside his hometown of Tobias.

That story was followed by a recap of the Panella-Bennett fraud case and the events of six months ago. But that was only to remind people of who he was and why his being at large was newsworthy.

Presently, he was described as the "development" in "this ongoing and bizarre case," which had ultimately resulted in the murder of suspected killer-for-hire Mickey Bolden, and the "likely but as yet unconfirmed kidnapping" of local businesswoman Jordan Bennett.

When the news went to a commercial, Josh muted the audio and stared vacantly at the screen while assessing how Jordie's kidnapping might impact his carefully laid plans, because he certainly hadn't counted on that happening.

What was particularly galling? The FBI, in their determination to recapture him, had exploited it. Joe Wiley, with Hickam standing square-jawed in the background, had read a statement from behind a miked podium in the lobby of the FBI field office. The agent hadn't come right out and pointed a finger at him, but his implication had been that Josh must shoulder blame for his sister's misfortune. That was playing dirty pool.

"It's obvious that Mr. Bennett didn't think through the potential consequences of his flight." With all the gaiety of a foghorn, Wiley went on to say how snitches who reneged oftentimes didn't live very long. "I don't believe Mr. Bennett realizes the peril he's placed his sister in. Nor does he recognize the jeopardy to himself. I urge him to surrender. He's safe only while in our custody."

He was warning of reprisal from Panella, of course. "Subtle as a sledgehammer," Josh said to the silent TV, scoffing the FBI agent's transparent scare tactics. Josh had already outfoxed that fox, hadn't he? "So up yours, Agent Wiley."

But his bravado was halfhearted at best. He couldn't wholly dismiss Wiley's warning. The bald truth? He *had* created a hazardous situation for himself. In fact, thinking about it made him a little queasy.

His gaze was drawn to the cell phone lying on the table. He was tempted to pick it up and call Jordie's number just to see what he'd get, if anything. But, as before, he nixed the idea. In the unlikely event that this guy Kinnard—who the hell was he, anyway?—had left her phone behind when he took her, the risk of calling it was great. He envisioned Wiley and Hickam and God knew who else huddled around it just waiting for it to ring so they could trace the call straight to his current location.

Geographically he was a little too close for comfort to chance that.

Otherwise, he felt reasonably secure about his hiding place, which had been waiting for him against the day when he would make good his escape plan. He'd prepared well. Before being hauled away to Tennessee, he paid the utility bills for a year in advance. He'd made certain the pantry and freezer were stocked. The food was six months old, but he'd never paid much attention to expiration dates and had probably eaten older.

Sooner or later, one of the people with whom he'd crossed paths since Tuesday would connect the hitchhiking burnout to Josh Bennett, accused felon, turned informant, turned fugitive.

If the cashier or the blowhard in the convenience store IDed him, the authorities would know he was back in the state. But from that Hicksville store, he'd covered his tracks well.

Beneath the huge oak tree in the woods, he'd made slight alterations in his appearance. From there, it was a three-mile walk to a public storage facility where he'd left a car six months ago. He'd waited until no one was around, then had opened his storage unit and reconnected the car's battery cables, and with minor encouragement, the engine had kicked on.

Sure, there were security cameras all over the place, but he'd taken measures to prevent them from being a problem. If by some miracle, he was identified entering the place on foot and leaving in a vehicle, he had switched license plates twice on the way here, so he was confident they would never find him.

There wasn't a person alive who would think to look for him here, not even Jordie. The nearest occupied property was over two miles away. As long as he kept to the ground floor, and used only a minimum of light each night, he should be okay here indefinitely.

Jordie's kidnapping was an unexpected snag, but he couldn't let it unravel him. He *wouldn't* let it unravel him. He only had to hang in there until he could implement the last step of his plan. Then he would be clear and worry free forever.

However, the context of Joe Wiley's sound bite was spoiling his optimism. What did the FBI know that he didn't?

Something about Panella that would trigger another avenue of investigation?

Something about Jordie's abduction that they weren't sharing with the media?

The TV had a DVR. He had recorded the newscast. He watched it again now.

And then again, and once more, becoming a little more paranoid and panicked each time Joe Wiley said, "the potential consequences of his flight..."

Chapter 16

———◄◉►———

After what Shaw had said, Jordie had difficulty looking him in the eye. In her peripheral vision, she saw him pull the familiar knife from his pocket. Then he stood there, waiting.

She wished she could muster the obstinance to make him wait, to make him order her, but she was too anxious to have her hands freed, so like an obedient and well-trained pet, she turned around. With an efficient snap, he cut through the cuff.

When she came back around, he was rummaging inside the trunk of the car. He returned to her carrying several things, including one of the unused camouflage-print bandanas.

"How many are you down to?"

"I have a few more."

She wondered which would run out first, the bandanas or her time.

He passed her the bandana and a small bar of soap, the kind furnished in an inexpensive hotel, no larger than a wafer and still wrapped in glossy white paper. He then handed her a bottle of water. "Be frugal with it."

When she realized that he was suggesting she wash, the idea

of it was so appealing, she wanted to weep with gratitude. On the other hand, the extended kindness made her wary, and her expression must have conveyed that.

He motioned behind him. "As long as you behave yourself, you can have that half of the building, and I promise to keep my distance and my back turned."

"Why should I trust you?"

"You shouldn't."

She looked past him into the gathering gloom at the back of the building. Although the early dusk would partially conceal her, the deeply shadowed space wasn't inviting. Being clean, however, was.

She stepped around him and walked into an area of the cavernous building where the darkness was deepest. At eye level on the rough wall, a two-by-four ran horizontally to form a narrow ledge. She unwrapped the soap bar and placed it there along with the bottle of water.

She glanced over her shoulder. Shaw was folding up the tarp, which she took as a good sign. He wouldn't be doing that if he planned on needing it soon. Nor would he be enabling her to wash. In any case, he wasn't looking her way.

Holding the corner of the bandana between her teeth, she pulled her top over her head, and, before she could talk herself out of it, peeled off her jeans. She had difficulty getting them past her sandals, but she wasn't going to put her bare feet on the floor if she could avoid it.

Really there was no difference between being in a bra and panties and wearing a bikini. But feeling exposed and vulnerable, she hastily poured a palmful of water and worked up a lather with the soap between her hands.

When she'd washed every place she could reach, she soaked the bandana and used it to wipe away the soap. With the last of the water she wet the cloth again, then went over herself a second time.

"Time's up."

She froze and gave him another glance. His back was to her. He was pulling on his shirt. She called to him that she was almost finished.

"I'm counting down from sixty," he said.

"That's not enough time for me to air-dry. The humidity—"

"Fifty-seven."

She cursed under her breath and hurriedly pulled on her jeans. Her skin and underwear were damp. Even so, she felt considerably better. Trying not to dwell on the dried bloodstains on her top, she pulled it on and pushed her arms through the armholes. She scooped her hair from the neckline and gathered it into a ponytail, tying it with the wet bandana.

"Thirty-four."

She reached for the bar of soap and, in her haste, dropped it to the floor. "Damn!"

"Twenty-two. Twenty-one."

She crouched and groped along the floor looking for the soap.

But she discovered something else. Something completely unexpected.

Immediately, she recognized it for what it was, but if she hadn't been this close to it, it would have gone unnoticed, because it was stuck between the bottom of one of the vertical slats and another two-by-four that ran along the floor like a baseboard.

She took hold, but it was tightly wedged in the crack between the two pieces of lumber, which, despite their age, were unforgiving. She applied herself to pulling it free, but if she managed to, where could she hide it until she had an opportunity to use it? The timing had to be perfect. She would have to be close to him, and lightning quick, because she wouldn't get a second chance, so the jab would have to count and be—

"Ten, nine, eight."

She gave one final tug.

"Seven. Six."

"I'm coming." She used her last five seconds to calm her breathing, then stood up and started toward him. "I feel much better, thank you. It was wonderful, truly. Who knew that a sponge bath could be—"

"What have you got behind your back?"

"Nothing. I'm just tucking in my top—"

She didn't even get the last word out before he was on her, turning her around and seizing her wrist. He pried open her fist. In it lay the bar of soap.

"I wanted to keep it," she said meekly. "You may have fewer of these than bandanas."

Her heart didn't stop thudding until he finally released her from an incisive stare. "I'm gonna eat," he said. "You can or not."

He let go of her hand and moved away. She trailed him, but her mind was on the weapon she'd had to leave wedged between the planks in the wall. In order to relocate it in the darkness, all she had to do was look for the empty water bottle she'd left at eye level on the makeshift ledge.

Her problem was going to be getting to it at all.

Jordie was up to something.

If Shaw hadn't discerned that the second she came toward him with that chipper smile and babbling monologue, the way she was wolfing down the beanie wienies would have been a dead giveaway. Her conversation was still lively.

"My skin was gritty with dried sweat. Didn't washing off make you feel better?"

"Nothing like cleanliness."

"And now this fine cuisine." She shot him a smile that was almost flirtatious.

Yeah, something was behind her change in mood and batting eyelashes.

She emptied the small can and licked the bowl of her spoon clean. "Want something else?" he asked.

"No thank you."

He took the can from her, tossing it and his own empty into the trunk before lowering the lid. When he did, the light went out, and so did Jordie's fake smile.

She looked around with worry. "What happens when we lose all daylight?"

"It'll get dark."

"But...we...we can open a car door so we'll have the dome light. Or keep the trunk open."

He shook his head. "Too much drain on the battery."

"I saw one of those big square flashlights in the trunk."

"For emergency use only."

"You could—"

"A light can be seen for miles, Jordie."

"From as far away as the main road? How far is it from here?"

"No light."

"So we'll just sit here in the dark all night?"

"You scared of the dark?" When she didn't answer, he said, "It's always dark when your eyes are closed."

"I slept too long today. I won't be sleepy for hours."

"Then I guess we'll have to think up something we can do in the dark. For hours." He walked to where she sat on the upended crate. "Oh, sorry. Did that sound like another lewd innuendo? Didn't mean for it to."

She shot him a sour look.

"Actually, I was thinking we could call Panella back," he said. "That would kill some time."

Watching her watch him, he replaced the battery in Mickey's phone and clicked it on. As the phone booted up, he studied her face in the minimal light of the screen. "What were you doing back there?" Using his chin, he motioned toward the back of the building.

"Taking a sponge bath."

"What else?"

"I was avoiding the mouse droppings."

"That's all?"

"What else could I have been doing?"

"I don't know, but I don't like surprises."

"So you've said."

She was looking straight into his eyes, challenging him. He got to the call memory and pressed his thumb against the screen, then put the phone on speaker.

Panella answered after the first ring. "All right, asshole," he said in his garbled voice. "Two million."

Jordie drew in a startled breath. Her lips remained parted. Her eyes seemed to dilate.

Panella was saying, "I've already notified an offshore bank that I'll be making a wire transfer in that amount. After I get indisputable confirmation of the kill, of course."

"I'll text you a photograph."

"No."

"Didn't think so," Shaw said. "So how do I confirm to you she's dead?"

"I'm making arrangements for that."

"Um-huh. I'll bet you are. Like the arrangement for me that you and Mickey had planned." When Panella didn't respond, Shaw said, "Not that I mistrust you, Panella, but I'm gonna require a show of your good faith."

"What would show my good faith?"

"Half up front."

"Forget it."

"Half up front, or I take one of those options I outlined to you earlier."

"Know what would show *your* good faith? If you'd stop screwing around and get the job done. Now. *Before* her double-crossing brother gets himself recaptured. It doesn't have to be fancy. I just want Josh Bennett to know she's dead. Soon."

Shaw waited several beats, then said a brusque "I'll get back to you" and clicked off.

For the entirety of the conversation, he hadn't broken eye contact with Jordie. After he hung up, ponderous moments passed with neither of them moving, then she took off like a sprinter. He barely managed to grab her shirttail and hold on as he pulled her back. She came around swinging, her fist landing hard on his cheekbone.

"Goddammit!" The pain brought sudden tears to his eyes. He lost his grip on her top, and she got several yards away from him before he lunged after her. He caught her from behind in a bear hug and pinned her arms to her sides.

"Stop it! Listen! You don't have to die!"

She kept struggling, until she realized the futility of her struggle and what he was saying sank in. Her ponytail swept across his face as she whipped her head around and looked at him over her shoulder. "What?"

"Are you gonna listen? Or act like a madwoman until you force me to shoot you just to get rid of you?" She didn't say anything but ceased straining to break his hold. Not completely trusting her capitulation, he relaxed the bear hug, but took her arm and pulled her back to the crate. "Sit down."

She backed onto it, but looked ready to spring off it at any second, and he noticed the furtive glances she kept casting toward the back of the building.

He touched his throbbing cheekbone with the heel of his hand. The skin hadn't split, but it was swelling. "That hurt like bloody hell."

"Don't expect an apology."

He removed the battery from Mickey's phone, but as he

slid the two components into one pocket, he withdrew another phone from his other pocket. Recognizing the Extravaganza logo on the case, she sat up at attention.

"That's mine."

"That's right."

"You told me you'd hidden it."

"I retrieved it this afternoon while you were asleep."

He opened the back of her phone and inserted the battery. "By powering it up, I'm taking a chance that the signal will be triangulated and bring the law right to us. But I want you to see something. Your fate really is up to you." He clicked the phone on. When he got to her call log, he turned the screen toward her.

"Last night, nine twenty-three, incoming call. No ID, no number. But you called it back three minutes later, and again at nine forty-seven. I'm guessing that call was made while you were driving, because your house is several miles from that bar out in the boonies. At roughly ten o'clock you walked in and took a bar stool, looking as out of place as a frosted cupcake atop a pile of cowshit.

"Only one person would get you to a honky tonk like that in record time. Now..." He bent over her, bringing his nose to within inches of hers. "Where is brother Josh?"

She wilted. "That's my saving grace?"

"That's it."

"Then I'm dead."

"That's entirely up to you. You die or you live. I either take Panella's measly two million, or you direct me to Josh and his thirty."

"I can't! I've told you a hundred times that I don't know where he is!"

"You also told me that nobody called you to that bar," he shouted, shaking the cell phone near her face. "You lied about that, you're lying now."

She sat back and folded her arms across her chest. He noticed the red marks and bruises on her wrists left by the cuffs, and that gave him a pang of regret, but he didn't let it stop him.

"Josh put in a distress call, didn't he, Jordie? An SOS. He asked you to come pick him up at that out-of-the-way bar."

"No."

"And drive him to a hiding place?"

"No."

"Or maybe he didn't have a hiding place yet and needed your trusted input. Were you going to have a brother-sister confab and discuss options?"

"No."

"Was he going to leave a message for you at the bar, let you know where he was headed?"

When she didn't reply to that, he tilted his head. "Was that it?"

"No."

"Where was he going?"

"I don't know! Stop with the questions. You're only wasting your breath. I haven't talked to Josh. He didn't call me last night."

"You're lying."

She gave her head a firm shake.

"Then if it wasn't Josh, who did you talk to on the phone?"

"Nobody," she said, but the turbulence in her eyes evidenced how fast the wheels of her mind were spinning.

He pressed, but asked softly, "Who did you talk to?"

"Why should I tell you anything?"

"Because you know what will happen if you don't."

"I know what will happen if I do!"

"We'll go to Josh—"

"You'll kill both of us."

"And pass on the thirty million? I don't think so."

"Josh hasn't got the—"

"Who called you?"

"—money."

"Who did you talk to?"

"No one!"

"Tell me now, or by God, I'm taking Panella's deal."

She sucked in a breath, wet her lips, and said huskily, "I didn't talk to anybody."

"Jesus, Jordie, don't—"

"But I—"

"—be stupid."

"But I did get a call."

Chapter 17

A rumble of thunder interrupted the sudden and taut silence between them. Shaw didn't seem to notice. Her admission had cemented his attention on her.

She asked, "May I have some water, please?"

He straightened up and walked over to the car. Leaning into the driver's seat, he reached beneath the dashboard for the trunk release. The lid popped open, the light inside came on, and Jordie was grateful for it and the dome light. With only the slate-gray remnants of daylight eking through the cracks in the walls, it had grown almost completely dark inside the building.

The back half of it was especially dark.

He returned to her with a bottle of water. She thanked him and drank deeply. When she'd had all she wanted, he took the bottle from her. "We're running low." He drank the rest, threw the empty bottle into the trunk, then came back to her.

"Male or female?"

"What?"

"The person who called you."

"Male."

"But it wasn't Josh?"

"I don't think so. It might have been, but I don't think so. His voice was muffled."

"Panella and his silly machine?"

"No. Nothing like that. Just—"

"—muffled."

"Yes."

"What did this muffled voice that might or might not have been Josh say?"

She ignored his patent skepticism. "He said, 'If you want information about your brother, come now.' He emphasized the *now* and told me where the bar was located. He didn't give me a chance to ask or say anything before disconnecting."

He thought all that over. "What did he say when you called back?"

"I did so directly because I needed better directions on where to find the bar. His had been rushed and imprecise. But when I called, he didn't answer."

"Although he'd just called you?"

She raised her shoulders. "He didn't answer."

"Regardless, you wasted no time setting out."

"That's right." She considered telling him about the car which she was almost certain had followed her, but thought it best not to volunteer anything. "As you assumed, I called him again en route when I got turned around on one of the back roads. He didn't answer then, either. That's the *truth*. That's all I know. I swear it."

"That's the truth?"

"Yes."

"All you know?"

"Yes."

"Then why hold out on me? Why didn't you tell me this last night when I asked—repeatedly—why you went to that bar?"

That touched a nerve. "Well, just possibly my reticence had

something to do with you snuffing your partner, kidnapping me, tying me up, and marching me into a dark woods for what I feared was my execution."

Building up a full head of steam, she continued. "I was scared out of my mind! I'd just seen you kill a man, and you were suggesting that I"—she slapped her hand against her chest—"was part of a plot to set you up as a fall guy. I was afraid if I told you about the call, you would demand to know more, and I couldn't tell you any more, because *I don't know any more!*" By now she was shouting.

Unruffled, he watched her for a moment, giving her time to simmer down, then said, "Let's see."

"What?"

"Call back. See if he answers this time." He extended her the phone.

An active phone. A lifeline. He was offering it to her. But she would never be able to complete a 911 call before he stopped her, and she didn't dare redial the unknown caller who'd summoned her to the bar. If the person on the other end *was* Josh . . .

She left the phone lying untouched in Shaw's palm.

"No?" he said. "Then I'll call again."

"Again?"

He turned the phone so she could read the screen. "See? Last night. Ten fifty-two. I was approximately a half hour's drive away from the bar when I pulled off the road to switch license plates. I took the opportunity to check your phone. Out of curiosity I called Unknown."

She looked at him expectantly. "What did you get?"

"Rings. No answer. No voice mail. Just like the three times I've called it since then." He showed her the history of his attempts, the most recent being that afternoon while she slept. "Maybe we'll get lucky this time." He tapped the screen and held the phone so she could hear the rings. Her heart thumped with fearful anticipation, but the call went unanswered.

After seven or eight rings, he disconnected. She didn't know whether to be disappointed or relieved, but his scrutiny of her was unsettling.

"No one approached you in the bar except that idiot who slipped you the phone number."

"He had nothing to do with anything," she said. "It wasn't him who called me."

"How do you know?"

"Did he look trustworthy to you, or like someone who could carry out a dangerous mission for Josh?"

In spite of her scoffing, Shaw's stare didn't waver.

She added, "I think when he came over to me, he must've scared off the person who called. Which was the main reason I became so irritated with him."

"He scared off the mysterious caller who was going to give you information about Josh."

This time she acknowledged his sarcasm. "You think I'm lying."

"I didn't say that."

"Your tone implied it."

"First you complain about my innuendos, now my tone. Makes me wonder if I'll ever be able to satisfy you. Ooops." He exaggerated a wince. "Another innuendo."

She came straight off the crate to her feet. "I think *you* scared him off."

"When I shot Mickey? Wrong. Because by then you had realized you'd been stood up and had hightailed it out of there."

"I hightailed it because I realized how irrational it was to have gone in the first place. When I got that call, I didn't know Josh had escaped. I thought that perhaps someone would deliver a message from him, or give me a way to reach him. Something like that."

She could tell he wasn't buying it. Sighing, she returned to her seat on the crate and rubbed her temple. "Honestly, I don't know what was going through my mind. I reacted without thinking. The moment I walked into that place, I realized how stupid it was to have gone streaking off into the night.

"The longer I sat there, fending off that creep, the more likely it seemed that the call had been a hoax, someone playing a cruel joke on me. I was still thinking it was a prank until I turned around, saw you and Mickey coming toward me, and realized that Billy Panella was behind the whole thing."

"He was behind the hit, not the phone call."

"Oh, right. My arrival was a shock. I showed up, and you had to scrub plan A." She gestured with helplessness. "We're back to where we started. I don't know who called or why he sent me to that bar."

He didn't react for the longest time. Eventually he shrugged and said, "Okay," but his flippancy suggested that it wasn't at all okay.

"You've got to believe me!"

"I said okay." Methodically he removed the battery from her phone before putting both in his front pocket. Encircling her biceps with his hand, he pulled her up off the crate and drew her toward the door. "It's starting to rain. You need to go outside while you can."

"Please, listen, I—"

"I was listening."

"But I don't think you believe me. Do you?"

When they reached the door, he pushed it open, then stood there, his breathing hard, his fingers growing steadily tighter around her arm.

"I'm not lying, I swear."

Suddenly he brought her around to face him. He'd never looked more intimidating or forbidding.

"I'm telling you everything I know. Please believe me. Believe—"

"Hush, Jordie."

The command was softly spoken but imperious. He brought his mouth down on hers ungently and without restraint. The back of her head was encompassed by his hand and held in place with inescapable strength. His other hand settled on her neck.

While his thumb stroked the sensitive underside of her chin, his stern lips pressured hers to separate, and when they did, the sleek glide of his tongue against hers caused an overspill of heat throughout her. Angling his head the other way, he made an even deeper foray into her mouth.

But then he groaned with frustration and raised his head. "I had to do that. Just once."

Abruptly he let go of her and pushed her through the open door, soundly pulling it closed behind her.

Before she fully registered what had happened, she was outside, standing in the falling mist, staring into the darkness, her entire body pulsing. With trembling fingers, she touched her damp lips, and even as she did, a whimper escaped them. A whimper of longing, mortification, torment. His breath had been hot on her face, his body hard, his voice gruff, his eyes alight in the darkness. All of him, masterful and possessive.

I had to do that. Just once.

Once.

The qualifier made it clear.

He was going to kill her.

Chapter 18

It was after nightfall by the time the helicopter set down near the convenience store where Josh Bennett reportedly had bought groceries, some toiletries, and a lottery ticket. Joe and Hick had asked to interview the store clerk and the customer at the site. The two were waiting for them at the register when they entered the store.

Both seemed excited to be in on something as big as the recapture of the man who'd turned FBI informant and then had the audacity to bail. As the loud, barrel-chested man shook hands with them, he said, "Josh Bennett screwed y'all, too, didn't he? Just like he and Panella did all those other folks."

When asked, he described Bennett's appearance that morning and gave them his impressions of the fugitive. "Truth be told, I was paying more attention to what was on the TV."

When it came the cashier's turn, she actually expressed concern for the runaway. "I sensed there was something the matter with him."

"Was he injured, ill, what?" Joe asked while Hick was busily typing their responses into his iPad.

"No, he seemed fine when he came in. He didn't start looking sickly till he was filling in his lottery numbers. That's when we started watching the news. I guess that's how he learned about what happened to his sister last night. Must've been a shock. You gotta feel a little sorry for him."

Hick and Joe looked at each other, tacitly agreeing that they couldn't work up one iota of sympathy for Joshua Bennett. Joe went back to the cashier. "Did he mention anything about the kidnapping or murder?"

Both she and the man shook their heads. She said, "He just wrapped up his business like he was in a hurry to get going. He was jumpy. Sweating. He was wearing khakis, sorta like the military. I figured him fresh back from Syria or someplace. You know, post-traumatic stress."

"Did he appear to be armed?" Joe asked.

The man answered. "No. But can't say what was in his backpack."

The two had little more of value to report, although the man remembered seeing Josh set off on foot after he left the store. "He was walking along the shoulder, headed west. He had on the backpack and was carrying the bags of stuff he bought. It crossed my mind to go after him and offer him a lift, but then I got distracted buying my own lottery tickets, and by the time I went out and got in my pickup, he was nowhere to be seen."

Joe asked to see the video from the store's security cameras. He, Hick, and a handful of local law officers watched it several times, but it revealed nothing of significance beyond what the witnesses had already told them.

However, Hick did comment on the change in Bennett's appearance. "I'm not sure I would have recognized him immediately."

Joe reluctantly agreed.

Law enforcement departments from nearby municipalities and the parish SO, as well as state troopers and U.S. marshals, had been mobilized to begin a search, although no one was optimistic about picking up Bennett's trail until daylight.

So it was with some surprise that Joe received word that debris had been discovered in a clearing in the woods not far away. "Don't let anybody touch anything till we get there."

The clearing was a distance from the highway and accessed by a footpath which everyone was careful to stay off of as they thrashed their way through the dark woods.

The deputy who'd made the discovery led the way to a live oak tree that Joe estimated to be at least a century old, if not twice that.

"Everybody who grew up around here knows this path and this tree," the deputy told them. "Teenagers buy beer at the convenience store, usually with fake IDs, come here to drink, make out. In high school we called it the knock-up tree because...well, you know. That's how come I remembered it and thought to check. Sure enough."

He shone his flashlight on the litter scattered over the network of large roots that snaked along the ground at the base of the tree. Joe didn't get his hopes up. The trash could have been left by Josh Bennett or just as easily by lustful teenagers with illegally purchased six-packs.

With care, he squatted and studied the various product wrappers and empty plastic bags. Among them, he picked out a cash register receipt. It was from the store, and the time stamp coincided with when Bennett had been there. One of the purchases was a Lotto ticket.

The deputy said, "Something else I noticed on the path. There's one set of shoe prints coming in this way, another set going back out toward the highway."

"He changed clothes while he was back here?" Hick asked.

"That'd be my guess," the deputy replied. "Smart guy like him, prob'ly knew he'd been caught on security cameras inside the store. He'd want to switch clothes quick."

Joe agreed. He also noticed among the litter the empty package of a razor. He pointed it out to Hick.

Hick said, "He got rid of his ugly scruff."

Joe stood up and looked back toward the path. "Say he did come back here and changed at least his shoes, shaved, stuffed his purchases into his backpack, and walked back to the highway. What then?"

"Hitched a ride," suggested one of the officers grouped around the clearing.

"Ankle express," said another.

The deputy who'd found the debris said to Joe, "If he was on foot, search dogs might pick up a scent. We could get a canine unit out here in the a.m. "

"How about ASAP?" Joe asked. "The dogs don't know it's dark."

The deputy hesitated. "It's a private contractor. Y'all paying?"

"We'll pay."

The officer touched the brim of his hat. "I'll make the call."

Leaving the others to bag evidence, Joe and Hick began tromping back toward the highway. Joe's cell phone rang. He answered. "Joe Wiley."

"That sketch of me you showed on TV is for shit."

Joe came to a dead standstill. "Josh?"

When Hick heard the name, he swung around. Joe angled the phone away from his ear, so Hick could listen in.

"How'd you get my cell number?" Joe asked.

"I remember it from six months ago. I'm smart that way."

"Calling me to turn yourself in is the smartest thing you've ever done."

"I'll never turn myself in."

"Then are you calling only to critique our sketch artist?"

"Is Jordie dead?"

The blunt question and the perceptible emotion behind it surprised Joe. "I don't know, Josh. I hope not."

He made a choking sound. "I think she's dead and you're just not announcing it yet."

"Tell me where you are. I'll come to you and we'll talk about it."

"As if."

"You left a trail from the convenience store. Agent Hickam and I aren't too far behind you. We'll keep at it until we find you."

"Stop wasting your time tracking me and *find my sister*!" On the last word, his voice cracked.

"We're doing our best."

"You think he's already killed her, don't you? That guy Kinnard. Shaw Kinnard. They showed his picture on TV."

"He's bad news. Mean bastard. But he and Mickey Bolden were only hired guns, bought and paid for by Billy Panella. You know that as well as I do."

"You're only trying to scare me. Billy doesn't care about me anymore."

"Josh, you worked for the man. Did he ever let a slight go unpunished? And you ratting him out was a lot more offensive than a slight." Taking advantage of the gulping swallows coming through the phone, Joe laid it on thick.

"Geography won't be a hindrance. Panella's got a surplus of money. Thirty million will buy a lot of contract killers. He can send one right after the other. They'll come in waves. He's already sending two at a time. He won't die happy till you die miserable."

Josh began to sob in earnest. "He always threatened to kill Jordie first. He swore he would if I ever double-crossed him."

"Looks like he's made good on that threat, doesn't it? Guess who's up next? You. Unless you let the government protect you."

"Protect me? Ha! You'll put me in prison."

"Maybe you can strike another deal with the DOJ. But you lose any bargaining position you have if you continue to run.

And without us shielding you, you're fair game for Panella. So tell me where you are. Agent Hickam and I will come get you. You'll be safe."

"I am safe. I want Jordie to be safe." He gave a liquid sniff, then mumbled, "Maybe we could work together."

Joe looked sharply at Hick, who raised his eyebrows with interest. "What do you have in mind, Josh?"

"First, you've got to tell me the truth. Is Jordie dead?"

"God's truth, I don't know."

"But you think he's killed her, don't you? Don't you?"

Joe figured that Josh Bennett was angling to cut another deal, and the sly little shit had proved to be a stubborn negotiator. Would it be better to hedge or to level with him?

He knew Hick was following his thoughts and silently consulted him. Hick tipped his head as though to say *Your call*.

Joe decided to give it to Josh straight. "Given this man's reputation, the odds are not in Jordie's favor."

Shaw Kinnard was going to kill her and collect his two million dollars. That was what would happen unless she could escape him, or prevent him.

Navigating the labyrinth of channels behind the building was out of the question. She had no idea how deep the water was, and determining its depth would be hazardous enough. Just by wading into it, there were any number of ways by which she could perish: alligators, poisonous snakes, and becoming ensnared underwater in the tangled roots of vegetation that grew above as well as below the opaque surface.

She also had no idea how far-reaching the swampy waterway was or to where it led in any direction. If she were to survive in it, she could meander for days and get exactly nowhere before the elements claimed her life.

Looking behind her, she considered the gravel lane by which they'd arrived. But how far away was the main road? She'd thought she had posed her question about the distance to it quite cleverly, but Shaw had seen through her disingenuousness and had avoided telling her. If she attempted to make it there on foot, he could easily run her down in the car.

She didn't have wings.

So escaping by water, land, or air was out. Which meant she had to prevent him from killing her.

Her only possible means of doing that was inside the building.

She reviewed her limited options once more, but no new ideas came to her. She was only delaying the inevitable. With trepidation, she reached for the broken latch and pulled open the door. The building was in total blackout, the air inside as dank as a cave.

"Come in." His voice was disembodied. She couldn't see him.

"I can't see where I'm going."

After a lengthy silence when all she could hear were her own heartbeats against her eardrums, he opened the car door and the dome light came on. It did more to emphasize the surrounding darkness than to relieve it.

He was standing on the opposite side of the car, only his head and shoulders visible above the roof of it. "Did you get wet?"

Until he asked, Jordie hadn't even noticed that her hair and clothing had indeed absorbed the mist while she'd been outside contemplating the only hope she had of surviving.

The mere thought of what she must do sickened her. But more sickening was the thought of dying like Mickey Bolden.

The bandana with which she'd tied her ponytail felt soggy and heavy against the back of her neck as she nodded in reply to his question. "Yes, a little."

"Maybe there's something in the trunk you can use to dry off."

Her heart thumped hard. He'd just given her an excuse to
go back to the spot where she'd taken her sponge bath. But she
didn't want to appear too eager to get there. "What have you
got?"

"Take a look." He bent down out of sight only long
enough to reach beneath the dashboard and pop open the
trunk again.

She hesitated, then started toward the car. "I might have to
use the last of your bandanas."

"Short as that supply is, I'd hate to give up more."

"I'll buy you another dozen."

It suddenly stuck her what an inane conversation this was to
be having at this moment. But what did one say to someone at
a time such as this? What would be appropriate? Nothing she
could think of.

However, it seemed vital that she continue talking to him.
The sound of her own voice somehow bolstered her resolve. It
was proof that he hadn't shot her outright when she reentered
the building and that she was still alive. For as long as she was
drawing breath, hope remained. In dwindling quantities, perhaps. But for now there was still a glimmer of it.

She got as far as the rear bumper on the passenger side. He
was still standing in the open wedge of the driver's door, his left
forearm propped on the roof, looking deceptively casual. His
eyes were the giveaway to exactly how alert he was. They reflected the faint light like razor-sharp blades, scarily motionless
as they watched her.

Attempting to appear unafraid, she moved around to the
open trunk and took a swift inventory. What she saw were the
remaining canned goods, a half-dozen unopened bottles of water, their empties, the blue tarp. She didn't spot her phone. Nor
the tire iron. Was it beneath the tarp? If not, where was it? What
had he done with it? "Find them?" he asked.

"Yes." She reached into the trunk for the package of bandanas. She pulled one from it then dropped the package back into the trunk.

Trying to look unhurried, she turned and started walking toward the back of the building. "If you'll keep the light on for a few minutes longer, I'll just go back here and use—"

"Jordie."

"What?"

"What's your rush?"

"I'm wet."

"Stop."

"What?"

"I said stop!"

She turned around quickly. "Why?"

He was walking toward her, his right hand held down at his side close to his thigh. "Is this what you're going after?" He raised his right arm. Her heart stopped in expectation of seeing the pistol in his hand.

Not the arrow.

She gasped.

With breath-stealing swiftness, he raised his right knee and broke the shaft over it, then threw the two pieces to the floor.

Jordie gave a strangled cry, spun away, and raced toward the back of the building.

He was right behind her and closing in. "I wondered what had captured your interest back here. I found it just now while you were outside."

When she came even with the empty water bottle sitting on the two-by-four ledge, she practically threw herself against the wall.

"Did you really think   "

She dropped to her hands and knees and crawled forward a few feet.

"—that I wouldn't know you were up to something?"

Splinters pricked her hands as she blindly felt along the rough wood wall.

He crouched down. She turned to face him, flattening herself firmly against the wall, her hands behind her. "It's no use," he said. "I found your secret weapon. What were you planning to do with that arrow? Restring the bow and shoot me with it?"

Tears welled in her eyes. She was trembling with fright.

"Come on. Get up." He placed his hands on her shoulders and tried to pull her to her feet, but she resisted.

His face had become a watery blur because of her tears. But she could clearly see the scar carved out of his scruff, and the lips that looked so austere but which kissed with remarkable passion.

She also made out the stunned disbelief that froze his features when she thrust her right hand against his midsection.

They stared at each other for several seconds, then moved at the same time, he falling back several feet and landing on his butt, she slapping both hands across her mouth to keep in a wail of horror over her own violent action.

He continued to gape at her with bafflement, then bent his head down to look at the broken outboard propeller jutting from his abdomen.

Chapter 19

Shaw swore savagely and raised his head to glare at Jordie, who remained with her hands covering her mouth for several seconds more, then she sprang toward him.

"Get the fuck away from me." He'd tried yelling it, but his voice had already gone thready.

She reached beneath his shirttail and wrestled the pistol from the holster. He needed his hands to support himself, so he let her take the gun without a fight. Shakily holding it between her hands, she aimed it at him.

"Don't move or I'll shoot you, too."

"Not with that, you won't." Hissing in pain, he levered himself into a full sitting position. He could feel beads of sweat popping out on his forehead. Any other time, her inexperienced handling of the firearm would have made him nervous. Now, he grit his teeth against the agony in his middle and said, "I took the cartridge out."

She stopped fiddling with the pistol and gaped at him. "What?"

"Safety precaution. You were getting too interested in it."

"Where are the bullets?"

"Hidden."

"Where?"

Ignoring her, he visualized a chart of the human anatomy and tried to remember the organs which, if punctured, would cause him to bleed out. The broken propeller blade had stabbed through his shirt under his last rib on his left side. It would have missed his pancreas, liver, and stomach, all of which were too high and center. Left kidney? Too high and posterior. Large intestine? Possibly. If he was lucky, the blade was too far left of it and had missed.

Worst-case scenario, it had struck that large artery—what the hell was the name of it?—that passed through the abdomen and funneled down into the groin to become the femoral. If that major blood vessel had been opened, even nicked, he wouldn't be a problem for Jordie Bennett much longer. The time he had left would depend on the size of the leak.

He cursed again. "You might not need any bullets."

She left him and ran to the car. He heard her fumbling around in the trunk, then swearing as she tried to click on the spotlight. "Dammit! Did you take the batteries out? Where are they? Did you hide them?"

"I was busy while you were napping."

She came back, dropped to her knees beside him, and pushed her hand inside his jeans pocket. Coming up empty, she moved to the other where she found his pocket knife and Mickey's phone. She tossed the knife out of Shaw's reach, her interest solely on the phone. But when she tried to turn it on and realized it was dead, she turned it over and removed the back as she'd watched him do several times. Seeing that it was empty, she turned frantic. "Where is the battery?"

He shook his head.

"Are you crazy? Tell me. I have to call 911."

Shaking his head had only made him more lightheaded and dizzy, so he didn't respond at all.

"If you don't get help, you could die."

"Isn't that what you wanted?"

"No! I didn't want to kill you. I only wanted to stop you from killing me."

"I wished you'd just asked pretty please instead of shoving...ah, shit, it hurts."

She caught his chin in her hand and forced his head around to look at her. "Tell me where you hid the phone battery."

He jerked his chin out of her grasp. "Bring me a bottle of water and the rest of those bandanas."

She looked at him with consternation but got up, went back to the car, and in under a minute returned with the requested articles. He managed to remain sitting, although at a slant, as he took the water from her, removed the cap, then poured it over the piece of metal that had his shirttail pinned to his torso. She watched with alarm as he grasped it with thumbs and fingers of both hands.

"What are you doing?"

He blinked sweat from his eyes. "Move back. If you sliced an artery, you're gonna get squirted."

"You're going to pull it out?"

"Have a couple of those bandanas handy. Soon as the blade is out—"

"You can't do that!"

"I'm not looking forward to it."

It was a toss-up whether or not to remove it. It could be acting as a plug to prevent serious bleeding. But if the damn thing was as rusty and dirty as the rest of that outboard, and he left it in there, he'd die of infection or tetanus, and neither would be easy or quick. If he died in a geyser of arterial blood, at least it wouldn't take too long.

"Please," she said, her voice ragged. "Let me call—"

Before she talked him out of it, he pulled on the portion of the propeller sticking out of him, testing how firmly and deeply it was embedded. Just that tug almost caused him to black out. He inhaled deeply several times, braced himself mentally, then pulled as hard as he could. The jagged metal tore through his flesh as it came free. Blood spilled warmly down his belly.

A thousand noisy flapping wings swarmed toward him, obscuring his vision. Bells tolled inside his head. His skin became slick with sweat. His stomach heaved, filling the back of his throat with stinging bile. He gave up his fight with gravity and collapsed onto his back, favoring his left side.

He was vaguely aware of Jordie popping open the buttons of his shirt, then of her bending over him, packing the wound with the squares of camo print.

"Jordie?"

He wasn't sure if he spoke her name or merely thought it.

But he must've said it because, she snapped, "What?"

"Why—"

"Shut up, I'm busy."

"Why—"

"Don't talk to me!"

"Why aren't you running for the road?"

She stopped what she was doing and looked into his face. He could tell from her expression that the idea hadn't even occurred to her.

Her naked bewilderment lasted for several heartbeats before she set her jaw and said, hoarsely, "It's raining," then bent back over him and resumed her effort to stanch the wound.

———◆———

She found several batteries in the sunken compartment of the trunk where the spare tire was stored. When she put them in the spotlight, it came on. She used it to search the car thoroughly—

glove compartment, under the seats, even under the hood. But the search didn't yield anything.

Since the dome light was growing steadily weaker as the car battery drained, she shut the doors and the trunk, but not before collecting a whole bottle of Advil and anything else she thought would be useful toward saving Shaw's life.

She carried the tarp over to where he lay. He was conscious, because when she shone the spotlight on him, he snarled and told her to turn the effing thing off.

"I've got to see what I'm doing."

She set the spotlight on the floor beside him but out of his reach and made two other trips to the car, carrying back with her items she'd taken from the trunk. When she'd assembled everything, she spread the tarp out on the floor near him. "Do you think you can move onto this?"

He looked at it, then at her, and shook his head.

"This floor is filthy."

"So's that tarp."

"I made sure the clean side is up."

He harumphed. "Like that matters." Weakly he gestured toward the bloody piece of metal she'd stabbed him with, now lying on the floor a few feet away. "That thing has enough bacteria on it to kill an elephant."

"Then let me call 911."

"No."

"Do you want to die?"

He gave her a hard look, then made an effort to scoot onto the tarp. He clenched his teeth and growled in pain.

"Here, let me help." She moved to his side and slid one arm beneath his shoulders, the other beneath his waist. "I'll support your upper body while you use your feet—"

"Just do it."

It took three tries, which must have been agonizing for him, but she got him onto the tarp. By the time he went limp, he was sweating from every pore, and his lips were compressed so tightly they were rimmed with white.

As gently as possible, she began removing the blood-soaked bandanas from the wound and when the last one came away, she had to swallow her gorge. The open gash was four inches long and about three-quarters of an inch wide at its widest point. The flesh inside was an angry red.

He came up on his elbow only high enough to assess the damage. He took one look, then lay back down. "Your bad. You missed the artery."

"How do you know?"

"Because I know how to kill a man."

Even though she'd missed a major vessel, the wound was quickly filling up with blood. She pressed another folded square against it. He spat an obscenity, then clamped his jaw so tightly the bones stood out. She guided his hand down and placed it over the cloth. "Keep pressure on it."

Moving hastily, she retrieved the pocket knife and opened the blade, then doused it with water from one of their remaining bottles. They were down to only three bandanas. She used the knife to cut one of them into strips.

"What are you doing?"

She begin tying the ends of the strips together. When she was done, she pulled all the knots tight, then gauged the length of the strip she'd formed against his waist size. "It helps that you're slender. Raise up."

He must've realized what she had in mind. He lifted his hips high enough for her to thread one end of the strip behind his back. Pulling it taut, she tied the two ends over the square covering the wound.

"That's the best I can do until you let me call 911."

He closed his eyes and breathed hard through his nostrils as though to stave off waves of pain. She pushed four Advil tablets into his mouth and uncapped a bottle of water. "Here. Drink."

He raised his head to take a few sips. She poured too quickly and water dribbled from the corners of his lips. Without thinking, she wiped the trickles off his scruffy chin, off the C-shaped scar, then off his neck.

"Thanks."

"You're welcome." She sat back on her heels. "Shaw—"

"Forget it."

"You don't know what I was going to say."

His eyes remained closed. "No, but that's the first time you've addressed me by name, so I know I won't like anything you say that starts that way."

"Let me call for help."

He merely shook his head.

"Please."

"Turn out the light."

"No."

He opened his eyes. "You're using up the...the batteries, and they're all I've got."

"Sure they are."

He sighed. "I swear."

He seemed close to passing out. He was having trouble keeping his eyes open and focused. His speech was slow, as though he had to search for each word, and holding a thought seemed increasingly difficult.

He repeated softly, "Turn out the light."

Since she hadn't found extra spotlight batteries anywhere in the car, she reasoned that he might be telling the truth. She switched off the spotlight, plunging them into darkness.

For a time neither said anything, then he murmured, "If I go under, will you take off?"

"In all honesty? I haven't decided."

"Sucks to be you, Jordie Bennett. Always torn between morality and self-interest."

"Perhaps I should become more like you."

"Amoral, you mean."

"If you were amoral, I would be dead."

"Greed has kept you alive, not morality." He shifted his weight slightly and moaned. He panted through the pain like a woman in labor. After a minute, he said, "If I pass out, will you turn this place inside out looking for the car keys?"

"Probably. And my phone. What did you do with my phone?"

"It's a secret. When did you find that propeller blade?"

"While I was washing."

"I shouldn't have been so nice to you."

"It was wedged between two boards in the wall. I couldn't get it out while you were counting down. I had to leave it there."

"When I discovered the arrow—"

"I never saw the arrow until you broke it over your knee."

"I thought I'd trumped you."

"So did I. I knew I had only one chance to get to that broken propeller."

"And you took it."

"Yes."

"That was brave. But remember... if you're ever in a similar situation..."

When his voice faltered, she prompted him. "What?"

"Go for the kill."

"I'll bear that in mind."

She heard the rustle of the tarp beneath him as he moved restlessly, then he lay still and silent for a time. Finally, he said, "You...you..."

She pulled her legs out from under her hips and leaned down closer. "Yes?"

"You could have killed me a dozen times over by now. What's kept you from it?"

"I told you, and I meant it, that I didn't want you to die."

"Because of the kiss?"

"The kiss?"

"You remember it. Sexy as hell? When we went from zero to sixty in about a second and a half? Virtual foreplay?"

"I don't recall it like that."

"Hell you don't."

"I just don't want you to die, that's all."

"Okay, okay. Thanks for that."

He groped in the darkness until he found her left hand, drew it to him, and laid it on his chest. The hair on it was soft, the skin hot. It was rising and falling rapidly and erratically. He rubbed the back of her hand and rolled slightly onto his right side, the one uninjured.

"But in case...in case you were to change your mind..."

Too late she realized what he was doing. He clipped the plastic cuff around her left wrist and his right. She made an inarticulate sound of outrage, mostly at herself for being so easily tricked by talk of sexy kisses.

She pulled hard on her hand, knowing already that it was futile. Then she remembered the knife. She had set it down after using it to cut the bandana into strips. She began searching for it with her free hand.

But he was ahead of her on that, too. "It's in my seat pocket," he said, "where the cuff was. It was careless of you to set it down within my reach after you used it."

"I was trying to keep you from bleeding to death!"

"If I do, you'll be able to roll me over, get the knife, and cut yourself free. But the only way you'll get to it is if I'm dead."

"Please don't do this. I can't help you if I can't move around."

"Right now you can help me by lying still and being quiet."

"Be reasonable, Shaw. It's over. You have a serious, possibly mortal wound. We have no way of knowing the extent of the internal injuries." She went on like that for at least a full minute, pleading and arguing with him before she realized that he wasn't arguing back.

When Shaw woke up, rain was beating against the tin roof like a shower of ball bearings. But it was pain not dulled by ibuprofen that had awakened him. Jordie had placed the spotlight even with his waistline, the beam directed onto his wound. She was palpating the area around it.

"Will you please stop that? It hurts like a son of a bitch."

Her brow was furrowed. "Shaw, listen to me, you're—"

"What time is it?" He crooked his left arm and blinked the numerals on his wristwatch into focus. It wasn't too long till dawn which was why the darkness was no longer absolute black, but a dark gray. There wouldn't be a sunrise, however. Not the way the rain was coming down.

"Are you lucid?" Jordie asked.

He looked at her and nodded.

"This is worse. It's getting infected."

Although he had to clench his jaw to keep from moaning, he struggled up so he could check for himself. Jordie had untied the makeshift binding and removed the blood-soaked bandana, exposing the torn, raw flesh. The area surrounding the wound had become puffy and red.

"You're burning up," she said.

Yes, he realized that he had a fever. His skin felt itchy and too tight; his eyes were stinging; he had a raging thirst. "Pass me that water bottle."

She was quick to do so, reaching for it with her right hand, since her left was still shackled to his. As he raised the bottle to his mouth, he halted it midway. "What was that?"

"What?" She followed the direction of his gaze to the door. "Lightning. It's been flashing off and on for at least an hour." Coming back around, she said, "Shaw, you've got to give up. Let me cut myself free. Tell me where the phone battery is. Or the car keys. I'll drive you—"

"Shh!"

"Don't shush me. You've got—"

He pulled her down beside him and rolled partially on top of her so he could reach the spotlight with his left hand. He clicked it off.

"What are you doing?" She tried to throw him off, but he kept her pinned down, his left thigh thrown across her.

He trained his feverish eyes on the door where he saw another flicker of light, but the rumble he detected above the racket of the rain on the roof wasn't thunder.

"Shaw—"

"Be quiet!"

"Let me up!"

Instead he clamped his left hand over her mouth. "Car," he said. "If you say a word, if you even breathe hard, whoever is in it will likely die. His or her blood will be on your hands. Got it?"

She hesitated for only a second, then bobbed her head as much as his restraining hand would allow.

He removed his hand from her mouth and blinked hard to keep from passing out from the pain as he struggled to sit. He drew his right knee up and with his free left hand reached beneath the stringy hem of his jeans and into his boot, and pulled out the Bobcat.

When Jordie saw the palm pistol, she gasped.

He said, "What kind of hit man would carry only one gun?"

"Is that one loaded?"

"Always."

The headlights that he'd seen approaching cut an arc across the front of the building, then remained stationary, but on. For the longest time, nothing happened. Which signaled to Shaw that it was a cop. A curiosity seeker would be less cautious. A cop on a manhunt would be calling in his position before coming to explore further.

Beside him, Jordie remained tense as she, too, kept her eyes on the closed door.

Shaw strained to catch the sounds of a car door opening, approaching footsteps, but the noise of the rain striking the roof drowned out everything else, until a voice with a noticeable Louisiana accent called out, "I'm Deputy Clint Morrow, Terrebonne Parish Sheriff's Office. Identify yourself, please."

Beside Shaw, Jordie was trembling, but she didn't speak.

"I know you're in there," the deputy said. "A fisherman saw the light going on and off."

Shaw looked at Jordie with reproach, but she didn't make eye contact, just kept staring at the door.

It was slowly pulled open, the creak of the hinges distinct despite the rainfall. A man, crouched with pistol drawn, appeared in the opening, silhouetted against his car's headlights, a tall form beneath a cowboy hat. He took one step into the building, but Shaw ordered, "Far enough."

He halted. "Shaw Kinnard?"

"The pleasure's all mine. You have a family, Deputy Morrow?"

"What?"

"You heard me. If you want to see your loved ones again, back away. Otherwise I'll shoot you."

"And then I'd see your flash and shoot you."

"No you won't. Because you might hit Jordie Bennett who's handcuffed to me."

The deputy hesitated then ducked out of sight. "Ms. Bennett," he called from outside, "are you all right?"

She looked at Shaw, who nodded his permission for her to speak.

"Yes. But…but I am handcuffed to him, and he has a gun, and—"

"Enough!" Shaw said.

"We need an ambulance!" she shouted.

"Who's hurt?" the deputy shouted back.

"Don't say another word." For emphasis Shaw yanked on her handcuffed hand. He envisioned the deputy speaking softly but urgently into the mike clipped to his shoulder, alerting a dispatch operator to the hostage situation, requesting backup and EMTs.

"He's good," Shaw said with grudging respect. "Took him less than the three days I allotted. Of course he had your help with the spotlight."

Jordie looked at him with evident anxiety. "What are you going to do?"

He thought about it for a moment, keeping pain, nausea, and unconsciousness at bay by a sheer act of will. "Getting captured is one thing. It happens to the best. But being played for a fool is something else."

Moving swiftly, he hooked his left hand around the back of her neck and pulled her face to his, aligning their foreheads and pressing hard. "I turned down two million dollars, plus what I fantasized would be a really great fuck, in the hope that you'd take me to your brother and his thirty mil. You can tell me now. Would you ever, *ever*, have done that?"

"I couldn't." She angled her head back so she could meet his eyes directly. "I don't know where Josh is. Or the money. Or Panella. I don't know anything. I never did."

They held that way for a moment, then he stifled a laugh of self-deprecation and withdrew his hand from her neck. "Morrow! You ready to parley?"

Chapter 20

———◦◉◦———

Agents Wiley and Hickam had a bumpy helicopter ride back to New Orleans. Marsha wouldn't have liked knowing they were dodging lightning and wind shears. Joe himself was relieved when they set down at the heliport.

They drove directly to the office, where Joe surrendered his phone to a techie who swapped it out with another, to which Joe's calls were rerouted. Specialist agents would attempt to pinpoint Josh Bennett's location using the call he'd made to Joe's cell, but Joe didn't hold out much hope for success. Joe had called the unknown number several times since Josh clicked off, but it hadn't been answered.

"He probably stripped that phone of its battery and SIM card as soon as he hung up," Joe said to Hick as they paused at their side-by-side cars in the parking garage.

"Where did he get a phone? When?"

"Where? Anywhere. When? Hell I know," Joe grumbled. "He may have had it secreted somewhere all along. He could have a dozen of them. An inexhaustible supply of disposable SIM cards."

"He sounded scared, though."

"Well he should be. If he talks himself into believing that Panella is willing to let bygones be bygones, he's an idiot."

"I don't think he's an idiot."

"Neither do I. For all his bluster, he's scared. Why else would he volunteer that information about Jordie?"

"Do you think it's true?"

Joe rubbed the back of his neck. "Don't know. But—" He broke off when his phone chirped. He reached for it quickly, thinking that maybe the fugitive was calling back. But after seeing the caller ID, he said to Hick, "Morrow," and braced himself for bad news. Had Jordie Bennett been found? Or only what was left of her?

"Hey, Morrow." Joe listened for several seconds then frantically motioned Hick toward the driver's side of his car, saying into the phone, "We're on our way."

Even if he and Hick would have been comfortable taking the chopper back out, Joe wouldn't have asked a pilot to risk flying in this weather. So they had to drive, and it was like doing so underwater. Windshield wipers were useless against the cascade.

An hour and a half outside New Orleans, Hick was leaning forward over the steering wheel and gripping it with both hands. Joe said, "Is there a black equivalent to 'white-knuckling'?"

Without taking his eyes off the road, Hick gave a wry smile. "Don't know of one, but it applies."

"Should be coming up on the turnoff soon."

To Deputy Morrow's knowledge there wasn't a physical address for the barnlike structure in which Shaw Kinnard was holding Jordie Bennett hostage. But he'd provided Joe with the nearest highway intersection, which Hick had located by using the car's GPS. From there, Morrow had given him oral directions by phone.

Now, as they rounded a bend in the rural road, Hick said, "This must be the place."

Through the rain, light bars of several squad cars were flashing their tricolor warning. Some of the vehicles were parked end to end along the shoulder; one was sideways in the middle of the road. A state trooper, outfitted in a slicker, alighted from the passenger side and came over as Hick rolled to a stop and lowered the driver's window.

A waterfall of rainwater flowed from the brim of the trooper's hat as he dipped his head and peered in at them. "Agent Wiley?"

"I'm Wiley. This is Agent Hickam."

The trooper acknowledged them in turn and introduced himself. "The building's about half a mile up the road, which has turned to mush in this rain."

"Is this the only road in and out?"

"Yes, sir. Dead-ends at the building, which backs up to wetlands."

"We don't know if he has a vehicle, but we have to assume so. If he somehow eludes us—"

"He'll have to get past all of us here, and that ain't gonna happen."

Joe liked the trooper's confidence. "We don't know what kind of arsenal he has, so be careful."

"Y'all, too."

The trooper backed away and signaled the driver of the unit parked sideways to pull forward. Once they were past the roadblock, Hick followed the trooper's flashlight as he motioned him into a left turn.

The road *was* mush. They slip-slid for the approximate half mile until they came to a ditch on the verge of overflowing. Beyond it loomed a structure described to Joe by Morrow as a cross between a barn and a garage on steroids.

Parked in front of it were numerous squad cars, several official SUVs, and two ambulances. Law enforcement personnel
were outfitted in rain gear, making it difficult to differentiate the
various departments represented unless their backs were to Joe
and he could read the reflective letters on their slickers. Most reassuring to him was that there were plenty of them, signifying a
lot of firepower.

As Hick carefully steered their car across the road spanning
the swollen ditch, one of the officers separated himself from the
rest and came slogging toward them. It was Morrow. Beneath
the brim of his hat, his face was set with tension.

Joe motioned for him to join them inside the car. He opened
the backseat door and got in, mumbling an apology for slinging
rainwater. Joe asked him if there had been any change since
they'd last talked.

"Nothing."

"So you don't know for sure that she's still alive."

"She was when I got here. Last thing Kinnard said was that
he would surrender to you and you only. Since he laid down that
condition, there's been nothing from him but silence, and I've
tried several times to engage him. Her, too. Not a peep. But if
he's killed her, he didn't use a gun. No shots have been fired."

"She didn't tell you why an ambulance was needed?"

"No. I asked several times which of them was hurt. Got no
answer. I guess the son of a bitch meant it when he said he
wouldn't talk to anybody except you."

Joe considered the hulking building and dragged his hand
down his face. "Okay. Showtime. Pass me that slicker, please."

Morrow took it from the backseat and handed it up to him.

"If you think I'm letting you go in there by yourself, think
again," Hick said.

"That's what the man wants."

"Screw what he wants. You investigate stock fraud and other
scams. This is a job for the cowboys."

"Which he swore to shoot one by one if they stormed the place," Morrow said.

"Till they kill him," Hick argued.

"Or he kills her."

Joe's words fell like bricks and crushed Hick's argument. He said *shit* under his breath and turned to address Morrow. "You're sure there's no other way in or out?"

"Not unless there's a tunnel underneath, and, you know, dig a hole in Louisiana, it fills up with water, so I don't think a tunnel is likely. Risk is too high to try going in through the roof in this weather. No other doors, and I've had men examining the exterior walls plank by plank looking for a concealed one. None of the lumber is rotten enough for us to bust through without giving him plenty of advance warning."

The deputy hitched his chin toward the front of the building. "That door is the only access. It's stood ajar like that since I backed out of it. I thought he might poke his head around, take a look-see. But if he's come near that opening, we missed it. No motion inside at all."

Hick exhaled in frustration and looked at Joe. Joe gave him a vapid smile. "I'm wearing a vest."

"He's a head-shot guy."

Neither of the other two said anything to contradict or qualify that, and Joe sort of wished that one of them had. "Well, we gotta get her out of there." Without further ado, he checked his pistol, tucked it into the holster at the small of his back, then pulled on his slicker.

Once he and Hick had protected themselves as well as they could from the downpour, the three got out and approached the building, using the parked vehicles as cover. Morrow's squad car being the closest to the door, they crouched behind it.

Hick chambered a bullet in his pistol. "Just so you know. He kills you, I'm sending him to hell."

In all seriousness, Joe said, "I would appreciate that. Thanks."

"Then I'm making a move on Marsha."

Joe looked at him with disdain. "That certainly gives me the will to live."

"But your crap wardrobe goes straight to Goodwill."

Morrow had retrieved a bullhorn from his car. He duck-walked over to where they were hunkered and passed it to Joe. "Press that button and talk into it."

Joe took the bullhorn from the deputy and looked at Hick. "You have a patron saint you pray to on a regular basis?"

"Several."

"Now would be a good time."

"Plus, my aunt on my mama's side dabbles in voodoo."

Grimly Joe said, "Even better."

Shaw had been aware of the assemblage beyond the door, but neither he nor Jordie had remarked on the arrivals of other ve-hicles, the new sets of voices, the lights periodically slicing across the entrance and penetrating the holes and cracks in the walls.

He'd heard the men scuttling along the exterior, looking for a way in, or a possible escape route for him. They were wasting their time. There wasn't one.

It was coming up on two hours since the deputy had arrived, and time had become an important factor. Shaw was fully aware that his body was being poisoned by bacteria. Several times Jordie had pleaded with him not to wait for the FBI agent to ar-rive, but rather to surrender himself to the officers already there, to let paramedics take emergency measures before transporting him to the nearest hospital.

It had been a tempting proposition, but he remained unde-terred. "We wait on your fed."

Having grown increasingly lightheaded, he'd been lying down for the past twenty minutes. Jordie sat beside him, her knees raised, her forehead resting on them in a posture of despair.

He thought back to how she'd looked in that seedy bar. A knockout. Upon getting his first up-close look at her, his center had tightened and warmed with awareness and want, and he'd thought, *Damn.*

Of course the male animal in him had immediately zeroed in on seeing her naked.

But his more objective professional side had also kicked in and registered the details of his target: the casual but smart outfit, the pale manicured fingernails, the dark and satiny hair left to do its own thing, plush lips brightened only with a transparent sheen. All of which had told him that she was well maintained but unembellished. Classy without fuss or muss.

Comportment-wise, she'd been cautious, but controlled. Cool.

By contrast, her clothes were now stained with blood. It was caked underneath her fingernails, some of which had been broken when she was scrabbling for the propeller fragment. Her hair had lost its shine and was gathered into a makeshift ponytail; her lips were dry and tightly seamed together.

He'd reduced her to this. No two ways about it: He was a bastard.

She stirred, raised her head, and looked down at him. No longer controlled and cool, she looked desperate and close to unraveling. "You won't kill anybody else, will you?"

"All depends on how it goes."

She sniffed. Until then, he hadn't realized that she was crying. For the first time since Mickey had been shot dead right in front of her, she was shedding tears but doing so silently and with admirable dignity.

"I don't want anyone else to die because of me," she said. "Please. Don't do that to me. Promise."

He held her gaze for several seconds, then closed his eyes. "No promises, Jordie."

She made a near inaudible hiccupping sound, but said no more and bent her head over her knees again.

"Know what I keep thinking about?" he asked. "Panella."

"What about him?"

"I'll bet he's fit to be tied, wondering if you're dead yet. He probably expected me to get back to him within minutes of our last conversation and tell him you were history and ask how to go about collecting my money. You know he's gotta be climbing the walls. He doesn't like to be crossed."

"No. He doesn't."

"Huh. Spoken like you know that for fact."

She didn't respond. Shaw raised his right hand, the one cuffed to hers. Hers remained limp against his as he gently tugged on a strand of hair that had worked itself out of the bandana holding her ponytail. He kept pulling at it until she turned her head back to him.

"You got on Panella's fighting side? How come? Wha'd you do?"

"I avoided him."

"I've seen pictures. He's not bad looking. In fact, Mickey called him a pretty boy."

"Only on the outside."

"So you do think he's attractive."

"I admit he's handsome, but I dislike him intensely and have made no secret of it."

"Ah."

All this time, he'd been absently playing with the strand of hair still in his grip. Now she pulled it away from him. "Don't say 'ah' like you know what I'm talking about. You don't."

"I can take a couple of guesses. One, Panella treated Josh like a lackey. That crawled all over you."

"True. They were supposed to be equal partners, but the Panella Investments Group bore only one name, and there was no question as to who was in charge. Panella relied on Josh's acumen. Without it, he couldn't have made the numbers work for as long as he did.

"But he treated Josh like a doormat and Josh permitted him to. He did what he was told and rarely crossed Panella. I hated that. But their working relationship was between the two of them. I stayed out of it."

"Did you?"

"Yes."

"I doubt it. Want to know why? Because Panella seems to resent you almost as much as he despises your brother." He waited for her to comment and when she didn't he asked for one.

She said, "There's no love lost between us."

"Hmm. Interesting choice of words. I asked Mickey what your relationship was with Panella. He said he didn't think you had one. That you were just Josh's next of kin, and, as such, you were a pawn, and that was all there was to it."

"There you have it."

"No, I don't think so. In my experience, if a man wants a woman dead to the tune of two million, his reason usually involves R-rated activities. What I'm thinking—and tell me if I'm getting warm—"

"Just drop it, please?"

"Panella had a lech for you."

She didn't say yea or nay.

"You turned him down."

She didn't respond.

"Which irked him, and he's still irked. But he must have gotten some satisfaction from scaring off your boyfriend."

Her reaction to that was swift and angry. "What do you know about it?"

He gave a meager, nonapologetic shrug. "Mickey liked to gossip, and we had time to kill."

"While you were tailing me all over Tobias."

"What happened with the boyfriend? Panella edged in on him?"

"No. There's never—ever—been anything remotely romantic between Panella and me. From either side."

"Then why aren't you and the boyfriend still together?"

"What does it matter?"

"Maybe it doesn't. But humor me." He nodded toward the door. "I'm a man on his way to the gallows."

"In which case one would think you'd rather talk about something else. Your immortal soul, for instance."

"It's doomed. No amount of talking will change that. Besides, I want to talk about this."

"I don't."

"What happened with—"

"He got married."

The waspish answer momentarily silenced them. Then, in a more even tone, she repeated. "He got married. Saint Louis Cathedral. All the trimmings. The union of two families with roots deeply imbedded in New Orleans society."

Watching her closely, he said, "Bitter pill?"

She gave a rueful smile. "No. I bear Jackson no ill will. He's a nice man. Too nice to have become involved in a scandal."

"The scandal being that your brother was a crook."

"Jackson and his family couldn't be associated with something that unsavory. He and his father are bigwigs in the financial community. Highly regarded and respected for their integrity. They serve on the board of a major bank.

"In fact, that's how Jackson and I met. He was put in charge of organizing the bank's Mardi Gras fete and retained Extravaganza to plan it. He and I worked together on it, and I wound up being his date for the occasion. The party was a huge success and so was the date. We were together for more than two years. Then Josh's malfeasances came to light."

"Suddenly you're a taint on Jackson's good name. Jackson takes a hike."

"Essentially." She reflected for a moment. "Although I understood why he broke up, it did hurt at the time. In hindsight, however, I realize that everything worked out as it should. His bride is perfect for him. All sweetness and light. Not a breath of scandal. She has no aspirations beyond presiding over social and charitable events and being Mrs. Jackson Terrell. I would have soon grown bored with that life."

"Not enough challenge for you."

"I suppose. I wouldn't know how to function in a vacuum, without responsibilities, deadlines to meet, clients to pacify, vendors to haggle with."

"A spineless brother to defend."

She gave him a baleful look and said coldly, "Yes. That's exactly right."

He backed off that. "You enjoy your work?"

She was still hacked, and he wasn't sure she would answer, but eventually she said, "I love it. I have an excellent staff."

"How many people?"

"Eight full-time. Others work only the events. They're all talented and hardworking. They didn't tuck tail and run when Josh began making headlines." Her eyes began to fill with tears again. "In fact, they remained fiercely loyal. I regret the hell they must be going through right now, not knowing whether I'm dead or alive."

"You can blame me."

"I do." Her expression turned even bleaker. "You've asked me a lot of questions. Am I'm entitled to ask you *one*?"

"You can ask. Don't know if I'll answer."

"If..." Her voice became husky with exhaustion, anxiety, fear, and a mix of other emotions he couldn't isolate and identify but wished he could. "If you finally had come to accept that I couldn't deliver Josh to you, and if I hadn't done this..." She nodded down at the wound. "If you were certain that Panella would have paid your price..." A single tear slid from the corner of her eye and ran unchecked down her cheek. She took a catchy breath. "Would you have killed me?"

Chapter 21

Her question hung in the air between them.

Suddenly the quiet was shattered by his name being boomed through a speaker and reverberating through the building. He sprang bolt upright and almost blacked out from the reflexive movement and the riot of pain it caused. But his left hand was steady as he aimed his pistol toward the door.

"This is Special Agent Joe Wiley, FBI. Shaw Kinnard?"

"Yeah. And I'm not deaf. Turn off that damn bullhorn."

After a pause of several seconds, the agent spoke to them in a voice no longer amplified but loud enough to carry. "All right, you asked for me, you got me. I'm coming in."

"Alone and unarmed," Shaw said.

"I'm both."

Jordie slouched with relief. "Thank God," she breathed, and said to Shaw, "You can put the gun down now."

"Not a fucking chance."

"But he said—"

"He's lying."

A silhouette appeared in the open doorway, arms extended at

his sides, fingers spread wide to show that his hands were empty.

She whispered, "See? He's keeping his word."

"Not to me he isn't."

"But—"

"Ms. Bennett?" the agent called.

Shaw nudged her with his elbow. "Don't say anything until you hit him with the spotlight."

Jordie looked at Shaw with misgiving. "Why? What are you going to do?"

"Hit him with the spotlight."

"So you can see to shoot him?"

"I could already have shot him, and if I'd fired, he'd be dead. Now shine the light on him."

Still uncertain, she picked up the spotlight, turned it on, and pointed it toward the agent, who blinked against the bright beam but didn't recoil from it.

"That your guy?" Shaw asked her.

"Yes."

"You sure?"

"Positive."

"Okay. Answer him."

She cleared her throat. "Agent Wiley? I'm here."

"You all right?"

"Yes. I'm fine. But Mr. Kinnard is seriously wounded."

"How so?"

"I . . . I—"

Shaw said, "She stuck me in the gut."

Joe Wiley took a moment to process that. "You're bleeding out?"

"Not quickly. But I think my entrails are filling up with pus."

"Then you're out of options except to surrender peacefully."

"Wrong. I could opt to kill you where you stand."

"You do and it's likely that you and Ms. Bennett would also be cut down."

"At least I'd die trying."

"It still amounts to a hopeless outcome." Joe Wiley let that sink in. "Surrender, Mr. Kinnard. You'll receive immediate medical attention. You have my word."

During their exchange, Jordie had kept the spotlight trained on the federal agent, afraid of what either he or Shaw would do if she switched it off. She feared a hair-trigger reaction to the sudden darkness that could result in an eruption of catastrophic gunfire.

She looked at the small but menacing pistol still gripped in Shaw's hand, then into his fever-glazed eyes. *Please.* She didn't even speak the word. It was merely a beseeching movement of her lips, and it persuaded him.

He lowered his gun hand, drew in a deep breath, and released it slowly. Turning his head to bring their faces close, and speaking in a voice only she could hear, he said, "To answer your question. . . The moment I laid eyes on you, your life was spared."

She took that in, her throat constricting with emotion. "So all this time I've been safe from you?"

"Safe from me?" He gave a grim smile and shook his head. "Not for a single second."

He held her stare for several beats more, then, moving quickly, reached behind his back, took the knife from his seat pocket, and flicked it open. "Hold still." He cut the cuff from their wrists. "Now go."

"Shaw—"

"Go!" His whisper was harsh, emphatic.

Sounding alarmed, Wiley shouted from the doorway. "Ms. Bennett, what's going on?"

Shaw said, *"Go!"*

"What are you going to do?" she asked.

"Jesus!" He reached for her hand and slapped the pistol into it. "Now will you get the hell away from me?"

She hesitated a second more, then made to stand up, but Shaw grabbed her arm. "Alert him, so he won't blast you."

"Agent Wiley," she called shakily. "I'm coming out. I have his gun. He gave it to me. All right?"

"Hold it where I can see it."

Shaw released her arm and gave a brusque nod. Again, she wavered, then stood up, turned away from him, and started walking slowly toward the door, holding her right hand away from her body.

In one glance, Joe evaluated the physical condition of the woman coming toward him, and his immediate impression was that she was a much diminished version of the Jordan Bennett he remembered from months before.

She was walking unsteadily. As she neared him, she raised her hands in surrender. Both her hands and her clothing were liberally bloodstained. In her right hand she was holding a small pistol.

"Set the pistol on the floor."

She did.

"Are you hurt?"

"No."

"Okay, just like that," Joe said, "with arms raised." He jerked his head toward the open door behind him. "*Now*. Hick?"

"Here!"

"She's coming out."

She scurried past Joe and through the door. Joe stayed where he was, but he could hear Hick speaking to her quietly and urgently. After a moment, Joe spoke softly over his shoulder. "Hick, can you hear me?"

"Yes."

"She all right?"

"Shaking like a leaf. Dazed. Otherwise okay."

"What'd she say about him?"

"Badly wounded."

"Is he armed?"

"She says he has what sounds like a nine-millimeter, but it's empty, and he hid the cartridge. Or so he told her."

"Any other weapons?"

"A pocket knife. But in her opinion it's not much of a threat."

Joe thought, *Yeah, but she's not a hired assassin.* "She left his palm pistol on the floor here, about ten yards inside the door. Be sure it's bagged."

"Got it."

Joe took several deep breaths to bolster himself mentally and physically for whatever might occur in the next few minutes, then called out Kinnard's name.

"I was beginning to think you'd forgotten about me," he said from out of the hollow gloom. "What's taking so freakin' long?"

"Turn the spotlight around so I can see you."

"I'm not armed."

"Convince me."

He directed the light off Joe and onto himself. Nevertheless, Joe still could barely make him out, and he didn't trust the fucker as far as he could throw him. He reached back and slid his pistol from its holster. As he started forward, an inane thought flashed through his mind: Marsha would kill him if he got himself killed.

As he moved farther into the building, he gained a clearer view of the man sitting on what appeared to be a blue tarpaulin. He was angled thirty degrees to his right, bracing himself on that arm. His left hand was pressed against his left side, which he was obviously favoring.

"Raise your hands," Joe said.

Grimacing, he shifted into a more upright position and removed his left hand from his side, then did as ordered. The skin across his sharp cheekbones looked stretched tight, waxy, and pale. Sweat had plastered strands of hair to his forehead. Blood had soaked into his clothes and was smeared beneath him on the tarp.

He was blinded by the spotlight, so as Joe came nearer, he had the advantage of being able to see Kinnard better than Kinnard could see him. He halted while still out of arm's reach. "Lie down and turn over."

"Bet you a thousand bucks you lied about coming in unarmed."

Joe gripped his extended pistol tighter. "Hands behind your head."

"On my stomach? Hands behind my head? That'll hurt like a mother."

"I don't give a shit. Do it."

Either he was a damn good actor, or he really was in excruciating pain. Even the slightest motion caused him to gasp. He paused several times, switching between holding his breath and panting. It took him a full minute to do as Joe had ordered, but when he was in the position, Joe called out for Hick and the others.

Joe himself was nearly mowed down by the special ops officers in assault gear who charged into the building and rushed past him to form a ring around Kinnard, shouting at him not to move, their weapons primed to fire if he did.

Hick jogged up to Joe, who lowered his pistol to his side, noticing that his hand on the grip was wet with nervous sweat. "You called the cowboys after all."

"The whole damn cavalry," Hick said. He squatted and picked up the palm pistol before it got lost in the shuffle.

As Kinnard was being cuffed, he was Mirandized by a deputy, then paramedics were allowed in and, for the next five minutes, he was in their charge. While they performed triage and got an IV started, Joe glanced through the door to the outside.

Several officers, including Deputy Morrow, were grouped around Jordie Bennett. Someone had draped a slicker over her. Joe could see her lips moving, so he knew she was responding to Morrow's questions, but she was staring straight ahead through the yawning door of the building, past him and Hick, as though in a trance.

"She looks spooked," Joe said. "Does she need medical attention?"

"She says no."

"They should at least put her in a car, get her out of the rain."

"They tried," Hick said. "She wouldn't budge."

Joe turned and met Hick's gaze. Hick raised his eyebrows and shrugged.

"Find out what she's telling Morrow. They're probably doping Kinnard with painkillers, and I want to talk to him before the juice takes effect."

Hick went back outside. Joe walked past Kinnard's car, which was already being gone over by investigators from Morrow's department. Others were setting up portable lights so they could search the building, although there didn't appear to be much to search. No hiding places that Joe could see.

He stepped over two halves of a broken arrow and called a detective's attention to it. The detective squatted down. "It's a toy, the kind that comes in a kid's starter set."

"Any blood on it?"

"Not that I can see."

"Collect it anyway."

Another of the officers approached Joe with a bagged object. "Thought you'd want to see this."

Joe looked at the thing in the bag. "What is it?"

"Her weapon."

When the detective told Joe what it was, he shook his head in awe. "No wonder he's hurting. He gonna make it?"

"He's asking, too. Paramedic told him it depends on what

all was sliced and diced by this propeller. Also on how tough he is."

One of the detectives who'd been examining the car joined them. "Agent Wiley, we just pulled this out of the tailpipe." He handed Joe an evidence bag. "Cell phone battery. We figure it belongs to the phone we found near him on the floor." He also passed Joe the evidence bag containing the phone.

"Thanks." ·

Joe walked over to where the paramedics were transferring the suspect onto a gurney. Morrow's man cuffed both his hands to the rails. During the process, Kinnard was jostled. That brought on an outburst of vile and profane language the likes of which Joe hadn't heard since Marsha had delivered their son breach. One of the paramedics assured Kinnard that the pain med he was getting intravenously would soon begin working.

Kinnard nodded at the paramedic, but his gaze had moved beyond him and connected with Joe's. He looked him up and down and gave a derisive snort. "I didn't know the FBI was so hard up."

Joe smiled. "I caught them on a slow day."

"Must have. They actually issued you a weapon?"

Joe turned his back and raised his rain slicker to reveal the holster, where he'd replaced his nine-millimeter.

When he came back around, Kinnard asked, "You ever actually fired it?"

"Practice range." When Kinnard registered his scornful opinion of that, Joe added, "At least I never got stabbed with a broken boat part. By a *girl*." He paused, then added, "'Course, a man who takes money to kill a woman doesn't have any balls."

Kinnard gave another snuffle of contempt and closed his eyes.

Not to be ignored, Joe nudged the sole of his cowboy boot. "Whose phone is this?"

Kinnard opened his eyes, looked at the evidence bag Joe was holding up to him, then closed his eyes again. "Get fucked."

"If I call the last caller, who am I gonna reach?"

"I don't want to spoil the surprise."

"Okay, be a smart-ass. It's not my shit being pumped through my system. It's not me who'll be charged with kidnapping and three homicides." When Kinnard's slitted eyes opened wider, Joe said, "Two dead guys in Mexico. One dead Mickey Bolden. An abduction. You've had a busy week. And on account of it, my personal life was put in time-out. When I finally do go home, I look forward to getting fucked." Joe leaned down, smiled, and whispered, "You already are."

Chapter 22

Joe ushered Jordie Bennett to his and Hick's car and helped her into the backseat. He asked again if she was all right, if she needed anything, but she responded to those inquiries with head movements.

They covered the half mile to the main road in silence. Joe saluted the state trooper he'd spoken to earlier as they drove past, and now Hick aimed them toward New Orleans. He wasn't as intent on his driving as before, because the sun had come up and, although the day was gray, the deluge had slowed to a manageable drizzle.

Speaking for the first time, Jordie asked, "Will he be all right?"

Before turning to address her question, Joe caught the meaningful look Hick cast him out of the corner of his eye. "Are you referring to Shaw Kinnard, Ms. Bennett?"

She nodded.

Joe had conferred with one of the paramedics before they'd sped away with Kinnard secured in the ambulance. Deputy Morrow had gone with them. "I was told that he's stable, which is about all they could tell of his condition till a surgeon gets in there and takes a look. A trauma team is standing by."

"In New Orleans?"

"Houma." Seeing her doubtful expression, he added, "Nearest one."

She turned her head aside and looked out the rain-streaked backseat window.

"Did Kinnard mistreat you, Ms. Bennett?"

Her head shake indicated that he hadn't.

"I noticed the marks on your wrists."

She rubbed the left one with her right hand. "He kept them bound in those plastic things."

"Flexcuffs?"

"He kept them on me that whole first night, except to let me go to the bathroom. He gave me more freedom after we got to the garage."

"When was that?"

"Yesterday. Sometime in the morning. We'd driven all night."

"You didn't cover very much ground."

"I guessed as much. Once he took the blindfold off, and I—"

"He blindfolded you?"

"For a while."

"Why'd he go to that particular place?"

"He didn't say." After a beat, she turned her head away from the window and toward Joe. "Maybe he should be taken by CareFlight to a major hospital in New Orleans."

"He's a survivor. Been in a lot of scrapes."

"Yes. That scar on his chin . . ."

Hick cut Joe another look, which he pretended not to notice. "Right. That scar helped identify him. He has a history of violence. You're lucky to be alive, and, frankly, your concern for his welfare is misplaced. If you don't mind me saying so."

"Well, I do mind you saying so," she snapped. "I could have killed him."

"Wasn't that what you had in mind when you stabbed him?"

"Yes. No. I... I don't know." The starch going out of her, she rubbed her eye sockets then turned back to the window. "I reacted out of fear for my life. But when I attacked him, I didn't wish him to die, and still don't."

Joe stalled by coughing behind his fist. Finally he said, "You're more forgiving than I'd be in your situation. I'm relieved and grateful he didn't kill you outright. I was afraid we'd find your remains, not you."

"I feared that, too. At first. But then he kept putting off killing me, and I began thinking that he couldn't do it."

"Even though he'd killed Mickey Bolden directly in front of you."

"I grant you, that was horrendous."

"Most of the blood on your clothes must be Kinnard's because it's fresh. But some of those stains aren't that recent. Bolden's?"

She glanced down at her front, closed her eyes briefly, and murmured, "He washed it off my face."

"Come again?"

"I don't remember it. I was still unconscious."

"He knocked you unconscious?"

"I don't remember that, either. He told me later. A tap, he said. When he stopped to switch license plates, he washed the blood spatters off my face."

Joe and Hick exchanged another look, then Joe settled more comfortably into his front seat. "We've got a long drive ahead of us, Ms. Bennett. Why don't we pass the time by you talking Agent Hickam and me through the past thirty-six hours, minute by minute. You don't mind if I take notes, do you?" He held up Hick's iPad, and she shook her head.

"Okay then..." Joe opened up a word processing app.

"What were you doing in the bar? Why'd you go there Friday night?"

Her immediate response was a soft, but humorless laugh. It wasn't the reaction Joe had expected. He peered at her over the seat and was aware of Hick suspiciously eyeing her in the rearview mirror.

Sensing their interest, she said, "You're not the first to ask me that," then after a pause, said, "I got a phone call, directing me to that place."

"Call from who?"

"I don't know."

"Your brother Josh?"

"If it was Josh, I didn't recognize his voice."

"Could it have been Panella?"

"I suppose, but Mr. Kinnard didn't think so. He said Panella was behind the hit, not my going to the bar. It was a surprise to him and Bolden when I showed up there."

They went round and round about that unexplained call for five minutes or so, but she insisted she couldn't identify the individual who'd summoned her to the bar.

"Mr. Kinnard didn't believe me, either," she said with obvious weariness.

Eventually Joe decided to let it go for now and asked her to move along to when she arrived at the bar.

In a drone virtually devoid of emotion or inflection, she related her story. Her description of the sequence of events coincided with the testimonies of witnesses, in particular Royce Sherman's account.

Joe said, "You didn't know him?"

"No."

"He admitted to slipping something into your pocket. He said it was his phone number. That true?"

"I guess it was his number. I wasn't aware that he'd given me anything until Sh— Mr. Kinnard took it out."

"Took it out of your seat pocket?" Joe asked.

She divided a look between him and Hick, then bobbed her head once.

Following an awkward silence Joe asked for details about Bolden's murder. Her recollection matched the evidence they'd retrieved and what they'd surmised. Then he asked about her overnight drive with Shaw Kinnard.

"After I regained consciousness, he stopped and let me relieve myself. One other time he stopped to put on the blindfold." Shortly after that, they arrived at Kinnard's destination. "He said, 'Today it's a hideout.' It wasn't until we got there that he put the battery in the phone so Panella could call."

"Call Bolden's phone?"

"Yes. If you hit the Redial, Panella will answer. He's waiting to hear that Mr. Kinnard went through with it."

He and Hick had discussed whether or not to try to connect with Panella, but decided in favor of postponing that redial until they had the phone hooked to every conceivable monitoring device. There was another solid reason for Joe's delaying contact with Panella: He wanted to hear everything Jordie Bennett had to say first.

He asked her now about the tone of the conversations between Kinnard and Panella. "Did you get a sense that they'd ever met face-to-face?"

"No. The contract went through Mickey Bolden."

"Did you overhear what they said?"

"Yes. Most of the time the phone was on speaker."

"Did Panella ever give a hint of where he is?"

"No. None." She reflected a moment. "It seemed surreal to be listening to two men bargaining over my life. Panella's creepy voice."

"Creepy voice?"

She described it to them and said, "It made him seem all the more monstrous when he agreed to pay Mr. Kinnard the two million."

"Excuse me?" Joe said.

"Two million?" Hick exclaimed.

"That's what Mr. Kinnard demanded and Panella agreed to it."

Joe tried to wrap his mind around the staggering amount. Kinnard had gall to ask for that much. It had to be way above his normal rate. But then he would know that Panella was good for that amount and more. He said, "I'm more amazed than ever that Kinnard didn't cash in."

"You mean kill me," she said, and when he nodded, she continued. "Last night, just after dusk, I became certain he was about to."

"What made you think so?"

She glanced down at her lap, up at Hick's gaze in the rearview mirror, finally coming back to Joe. "Just an intuition."

"An intuition?" he repeated, ending on an inquisitive note to which she didn't respond.

Her gaze, her demeanor remained evasive. Joe wondered what she wasn't sharing. Hick was squirming with curiosity, too, but he didn't press her. For right now, they wanted the overall picture. They'd hammer her for details later. He did, however, ask her what had led up to her stabbing Kinnard and how she'd managed it.

"He'd...he'd found an arrow. He thought he'd outsmarted me, that he'd found my secret weapon."

"He didn't know about the broken propeller."

"No. I went back to it, and managed to pry it free from the crack between the boards, and...and...jabbed it into him as hard as I could."

She stopped and lowered her head to stare at her clasped hands. Deputy Morrow had given her a bottle of hand sanitizer to clean them with, but bloodstains were still evident.

She described how Kinnard had pulled out the blade and she'd packed the wound as well as she could, how his condition continued to worsen throughout the night, how his fever spiked.

"Then that deputy sheriff arrived," she said. "I begged Mr. Kinnard to surrender. I told him that I didn't want to be responsible for another death. For anyone's death, including his. That's when he asked me for the name of the most senior FBI agent who'd interviewed me about Josh. He said he wouldn't surrender to anyone else. I gave him your name. You know the rest."

Joe was aware that she'd left a dozen or more gaps wider than the Grand Canyon, but she looked done in, and by now they were on the outskirts of the city.

He said, "Thank you, Ms. Bennett. I know you're exhausted and that having to talk about the experience couldn't have been pleasant." He looked over at Hick. "You have anything specific to ask?"

"I do." He addressed her in the mirror. "That unknown caller on Friday night. You said that before Kinnard hid your phone, he tried to reach the person."

She nodded. "Like every other time, no one answered. He thought it was probably Josh who'd called me, trying to set up a rendezvous with either him or a messenger who would give me information about where he was going, something like that."

"You told him it wasn't Josh."

"I told him I couldn't be certain, but that I didn't think so."

"He pressured you to tell him who it was."

"That's right. He wanted me to admit that it was Josh."

"Why? Why was Kinnard so hip to connect with your brother?"

"He thought Josh might pay more to keep me alive than Panella was paying to have me killed."

"More than two million?" Joe asked.

"Mr. Kinnard is convinced that Josh has the stolen money, not Panella. I tried to disabuse him of that."

"But his intention was to bargain with Josh for your life?"

"Yes. But he never got the opportunity."

"Josh didn't answer Kinnard's calls."

"No one did. And for the hundredth time, I don't know that it was Josh."

Joe looked over at Hick before coming back to her. "Why don't you simply tell us where he is, Ms. Bennett?"

"Where Josh is? I don't know!"

"Not Josh. Tell us where to find Billy Panella."

"Panella? I have no earthly idea."

It wasn't until that moment that she became aware that they had pulled under the porte cochere of a downtown hotel. She looked at the two of them with bewilderment.

"What's this? Why are we here?"

"We took the liberty of booking you a room."

"Why?"

"So you can get cleaned up, rest, sleep, have a couple good meals, take it easy. We'll need to interview you again tomorrow."

She looked at Joe, then over at Hick, then back at him, now less puzzled than wary. "I have a small apartment attached to my office at Extravaganza for when I stay over. I thought that's where you were taking me."

"Extravaganza has media camped around it in a quarter-mile radius. So does your house in Tobias. Staying here will be hassle free. You'll have room service. It's closer to our office where we'll reconvene first thing. A female marshal is bringing you some clothes from your Tobias house. In fact—" Joe checked his wristwatch "—she should be waiting for you in your room."

"I'll go check." Hick got out, showed his badge to the doorman and asked him to leave the car where it was for the time being.

Joe reached for his door handle, but Jordie Bennett stayed him. "Wait a minute. What's this really about?"

"I told you—"

"You told me a great lot of nothing. Are you placing me under house arrest?"

"What? No," he said, and realized how phony he sounded. "This is strictly a precaution, meant for your protection."

"From what?"

"The media."

She looked at him with disgust and a shade of disappointment. "I know how to handle the media. Try again."

"You and my wife," he mumbled. "She sees through me, too."

His folksiness didn't impress or faze her. She kept glaring at him, demanding a no-bullshit answer.

He surrendered with a sigh. "I heard from your brother."

"What?" She exhaled so hard that her chest went a little concave. "When?"

"Last night. He called me directly on my cell phone while I was beating the bushes—literally—looking for him." He explained the circumstances. "This was before Morrow summoned me to deal with Kinnard and your rescue."

"Where was Josh? Was he all right? What did he say?"

"Well, he didn't give himself up. Last he was seen, he was on foot. This morning they brought in track dogs to try and pick up a trail."

"Dogs?" she asked in horror.

"He's a fugitive, Ms. Bennett. Thumbed his nose at me. Told me we should give up looking for him. Swore we'd never catch him and that he'd never surrender. But he's still trying to cut deals. This one? If I would guarantee your safe return, he would give me Panella's last known whereabouts."

"He's known all this time and has been keeping—"

"That surprises you?"

"If he knew, why's he held back?"

"Because he's a felon. He hasn't been convicted of his alleged crimes yet, but you and I both know that he's a damn crook. He's an even better liar and manipulator."

She didn't defend or argue those charges, so Joe continued. "All along I've figured Josh was holding a few aces, so that if and when he got in a tight squeeze—which your abduction was—he'd have something to play. He pulled one out of his sleeve last night."

"What did you play? You couldn't guarantee my safe return."

"No, I couldn't. Honestly? At that point in time, I thought you were probably dead already and your body sunk in a swamp somewhere. I told Josh that. The only guarantee I could give him was to do my best to find you, dead or alive, and I promised to keep at it until you were either rescued or your remains recovered. He hemmed and hawed. Waffled. You know how he is. Eventually, he took the deal."

"He told you where Panella is?"

"He claims not to know that, but he told me where Panella was headed when he took off. Costa Rica."

Joe watched her for a reaction, and when she didn't register so much as a blink, he went on. "It was to be only his first jumping-off spot on his way to South America, according to Josh, who said he knows this because his last official duty while in Panella's employ was to wire some walking-around money to a bank down there."

"At least you'll know where to start looking for him."

"We've already started. What we've turned up so far?" He rubbed his brow as though it pained him to tell her what he must. "The only time on record that Billy Panella was in Costa Rica was about a month before we busted open his scam. He spent a long weekend at a swank resort outside of San Jose." He lowered his hand and looked at her directly. "With you."

Her lips parted, but nothing came out. Eventually she closed them.

Joe gave her a ten count to see if she would deny it, qualify it, something. When she didn't, he got out, opened the backseat door, and reached in to take her arm. "Till we get to the bottom of this, you're registered here under the name of Ms. Jones, and your roommate is a federal marshal named Gwen."

Chapter 23

Late Sunday afternoon, the Terrebonne Parish SO determined that all the evidence had been collected from the now-famous bar. The crime scene tape was removed and the establishment was permitted to reopen.

Word spread quickly, and soon the parking lot couldn't accommodate the customers who drove for miles to see where Friday night's drama had taken place.

The bartender recruited customers who could be trusted with the cash register to help him fill orders while he retold his story that contained the juicy details media sources had omitted from their reports.

But the evening really belonged to star witness Royce Sherman. The pool table where he'd been playing with his buddies when he decided to approach Jordan Bennett became center ring.

"Little did I know that my move on her would sic the feds on my ass. Not to mention"—he slung an arm across his live-in's shoulders in a gesture so broad that he sloshed his third Jack and Coke on her new tank top—"getting me in dutch with my old lady here."

His old lady wasn't amused, but his audience was spellbound as he gave them a spectacularly appended version of his conversation with Jordie. He relished his newfound celebrity. No one would ever call him a loser or ne'er-do-well again. His name had appeared more than once in the *Times-Picayune*. Even his mean ol' daddy had been impressed when an interview with him was aired as the lead story on the ten o'clock news Saturday night.

As the evening wore on, the crowd became thicker. No one noticed the man who came in with a group to which he didn't belong, then separated himself from it and sought out the darkest corner of the bar in which to lurk.

It was the farthest point from the jukebox. He didn't go near the gregarious bartender, never ordered a drink, just watched Royce and listened to his tale, which grew a little taller with each retelling, and Royce's role got larger.

"I didn't know nothin' about the fraud case. I had to Google Billy Panella to find out his connection to this gal." Here, his eyes bugged. "Whoa! Dude. Her brother's gotta be the dimmest bulb in the box to double-cross this Panella character. That TV reporter asked me did I think Panella sent Bolden and that other guy to exact his revenge on Josh Bennett. Hell yeah, I told him. But I threw a wrench in it by talking to her. If his sister's still alive, Bennett's got me to thank."

"You can say that again, Royce," muttered the man backed into the corner.

Royce's old lady finally had enough of his braggadocio. She suggested that it was time for them to go. When Royce said he wasn't ready yet, she *insisted* that they go. Royce ignored her. She then shouted an ultimatum: Either he leave with her right then or not bother coming home at all.

Royce saluted her a *so long*. This time, he slung his arm across the shoulders of a starry-eyed young woman who'd been more appreciative of and attentive to his story.

Royce's live-in stalked out, accompanied by two female

friends who lent full support to her grand exit. The man in the corner overheard them urging her to change her door locks and telling her that she would be better off never to see that asshole again.

Another hour passed. Royce Sherman became drunker, and the young woman more in thrall of him. In a particularly amorous move, she reached up and used his stringy goatee to pull his face down to hers. They kissed while the crowed hooted and hollered encouragement.

The spectacle almost caused the man in the corner to miss the incoming call on his cell phone. While glad that the phone, which had been dormant all day, was finally vibrating inside his pants pocket, he was equally annoyed that the call was so late in coming. He sidestepped his way along the wall till he reached the door, then gratefully pushed through.

He took the phone from his pocket and, as he threaded his way across the parking lot toward his car, glanced down at the phone's LED. Unknown Caller. But it could be only one person: Shaw Kinnard. And he would be calling for only one reason: He'd killed Jordie and wanted to be compensated.

He was about to answer when he paused to reconsider. In any transaction, whoever held out the longest gained the upper hand. Up till now Kinnard had had it. This time, let him grow anxious.

He only had to wait for three minutes before the phone vibrated again. Leering with self-satisfaction, he took the electrolarynx from his pocket and pressed it against his voice box. "You had better be calling to tell me she's dead."

"'Fraid not, Billy."

It wasn't the hired gun's voice.

"This is Special Agent Joe Wiley, FBI, New Orleans office."

"Fuck!" The expletive was out before he could control his reaction. While he was at it, he filled the feeb's ear with a few more.

Seemingly unimpressed with the profane litany, the agent talked over him in a conversational tone. "The media hasn't broken the story yet, so you're getting an exclusive. Shaw Kinnard has been arrested. Jordie Bennett is alive and well and in our protective custody. So your reprisal scheme is kaput. And it only gets better, Mr. Panella.

"Josh Bennett is still at large, *but* he's been in touch with me personally, and—you probably won't find this surprising—once again he's ratting you out. You know that he's a chicken liver at heart. He'll sell you—"

Seeing red, he didn't wait to hear the rest of whatever the federal agent had to say, but immediately disconnected, then flipped the phone over and removed the battery. He walked toward the bayou until he got close enough to make a good overhand pitch that plopped both the phone and the battery into the water.

Every blood vessel expanding with fury, he returned to his car where he could sit and mull over the call and its dire implications. He couldn't dismiss or underestimate them. The news of Jordie's rescue might not have been broadcast yet, but the fed had sounded too smug not to be believed.

This was definitely a kick in the teeth. Clearly, retaining Mickey Bolden and his onetime partner had been a mistake. But that was water under the bridge. He must think forward, not backward.

He stewed and reviewed and ultimately determined that there was an upside. Shaw Kinnard was a write-off. The authorities had him for a capital crime. The nature of the beast was to lie, so nothing he said would be believed. And, anyway, he was a Johnny-come-lately on the scene. He didn't know anything of substance about the Panella-Bennett partnership.

The downside was that Jordie did. And Jordie was alive and well and in the FBI's protective custody.

She still had to die, but he wasn't going to rely on anyone else to do it. Enough with the hired help. He couldn't trust either their competency or their loyalty. Besides, taking on the chore himself was an exciting prospect. Death throes had a way of shattering cool reserve like hers. It stirred his blood to think of instilling mortal fear in the condescending bitch and then watching the life fade from her big blue eyes. He would enjoy that very much.

Naturally there was some risk to coming out from hiding, but the reward outweighed it. From now on, whenever he wanted something done properly and in a timely fashion, he would do it himself.

Starting now.

———◆———

Beside him Jordie lay naked and soft.

Well, soft except for the tips of her breasts that tightened as she rubbed them against his chest. He took one between his fingers and worried it gently. She made a purring sound. He pressed his tongue into her mouth to catch that sweet vibration.

Someone almost ruined their kiss by bumping into the bed, and Shaw wanted to snarl at the offender for the interruption, because Jordie's kiss was delicious. She wasn't a passive kisser, either, but an active and ardent participant. Her mouth compressed around his tongue, and he knew then how amazing it would feel once she took his penis. When they got to that. For now, however—

"How's he doing?"

"Oh, hello, Doctor. I thought you'd left for the night."

"I was about to, but decided to check on him once more before I go."

"He's been stirring, but hasn't woken up. His vitals are good."

"Temperature?"

"Normal."

Somewhere far in the back of his mind, Shaw acknowledged that kissing Jordie was a bad idea, but now that he was doing it, not for the life of him could he stop. Although, classifying this as a mere kiss was like comparing a candle flame to a wildfire. This kiss was the stuff of wet dreams. He had unrestricted access to her. Mouth, the sexiest. Breasts, so easily aroused. The more of herself she allowed him, the more he wanted.

If word of his obsession got around, he'd become a laughing-stock. His reputation was that of a hard-ass, a badass. Ruthless. Merciless. An unfeeling and unshakable son of a bitch. No one would expect bad Shaw Kinnard to go soft over a woman.

Oh, Jesus. *Was* he soft? No. He was hard. Wasn't he?

He wasn't sure. Things down there didn't feel quite right. There was a persistent, throbbing heaviness in the lower part of his body, which was somewhat reassuring. But it didn't feel like a normal erection. Strangely, he was reluctant to explore the source of that odd pressure. All he actually wanted to explore was Jordie, every enticing curve and hollow of her.

"I'm sorry, sir, you can't come in here."

"I'm Deputy Sheriff Clint Morrow."

"And I'm the surgeon who just repaired this guy's gut. He's still in recovery ICU. You have to leave."

"He's my prisoner."

"He's my patient."

Indifferent to their squabble, Shaw ignored them. He wanted to touch Jordie where it counted, and, judging by the way she was shifting against him, with restlessness and urgency, she was wanting him to.

He slid his hand down her smooth belly and cupped her sex. *Yes, Shaw, yes.*

Music to his ears. Because after what he'd put her through, she should hate him. She should be afraid of him, but she wasn't. She was arching against him with what could only be desire and whispering naughty encouragement against his lips.

"Kinnard? Kinnard? Can you hear me?"

"Deputy Morrow! What are you doing back in here?"

"Just checking to see if he's come around."

"He hasn't. And I heard the doctor ordering you out."

"Can Kinnard hear me?"

"He's unconscious."

"He could be faking it."

"He's still under anesthesia. In any case, you must wait until after the doctor has checked him in the morning, and only then will he determine if the patient is up to being interrogated. It's not like he's going anywhere. Are these restraints really necessary?"

Somebody tugged on Shaw's hand. It didn't move. Not that one. The other one was stroking Jordie in that softest of soft places on a woman's body. She was pressing herself up into his palm with want and invitation. He extended his middle finger down into the cleft, collected her moisture on the pad of his finger, and tantalized that most sensitive spot. Dipping his head, he did the same to her nipple with his tongue.

Teasing strokes in perfect concert. Pleasuring by painting small circles.

She clutched handfuls of his hair, chanted his name in gasps and sighs, implored him not to stop.

"The restraints stay on. Both hands. Be sure the rest of the nursing staff understands that. Don't be taken in. He's dangerous. Two nights ago, he shot a man in the back of the head."

"Well, he's not going to shoot anybody tonight. Please, Deputy. I'm the one who'll get into trouble if I allow you to stay in here. Please leave. He won't be fully conscious for hours yet."

They left. Thank Christ. Now he could enjoy this erotic dream in peace.

Jordie's breath had turned uneven. In shockingly explicit language, she begged him to put his fingers inside her. He was all too happy to oblige.

Holy hell. He'd thought her mouth was wet and hot and snug.

She clenched, drawing his fingers deeper. He eased them back, and when she whimpered in protest, he pushed them into her again. Higher. She clenched tighter.

And then in the miraculous way of dreams, he was suddenly on top of her, and it wasn't his fingers but his cock embedded in her. She was squeezing it each time he thrust into her. God, it felt good.

Never one for prolonged foreplay—or kissing, for that matter—he'd always just as soon skip the preliminaries and get on to the main event. Not this time. Not with Jordie. He was in no hurry. He liked this unrushed fucking.

Best of all, he wasn't going anywhere. He could keep at this for a long time. Till morning. Hours yet.

Jordie came awake as suddenly as though someone had shoved her out of sleep.

She expected to find herself reclined on a cloth-upholstered backseat, her hands and feet bound. It took several seconds for her to remember that she was in a hotel room. Creature comforts included fresh bedsheets and a pillow stuffed with the softest down. The temperature wasn't sweltering; instead, she was chilled by air-conditioning.

However, while she was no longer a hostage in a nasty garage, she wasn't in this hotel suite by choice.

According to the clock on the bedside table, it was four thirty a.m. Throwing off the covers, she left the bed and went into the bathroom. After using the toilet, she closed the lid and sat on it, elbows on her knees, head in her hands.

Was Shaw all right? Would he recover? Was he even alive?

Not knowing his current condition or prognosis was sheer torture.

Gwen Saunders, the U.S. marshal with whom she was shar-ing the suite, had received calls at various times throughout the long afternoon and evening, but she had never divulged the na-ture of those calls to Jordie.

When Jordie had pretended to nap, she had intentionally left the bedroom door ajar, hoping to pick up enough tidbits of the one-sided conversations to piece together some solid answers to all the questions plaguing her.

But either Gwen was aware of her eavesdropping or she had an unusually soft speaking voice. When Jordie had given up the pretense of napping, emerged from the bedroom and asked the marshal point-blank if she had received any word on Shaw Kin-nard's condition, her answer had been "The last report, he was still in surgery."

That was all Jordie had gotten from her, and she had no way of knowing whether or not that was the truth. "Still in surgery" could mean that he had died on the operating table and they had left him there.

The marshal was no more forthcoming about Josh. After Jordie had asked several times if there had been any further contact with him, the marshal told her that Agent Wiley had repeatedly called the number from which Josh had called him. "He hasn't answered, and he hasn't called back."

The story of her rescue hadn't been reported until the last news broadcasts of the night. Maybe Josh, wherever he was, had learned of it by now. Perhaps he'd tried to reach her directly. With that possibility in mind, she'd asked Gwen if her cell phone had been recovered.

"It was found in Kinnard's car."

"But I searched that car. Thoroughly."

"Apparently he had cleverly hidden it."

"I'd like it back, please."

"I'm sorry, Ms. Bennett. It was taken into evidence."

Evidence of what, Jordie wondered. Evidence against whom?

Gwen hadn't specified, and Jordie was afraid to ask for fear of what the answer would be.

In any case, it was doubtful that Josh would be foolish enough to call her phone. He would know the authorities were closely monitoring it in the hope they could use an incoming call to pinpoint his location.

After consulting Agent Wiley, Gwen had permitted her to communicate with her office staff on the condition that she talk to them on speaker. Her employees became uncharacteristically emotional when they heard her voice. They expressed relief and gratitude that she was unharmed.

No one mentioned Josh, so she was spared having to address that issue with them. Nor did she provide them any details of her abduction and rescue, primarily because Gwen had instructed her not to. "Something you say innocently might impede the investigation."

Jordie didn't see how that was possible, but she didn't argue, because she wasn't ready to talk about those thirty-six hours spent with Shaw Kinnard anyway.

She had no idea when she would be allowed to return to work and resume normal life. After talking with her staff, she felt detached from reality and drained of energy. The remaining hours of the day had seemed to stretch emptily and endlessly ahead of her.

She'd availed herself of the suite's Jacuzzi tub and had shampooed so vigorously she'd made her scalp sting. She used a spare toothbrush to scrub the caked blood—Shaw's blood—from beneath her fingernails.

Gwen had collected changes of clothing and toiletries from her house in Tobias, as Wiley had said. Jordie was glad to swap clean clothes for those hopelessly blood-stained, although she was strangely reluctant to hand them over to Gwen when she asked for them. Jordie couldn't account for why she was inclined to hug them against her chest and not let go.

Since her arrival, they'd ordered two room service meals. Jordie should've been ravenous, but she'd listlessly picked at the food. After drinking a half glass of minibar white wine, encouraged by Gwen, she'd pleaded exhaustion and gone to bed.

It surprised her now that she'd slept at all, but she supposed that her body had demanded it whether she'd desired it or not. The sleep had restored her physically, but she'd come abruptly awake with her anxiety intact.

Staring at the cold floor tiles between her bare feet, she thought how badly she dreaded tomorrow and the unwelcome surprises it could have in store. Then she realized that it *was* tomorrow. She had no alternative except to face it.

When she stepped into the bedroom, Gwen was standing backlit in the doorway that opened into the living area of the suite.

U.S. Marshal Gwen Saunders was of average height, her frame padded by fifteen pounds of extra weight, which she carried well and unselfconsciously. She wasn't unkind, just... official. She was on high alert even at four thirty in the morning. Not that Jordie could blame her. Josh's escapade hadn't inspired much trust between the Marshal's Service and the Bennett family.

Gwen asked, "Everything okay?"

"I just needed the bathroom."

"Can I get you anything?"

"No thank you."

"I received a text from Joe Wiley after you went to bed."

Jordie's heart tripped. *Shaw?*

"He'd like us to be at his office at nine thirty," Gwen said, dashing her hope, and fear, of getting an update on Shaw. She went on to tell Jordie that she'd ordered a Continental breakfast to be sent up at eight. "Unless you want me to order something else."

"No, that's fine."

Gwen asked what time she wanted to be woken up. Jordie gave her a time. "But wake me if you receive any news."

The marshal nodded but made no promises. "Get some more rest." She pulled the door closed as she went out.

Jordie got back into bed, rolled onto her side, and curled into the fetal position.

What a godawful mess.

By escaping, Josh had set things into motion, but it was unfair to lay her present circumstances entirely at his feet. She was also culpable. When the FBI agents had questioned her six months ago and asked specifically about her relationship with Billy, she should have told them about that cursed trip to Costa Rica. Of course, she hadn't known then about the funds that Josh had transferred down there to facilitate Panella's getaway.

She'd also made an egregious mistake by going to that redneck bar on Friday night. When Josh was being taken away and she'd told him, "I'm done," she should have meant it. She should have ignored the anonymous phone summons.

Instead, she had responded as years of conditioning had trained her to. Old habits weren't hard to break—they were *impossible*. Or so it seemed. Josh needed her, so she went running, this time plunging headlong into the appalling situation in which she now found herself. She was under the suspicion of the FBI.

And then there was the conundrum of Shaw Kinnard. Regarding her kidnapper, her heart and her reason were at odds. No, that was inadequate phraseology. She was foundering in an emotional maelstrom.

She'd witnessed him commit cold-blooded murder. Although he hadn't treated her cruelly, never once had he let her forget that she was his hostage and under threat of death. He had kept her frightened and unsure. Her fate had been at his whim.

The moment I laid eyes on you, your life was spared. Truth? Or just nice words to keep her off balance? She'd been inclined to believe him. She'd wanted to badly, not as a hostage, but as a woman.

And that was the most frightening aspect of the entire experience. That was what had her caught in a whirlpool of conflicting and incomprehensible emotions.

As she'd watched the ambulance speed away with him in shackles, she should have been weak with relief. Instead, all she'd felt was despair. She'd inflicted his wound, but it pained her that he was suffering so terribly. If he lived, he would face harsh punishment for his crimes. Knowing that should have been gratifying. It wasn't.

The thought of his forbidding face didn't cause her to shudder with revulsion, as it should have. Instead, she ached to look into it again. Recalling his touch, she didn't flinch. Rather, she had a bone-deep yearning to be touched again. She didn't try to erase his kiss from her mind but avariciously clung to the memory of it, deeply regretting that he had limited himself to only one.

She should have been brimming with happiness just for being alive. And she was.

But there was no real joy in it, because of her profound sense of loss over possibilities unrealized.

Chapter 24

———❖———

Josh anxiously awaited daybreak.

He sat at the kitchen table, fiddling with a box of toothpicks, nearly jumping out of his skin at every sound. He was reminded of a popular bumper sticker from a few years back: YOU'D BE PARANOID TOO IF EVERYBODY WAS AFTER YOU.

The darkness made him jittery, but he was afraid to turn on the lights, now even more so than before. A light had brought about Shaw Kinnard's capture. That was just one of the surprising tidbits that had been on the late newscasts.

According to the report, a fisherman had spotted light inside a building that had been abandoned for years. He had alerted local authorities to it, and that had led to Jordie's rescue and her abductor's arrest.

Good fortune for her. Disaster for the perpetrator.

Since Josh fell into the latter category, he'd taken the lesson to heart, switched off the TV immediately, and had kept every light off since. Total darkness was safer, but hell on his nerves. Throughout the wee hours, he'd crept from window to window of the house, afraid that when he looked outside he would see armed men in uniforms sneaking up on him, surrounding the house, spreading a net he couldn't escape.

He wasn't that good with guns, but he kept a loaded pistol within reach on the table next to the box of toothpicks. He was glad he'd planned ahead and had left the gun here in the house along with the frozen TV dinners and stocked pantry. It gave him peace of mind. With it close at hand, he didn't feel so naked and exposed.

He detested being naked and exposed. Even in his own shower. Because occasionally, as much as he tried to avoid it, he would accidentally catch a glimpse of himself in the bathroom mirror and see his grotesque scars.

The passage of time had faded them. They were no longer red and pink but slick and white and shiny, like repulsive worms crisscrossing his back. He remembered being told how lucky he was that his clothing would conceal them. Even Jordie had told him that once.

"Nobody will ever know they're there, Josh."

He had yelled at her that *he* knew they were there.

That indisputable fact had shut her up. She'd never tried that platitude on him again.

Frustrated over the reminder of his deformity, he knocked the box of toothpicks over the edge of the table. They spilled onto the floor. Still feeling restless, he reached for one of his cell phones and bounced it in his palm. He'd removed the battery from the one he'd used to call Joe Wiley. This was a new phone, new battery, and it was charged.

He was tempted to call Wiley again, ask him if what they'd reported on TV about Jordie was true and that she really had come through her ordeal unharmed. He also wondered if Wiley had asked her about Costa Rica yet.

She would probably be mad at him for telling the FBI agent about her and Panella's little getaway. From the day she'd returned from Central America, the junket had been a closed subject. Taboo. Off-limits. Josh's tentative inquires about it had been met with frigid silence. She was probably still touchy on the topic.

But he'd had to give Wiley something last night, hadn't he? Would Jordie rather have remained at the mercy of Shaw Kinnard, hardened criminal? They'd said on TV that he had been "gravely wounded," but they hadn't disclosed the nature of his injury or how he'd sustained it.

Josh hoped he'd died.

He knelt, gathered up the toothpicks by feel, and replaced them in the box. Then he made another circuit of the ground floor of the house, tiptoeing through the dark rooms, taking peeps out the windows. No need to check the second floor. He'd done so twice.

Outside, nothing was moving. He was okay.

But the suspense to know about Jordie was killing him. Yielding to temptation, he returned to the kitchen, picked up the phone, and tapped in Joe Wiley's number. After three rings, the agent answered, sounding groggy, as though the call had woken him up.

"I heard about Jordie. Is she really all right?"

"Hi, Josh. I wondered when you'd break down and call me. I had a bet going with my wife that you—"

"*Is* she?"

"She's fine. But why don't you come see for yourself? I'll come get you, drive you straight over to her."

"Is her kidnapper dead?"

"Last I heard, no. But you're not the only one who hopes he'll die."

Josh recognized that statement as a dangled carrot. Nevertheless, he couldn't resist it. "I'm sure Jordie does. Did he do something to her? Hurt her?"

"She says no. But I wasn't referring to her. I talked to Billy Panella tonight."

Josh snorted. "Liar."

"A few hours ago."

"Liar!"

"Have you ever known me to lie to you, Josh? Think about it. I've always leveled with you even when I didn't want to."

"Panella's in South America."

"Possibly, but I brought him up to speed on what's going on here."

"You're just trying to scare me."

"You decide if you should be scared or not."

"What's that mean?"

"When I told Panella that Kinnard was in custody and that Jordie was alive and well, he said the F word. And the tirade didn't stop there. I had to look up some of the words."

"That's not scary," Josh said. "He always says the F word when he's mad, and he was mad because his plot to kill Jordie failed."

"This time. I figure he'll try again, because . . . well, here's the thing, Josh. I sorta let it slip that you were once again trading his secrets to get on our good side."

"Oh, Jesus."

"Are you scared yet? You've got good reason to be."

Josh began to blubber.

"Be smart, Josh. Tell me where you are."

Shaw resented sleep. He considered it a waste of time and disliked the vulnerability that necessarily accompanied it. He slept only when he had to and never for more than a few hours.

But he hadn't been conscious for long before wishing he could slip back into oblivion. Any given morning a hospital was a busy place, but it seemed that everybody on staff at this one had some business in his room.

Probably they just wanted to take a gander at the man hand-cuffed to his bed.

His vitals were taken. Twice. His blood was drawn. At least a quart. His floor was mopped. The guy seemed to delight in banging the mop into all four wheels of his bed. His IV was checked a dozen times by a dozen different people. His dressing was changed. The row of staples, like a miniature railroad track holding him together, was probed to test its durability. His piss output was measured and recorded before the bag was replaced.

Shortly after that humiliation, a male nurse showed up to give him a bed bath. He bent Shaw like a pretzel, causing him to swear viciously. "Where'd you get your training? Guantanamo?"

The next guy who breezed in was dressed in blue scrubs. "Remember me?"

"No."

"Didn't think you would." Skinny and spry, he introduced himself as the surgeon who'd worked on him the day before. "We did several X-rays and scans, didn't find any organ damage. Your large intestine was missed by this much." He left a half inch between his thumb and index finger. "You also got by without a major blood vessel being cut. The wound was nasty, getting in-fected. I cleaned it out. Could have been a lot worse."

Shaw said, "What's the bad news?"

"Your oblique was sliced through like a steak. Using a dull knife. Had to take lots of stitches, layers of them, starting deep inside and working out. So it's gonna be sore for a while. Take it easy. No heavy lifting. No strenuous exercise."

He seemed to remember the restraints keeping Shaw secured to the bed, and looked like he wished he could take back that last bit. He continued briskly. "You were given a tetanus shot. If you start running a fever, get checked for infection. We're giving you IV antibiotics, and you'll leave here with a butt-load of them plus capsules to last several weeks. Take them till they run out. Any questions?"

"When will the staples be removed?"

"Tomorrow if all is looking good. They're only a safety net. A physical therapist will get you up today, start you moving around."

Shaw rattled the handcuffs.

"They've stationed a deputy outside the room," the surgeon said. "He'll be on hand to...assist."

"When can we pull that thing out of my dick?"

The surgeon gave a lopsided grin. "I'll send somebody in. But if you can't pee on your own, back in it goes."

"Then I'll make damn sure I pee on my own."

"Good luck to you."

He breezed out. Fifteen seconds later, a uniformed man stalked in.

Shaw rested his head on his pillow and closed his eyes.

"Morning."

Shaw didn't return the greeting, but the officer didn't take the hint. Shaw sensed him advancing into the room, stopping at the foot of the bed, looking down on him. "I rode in the ambulance with you yesterday, but you were pretty out of it. Clint Morrow, Terrebonne Parish—"

"I remember you," Shaw said. "The man who tracked me down."

"Wasn't much of my doing. I got a good lead."

"What was a fisherman doing in a swamp during a thunderstorm? Let me guess. Some crazy Cajun."

"Takes all kinds."

"My luck," Shaw muttered.

After a brief pause, Morrow asked how he was feeling.

"How do I look?"

"Like shit."

"That pretty much covers it."

The deputy waited a beat, then got down to business. "I need you to answer some questions."

Shaw raised his head, opened one eye, and took a look around the room. "I don't see a lawyer." He closed his eye and returned his head to the pillow.

Undeterred, Morrow began relating facts that Shaw already knew about the fatal shooting of Mickey Bolden. "Do you want to comment on any of that, Mr. Kinnard?"

"Still don't see a lawyer. But if you stick around long enough, you might get to watch them remove my catheter."

"When did you become acquainted with Bolden?"

He asked a few dozen questions. Shaw responded with sighs, yawns, and once by asking if Morrow would mind scratching an itch for him. "It's a lot to ask, I know, but it was washed during my sponge bath."

"Okay, talk smart," Morrow said. "Sooner or later you'll realize that it's in your best interest to cooperate."

"No, it's in *your* best interest for me to cooperate." Looking beyond him, Shaw added, "Unless I miss my guess, she's here to run you out."

Morrow turned to the nurse who'd entered the room. "I'm sorry, but your ten minutes are up," she told him. "You can come back this afternoon between one and three."

Shaw said, "That is if you have absolutely nothing better to do between one and three, because I'm not talking to you without a lawyer present."

"Actually I do have something better to do. Agent Joe Wiley—you remember him?"

"Prince of a guy."

"He invited me to sit in when they question Ms. Bennett. You..." He looked pointedly at Shaw's cuffed hands. "You'll keep." He put on his hat and brushed the brim of it with his index finger. "Ma'am," he said to the nurse and started for the door.

"Wait a minute." Shaw tried to sit up but was able only to lever himself onto his elbows. "Is Josh Bennett still at large?"

Seeing the deputy's hesitation, Shaw said, "His capture wouldn't be kept secret. It'll have been on the news. I can ask her," he added, indicating the nurse, "or you can just tell me."

Morrow said, "Still at large."

"And the feds think his sister can lead them to him?" He made a scoffing sound. "Wish them luck."

Morrow came back to the bed. "Why do you say that?"

Shaw gauged the deputy's apparent interest, then said to the nurse, "Beat it."

Her sizable chest swelled with indignation. "I beg your pardon?"

Shaw fixed his coldest, most intimidating stare on her. She gathered her dignity and marched out. He returned his attention to Morrow. "Jordie Bennett doesn't know anything. Not about her brother. Not about Panella."

"That's what she told *you*."

"I was trying to squeeze more money out of the deal. I grilled her under pain of death. I put her through hell. Didn't she tell Wiley all this?"

"She alluded to your death threats and persistence. But there were gaps in her story that Wiley wants filled."

"What kind of gaps?"

The nurse reappeared, bringing with her a staff supervisor and the deputy guarding his room. The guard said, "Sorry, Sergeant Morrow. They're kicking you out."

Morrow said to Shaw, "I'll be back later."

"Wait a goddamn minute! These gaps in Jordie's statement. Are they regarding her brother? Panella? What?"

"Probably all of the above. You included."

"If she'd known anything about Panella or her brother, she would've told me."

"Or stabbed you." Morrow held Shaw's gaze for several seconds, then the corner of his mouth hiked up in a quasismile. "Kinda makes you wonder who rooked who, doesn't it?"

He turned to go. The people grouped in the open doorway parted for him. In a voice too low to hear, he said something to the deputy, then walked away. The others dispersed. The nurse Shaw had insulted shot him a spiteful look and pulled the door partially shut.

As he resettled on the hard pillow, his thoughts swirled around Jordie, star of his drug-inspired, X-rated dreams, sister of a criminal, object of Billy Panella's affection.

Although she'd denied that, it was logical to assume. Panella had the hots for her, she'd spurned him, and he—

Or *had* she spurned him?

Morrow hinted that Shaw had been a chump to trust her. Obviously the FBI doubted her trustworthiness. She'd left gaps in the account she'd given Joe Wiley, and it was bedeviling Shaw to wonder what they were.

Hearing murmured voices just outside his room, he raised his head as the door was eased open. When he saw who his new visitor was, he swore under his breath.

"Not a very nice greeting." Xavier Dupaw, assistant district attorney of Orleans Parish, came to the side of his bed and took him in from head to toe, *tsk*ing. "My, my. Look at you."

The prosecutor tried and failed to contain a smirk. "You are in deep, *deep* doo-doo this time, Mr. Kinnard. Up to your ungroomed eyebrows in Panella's doo-doo." More *tsk*ing. "Of course, a day and a half spent alone with Jordie Bennett was a fringe benefit." He winked.

Shaw wanted to tear out the guy's jugular with his teeth.

"No wiggle room for you this time, my friend." Dupaw leaned down and whispered with devilish glee, "Let's get this party started!"

Chapter 25

J ordie kept the television in her bedroom tuned to the network morning shows, anticipating the local stations' break-ins. Because of their brevity, her rescue was only touched upon, and there was no mention of Shaw's condition. She paced until Gwen knocked on her door and told her that their Continental breakfast had arrived.

While sipping a cup of strong coffee, it occurred to Jordie how ill-advised it would be to meet with Agents Wiley and Hickam without having legal representation there. She didn't want to appear guilty of any wrongdoing. But she wasn't naïve, either.

She borrowed Gwen's phone to call the lawyer who'd been at her side when she was questioned six months earlier and therefore was familiar with the case.

Adrian Dover was in her forties, sharp, no pushover. Better still, recognizing the implications of Josh's escape and Jordie's abduction, she was willing to adjust her schedule and come to Jordie's aid on short notice. On Jordie's behalf, Gwen called Joe Wiley and asked if the interview could be moved back to noon, allowing Jordie time to confer with her lawyer. He granted the request.

A few minutes before twelve Gwen ushered Jordie and the attorney down a corridor in the FBI building and into an inter-rogation room, although it was not identified as such. Jordie had been through this drill before.

Wiley and Hickam were already there. Everyone was painstakingly polite. Jordie thanked Wiley for agreeing to the postponement. He said it was just as well, because one of the toilets at his house had overflowed, creating a minor flood in an upstairs hallway.

Jordie curbed her impatience for as long as she could before interrupting Wiley's anecdote about his wife's encounter with the indifferent and unhurried plumber.

"What is Shaw Kinnard's condition?" she blurted. "Did he make it through the surgery all right?"

The two men exchanged an uneasy glance.

Jordie's stomach plummeted. "He died?"

Wiley cleared his throat. "No. He came through the surgery okay and was expected to make a full recovery."

She tried to keep her relief from being too obvious. But then she caught the tense of the verb. "*Was* expected?"

No longer the genial family man harassed by a faulty toilet, Wiley now assumed his game face. "About fifteen minutes ago, we got a call from the Houma hospital's administrator. Preemp-tive, I think. He's covering his... behind."

"For what?"

"Kinnard is en route to a trauma center here in New Or-leans. His condition is a lot more serious this time."

Jordie's ribs seemed to shrink around her lungs. She couldn't take in sufficient air. "More serious than what I... what I did to him?"

"The admin guy described him as being critical. Of course, he's not a doctor."

She wheezed. "What happened?"

Wiley's frown deepened. "An assistant DA here in Orleans Parish, name of Xavier Dupaw, failed to indict Kinnard on two murder raps when he had the chance to. He's been eating crow ever since. He heard about Kinnard's capture and went to see him in the hospital this morning.

"No one knows exactly what was said between them, and, believe me, Dupaw can be provoking as hell. Whatever he said caused Kinnard to go apeshit, if you'll pardon the French. He started yanking on his restraints, yelling that he was gonna kill Dupaw if it was the last thing he ever did.

"The admin guy described quite a scene. The upshot of it? Kinnard was too aggressive and hostile to be left down there in Houma. Dupaw insisted that he be moved immediately to a more secure facility, a hospital with bars on the windows, concertina wire around the perimeter, and dozens of guards, not just one deputy outside his door, who Dupaw described as 'green as they come.'" He paused and looked at her with concern. "You want some water, Ms. Bennett?"

She shook her head.

"You sure?"

"Please go on."

He hesitated, then resumed. "The hospital staff objected to him being moved, said their patient wasn't up to it, that he wasn't out of danger yet. Since Kinnard is technically Morrow's prisoner, Dupaw enlisted his help.

"After some arm-twisting, Deputy Morrow got the surgeon's clearance to make the transfer. The admin guy signed off on it. That's where the ass covering comes in. He doesn't want to be held responsible for what came later."

Jordie's throat was too constricted to ask what had come later.

Wiley took a deep breath. He looked over at Hickam, who gave him a nod of encouragement to continue. "Somehow—we don't know the details yet, because we've been unable to confirm with Morrow. But somehow while in transit, Kinnard got hold of that green deputy's service revolver. Busted out of the ambulance and took off on foot. Almost made good his escape. Morrow managed to, uh, stop him."

"Stop him."

"We were told he ordered Kinnard to halt. He didn't. Morrow had no choice."

"He shot him?"

Wiley just looked at her, which was answer enough. "They packed him back into the ambulance and, since they were closer to New Orleans, continued on this way rather than returning to Houma. I think the admin guy in Houma is relieved that it's out of his hands."

"Because he doesn't expect him to survive."

"He didn't come out and say it, but that's what I gathered." Wiley ran a hand around the back of his neck. "I hate this for Morrow. He told me yesterday morning after Kinnard was apprehended that he was damned glad he hadn't had to use his weapon. Said he hoped to go his whole career without ever having to hurt anybody. He must've jinxed himself." He paused before adding quietly, "I'm sure we'll hear from him when . . . when he has something definite to tell us."

Jordie lowered her head and stared vacantly at the chipped edge of the particleboard table. Her ears were echoing the doleful beating of her heart.

"Shaw Kinnard was, *is*, a violent man, Ms. Bennett," Hickam said. "With heinous crimes to his credit."

She merely nodded.

Wiley said, "I know you have mixed feelings about this."

"Yes, I do."

"Why?"

She raised her head and looked at Wiley, who seemed genuinely puzzled. "He wasn't violent with me. He frightened me, but didn't do anything *heinous*. He was offered a lot of money to kill me." She raised her shoulders. "He didn't."

No one said anything for a stretch of time. Then Wiley said, "That's not the only development we've had this morning. The other relates to your brother."

She covered her mouth, whimpering, "Oh, God. No. Don't tell me—"

"He's alive," Wiley said quickly. "At least he was a few hours ago."

When he saw a question forming on her lips, he held up a hand. "I'll start the official questioning by telling you what we know. Uh, Hick, would you hit the switch on the video, please?" Then to her, he said with apology, "Procedure."

When the camera was on and recording, he continued. "The canines picked up Josh's trail in the woods and tracked him to a storage facility that was three miles from there, give or take. The security cameras at the facility caught him before he disabled the system."

"How did he do that?"

"It was old. Hardwired. We think he simply cut the power source. Management of the place provided us records. Josh rented the space using a fake name and paid for twelve months in advance. His unit was empty save for a motor oil stain in the middle of the floor."

"He kept a car there?" she asked.

"Looks like."

"He sold his car before being sent to Tennessee."

"And the single mother who bought it still has it," Wiley told her. "Hick checked on that this morning."

The other agent confirmed that with a nod.

"Your brother has a different set of wheels," Wiley continued. "We don't know what kind, because no one spotted him driving away from that storage outfit. But he's no longer so confident of his escape." He paused to take a breath. "He called me this morning a little before dawn."

Having had to absorb the shocking news about Shaw, Jordie

now suffered another jolt. She listened without comment as Joe Wiley recounted his most recent conversation with Josh.

"He sounded different from when I talked to him night before last," Wiley said. "He got really spooked when I told him that I had talked to Billy Panella last night."

Jordie flinched. *"What?"* The shocks just kept coming.

"I used Bolden's phone. Same as Kinnard did. Just hit Redial."

"Panella answered?"

"He expected it to be Kinnard demanding payment for services rendered. I identified myself and told him that his hired gun had been apprehended and that you were alive and well. Plan foiled."

"What did he say?"

"Garbled some obscenities, then hung up. Now that he knows we have Bolden's phone, the one he answered is probably in pieces."

Jordie murmured agreement to that. She was aware of Greg Hickam standing with his back to the wall, watching her intently and gauging her reactions to everything Wiley was telling her. Keeping her expression schooled, she said, "My brother is my main concern. Any indication of where he is, how he is?"

"If I knew where, he'd already be in custody. But I don't think he'll keep running much longer. He sounded strung out, jumpy, on the brink of falling apart. He was crying when he hung up."

"I'm sure he's scared."

"I think so, too," Wiley said. "Told him he should be. But what, in particular, do *you* think has him scared enough to bawl like a baby?"

"You don't have to answer," Adrian Dover said.

Jordie disregarded her. "He's scared of being recaptured because he knows the punishment he'll face."

"Years in prison."

"Yes, and that will be torture."

"It isn't meant to be fun, Ms. Bennett."

"Of course not. But for Josh, the lack of privacy is his worst nightmare."

"You're referring to his scars," Wiley said quietly.

She nodded and lowered her head sorrowfully. "They're unsightly, and Josh sees them as being even worse than they are. He's extremely self-conscious of them. Pathologically so."

No one said anything for the next several moments, then Jordie raised her head. "I can't bear the idea of imprisonment for my brother and his being subjected to, well, everything that it entails, but I'll do the right thing, Agent Wiley. I'll answer truthfully any questions you put to me."

Adrian Dover said, "Unless she exercises her constitutional right not to."

Wiley began, and for approximately an hour they reviewed everything Jordie had already told them about her abduction. She found it almost impossible to speak Shaw's name without her throat seizing up.

Various aspects of the time he'd held her captive were covered repeatedly, until she said in a cracking voice, "Must we go over this again and again? There's nothing more I can tell you."

Then from Hickam, "All right, then tell us about your trip to Costa Rica with Billy Panella."

The switch in topics was so abrupt it took her aback.

"That's not a question," Adrian Dover said.

"Excuse me. I'll be happy to put it in the form of a question." Hickam pushed himself away from the wall. "Ms. Bennett, did you accompany Billy Panella to Costa Rica?" He checked his iPad and cited the dates.

"Yes."

"What was the reason for the trip?"

The lawyer laid her hand on Jordie's arm and shook her head.

This time Jordie heeded her. "I've been advised by counsel not to answer."

"Did you know that Panella had funds stashed in a bank in San Jose?"

"Not until yesterday when Agent Wiley alleged it."

"Your brother made the deposit for him."

"So Agent Wiley alleged."

"You had no previous knowledge of this?"

"None."

"You didn't know about Billy Panella's plans to flee the U.S.?"

"You don't have to answer."

She turned to the lawyer. "I want to answer, Adrian." Then to Hickam, "I didn't know Billy Panella's plans regarding anything. We rarely even spoke."

"But you spent a long weekend with him."

She divided a look between the two federal agents, but didn't say anything because her lawyer was whispering in her ear not to.

Hickam said, "You still claim to have no knowledge of funds in that bank?"

"Correct. I have no knowledge of them."

Wiley sat forward, clasping his hands on the table and looking at her like the regretful bearer of bad news. "They remember you down there, Ms. Bennett."

"Who? Where? What are you talking about?"

"The bank employees in San Jose. You paid a visit to it with Panella."

"Oh. That." Her shoulders sagged forward. Adrian Dover cautioned her not to say anything, but she held up a hand to silence her. "I want this cleared up, Adrian."

She glanced at handsome, stoic Hickam, then met Wiley's sad-looking eyes. "Panella ordered a chauffeur-driven limousine to take us to lunch, a place on the mountainside overlooking the city. On the way there, he asked the driver to stop at a bank, where he said he had some quick business to attend to.

"I told him that I would wait in the car, but he insisted that I go into the bank with him." She took a deep breath. "He made a spectacle of us. Flirted with the tellers, glad-handed the officers, and cashed a check. I was embarrassed by his grandstanding and couldn't wait to get out of there."

She raised her hands. "That was it. I'm not surprised that the bank employees remember us, because it was a disgusting display of affluence. Him with his Armani suit and Patik Philippe watch. But that's all I know about a bank in San Jose. If Josh made a deposit—"

"He did." Hickam stepped forward and opened up an e-mail attachment, holding it where she could see it. "One week before Josh agreed to cooperate with us, he opened an account for Billy Panella with half a million dollars."

She looked at him, but didn't say anything, unsure of what he expected from her. Wiley said, "The thing is, Ms. Bennett... Show her, Hick."

He scrolled to another page.

"That's the amount in the account as of this morning. Half a million and change, the change being the interest that's accrued in the past six months." He leaned farther forward. "Panella hasn't touched it. No withdrawals."

Both he and Hickam were still looking at her expectantly. She raised her shoulders in a gesture of helplessness. "He must've changed his mind about San Jose. He went someplace else."

"And left this money there? Does that sound like him to you? Doesn't sound like him to me. To us. To Josh, who told us while sitting in that chair you're sitting in now that, although Panella made a show of spending to enhance his reputation as a brilliant moneyman, he kept track of every single cent. Squeezed the copper off every penny. He'd made a science of having his money multiply while he slept. Why would he leave five hundred thou in an account that earns less than one percent interest?"

They waited. She felt the walls closing in and was powerless to stop them. "I have no idea."

Wiley said, "Only thing we can guess? He plans on keeping it there till he can retrieve it or move it, and the timing just hasn't been right."

"I don't know what he plans," she said. "I never did."

"Who called you to that honky tonk last Friday night?"

Again, the switch in tone and subjects momentarily threw her. "I've told you repeatedly that I didn't recognize the voice."

Wiley leaned toward her. "And all he said was—"

"I quoted it to you exactly. You wrote it down." She gestured to the iPad now lying on the table.

Hickam picked up. "You're an intelligent woman, Ms. Bennett. You've got common sense. You're rational. A savvy businesswoman. Yet you expect us to believe that when a man you can't identify called and told you to rush to a seedy bar out in the sticks, you dropped everything and went tearing out there?"

Adrian Dover intervened. "This is becoming harassment, gentlemen. My client has affirmed several times that she doesn't know who that caller was."

"Was it Panella?" Wiley asked.

"No."

"How do you know it wasn't?" That from Hickam. "You said you didn't recognize his voice."

"I didn't! He only said a few words and then he was gone."

"Has Panella been cooling his heels somewhere until you and he could sneak off to—"

"Oh, good God, no!"

Adrian was urging her not to say another word.

Unmindful of her lawyer's advice she said, "I wouldn't go anywhere with him."

"You went to Costa Rica."

"If I had it to do over, I wouldn't."

"Why? What happened down there?"

"Don't answer," Adrian said.

"I hated Billy Panella then, and I utterly loathe him now. And the feeling is mutual," she said, stressing it. "He sent two men to kill me. Have you forgotten that?"

Hickam patted the air between them. "Okay. Right. He had Bolden and Kinnard waiting there for you. He laid a trap."

She negated that with a shake of her head. "Shaw Kinnard told me that it came as a shock to them when I walked in."

Hickam scoffed at that. "You believe *Kinnard*?"

She thought back to all the times he had tricked her with a lie or semitruth, and she'd been gullible enough to believe him. Maybe plan A had been to kill her at that bar.

Hickam didn't let up. "Panella called you—"

Shaw had said otherwise.

"—and invoked Josh's name to get you there."

She put her fingertips to her temples and massaged them. "I don't think it was Panella, but I suppose it's possible."

"If you loathe him, why would you heed his summons?"

"I didn't. I...I..."

"My client is declining to answer," Adrian said.

Hickam persisted. "If it wasn't Panella, it was your brother."

"I don't *believe* it was Josh, but I can't be certain."

"You went there to aid and abet one of them, Ms. Bennett."

Adrian Dover said, "Do not respond."

"Who did you expect to be there waiting for you?" Hickam asked. "Panella?"

"No."

"Then your brother."

"No." She shook her head in confusion. "Possibly. I don't know."

Adrian was pressing her arm, demanding that she say nothing more.

Hickam leaned across the table again and thumped it with his fist. "Not Panella. Not Josh. Then who? Tell us. Who called you?"

"I did."

At the sound of the new voice in the room, four pairs of eyes swung toward the door. There stood Shaw Kinnard.

Chapter 26

———◆———

Jordie and Joe Wiley lurched out of their chairs. Jordie's tipped
over backward.

But Wiley's partner moved faster than anyone. In under a
second his pistol was drawn and aimed at the bridge of Shaw's
nose, his finger on the trigger.

Behind Shaw, Xavier Dupaw shouted, "Don't shoot! He's
one of you. FBI. Special Agent Shaw Kinnard."

Shaw's focus remained on Jordie's wide, incredulous gaze,
but in his peripheral vision he saw that the woman sitting in the
chair next to her was blinking rapidly. Joe Wiley mouthed several
profanities and looked like he wanted to drive his fist through a
wall.

The guy with the nine-millimeter acted like he hadn't heard
the disclaimer. He still had a bead on Shaw's forehead.

Shaw didn't move except to cut his eyes over to him. "Want
to lower that?"

"Not really."

The prosecutor edged around Shaw and entered the room,
chortling, "You should see your faces. I guess we pulled it off."

Shaw watched Jordie's lips part in disbelief. Or disillusionment, maybe. In a barely audible voice, she said, "You're an FBI agent?"

"Guilty."

With obvious reluctance the black agent lowered his pistol. "You son of a bitch. I almost shot you."

Shaw turned his head and sized him up. "I don't like you all that much, either."

"Gentlemen, no need for hostility," Dupaw said. He turned to Shaw and added under his breath, "I told you that I should come in first to neutralize the situation, but did you listen?"

Joe Wiley stepped around the table. Shaw could practically see smoke coming from his ears, and, frankly, he didn't blame him. "If you're FBI, I'm a Chinaman."

"I caught 'em on a slow day." If Shaw had felt better, he might have grinned. But he couldn't muster the energy.

The woman beside Jordie had righted her chair and took her elbow in an attempt to guide her back into it. Jordie shook her off and remained standing. Shaw had only ever seen her in the jeans and top she'd worn into the bar. Today she was dressed for business in a navy pants suit with a pink scooped-neck top underneath the jacket.

But he was less interested in her wardrobe than in her facial expressions, which had evolved from dismay upon seeing him, to absolute fury upon learning how he had misled her, big-time.

He didn't blame her, either.

Wiley propped his hands on his hips. "Badge?"

"Can't carry one. But if you want to call Atlanta and check me out, I can give you a password."

"Do that."

Shaw gave him his code, the number to call, and the individual to ask for. The super-stud agent pecked the phone number into his cell and stepped out of the room to make the call.

Joe Wiley still regarded Shaw with blatant mistrust. "You work out of the Atlanta office?"

"When I work out of an office at all."

"I can vouch for him," Xavier Dupaw said with overblown self-importance. "I was about to indict him for that double murder. NOPD, you and Agent Hickam, everybody in Orleans Parish was pressuring me to do so."

"I was wasting time in jail," Shaw said to Wiley. "I had to tell him." He nodded toward the prosecutor.

Dupaw said, "Mr. Kinnard revealed himself to be a covert operative." The last two words were spoken in a stage whisper.

Wiley, frowning, grumbled, "We were sure you'd killed those two guys."

"I did," Shaw said. "They got wise to a DEA officer who was working the same case. To protect him . . . " He raised a shoulder.

Dupaw placed his right hand over his heart and said to Wiley, "I would have liked to share all this with you, but only I and the DA were entrusted with the classified information."

Wiley gave a snort of distaste over the prosecutor's condescension.

The other agent reentered the room. "He checks out." He looked none too happy about it.

Shaw turned to Xavier Dupaw. "You can go now."

The prosecutor blustered. "This is the thanks I get for coming to your rescue? If it weren't for me, you would still be chained to your hospital bed."

"Thanks. But you've served your purpose."

"This case is far from over."

"But it's not your show. It's federal. Crimes against the state were committed in another parish and outside your jurisdiction." Shaw motioned him toward the door.

Dupaw sputtered, but eventually shot his cuffs and stalked out, peevishly banging the door shut behind himself.

Shaw looked at Wiley. "Mind if I sit?"

He was woozy and didn't want to ruin his dramatic entrance by falling flat on his face in a dead faint. Wiley pointed him into a chair across the table from Jordie. Live coals didn't smolder as hot as she was. Her rigid posture, the stern set of her lips, her glare, all attested to her barely controlled wrath as she sat down.

Shaw expelled a long breath. "Look. Jordie. I know I put you through a meat grinder. But I was—"

"'Son of a bitch' doesn't come close to characterizing you." She practically spat the words at him, then turned her head aside as if the very sight of him sickened her.

The fraught silence that followed was broken by the woman beside her, who quietly introduced herself as Jordie's lawyer. Shaw acknowledged the introduction, but they didn't shake hands. He had much more to say to Jordie, but there was business to attend to, she wasn't in the mood to listen, and the real spoiler was that they were on opposing sides of a criminal investigation.

Wiley said, "Was Morrow in on this charade?"

Shaw nodded. "Couldn't have done it without him. He's a good man. Once Dupaw and I brought him into the loop, he facilitated everything. Ordered an ambulance, recruited a couple of guys from his department who he could trust to drive it. Got his dispatch operator to call the hospital administrator in Houma to inform him of the near-fatal shooting."

"He bought it," Wiley said.

"Good to know. The dispatcher told him it was a delicate police matter, some cock-and-bull like that, and ordered him not to put the media wise to it. Which he wouldn't have anyway, because it might set him in the hot seat for green-lighting my premature release and making his hospital look bad."

It had been necessary to take the surgeon into their confidence. He'd reluctantly removed the staples from Shaw's incision and given him a supply of oral medications and extra bandages to take with him. Morrow had them in his squad car.

Thinking of that, Shaw said, "Morrow remembered to re-trieve my boots from the hospital room closet before we left. I was rolled out, bare-assed in a hospital gown and handcuffed to a stretcher. Morrow went into a Walmart and bought me a change of clothes. Here I am."

"Cover still protected," Wiley said.

"Hopefully. For the time being anyway."

"Why isn't Morrow with you now?" Wiley asked.

"On the way here, he got an emergency call from his office. Couldn't delegate. Had to turn back. He dismissed the ambu-lance and drivers. Dupaw brought me the rest of the way in his car. Morrow said to tell you that he'd check in with you as soon as he could."

"Would have been nice for y'all to let us in on this," Wiley said.

"Morrow was handier. He'd left my room just a few minutes before Dupaw showed up. Morrow wanted to bring you in, but the fewer people involved in the ruse, the more likely it would work. I convinced him of that."

"How?"

"By telling him that was how it was gonna be." He let that settle then glanced at Jordie, who had resumed glaring at him. "Besides, Morrow knew you had your hands full here."

Wiley's partner chimed in, "And letting us in on it would have spoiled your big entrance."

Shaw looked up at him and decided to let the snide remark pass. "You're Hickam?"

"That's right."

"I was denied the pleasure of meeting you yesterday during my arrest."

The agent looked down at the spot where Shaw's shirttail was draped over his holster. "Where'd you get the piece?"

"When I asked for my weapons back, Morrow obliged."

"'Weapons' plural?"

"He keeps a pistol in his boot." That from Jordie, who nastily added, "What kind of hit man carries only one gun?"

Matching her testiness, Shaw said, "A dead one."

While the smoke was still clearing from that exchange, Joe Wiley asked, "What about the playboy and corrupt state policeman in Mexico?"

"They resisted arrest." He said it deadpan and nobody commented. "By the way, whichever agency that girl belongs to needs to bring her in and give her some better training."

"Girl?"

"The one who left the party with the three of us that night. She hadn't been at the villa for five minutes before I marked her as heat."

"Only call girl to leave her clothes on?" Wiley asked.

"No, first one out of them. She's too eager. She needs to learn subtlety. The idea is to make them try to impress her, not the other way around. If she doesn't learn that, she's gonna give herself away and die bloody. Find out which agency she works for and get word to them that I said so."

Hickam and Wiley exchanged a look with eyebrows raised, but Hickam made a note of it on his iPad.

"I left the bodies where I knew they'd be found, along with a secret sign so our plant inside the state police would know it was me who took them out and would handle the mop-up, including all the paperwork required in Atlanta. I beat it across the border that night."

"How'd you get across undetected?" Hickam asked.

"That's classified." Unfazed by the other agent's resentful glower, Shaw continued, "I beat it here quick as I could. I'd waited months for a call from Mickey Bolden and didn't want to keep him waiting."

Wiley and Hickam continued to ask about his journey from Mexico to New Orleans. Most of their inquiries he answered with, "Classified." And mainly, it was. But it was also a convenient dodge. He didn't want to waste time on something irrelevant while Billy Panella and Josh Bennett were still at large.

Shaw tipped his head toward Jordie. "Do you have her cell phone?"

"In Wiley's office," Hickam said.

"Would you get it?" Then, as an afterthought, he added, "Please?"

With a look, Hickam consulted Joe Wiley, who okayed him with a nod. Hickam left the room. The four of them sat in strained silence until he returned with Jordie's bagged cell phone.

Shaw said, "When I came in, you were grilling her about who called her to the bar. Check her call history. Friday night, there are two incoming calls from an unknown number."

"We've called it back several times," Hickam said. "Never got an answer."

"Call it again."

Hickam removed the phone from the bag, went to the log and tapped the screen. A few seconds later the phone inside Shaw's shirt pocket began to ring. He took it out and showed them Jordie's cell number in the readout. "This is a burner I bought the day I arrived in New Orleans, just before I hooked up with Mickey Bolden."

"Okay," Wiley said. "Friday night. What really went down? Why you'd call Ms. Bennett to the bar?"

"I'm coming to that." Suddenly struck with a wave of dizziness, he propped his elbow on the table and tunneled his fingers through his hair. He was tempted to rest his forehead in his palm and close his eyes. But, afraid he'd be unable to reopen them, he lowered his hand, ignored the throbbing in his side, and plowed on.

"When I talked to Mickey from Mexico and he told me that Josh Bennett was on the loose, I figured he was the target we'd been contracted to hit. Then I got here. Shocker. Bennett's sister was the target. Killing a woman? Jesus." He shook his head. "Underscored just what a cowardly scumbag Panella is.

"But I had to appear indifferent to Mickey so I could stay cheek by jowl with the asshole and learn what I could. Mickey and I spent all day Friday following Jordie around Tobias. She went home around six. We watched her house for a while. It looked like she was tucked in for the night."

"We had a sheriff's deputy surveilling her," Wiley said.

Shaw scoffed. "And doing a piss-poor job of it. He'd just as well have had a Maglite on his head. I spotted him right away, and I couldn't believe he didn't mark Mickey and me." Looking at Jordie, he said, "You knew he was there, didn't you? You shook him on the way to the bar."

"Go to hell."

He ignored the putdown. "Doesn't matter now, I guess." Turning back to his FBI colleagues, he continued, "Mickey and I went to a diner for supper, and that's when he laid out the plan."

"Plan A?" Jordie said with insincere sweetness.

Shaw looked at her, but didn't respond. Wiley asked, "What was plan A?"

Shaw went back to Wiley. "To hit her early the next morning at her house. Make it look like a burglary turned deadly. Dumbest idea I'd ever heard and told Mickey so. It was rushed, rash, and breaking into her house was an engraved invitation to leave evidence.

"But Mickey said that was the plan. End of discussion. That's when I realized that I'd be left dead, too. He'd brought me in specifically to take the fall. The clock was ticking. I had to stop it."

"By calling her?" Hickam asked. "Why didn't you tip the sheriff's office, or us?"

"I'll get to that," Shaw said, hedging. "I went along when Mickey suggested we grab a drink at that joint before checking into a motel. Before we went inside, I excused myself and followed the arrow pointing around back to the toilet." He looked at Jordie. "That's when I called you."

"How'd you know how to reach her?" Wiley asked.

"Panella had given Mickey the skinny on her, everything, including her cell number. Mickey shared it all with me 'cause he thought I would be dead in a few hours, so what did it matter?"

"So back to why you called her..." Wiley said, leading him.

"Mistakenly, I thought that crossing paths with her the night before the hit—especially with a local cop on her tail—would rattle Mickey and Panella enough to cancel it. At the very least postpone it. Which would have given me time to hang with Mickey, work from the inside, possibly track down Josh and, more particularly, Panella. But, instead of telling us to back off, Panella ordered Mickey to go ahead, to pop her then and there. I couldn't let that happen."

He paused and locked eyes with Jordie, willing her to remember what he'd told her before sending her out to Joe Wiley.

She said nothing for a moment, then a terse "Thank you for saving my life."

"You're welcome."

But he was far from forgiven. Still seething, she grated out, "Why did you do the rest of it?"

Without excuse or qualification or missing a beat, he answered. "Because I want that goddamn fucking Panella."

When he'd appeared in the open doorway, Jordie had barely contained a cry of joy. Now she wanted nothing more than to scratch out his damn lying eyes.

"I have nothing to do with Panella," she said. "Since you have the *skinny* on me, you should know that. Once Mickey was out of commission, why didn't you tell me you were FBI? Or just leave me there and drive away?"

"Because your brother is a friggin' fugitive, Jordie. You're the one and only link to him, and Panella is at the end of that chain."

"In other words, you decided to use me as bait."

"Okay. If you like that word better. I called you to the bar primarily to jinx the hit. But it served a dual purpose."

"What was the other?"

"To test your loyalty to Josh. I dropped his name; you burned rubber getting there."

"You bastard."

He didn't blink. "It's been said."

She rolled her lips inward, clinging to her temper by a thread which was unraveling a little more with each word from his mouth. Clearly, he shared Wiley and Hickam's suspicion that she had been, and possibly was still, involved on some level in her brother's criminal activity.

Joe Wiley said, "Ms. Bennett, did you know that Josh reneged on his deal with us and had run off?"

"No. Not until *he* told me."

Shaw said, "For whatever it's worth, Wiley, she seemed shocked when I told her that Josh had been missing for four days. I don't think she knew. But that didn't cancel the possibility of her knowing *something*. I knew she would be afraid of me because she'd seen me kill Mickey. I figured I could use that fear to get information from her."

Hearing him admit it snapped her control. She shot from her chair and, planting her palms on the tabletop, leaned across it toward him. "You badgered me for hours about that damn phone call!"

"Only after you lied about it."

"You terrorized me."

"I guess. To some extent."

"There's no *extent* to terrorism."

"You're right," he said, raising his voice to match hers. "I kept at you, thinking that I'd wear you down until you let some- thing slip about Josh or Panella, which could have proved vital to their capture."

"You browbeat me about that call, and all along it was *you*."

"What matters more than who called is that you responded. You came running in record time. You made sure you weren't followed. When your surveillance failed to show up, either inside the bar or out on the parking lot, you flunked the test."

"To hell with you and your test!"

"You shook that tail because you expected somebody to be waiting for you in that beer joint. *Who?*"

She was about to fire a comeback when her attorney gave the hem of her jacket a hard tug, pulling her back into her chair. Taking the advice being urgently whispered in her ear, she fell silent.

During her shouting match with Shaw, Wiley looked like a spectator at a tennis match, his head swiveling back and forth between them. Hickam kept up the infernal pecking on the screen of his iPad. She couldn't help but wonder what he was taking down. The session was still being video recorded. Was Hickam adding color commentary, details they would later use against her?

She strived to mask the emotions roiling inside her.

Eventually, Shaw resumed, addressing her. "When I stopped to switch license plates, I used your phone to call myself, so I could show you later that I had tried that number."

"You're full of clever tricks."

He raised a shoulder.

"And bullshit."

"Effective bullshit."

Her face burned when reminded of how effective his words, both sinister and provocative, had been. She wanted to kill him. "You called that phantom number several times, hinting that Josh might answer, knowing full well he wouldn't."

"Another tactic to try and break you."

"Well you failed, *Special Agent Kinnard*. You've got nothing to show for all your testing and clever tricks. You got nothing helpful from me."

"You'd be surprised what I found helpful."

"My brother is still at large."

"Which is why you're still in custody."

Chapter 27

———◦◉◦———

A taut silence followed that fiery exchange, which Joe and Hick had tacitly agreed to let play out without interruption. Adrian Dover softly asked Jordie if she would like to take a breather. "Maybe some water?"

She declined with a brusque no.

"I'd like some," Kinnard said. "I'm supposed to be getting fluids."

Joe got up and walked over to a small table stocked with bottles of water. "You should be readmitted to a hospital," he said as he uncapped one and passed it to Kinnard. "Under an assumed name, naturally."

"Maybe later."

When he finished drinking, Hick asked him where he'd had his burner phone hidden. "It wasn't on you. The barn was searched. Wasn't in the car."

"I left it in the woods where I stopped to switch car tags. Sealed in a ziplock and stuffed in a hole in a tree trunk. I told Morrow where he could find it. He retrieved it and brought it when he came to the hospital."

Joe thought, *This son of a gun doesn't miss a trick.* He wanted to throttle him, but he couldn't help but admire his craftiness. Of course, his life depended on outsmarting people. On deception.

Hick asked, "What about the barn?"

Shaw smiled wanly. "Belonged to my grandfather. He called it the garage. He had a couple of old Chryslers he restored and kept there. Before he died, he sold the cars, but the building came to me. I hadn't been there in years and was surprised to find it still standing."

"You grew up around here?"

"No. I only visited my grandparents from time to time."

He didn't volunteer where he hailed from, and Joe didn't bother asking. Neither did Hick. He probably would have told them that it was classified.

"The bow-and-arrow set was mine," Kinnard said, addressing Jordie. "It came with a canvas target stuffed with straw. I don't know what became of that. I never knew my grandfather owned a boat. Maybe he didn't. I don't know what that busted outboard was doing in there."

She didn't respond except to stare at him coldly.

Joe went back to something Kinnard had said earlier. "You want Panella."

"That scam he had going with Josh was little more than a hobby. He's into much more that than. After Katrina, he swooped in like a vulture and cashed in on the corruption and chaos. Racketeering, money laundering. No aversion to blood. My unit wanted him long before you guys got on to him.

"He's old-school. Tit for tat. Sicilian shit. For instance, on Panella's order Mickey Bolden slit a guy's belly open and threw him off a fishing boat into the Gulf."

As an aside to Jordie, he said, "That was no empty threat. It happened. Another agent witnessed it. Nothing he could do to stop it without blowing his cover." Coming back to Joe, he continued. "To get inside his operation, I made my initial contact with Bolden and told him that I was available for speciality work like that.”

“Like gutting people,” Jordie said.

Kinnard looked across at her. “Too messy. I’m tidier and more efficient than that.”

“Like blowing Mickey Bolden’s head to smithereens.”

“Would you rather have had him blow yours to smithereens? Or me to take the time to say, ‘Freeze, FBI, you’re under arrest’?” When she declined to say anything, he added, “I kill only the bad guys, Jordie. To keep them from killing other people.”

“But you still lie and deceive.”

“I do, yeah. Most times. Not always.”

The atmosphere between the two crackled. Joe couldn’t help but wonder the nature of some of the lies that Kinnard had told her while she was his captive. He tabled that interesting thought for the time being and concentrated on what Kinnard was saying.

“Bolden didn’t immediately take me up on my offer. I couldn’t look too eager or he would’ve smelled a rat. When that DEA agent got crosswise with the two key men, I had to take them out. I got myself arrested on purpose. It looked better, and jail is often safer than the streets. By the time What’s-his-name Dupaw released me, Panella had vamoosed to parts unknown and Josh was in protective custody pending testimony.

“So I worked the other case in Mexico, planning to wait out Panella like he’s been waiting out Josh. I think he forecast that Josh would renege.”

“Why do you think that?”

Jordie said, “Because Mr. Kinnard has this wild hair that Josh, not Panella, has access to the stolen money.”

Everyone looked at her. Wiley asked, “Does he?”

“No.”

Wiley looked back at Kinnard, who said, “My opinion differs, but we gotta catch him to find out.” He paused and touched his side as though it pained him. "Where are you on that? Any updates?"

Joe brought him up to speed, starting by telling him about Josh's unexpected call to him two nights before. "Here we were stomping around in the woods searching for him, my phone rings, it's the man himself."

He recounted that conversation, including mention of the bank account in Costa Rica, but omitting that Jordie had accompanied Panella on a trip there. He finished by telling him about the call he'd got before dawn. "Surprised me again."

"What'd he say?"

"He wanted verification that Jordie was safe."

Kinnard frowned. "That first call. Was he telling the truth, you think? Granted, Costa Rica would be a good stopover for somebody wanting to disappear. Gulf on one side, Pacific on the other. Rain forests and mountains to hide in. But have you confirmed that this bank account exists?"

"As of this morning, the money's still there. Intact. Never touched."

"No shit?"

"Our thought exactly," Hick said, and Joe noticed that he shot a glance at Jordie.

Kinnard, lost in thought, didn't catch it. "And Josh called you again this morning, indicating to me that his nerves are wearing thin. Whether or not he's got the money, he still betrayed Panella. He's rethinking his decision to abandon the protective arms of Uncle Sam."

"If he wasn't rethinking it before, he is now that I told him I talked to Billy Panella last night."

Kinnard looked at him with a start. "You *what?*"

"He thought it was you calling." Joe told him how the conversation had come about and related it in its entirety. "We had all the geegaws hooked up to the phone. Got nothing. Panella hung up in less than thirty seconds."

Kinnard absently rubbed the scar on his chin. "His attempt on Jordie's life was a bust. Josh still knows all his secrets and is inclined to make deals." Addressing them all, he said, "Our friend Panella can't be happy with the status quo, especially if he was left holding an empty bag. Do you realize how dangerous that makes him?"

"We do. That's where we were when you came in," Joe said. "Hick and I were encouraging Ms. Bennett to share with us any information she has regarding either Panella or her brother's whereabouts."

"Morrow told me you were questioning her." Kinnard looked across at her, but he referred to her in third person. "That's one reason I left the hospital in such a hurry. For a day and a half, I tried everything I could think of to get information out of her. Some of my tactics were unpleasant, even crude." He waited a beat, then looked at Joe. "If she knew anything, I believe she would have told me."

She hadn't told him about her weekend getaway with Panella. Joe would bet one of the swindler's millions on that. If Kinnard knew about that, he wouldn't be letting her off the hook now.

Another one of those awkward silences ensued. Kinnard was staring hard at Jordie as though compelling her to look at him. She kept her eyes downcast, looking only at her lap.

Eventually Adrian Dover stirred. "That's it then. Is my client free to leave?"

Joe said, "Ms. Bennett is free to go now, but she remains in our custody. Hick, tell Marshal Saunders she's ready to return to the hotel."

Hick stepped out and called down the hallway to the marshal.

Jordie said nothing as she stood up. Evidently she planned to walk out without acknowledging any of them, especially Shaw Kinnard. But when he spoke her name, she hesitated on the threshold before turning around. And if looks could kill.

Kinnard said, "You can't protect your brother from Panella, Jordie. He'll send the next Mickey Bolden, then the next, until he gets him. He won't give up until Josh's entrails are strung along behind him in the Gulf."

She held his stare for the length of a slow freight train, then said, "I wish I'd gone for the kill."

She and the lawyer walked out as Hick came back in, his cell phone to his ear. He mouthed, *Morrow.*

Joe, who'd stood up as a courtesy to the ladies when they left the room, sat down again and scrutinized Shaw Kinnard. He looked worse off now than he had when he'd made his grand entrance, and he'd looked like hell then. He was pale, the lines in his face more deeply carved, cheeks sunken.

Nevertheless, from deep within their shadowed sockets, his eyes projected a cold glint that signaled danger despite the signs of his physical debilitation. Joe didn't have that quality. Nobody would ever move out of his way simply because he focused on them.

If Kinnard had been affected by Jordie Bennett's parting shot, he didn't show it. To look at him, you'd think the words had bounced right off him like he was wearing armor. Of course, in order to work as deep cover as he did, detachment was essential. Everything was sacrificed to the job, even normal human emotions.

Joe thought about the comforting clutter in the den of his house, the constant commotion his kids created, the particular squeak his and Marsha's bed made when they moved on it together, and he didn't envy Shaw Kinnard his gravitas. It came at a price. Too high a one, in Joe's opinion.

He motioned toward the door through which Jordie Bennett had just passed. "I don't think she likes you."

"Nobody does. I'm used to it."

"She seemed to yesterday, though."

Kinnard snapped him a look of alerted interest. Maybe his armor wasn't so impenetrable after all.

But before he could speak, Hick abruptly ended his phone call and said, "We gotta get to Tobias."

Joe shot to his feet. "Bennett?"

Hick shook his head. "Royce Sherman."

"Who's that?" Kinnard asked.

"The guy who accosted Ms. Bennett in the bar."

Kinnard was so wobbly he had to use the table to stabilize himself as he stood up. "I'd like to talk to that jerk-off myself."

"Not gonna happen," Hick said. "He's in the morgue."

Chapter 28

Upon learning that the young man who'd played a key role in Friday night's events had turned up dead, they wasted only a few minutes arguing over whether or not Shaw would accompany them to Tobias.

Wiley and Hickam were resistant to the idea. He was adamant. To save time, he told them whether or not he rode with them, he would get there. They gave in.

"We'll stop somewhere along the way and buy some things to better disguise you," Wiley said over his shoulder as they left the interrogation room.

"Good thinking," Hickam said. "I'd hate to get struck by a bullet intended for Mr. Armed and Dangerous here."

Although each step sent a spike of pain through his side, Shaw kept up with them until they reached Hickam's car in the parking garage. After climbing into the backseat, he surreptitiously lifted his shirttail and peeled back the dressing to check his stitches. They were holding.

No doubt Jordie wished she'd done more damage with that propeller. If she had it to do over, she probably would plunge it into his throat. She'd said as much, and he believed her. She despised him.

His work was too high risk for him to get life insurance. Not that he had anyone to name as a beneficiary, because his job was also hazardous to personal relationships. Before now, that hadn't bothered him. Often he used innocent people in order to put away bad people. If someone in his wake was left emotionally scarred, it was a cost of doing business. Dirty job and all that.

But when Jordie Bennett had looked at him with unqualified hatred, he'd felt more than a twinge of conscience. That was a first, and it was uncomfortable.

As they wheeled out of the garage, Wiley got a call on his cell phone. Hickam didn't engage Shaw in conversation, which was fine with him. He laid his head back and dozed, waking only when Hickam parked outside a discount store. Wiley was still on his call, doing more listening than talking.

Hickam was back in under five minutes, bringing with him a sack, which he tossed over the car seat into Shaw's lap. "Not a place where I typically shop. That's the best I could do."

He'd bought an ugly maroon hoodie and a pair of sunglasses with black plastic frames and cobalt blue lenses. Shaw said, "These are fine."

"I thought they might be." Hickam made a point of looking at the pearl snaps on the new chambray shirt Morrow had bought for him.

Ignoring the agent's implied insult to his taste, he yanked the price tag off the hoodie. "So what about Royce Sherman's demise?"

"Morrow was on the fly, so he gave me the facts in shorthand. I'll tell you what I know as soon as Joe gets off the phone."

As though on cue, Wiley, riding shotgun, clicked off. "Sorry. That was Marsha. My wife," he said for Shaw's benefit. "We have a toilet problem at home, and she's threatening to apply a wrench to the plumber's privates if he doesn't get it fixed. Soon. What'd I miss?"

"Nothing. I waited on you," Hickam said. "First thing, Morrow emphasized that it hasn't yet been determined whether or not Royce Sherman's death relates to anything that happened Friday night."

"How'd he die?" Shaw asked.

"Gunshot to the head. Left frontal lobe. Close range."

"Suicide?"

"No gun found near the body, no powder on his hands."

"Homicide then," Shaw said.

"Fair bet."

Wiley asked if there had been signs of a struggle.

"No. He had cash and one credit card on him, so robbery doesn't appear to have been the motive. Morrow said it looked like the killer walked up to the open window and popped him."

"At home?"

"Driver's seat of his pickup truck. He'd pulled off the highway onto a side road."

"What for?" Shaw asked.

"Nobody knows."

"To take a leak?" Wiley ventured.

"No evidence of that. Morrow doesn't think he got out of the truck."

Shaw asked him about a shell casing.

"None found. No other bullet, either. Looks like the shooter only fired once. With intent."

Shaw thought on that and almost missed Hickam's saying, "But Morrow has a possible motive. The bartender—" he paused and looked at Shaw in the rearview mirror "—he's the one who put us onto you."

"Doesn't surprise me. He's former military, right? Saw action?"

"He mentioned Iraq."

Shaw nodded. He'd noticed the bartender's scrutiny of him and Mickey, which had been surreptitious but sharp. Nothing made a man more observant than a war zone where the enemy didn't wear a uniform.

Hickam said, "When the bartender heard about Royce's murder, he immediately called Morrow. Told him Royce was in the bar last night for hours, acting like a celebrity, knocking back whiskeys like they were Kool-Aid."

"Was his ol' lady with him?" Wiley asked. Turning to Shaw, he added, "He had a live-in who ragged on him."

Hickam said, "She was there, all right, and did more than rag on him. They got into it. Put on a floor show for the crowd, the bartender said. She stormed out with two girlfriends. No sooner had she left than Royce started tangling tongues with another girl. Around midnight, he and the newbie staggered out together. All this has been corroborated by the witnesses they've been able to locate."

"What does Royce's ol' lady have to say about it?" Wiley asked.

Hickam told them that Morrow himself had gone to pick her up at her place of employment. "She oversees the paint department in a big-box store. Morrow said she dropped to her knees and started wailing when he broke the news. Said her shock and tears looked genuine, but he brought her in anyway. She swears she didn't see or speak to Royce after leaving the bar."

"She lawyer up yet?"

"No, but he sent deputies to round up the two friends who drove her home last night. They were questioned separately, and their stories match hers. They took her back to the apartment she shared with Royce where they killed a couple bottles of wine toasting the good riddance of him. Around four a.m., the friends decided they were too drunk to drive home, so they crashed there at her place and got up this morning barely in time to drag themselves to work."

"What's Morrow's read on her alibi?" Wiley asked.

"He tends to believe it."

"I do."

At Shaw's succinct statement, Wiley turned around to look at him. Hickam was watching him in the rearview mirror. He said, "It doesn't sound like a crime of passion. Not the way you described the scene. The shooter fired once? With intent?" He shook his head. "That's not a pissed-off girlfriend's kind of kill. A recently dumped ol' lady would have emptied the pistol into him, then called the cops herself and told them where to find his sorry dead ass."

Wiley nodded, looking glum. "Unless evidence places the recent ex at the scene, I've gotta say I agree."

Shaw addressed Hickam in the mirror. "What about the newbie? The bartender said they left together."

"They *exited* together. They could have parted ways in the parking lot."

"Or not," Shaw said.

"Or not. Because there were partial footprints outside the passenger door. But first responders found the pickup empty except for Royce. ME estimated time of death between midnight and two a.m."

"Who called it in?" Wiley asked.

"The side road is a private drive that leads to a house way back in the woods. The property owner is retired. He and his wife were leaving for an early lunch. Royce's pickup had them blocked in. The missus got out to check, so it could be her footprints outside the truck. They're making casts."

"The retirees know Royce?"

"No."

"Okay," Wiley said. "Leaving Morrow, where? All he has so far are the current two women in Royce's life."

"They're trying to track down the newbie," Hickam said. "But Morrow didn't have a positive on her name, much less where to find her. He has a lot on his plate. Pulling off that act to spring you," he said to Shaw in the mirror. "Now this. He asked us to give him a heads-up when we're five minutes out."

Again, Shaw laid his head back and closed his eyes while the two of them lapsed into a conversation about an asshole of a coroner and the brisk trade he was doing this week.

Shaw tuned them out and thought about Jordie—more specifically how rancid her thoughts about him must be. *Why did you do the rest of it?* she'd asked, referring to all the awful things he'd subjected her to. Fear, deprivation, humiliation, browbeating.

A kiss.

What really sucked? She would forever think that the kiss had been just another maneuver to try to get information from her, and not a matter of life or death. His life, not hers. He'd had to kiss her. Simple as that.

Although it wasn't simple at all. He was a federal agent. She was a material witness in a criminal investigation. Which, by the rule book, placed her off-limits in capital letters. But he bent rules all the time, and he had no control over his dirty dreams.

A half hour later, Wiley roused him from a light sleep. "Kinnard? We're almost there."

Wiley placed the heads-up call to Morrow. Shaw put on the hoodie, wincing as he pushed his arms through the sleeves, which caused a strain on his incision and all the internal stitches. The blue lenses of the sunglasses probably made his complexion look sickly. At least it felt sickly. He was clammy all over. His limbs were weak and shaky. His side hurt like the very devil.

He wished he could lie down, close his eyes, and stretch out along the backseat the way he'd stretched Jordie out, adjusting her inert arms and legs, lifting her hair off her cheek.

Swearing under his breath because he couldn't stop thinking about her, he flipped the hood over his head, opened the back-

seat door, and got out. Instantly he was enveloped by the
swampy heat, made worse by the fleece hoodie. Goddamn
Hickam had chosen it on purpose.

The sheriff's department annex was an old and ugly building.
At the back corner of it was an unmarked employee entrance
where Morrow was waiting for them. He frowned at Shaw. "You
shouldn't have come."

"We tried telling him," Hickam said.

"You look worse off than Royce Sherman," the deputy said.

"I'm okay."

"Listen." Morrow held up his hand in front of Shaw's chest.
"Nobody in this department knows what we pulled this morning
except the dispatcher and the two deputies who posed as the ambulance drivers. All friends of mine. Not even the sheriff himself
knows. It gets out, I'll probably get canned."

"Nobody'll hear it from me. I know you stuck your neck out.
Thank you again."

"You're welcome. But it's not just that. This building is full
of officers who were in on the manhunt for you. They wouldn't
take kindly to you being here."

"They should thank me for the overtime."

"What I'm saying is, I don't think this cool getup is going to
fool anybody."

"You'd be surprised. What people aren't looking for, they
rarely see."

Still concerned, Morrow said, "If an officer does spot you, he
might shoot first and ask questions later."

"If it comes to that, feel free to blow my cover."

"At least you shaved."

"Part of the hospital's grooming and personal hygiene service." His identifying scar didn't show up as well without a
scruff, so he hadn't objected when the guy who'd given him the
bed bath started lathering his face.

"Don't say I didn't warn you." Morrow ushered them into

the building and led them down a short hallway to a doorway with a wired window. "Take a look."

Wiley and Hickam looked first, then it was Shaw's turn. He tipped down the sunglasses in order to see better. Inside the interrogation room, two officers were unsuccessfully trying to calm down a young woman whose head was bent low over her chest as she sobbed into her hands.

"Linda Meeker," Morrow said. "The girl who left the bar with Royce Sherman last night."

At that moment, she lowered her hands and raised her head to accept a tissue from a female deputy.

Shaw's first sight of her face came as a surprise. He had expected an entirely different sort. "She's just a kid."

"Sixteen. Barely. Turned last month."

Shaw watched Linda Meeker's apparent distress for another few seconds, then said, "Friday night while I was at it, I should've killed Royce Sherman, too."

The other three turned to him, but he didn't take back what he'd said.

Morrow covered an awkward silence by clearing his throat. "In here." He led them to the neighboring door and entered a small office. "I share it with another detective. He's off today."

They crowded into the already crowded space. Morrow closed the door and began his explanation without preamble. "Linda Meeker came in about half an hour ago under her own volition but at the urging of a friend, who drove her here when they learned about the murder."

"Who told her?" Shaw asked.

"They overheard people talking about it at the Dairy Queen."

Nobody said anything, but Shaw, Wiley, and Hickam exchanged glances.

Reading their dubiety correctly, Morrow chuffed. "It gets better. All of what I'm about to tell you came from the friend, because Linda isn't talking. According to the friend, Linda owns up to underage drinking, intoxication, getting chummy with Royce, and walking out of the bar with him. But she couldn't very well lie about that because there are three dozen witnesses to it.

"From there, the story goes murky. The friend contends that she was waiting for Linda outside. Linda and Royce exchanged fond farewells and parted ways. He took off in his pickup. The friend drove Linda to her—the friend's—house where they were supposed to have been all along. Linda upchucked a couple of times. The friend put her to bed. They slept until after ten o'clock this morning."

Wiley said, "Then picked up news of the murder at the Dairy Queen."

"Right."

"Wrong." Shaw, who'd propped himself against the doorjamb when they came into the room, left it for the corner of Morrow's desk and planted his butt on it before he fell down. "That girl's hysterical."

Hickam said, "Understandable. The guy she was mugging with twelve hours ago has since been shot in the head."

"I get that, but still." Shaw conjured an image of Linda Meeker. "Her teeth were chattering. She's out of her mind scared."

"Of her daddy," Morrow said. "He's a preacher. Hellfire and brimstone. Live snakes. Like that. Linda and her friend attended last night's Sunday evening services at the tabernacle, but I guess Daddy's sermon didn't take. Rather than going straight to the friend's house to watch TV, they sneaked off to the bar. She says her daddy will kill her for drinking, much less for—"

"—tangling tongues with Royce," Wiley said.

"Words to that effect. The friend says the reverend isn't the forgiving type, that his punishment will be harsh. Even though Linda knew that coming to us was the right thing to do, the friend said she practically had to hogtie her to get her here."

Morrow raised his chin toward the interrogation room next door. "Those two officers have been at her, singly and together, since she walked into our lobby and identified herself. All she's done is cry. Sob. Hasn't told us squat. Refuses to talk about it."

Wiley thoughtfully pulled on his lower lip. "She's a minor. Have her parents been notified that she's here?"

Morrow nodded. "Immediately after she came in. Which didn't help with her hysterics."

Nobody spoke for several moments, then Shaw asked, "What's the preacher's ETA?"

Hickam looked at him with suspicion and frowned. "Why?"

Shaw ignored him and repeated his question to Morrow.

The deputy consulted the wall-mounted clock. "They live out in the country, ten miles from town. Plus, the preacher subsidizes the offering plate by pouring concrete during the week. Mrs. Meeker wasn't sure which project he was on today and was going to have to locate him through the contractor." He glanced at the clock again and raised a shoulder. "Taking all that into account, ETA is twenty, thirty minutes maybe."

Shaw pushed himself off the desk. "Get some handcuffs."

Chapter 29

———◈———

"You're not eating anything."

Jordie looked up from the room service club sandwich Gwen Saunders had foisted on her. "I'm not hungry."

"You didn't eat breakfast, either."

She realized the U.S. marshal was only trying to be kind, but Jordie resented being spoken to as though she were a child. Apparently her resentment showed. Gwen refrained from insisting.

She ate the last of her own sandwich and folded her napkin beside her plate. "Should I call them to remove the table then?"

"Yes, I'm done," Jordie said.

"I'll ask the waiter to wrap up the sandwich. Maybe you'll want it later."

She gave the marshal a weak smile, but her appetite wasn't going to improve until circumstances changed, and she feared that they would change only for the worse, not the better. When every projected outcome was bad, what was she to hope for?

After the room service waiter left, Gwen made sure the door to the suite was bolted, then sat down at a desk and booted up her laptop. Agitated and restless, Jordie moved to the window, pushed back the drapes, and gazed out over the downtown sky-line.

Looking to her left across Canal Street, she was afforded a bird's-eye view of the French Quarter's narrow lanes. On the river, a paddle-wheeler full of tourists chugged along. The side-walks were congested with pedestrians.

Other people were actually having a good day. They were go-ing about their business, eating, drinking, sightseeing, enjoying the company of friends and family, untouched by tragedy, un-scathed by calamities of their own making.

She envied them their sense of freedom, even if it lasted only for today. Not since that December day in her childhood had she felt entirely free. The life-altering event of that day followed her everywhere. Even on occasions calling for celebration, it was a tenacious companion that spoiled her enjoyment. Nothing she did was free of its influence. It had dictated every major deci-sion. Much had been sacrificed to it.

Now, because of those few fateful moments, she was se-questered and under the guard of federal law enforcement offi-cers. Her future was uncertain, her life in jeopardy.

She wasn't even free to go to work and do the job she loved. As they'd left the FBI building, she'd asked Gwen if they could stop at her office, just long enough for her to check the status of certain upcoming events that were sizable jobs and would greatly contribute to her company's annual revenue.

Gwen had denied the request pleasantly but in a nonnego-tiable manner. "I'm sorry, Jordie. Agent Wiley wants you to be...protected."

"Watched."

"Same thing."

"No it isn't. Not at all."

Gwen hadn't countered because the distinction was unar-guable. However, she had interceded on Jordie's behalf and gotten Joe Wiley's permission to let one of Extravaganza's employees deliver to the hotel mail and paperwork that was time sensitive, such as work orders that required Jordie's approval before projects could move forward.

It was a small victory, though. Because, once delivered, Gwen had opened each envelope and package, inspecting the contents before handing it over to Jordie.

She suffered no illusions. She was under guard. True, Joe Wiley didn't wish any harm to come to her, but he was also mistrustful of her, as well he should be. She should have told him about that trip to Costa Rica.

She hadn't wanted to go, but Panella had given her no other choice. She'd hated every minute spent in his company, had willed away the memory of those three days, and had almost succeeded in pretending that she'd never allowed herself to compromise as she had.

But by telling Joe Wiley about the trip, Josh had resurrected it and all its residual ugliness, and merely lamenting it wasn't going to wash with the authorities. In the context of their case against Panella, the consequences of her being in Central America with him could be much more severe.

The sun shone in warmly through the window glass, but she hugged her elbows as though chilled at the prospect of testifying in court about that trip. Ruefully she thought back on ordinary days when catastrophes had amounted to a late floral delivery, a shortage of tablecloths, a misprint on a program, a grease fire in a hotel kitchen. Put into perspective, those had been mild mishaps. She wished now for problems that easily solvable.

The ones confronting her now seemed insurmountable. Not the least of them was Shaw Kinnard, more specifically the emotional tumult his very name engendered.

When she saw him not bloodied and dying but alive, learned that he wasn't a notorious murderer but an FBI agent, her relief had been profound. But it was instantly squelched. When she grasped the scope of his duplicity and its impact on her, she'd barely restrained herself from lunging at him, clawing at his eyes, hurting him.

In addition to being infuriated, she'd also been sick with humiliation over her gullibility. She would never forgive herself for being taken in, for thrilling to his sexual innuendos, even a little. She'd actually begun to believe that they were more than light teases meant to provoke her. She'd begun to think that the feelings underlying them were deeper and more meaningful, to think...

Things that now seemed incredibly naïve.

Suddenly the sunlight was too bright. It was making her eyes water. She jerked the drapes closed and said to Gwen, "I'm going to lie down for a while."

"A nap will do you good. Let me know if you need anything."

"I will."

"Jordie?"

She turned.

"What happened between you and Kinnard while you were in that garage?"

"You know what happened."

Speaking more softly, the marshal said, "Off the record. Woman to woman."

"Nothing," she said huskily. "Nothing happened."

Gwen knew she was lying and looked at her with something akin to pity. "He was only doing his job."

"I know." She went into the room and shut the door, leaning back against it and whispering, "And he's very good at it." Tears that had threatened earlier now spilled over her lower lids.

Angrily, she wiped them away. She would not cry over him.

Pushing herself away from the door, she headed for the bathroom only to be brought up short by a familiar sound—the distinctive buzz of a vibrating cell phone.

A cell phone? Hers was still in the FBI's possession. Hickam had last used it to call Shaw's burner when he staged his big reveal.

The sound persisted. She followed it over to the bureau where she'd stacked the items her office personnel had sent. Swiftly she checked the contents of padded envelopes and pushed lids off boxes until she found a box of printed invitations. She noticed now that the shipping label bore a company name she didn't recognize. She dumped out shrink-wrapped parcels of invitations, envelopes, and reply cards.

The box continued to vibrate.

She dug into a corner of it and lifted out the false bottom. There lay the phone, shimmying against the white pasteboard. Someone had gone to a lot of trouble to get this phone to her.

Instinctually, she snatched it up and answered. "Hello?"

"Jordie?"

Her heart clutched.

They already had Linda Meeker seated in a chair in the hallway outside the interrogation room when Morrow stalked through the door of his office, pushing Shaw along in front of him.

The young woman was hunched over, crying softly, her shoulders shaking, but she looked up, startled, when Morrow shoved Shaw into a chair diagonally across from the one in which she sat. He produced a pair of metal handcuffs and clicked one around Shaw's right wrist and the other around the leg of the chair, rattling them menacingly against the chrome to make certain they were secure.

"Your lawyer had better show up soon or I'm putting you in lock-up. And get that stupid hood off your head." He pushed back the hood of Shaw's sweatshirt, then turned away and headed toward his office, pausing when he drew even with the girl. In a much gentler voice, he asked, "Anything I can get you, miss?"

She shook her head.

"Your folks should be here soon." He started to move away, then glanced back at Shaw. "You. Don't bother her."

Shaw flipped him off with his free hand and pulled the hood back up to cover his head. Morrow scowled but said nothing else before returning to his office and pushing the door closed.

Shaw muttered several cuss words, then let his gaze drift from Morrow's office door to the girl, who was regarding him warily. He stared back for several moments, then said in a low voice, "Lighten up, kid. No matter what they brought you in for, you'll probably get off doing community service. Maybe some time in juvie, and it ain't that bad."

She immediately looked down.

Shaw rested his head against the wall and closed his eyes, but left them slitted so he could watch her.

She continued to stare into her lap where her hands were clasped but restless. She'd picked at a loose cuticle on her thumb until it had bled. One minute passed, then another thirty seconds or so. Shaw was beginning to think that his plan wasn't going to work, when she shyly looked across at him again.

"Are you sick?"

He kept his head against the wall but rolled it to the side and tipped down the sunglasses to peer at her over the frames. "Not exactly. They pulled me outta the hospital on an assault warrant."

"You were in the hospital?"

"Till about an hour ago."

"What's the matter with you?"

"Got stabbed." With his free hand he raised his shirttail to show her the bandage.

Her swollen red eyes rounded slightly. "Who stabbed you?"

He coughed a laugh. "Last time I'll piss her off."

"A woman?"

"Girlfriend. *Former* girlfriend. She got me with a broken, rusty outboard propeller."

"Mercy."

He laughed again. "I said a little stronger word than *mercy*."

When she smiled, Shaw shot her one back. "Good to see you smiling. I heard you crying earlier. From in there." He indicated the interrogation room. "Sounded rough."

Her lower lip began to tremble and misery settled over her whole being again.

"Look, kid," he said, speaking softly, "don't let these assholes get to you. The deputy said your folks'll be here soon. They'll get you out. Whatever it was you did—"

"I didn't do anything!"

Shaw just looked at her, knowing she desperately wanted to tell what had happened, explain it, clarify it, justify it, whatever. So he gave her the opportunity by saying nothing.

"I mean..." She licked her lips. "I went to this place where I shouldn't have gone. A bar? My friend and me had fake IDs." Then, speaking in a confidential undertone, in stops and starts, she told basically the same story her friend had told Morrow.

By the time she got to the part about leaving the bar, she was crying again in great sobs that made her choke, because she was trying to be quiet about it.

"Hey, shh," Shaw said. "Shh. Don't be so hard on yourself. Whatever happened, I don't think it was your fault."

"But it *was*. My friend told me I shouldn't leave with a stranger."

"She figured him for a loser, and sounds to me like she was right."

"But I...I...I didn't listen. I'd had so much to drink. And he told me I was hot, and that he'd never got that...that...*aroused* just by kissing." She ducked her head, asking softly, "You know what I mean?"

He frowned guiltily. "Yeah, us guys say shit like that when we want to get on a girl. Sometimes we mean it, though. Maybe he did."

"I don't think so. Because as soon as he pulled off the road and parked the truck..."

The words came tumbling out of her along with quarts of tears. It took every ounce of self-discipline Shaw had to remain sitting there, pretending to be nothing more than a sounding board with no vested interest whatsoever in who'd killed Royce Sherman.

The longer she talked, the more emotional she became. When she got to the nitty-gritty and described the fatal shooting, Shaw thought his heart was going to beat itself out of his chest.

"I couldn't believe it," she said around a watery gulp. "But I knew he was dead." She wiped her nose on her sleeve. "I was so scared. Petrified, you know?"

Shaw nodded.

"I just sat there, frozen. I don't even know for how long. When I came to my senses, I panicked. I guess I should've called the cops, but I knew they'd tell my daddy, and he'd skin me and hang me out to dry.

"So I called my friend and told her to come get me. I ran to the main road and hid in the bushes to wait for her. And all the time, I was so scared he'd come back and kill me, too. The wages of sin is death. That's what I was thinking."

She was crying so hard Shaw feared her breastbone would crack.

"I'm still scared he'll track me down. That's why I didn't want to tell anybody. They'll put it on the news. He'll find out my name. Then he'll find *me*."

Shaw was like a racehorse waiting for the bell, but he kept himself slouched in the chair and shrugged with unconcern. "You said you didn't see him."

"I didn't. But he might think I did. And I'm afraid he'll—"

At that moment, the double doors at the end of the corridor burst open and a middle-aged couple came barreling through.

The girl shrieked and collapsed upon herself in the chair.

The man, obviously the wrathful preacher, was dressed in work clothes and heavy boots. Linda's mother had an apron still tied around the waist of her flowered dress. Several deputies were right behind them, trying to stop the preacher's march down the hallway. The two deputies who'd been in the interrogation room with Linda emerged from it, assessed the situation, and quickly hustled her back into the room.

In the midst of the uproar, Morrow went unnoticed as he unlocked Shaw's handcuffs. They went back into his office where Wiley and Hickam were waiting.

Shaw pushed off the hood and removed the sunglassses. "How much did you hear?"

"Most," Wiley said.

Morrow said, "He seduced her to go with him. Pulled off the side of the road to—"

"—get blown by a just-turned sixteen-year-old," Shaw said. "A shot to the head was almost better than he deserved."

Wiley said, "A vehicle pulled up behind them. Royce Sherman thought it was the police. He zipped up. She righted herself."

Shaw took it from there. "The perp left the headlights on, so they couldn't tell what kind of car he was driving or who he was as he approached. She claims she never saw his face."

Wiley said, "That's about the time she started crying so hard, we couldn't understand anything else she said."

"What she said," Shaw told them, "was that she's scared to death that the killer will come after her."

"But she can't ID him."

"Not by his looks." Shaw paused for effect. "But she might by his voice."

Nobody said anything for several seconds, then Wiley fell back a step. "Oh, Christ."

"Yeah," Shaw said grimly. "The killer spoke a few words to Royce before he shot him. Linda's not sure what he said because he talked funny. Like her uncle Clive. Who has this black thing he holds up to his voice box."

Chapter 30

———◦◦◦◦———

J ordie pressed the contraband cell phone against her ear and
sat down on the edge of the bed. Guiltily, she glanced toward
the connecting door to the living area of the suite and spoke in a
hushed voice. "Josh? How—"

"Are you watching TV? Have you heard?"

"What? Heard what? How did you know I'd get this phone?"

"I didn't. Just hoped. You're at Extravaganza now?"

"No. The FBI has me sequestered in a hotel. But they allowed some mail to be brought—"

"Turn on the TV."

"Josh, where are you? Are you all right?"

"Turn on the TV! If you're in a hotel, you have a TV. Turn it
on."

"Why?"

He puffed a sound of impatience tinged with panic. "Turn.
On. The. TV."

She reached for the remote on the nightstand. "All right. It's
on."

He told her the channel to tune in. As she navigated the

aggravating menus inherent to hotel televisions, she said, "I've been so worried, Josh. You shouldn't have run away. Are you all right?"

"No, I'm not all right. Especially not after this."

"After what?"

"He's gonna kill me!"

"Who?"

"Who do you think?" he asked, his voice going shrill.

She recognized the symptoms. He was in full-blown panic mode.

"Josh, listen, please. You are in terrible trouble."

"Well no shit, Sherlock."

She rolled her lips inward to contain a retort. "I'll help you. You know I will. But you must calm down and—"

"Calm down? *Calm down?* He's out there! I know it. And he'll kill me."

His doomsday predictions continued in Jordie's right ear as she strained with the other to hear the television's audio and piece together the story that had her brother completely un-hinged.

"Are you watching?" he asked.

"Yes." A photo of a young man appeared on the TV screen, astonishing Jordie with its familiarity. In the picture, he didn't have a goatee, but she recognized the insolent grin immediately. Until now, she hadn't even known his name.

"He was at the bar Friday night. He talked to me."

"Oh I know all about it," Josh said. "He was on TV the other night, blabbing to a reporter about your little interlude."

"Fortunately I missed that."

"He talked about sharing a drink—"

"We didn't share—"

"Bragged about his 'brush with death.' If news reports are correct, he was back at that same bar last night retelling the story."

"So what? He's milking his fifteen minutes. There's no cause to panic over—"

"I wouldn't be panicked if he hadn't turned up dead!"

Her heart tripped. "What?"

"Murdered, Jordie. Murdered. I thought you were watching TV."

"I am. I—"

"He was found shot in the head. It happened after he left the bar where he had an *audience* while boasting about meeting you. Now do you understand why I'm panicked?"

On the screen now was video showing a pickup truck. Its windshield was blood-spattered. It was in a woodsy setting surrounded by crime scene tape, squad cars, and uniformed men.

"That's awful," she murmured. "But he probably got into an argument with someone last night. I'm sure his murder had nothing to do with me."

"Are you stupid?" Josh shouted.

"How could it involve me?"

"Before I called you, they were interviewing this hairy, tattooed bartender. He said Royce Sherman was acting like a big shot, bragging about the role he'd played in the 'Panella-Bennett case.' That's how they phrased it."

"That's what it is, Josh."

"Don't tell me this guy's murder has nothing to do with you. With us." He made a choking sound. "I'm never going to get away from him, am I?"

"Panella?"

"Of course Panella! Who do you think?"

"Please calm down. Tell me where you are. I'll come—"

"No!"

"Josh, you cannot outrun the authorities."

"I already have. I'm not worried about them. It's Panella. You know what I think?" Without waiting for her to answer, he rushed on. "I don't think he ever left the country. I think he's been lurking around, waiting for me to—"

"—to do something crazy like leave the government's protection?"

"I knew it! I knew you'd side with them."

"Dammit, Josh, I'm on your side."

"And you're probably mad because I told Wiley about Costa Rica. I had to, Jordie. I didn't say anything bad about you. Only that you went with Panella."

She refrained from pointing out how damaging even that much might be. It also occurred to her that even though this was the first time they'd spoken in six months, Josh hadn't asked after her welfare. Knowing full well the ordeal she'd suffered this week because of him, he hadn't apologized or expressed concern over her situation. She wouldn't have expected him to. Nevertheless, it hurt.

As evenly as possible, she said, "If you want my help you have to tell me where you are."

"No way. Panella's close. I can *feel* him. He's probably watching you. If I told you where I am, you'd lead him right to me. He'll never give up. I know him. He won't stop looking for me till I'm dead."

"That's paranoia talking, Josh. Billy Panella is thousands of miles away."

"No. He's here. He killed that guy last night."

"That's ridiculous."

"No it's not."

She envisioned him shaking his head in the manner of an obstinate child, red-faced and unyielding, impossible to reason with.

"That dumb redneck interfered with Panella's plan to have you killed. Worse, he was shooting off his mouth about it last night. The bartender said he took credit for you being alive. To Panella that would be a personal affront. He wouldn't let that slide."

On the television, a news reporter was trying to get a sound bite from Deputy Morrow, whom she recognized from her rescue the day before. He was pushing his way through a throng, saying nothing except, "No comment at this time."

The undaunted reporter turned to the camera and said, "Although authorities are reluctant to disclose details of the homicide, unnamed sources have told our newsroom that Royce Sherman was killed execution style with a single gunshot."

Beginning to worm through Jordie was a suspicion that Josh's ranting wasn't so farfetched after all. What he was saying came uncomfortably close to Shaw's warning. *You can't protect your brother from Panella.*

Nevertheless, she hastily dismissed the possibility that Panella was nearby and doing his own killing rather than hiring professionals. That was too frightening a thought to entertain.

Besides, whenever her brother was having a meltdown of this caliber, one of them had to remain calm and rational. She said, "For the sake of argument, let's say that Panella never left the United States. Why would he care about a smart-aleck bragging about his encounter with me? He would have much more important things to worry about."

"That's right. He does. Me! He's got *me* to worry about. That's what I'm trying to tell you! He's going to kill me."

"If you're that afraid of him, Josh, turn yourself in."

"They'll put me in prison and throw away the key."

"Well, which are you more afraid of?" she asked angrily. "Prison or Billy Panella?" She could just see him worrying the corner of his lip between his teeth. At least he was no longer screeching. She reigned in her own temper and switched to a cajoling tone.

"You've placed yourself in a no-win situation, Josh. You played both ends against the middle and lost, leaving you only two choices. Turn yourself in, or continue living in fear of Panella until either he or a hired assassin ferrets you out.

Clearly, your best option is to surrender yourself to the authorities."

"And be punished for things that aren't my fault."

"They *are* your fault."

"You want me dead, don't you? You hope I die. You want me out of your life forever. You always have."

She bowed her head and rubbed her hairline where a headache was coming on. "Don't say things like that. You know they're not true."

"When Panella gets to me, when they find me with a bullet in my head, you'll have finally gotten what you want, which is rid of me!"

With that, the phone went dead.

———

After Shaw dropped his bombshell in Morrow's office, things happened quickly.

Morrow turned over the questioning of Linda Meeker to the two detectives who'd been interviewing her before. Her father's bellowing could be heard throughout the building, publicly denouncing her for a long list of sins that would land her in Hell.

If Shaw had had the strength to lay into the judgmental son of a bitch, he would have. But he barely had the stamina to walk to the car with Wiley and Hickam. He stripped off the hot-as-Hades hoodie and the sunglasses and practically fell into the backseat.

He got out of sight just in time. Before they were even clear of the parking lot, two news vans in an obvious race pulled up in front of the sheriff's office.

"Crap," Hickam said.

"It was only a matter of time," Wiley said. "Two murders originating in one backwoods bar within a few days? Had to make news even if it's dismissed as a bizarre coincidence."

"Morrow said he would personally flay and filet anyone who leaked the girl's name to the media," Shaw said. "But it'll get out."

"Morrow's gonna have people guarding her house," Wiley said.

Shaw was only marginally reassured. He trusted Morrow, but he thought about the sloppy surveillance that had been done on Jordie.

Hickam said, "It'll really turn into a circus if Panella's name gets attached to the crime."

"Morrow's going to keep that speculation out of the media," Wiley said.

"Except it's not speculation."

Wiley conceded Shaw's point. "It's scary to think he's in the area. But I'd be lying if I pretended I'm not a little glad. I'd love to nail the bastard once and for all without having to go to the edge of nowhere in order to find him." He looked at Hickam. "You notify the marshal's service?"

"Gave the guy a hard-on."

Wiley smiled and watched as the reporters and cameramen rushed the entry of the sheriff's office. "I hate leaving Morrow alone to stamp out that wildfire."

"He'll handle it. He's solid," Shaw said as he dug his thumb and forefinger into his eye sockets. He'd never been so tired.

As though reading his mind, Wiley said, "You're going back to the hospital."

Shaw lowered his hand. "Hell I am. We gotta move Jordie Bennett to a safe house."

"We don't need your help," Hickam said.

"Didn't say you did."

"We can handle it without you."

"You can, but you're not."

Hickam shrugged. "Fine. Your funeral."

"You wish."

"Hey, cut it out," Wiley said. "You two are worse than my kids."

For the past fifteen minutes Hickam had been looking like he could chew nails. He chose now to vent, speaking to Wiley as though Shaw weren't there. "That dog-and-pony show he put on back there wasn't a legal interrogation. Nothing Linda Meeker told him can ever be used in a court of law."

"Wasn't illegal," Shaw said. "Wasn't even an interrogation. I didn't ask her a single question. Not *one*. I didn't lead the conversation, she did. All I did was listen." He looked at Hickam in the rearview mirror and raised his eyebrows, inviting him to contradict him.

Hickam said, "Too bad that disarming tactic didn't work on Jordie Bennett. Neither did flexcuffs and a blindfold. Thirty-six hours with her, and you got zip."

Shaw rested his head against the back of the seat and closed his eyes. "She didn't have anything to tell."

"Unless you count her tropical vacation with Billy Panella."

Shaw opened his eyes and raised his head only high enough to meet Hickam's smug gaze in the mirror, and it made him terribly uneasy. "Wiley?" The other agent turned his head and looked at him. "What's Quick-Draw talking about?" He listened for five straight minutes, liking none of what Wiley told him.

Wiley finished by saying, "She can't deny being with him down there, but claims not to know anything about the money her brother deposited or Panella's plans to return for it."

"So you see," Hickam said, "by relocating her, we're not sure what we're preventing. Another attempt on her life? Or a romantic rendezvous with Billy Panella?"

In Shaw's mind, he was shouting, *Fuck me!*

But he didn't respond to Hickam's goading. He didn't say a word, only returned his head to the back of the seat and closed his eyes.

———◆———

Joe Wiley called Gwen Saunders from the hotel lobby to tell her that they were on their way up, so Jordie was seated on the living area sofa when Gwen unbolted the door and they filed in. Wiley was in the lead, then Hickam.

Behind him came Shaw, whom she hadn't expected to see.

When their eyes met, the connection was electric, anger and hostility arcing hotly between them. But for all the ferocity of his gaze, Shaw looked ghoulish, his eyes alight with fever, shoulders slumped, tread unsteady.

Joe Wiley pointed him into a chair, saying, "Sit down before you fall down." Then to Jordie and Gwen, "We've got some disturbing news."

"We heard about it," Gwen said. "Jordie was in her bedroom resting and saw the story about Royce Sherman's murder on TV."

"It's dreadful," Jordie said, "but I don't believe it had anything to do with me."

"We hoped it was a coincidence, too, but we rushed down to Tobias to check it out." Wiley tipped his head toward Shaw. "He talked to the young woman who was with Sherman when he was shot." He covered the main points of that conversation. "Then she told him something that knocked our socks off. The killer talked through an electrolarynx."

Jordie sucked in a deep breath and released it slowly. "So, it was Panella?"

The three men had been watching her closely to gauge her reaction, and she could tell they were shocked by the resignation behind her statement.

Hickam was the first to speak. "You aren't surprised?"

"Not all that much, no. I'll be right back."

She left her seat on the sofa, went into her bedroom, and retrieved the cell phone from between the mattresses where she'd hidden it until she decided what to do about it. This new information had made the decision for her.

She went back into the living room and held out the phone where the agents could see it. She explained how she'd come by it. "Josh knows I proofread all printed matter before sending it on to the client. It was safe for him to assume that the box of invitations would eventually wind up in my hands."

"What if somebody else had answered when he called that phone?" Hickam asked.

"He'd have hung up, I suppose. Or if he never had need of it, it would have gone unused, forever a mystery as to how it got into that box. When he heard about Royce Sherman, he panicked and called me. He believes Panella killed Sherman and is afraid that he'll be next."

Hickam took the phone from her and turned it on.

While they waited for it to boot up, she related her conversation with Josh. Her account was interspersed with questions from either Hickam or Wiley, who asked when she was going to get around to telling them about the phone and the call.

"I admit I hadn't decided whether to tell you at all. Josh was having a paranoid episode. I was tempted to keep that line of communication with him open."

"Is he suicidal?" Hickam asked.

"Even in the throes of a panic attack he's never threatened to take his own life, and he didn't today. But I believe he's on the brink of a complete breakdown. I thought that if I kept the phone, maybe I could eventually talk him down, persuade him to surrender. But in light of what that young lady told Shaw..."

At the slip of his name, she automatically looked in his direction. Since entering the suite, he hadn't uttered a word. No questions for her. No comments on anything she'd said. He had remained perfectly still in his chair, silent and listening, riveted on her, as watchful as a hawk.

Her involuntary glance at him now produced a purl of

awareness, low and deep and sexual. It made her furious that he still had the power to evoke a reaction like that. It made her angry at herself for being susceptible.

Going back to the others, she said, "In view of what the girl said about the killer's voice, Josh's hysteria is justified." She paused, then added, "Of course we could all be mistaken."

Dangerous place, denial.

As though Shaw had spoken the words again, she looked across at him. He hadn't moved. His predatory gaze was still steady on her.

She said, "Royce Sherman could've gotten under anyone's skin. Any number of people could have followed him from the bar to that side road."

"It was all I could do to keep from decking him when Hick and I interviewed him," Wiley said. "So I would tend to agree with you, Ms. Bennett. Except I just wonder how many of Royce's potential grudge bearers would use an electrolarynx?"

The answer being obvious, as were its implications, Jordie sat down on the sofa and folded her arms across her middle in a subconscious gesture of self-protection.

"I don't think Uncle Clive killed him," Hickam said.

"Me either." Wiley sighed and looked down at Jordie. "This public hotel has become too public for comfort. As a precaution, we're going to move you to a safe house."

"You checked me in under an assumed name, and only we in this room know that I'm here."

"I'm not willing to bet your life on that," Wiley said.

She didn't argue with him, but she didn't believe that relocating her would guarantee her safety. Panella had far-reaching tentacles and thirty million dollars' worth of resources. If he wanted to find her, he could.

All this time, Hickam had periodically been calling the unknown number on the cell phone. He called it again now. They could all hear it ringing, but there was no answer.

"I've called back several times," Jordie told him. "He hasn't answered."

"No hint of where he is?" Wiley asked.

"I begged him to tell me. He refused. He's afraid that Panella is watching me, that if I go to him, Panella won't be far behind."

Wiley scratched his head. "Josh must be in the general vicinity, or he wouldn't have seen that news story about Sherman. What I don't get? Once he retrieved the car from the public storage place, he could've gone anywhere on the continent. Instead he returned here where recapture is much more likely. Also the first place Panella would look for him. So why'd he come back? It's not like he has a passel of friends and relatives who'd give him a place to lay low. In fact, there's only one person on earth who'd do that."

On the last sentence, the agent's tone changed and he assumed an interrogator's stance in front of Jordie. She shifted her gaze to Hickam, who was holding the cell phone in his palm. Suddenly it looked incriminating. Going back to Wiley, she said, "I'm certainly not harboring him. How could I be?"

"By not telling us where he's hiding."

"I don't know! I've told you everything that was said during my conversation with him. I impressed on him that his best option was to turn himself in and take his punishment."

"He wouldn't hear of it," Wiley said.

"Not...not exactly."

"Then what exactly, Ms. Bennett? What did he say?"

You hope I die. "Nothing. He hung up. But at the very least I believe I got him to thinking about surrendering."

She looked at each of them in turn, gauging how much or how little of what she'd said they believed. The only return stare that unsettled her was Shaw's. She looked away from its unblinking incisiveness.

After a moment, Wiley said, "Well, every law enforcement officer in the state and beyond is looking for him. He'd be better off surrendering before he's caught, or injured in the process of being captured."

"Or before Panella finds him," Hickam said.

"Hope to God that doesn't happen. But we can't make a strong case for surrender until he contacts one of us again." Wiley gestured to the phone Hickam had laid claim to. "Now that he's connected with Ms. Bennett, he'll more likely call her than me, so get one of the techies to sit on that phone like a hen on an egg."

The meeting broke up after that. Hickam sat down at the desk and began making calls. Gwen excused herself to do the same. Wiley walked over to Shaw and ordered him out of the chair.

"I'm driving you to the hospital."

"Fuck that."

"Enough with the tough-guy shit. You're only human."

"Oh, I'm human all right."

"Okay, so give yourself time to recover."

"I'll recover."

"Not unless you rest."

"I'm staying."

"Look," Wiley said angrily, "I don't want you dying on me of pure bullheadedness."

"I'm not going to die." Looking past Wiley, he addressed Jordie directly. "Panella is. I'm gonna kill him."

Chapter 31

Gwen Saunders was joined by two other U.S. marshals—fit young men in jeans and black t-shirts—who were called in to assist with Jordie's relocation. Among the marshals, Wiley, and Hickam, it was decided to wait until after full dark to make the transfer.

Shaw supported the postponement. That gave them several hours to plan how they would go about it and which safe house in the area would provide the best protection.

Shaw left the logistics of the process for the rest of them to sort out and took Wiley up on his suggestion that he sleep during the intervening hours. He didn't feel the need to be hospitalized, but his body was demanding some downtime.

"Take Gwen's bedroom," Wiley said. "She's going to be busy and won't be using it."

Jordie was in a huddle with Hickam and the marshals. Sensing his gaze, she looked at him, then quickly away. She was still furious at him for playing her. Or maybe her trip with Panella was the reason for her refusal to acknowledge him. Either way, she couldn't avoid him forever. Even if she planned to, he wouldn't let her.

He went into the bedroom and shut the door. The surgeon had instructed him not to get his incision wet for at least a week. He showered anyway, holding a plastic laundry bag over the wound with one hand, soaping and shampooing with the other.

He exchanged the bandage for a fresh one, which was among the items in the kit given him by the surgeon before leaving the hospital. Morrow had returned it to him when they were in Tobias. Also in the kit were several blister packs of antibiotics and a bottle of pain pills. He took an antibiotic capsule, but skipped the pain pill. He needed sleep, but not a hangover.

When he emerged from the bathroom, there was a room service tray on the nightstand. He scarfed down the grilled cheese sandwich and bowl of chicken noodle soup, reminding himself to identify and thank the Good Samaritan later. After finishing the meal, he gratefully lay down.

He wanted badly to throttle Jordie for not telling him about her Costa Rican excursion with Billy Panella.

He wanted badly to fuck her anyway.

Sliding his hand into his jeans, he tested the equipment and discovered to his relief that, despite the catheter, the anesthesia, and his overall weakness, it was in working order.

He was fantasizing about it in sexual congress with Jordie when he dropped into a deep slumber.

A tap on the door woke him. He sat up quickly and hissed a curse for forgetting to favor his left side. The room was dark. He checked the time. He'd slept nearly six hours and could tell already that it had done him good.

Hickam was standing in the open doorway. "Showtime's in about twenty minutes."

"Thanks."

Rather than retreat, Hickam stayed. "Do you ever get tired of it?"

"What?"

"Manipulating people. Misleading them. Lying."

"Everybody lies."

"That's your excuse?"

Shaw set his feet on the floor and stood up. "I don't need an excuse. I've got a job."

He left Hickam standing there and went into the bathroom. He used the toilet, splashed his face with cold water, and swished with the wintergreen mouthwash provided by the hotel. But then he braced his hands on the rim of the basin and stared into it, Hickam's question swirling around in his mind like the tap water around the drain.

Raising his head, he gave his cold eyes and uncharitable visage a good, hard look in the mirror, seeing himself as other people must. "Goddamn Hickam," he muttered.

Back in the bedroom, he checked his pistols, holstering the nine-millimeter on his belt and slipping the palm pistol into the customized scabbard inside the shaft of his boot. He put two of the blister packs of antibiotics in his jeans pocket, then went into the living room, where the others were similarly preparing.

Wiley asked, "How was your nap? Side hurt?"

"Like hell, but I feel better. Anything important happen while I was out?"

"We contacted the printing company that did the party invitations. Took them no time at all to look up the order. It was placed and filled over six months ago. Event was bogus, and Josh used a fake name, but the invitations were shipped to the address where he was living when he turned himself in. Ms. Bennett cleaned out the apartment and paid off his lease. She claims not to have found any invitations or such."

"He probably received stuff there, but squirreled it away someplace else."

"That's my thought, too," Wiley said. "He stocked the essentials plus anything he might need in order to contact his sister."

Shaw, who'd never met Josh, asked, "Is that a compulsion, you think?"

"Contacting her, you mean? Yeah, I think so. He had the gumption to steal millions, but then cratered before we really got tough with him. He had the wherewithal to defy us and escape, but he can't resist calling and checking in, with us, with Ms. Bennett. What does that make him, gutsy or a goofball?"

"Both."

"Right. You never know what you're dealing with. Anyhow, Hick and I think he had his own safe house somewhere around here all set up and waiting for him."

"Won't argue that. Speaking of safe houses, how safe is the one you're moving Jordie to?"

"Safe," Wiley replied, looking peeved for having been asked.

"What's the game plan?"

"Three black SUVs leave the hotel garage one behind the other. Motorcycle police block traffic for their exit. Once they leave the hotel, each peels off in a different direction."

"You don't think that will draw attention?"

"Exactly. If Panella is out there, he'll think she's in one of the SUVs. Also as a decoy, we're leaving Hick's car in the garage where we parked it when we got back from Tobias. But one of our agents left another car parked on the street. As soon as the SUVs peel out, Hick'll bring that car into the garage and pick up Gwen, Jordie, and me at the elevator."

"How many officers watching the hotel?"

"A dozen uniforms. That many more undercovers in and around the lobby and at all the entrances."

"They know to be looking for Panella?"

Wiley nodded. "To refresh memories, we circulated the last known photograph of him."

"What's my job?"

"To make yourself scarce until morning. You have somewhere to stay?"

"Plenty of flophouses in New Orleans."

"We'll reconvene early in my office. Hick and I will show you everything we have on Josh Bennett. Maybe you can spot a clue we've overlooked that would lead us to his hidey-hole."

Shaw thought over the difficult chore ahead of them. He wasn't typically a team player, and he wasn't being embraced by everyone on this team, where cooperation was absolutely necessary. He looked over at Hickam, then came back to Wiley with a silent question mark.

Wiley, following both his glance and his thought, said, "He doesn't like you."

"I'm crushed. But is he gonna continue being a pain in my ass?"

"I'll talk to him, encourage him to keep an open mind where you're concerned, because your particular skills might come in handy. Hick and I aren't fond of Josh, but we don't want Panella getting to him before we do."

"I want to nail Panella."

"So you've said." Wiley cocked his head to one side. "This hasn't turned personal, has it?"

Shaw just looked at him.

Wiley sighed. "I was afraid of that." Then he eyed Shaw up and down. "Try to stay out of trouble overnight. Don't scare anybody. And whatever you do, don't get arrested. I can't take two doses of Xavier Dupaw in one day."

Shaw gave him a wry grin of understanding.

Gwen Saunders approached them. "Mr. Kinnard, are you out of my bedroom? I need to get my things."

"Call me Shaw, and thanks for letting me crash in your room. Did you order the food for me?"

She smiled. "You looked like you needed sustenance."

"I did. Thanks. Where's Jordie?"

"We got a vest for her. She's putting it on." She indicated the closed door on the other side of the suite, then headed toward her own bedroom.

Hickam summoned Wiley over to a table where he was conferring with the marshals over the layout of the hotel and the routes they would take for their exit. Shaw pretended to be choosing an apple from a basket of fruit on the minibar. When no one was looking, he slipped into Jordie's bedroom and closed the door.

Without looking around, she said, "I'm coming."

She had changed out of the pants suit into a pair of black jeans, a button-up white shirt, and sneakers. She was bent over the bed, zipping up a duffel. When done, she turned around and, seeing Shaw, drew up tall, her eyes narrowing with animosity. She pulled the duffel off the bed and walked to where he stood against the door.

"Get out of my way."

"I had to make you believe it, Jordie."

"I said, get out of my way."

"There were times I hated myself for—"

"Then that makes two of us."

"Other times I hated you for making objectivity impossible."

"Oh, that's pretty. Be sure to write it down so you don't forget it. You can use it to manipulate your next hostage. That is, after you run out of cute innuendos, half truths, flat-out lies, and assorted other scare tactics." She made to go around him, but he sidestepped and blocked her.

"Not all of it was manipulation and lies."

She huffed a laugh. "Nothing you say will ever make me believe that."

"Good. I'm tired of talking."

He cupped her face between his hands, pushed his fingers up into her hair, and held her head in place as he turned them so that her back was to the door.

She went rigid. "If you don't get your hands off me, I'll yell this bloody place down."

He lowered his face close to hers. "When I was lying there with that propeller sticking out of my gut, you didn't run. You didn't escape. Why not?"

"If I had it to do over—"

"You do. Here. Right now. You can yell this bloody place down. But I think that if you wanted to, you would have already." His whisked his mouth across hers.

"Don't."

She tried to turn her head aside, but he held it fast between his hands and kissed the corner of her mouth.

"Stop it. I mean it, Shaw. I don't want this."

"No, you don't *want* to want it. Big difference."

Then he angled her head and kissed her the way he'd imagined, the way his drugged mind had fantasized it, the way he'd craved to from the first time he got a good look at her face.

He didn't care how many ethics codes he was violating, or how many federal agents were in the next room, or—God forgive him—if Billy Panella himself was on the other side of this door, unless she put words into action and stopped him, he was going to get carnal with her mouth. He was going to mate with it for as long as she and time allowed.

She didn't stop him. When he pressed his tongue into her mouth, it met with no resistance. After a slow dance with hers, he withdrew it just far enough to touch the tip of it to the center of her upper lip, just inside, just barely a flick. It was so blatantly erotic that her breaths started coming as hard and fast as his. Wanting more, he sent his tongue deep again.

She let go of the duffel bag. It dropped softly onto the toe of his boot. He pushed it aside, inched closer to Jordie and leaned into her, making adjustments in alignment that fit them together like puzzle pieces and caused her breath to catch. He hated the damn bulletproof vest that shielded her breasts from the pressure of his chest.

Her hand came up between them. She ran her thumb across the scar on his chin, then scraped it lightly with her teeth. He took a love bite of her wet, plump lower lip. Then they were kissing again, frantically. Maybe it was the mad recklessness of this whole thing that made it so goddamn good.

But he thought it was more the woman than the circumstances that had him about to combust.

He slid one hand down her front, pausing to grind the heel of it against where he approximated her nipple would be, before moving it lower, pushing it between her thighs and caressing her there. She gasped and arched into his gently massaging hand.

Lifting his face away from hers, he whispered roughly, "I'm going to have you, Jordie."

Her eyes were still angry, but now also lambent with arousal as she stared into his.

"You know it as well as I do, don't you?"

Slowly, she nodded.

A knock sounded on the door. "Ms. Bennett?" Hickam said.

Shaw squeezed her lightly before withdrawing his hand. He backed away from her then nudged her aside and opened the door. "She's ready."

Before Hick left the suite, Joe reviewed some last-minute details with him. "Got your earpiece in?"

Hick tapped his ear.

"Keep it open. I'll advise when we get on the elevator."

"The spare car is parked across the street and about half a block down from the entrance to the garage." Hick held up the key fob that another agent had delivered to the hotel earlier. "Soon as the SUVs clear the garage, I'll wheel in there." He looked over at Shaw Kinnard, who was munching an apple. "When you sent me to fetch Ms. Bennett, he was in the bedroom with her. He opened the door. Steam escaped."

Before Joe could remark on that, Kinnard approached them. "Sure you don't want my help?"

"We got it." Hick lifted the maroon hoodie from off a chair and passed it to him. "Don't forget this. You don't want to be recognized and apprehended as you roam the streets tonight."

Kinnard made his opinion of the blankety-blank fleece furnace clear, but, anchoring the apple between his teeth, he pulled it on.

Hick left, taking the ladies' bags to stow in the trunk. The marshals went with him to take up their positions in the parking garage.

Kinnard finished his apple and tossed the core into a trash can. "Guess I should shove off."

"Transportation?"

"I'll figure something out."

Joe had no doubt of that.

Kinnard didn't say good-bye to Jordie but paused at the door of the suite and shot her a telling look before going out. Joe pretended not to notice and walked over to her. "All set, Ms. Bennett?"

"Did you tell him about Costa Rica?"

"Who, Kinnard?"

"Did you?"

"He needed to know, especially now that it appears Panella isn't in a distant land after all." He paused, then asked, "Are you afraid he'll retaliate?"

"He can't. He's a federal agent."

Joe waited a second then said drily, "I was referring to Panella."

"Oh."

While the egg was still congealing on Jordie's face, Gwen, who'd been on her cell phone, quickly clicked off. "They're ready downstairs."

The three of them left the suite and walked along the corridor to the elevator that provided hotel guests direct access to the parking garage. Joe, speaking into the mike on his lapel, communicated to all officers involved that they were on their way.

No one said anything as they rode the elevator down, but Joe covertly studied Jordie's reflection in the brass door. Her expression was thoughtful, her brow slightly furrowed. He wondered what, exactly, had made her so contemplative.

Maybe it was concern over Kinnard knowing about her romantic getaway with Panella, whom he had sworn to either put away or blow away. Meanwhile, she and Kinnard were steaming up bedrooms. Strange dynamics for a budding romance.

He'd called Marsha earlier to tell her that he would be late—again. He recapped everything that had happened in Tobias and shocked her with their discovery about Shaw Kinnard.

"He's good. Fooled Jordie Bennett. The rest of us, too. Hick almost shot him."

"What's he like?"

"Like?"

"As a person."

Joe hem-hawed a description, circled the wagons, backtracked, tried again. Marsha interrupted and asked, "Is he Maverick, Iceman, or Goose?"

"Is this a trick question?"

"Which is he?"

"I don't know, Marsha. He's—"

"Of the three."

"Then Iceman."

"Okay."

Before hanging up, he'd asked, "Which am I?"

"Goose. Definitely."

A slightly disappointing answer.

When the elevator stopped and the doors slid open, the two young marshals were there to greet them. One held up a hand. "Hold tight. SUVs are rolling."

Through the open elevator door, Joe watched the three vehicles whiz past. They looked intimidating and official with darkly tinted windows and flashing lights in their tricked-out grilles. After a few moments, one of the marshals said, "SUVs are clear of the garage. Motorcycle cops are opening up the street."

"Okay, Hick, we're good to go," Joe said into his mike.

Then, one of the marshals said, "Hold it. We've got a clown at three o'clock."

Gwen backed Jordie into the corner of the elevator. Joe whispered for Hick to wait, drew his weapon, and peered around the open door toward the street entrance where the "clown" was strolling in on foot. Undeterred by the automated red-and-white-striped arm at the ticket dispenser, he went around it without breaking stride.

He had on a maroon hoodie, sunglasses with blue lenses, several strands of Mardi Gras beads, and was laughing into the cell phone held against his ear.

"Shit." One of the marshals relaxed his obvious tension. "It's Kinnard."

No sooner had he recognized Kinnard than an undercover policeman and a man in uniform rushed into the garage. "He's ours," the marshal called out to them. "We got it covered in here." They waved and retreated.

"Good to go, Hick," Joe said into the mike.

Kinnard dropped the pretense and pocketed his cell phone. He pushed back the hood and pulled off the sunglasses as he approached the elevator.

Joe said, "You're screwing the plan."

"Bad plan. Where's Jordie?"

Joe motioned into the elevator. Coming abreast of it, Kinnard looked inside and acknowledged her with a nod, then asked Joe, "Where's Hickam?"

"On his way. You have an alternate plan?"

"You ride shotgun. Gwen and I will flank Jordie in the backseat." He looked toward the entrance. "If I waltzed in here, Panella can."

"The officers were hot on your heels."

"Yeah, but..." He gave the garage a visual sweep. "It's dicey."

"Panella's too slick to walk into—"

"But he might send another Mickey Bolden, who's desperate for money and has nothing to lose by trying. Where the *fuck* is Hickam?"

"He should be here any sec."

"I agree. He *should*. How far away did he park?"

"Half a block."

"Half a block?" Kinnard's head came around and locked eyes with Joe.

They held each other's stare for no more than a heartbeat before they moved at the same time and ran toward the entrance through which Kinnard had just come. As Kinnard pulled his nine-millimeter, he called back to the marshals, "Don't let Jordie out of your sight."

When they got outside, Joe yelled toward the two officers who'd followed Kinnard into the garage. They turned and fell in behind them.

Kinnard kept pace with Joe. "What does the new car look like?"

"Like Hick's," Joe panted.

"Dammit, it's dark down here."

"That was the idea."

They spotted the sedan simultaneously and sprinted toward it. From several yards away, Joe saw that Hick was in the driver's seat, unmoving. He came to an abrupt stop, crying out, "Oh no no no *no!*"

Kinnard covered the remaining distance at full tilt. He actually skidded to a halt and banged into the side of the car as he yanked open the driver's door. Hick didn't stir. He was slumped sideways toward the passenger seat. There was blood on his face, his neck, shoulder. The left sleeve of his suit jacket was saturated. His dangling hand was dripping red.

Shaw reached in. "He's got a pulse," he shouted back.

Joe didn't remember until later when he saw the bruises on his kneecaps that he had literally dropped to them in relief. At the time, he'd been fumbling with the mike on his shoulder, shouting into it "Officer down!" and ordering the two policemen coming abreast of him to put in emergency calls.

Within seconds officers came running from every direction. Joe pushed himself up and stumbled over to the car, where Kinnard had his fingers dug in deep against Hick's neck. Blood was seeping through them.

Joe blinked a combination of sweat and tears out of his eyes. "Is he conscious?"

"No."

"The carotid, you think?"

"Fuckin' Panella."

"Is he going to make it?"

Kinnard was about to say something, but then turned his head, and looked into Joe's face, and made a quick edit. "Better have his suit cleaned before he comes around. He's gonna be pissed that it got messed up."

Joe wanted to thank him for that. But his throat was too tight to say anything.

It seemed like forever, but was actually only a few minutes later that an ambulance roared up and squealed to a stop. Joe and Kinnard were pushed aside as paramedics pulled Hick from the car and went to work on him. Before Joe could quite reconcile that this was actually happening, they'd strapped his partner onto a gurney and placed it in the ambulance.

His instinct was to climb in behind them and ride along. Hick might not make it. If he weren't already dead, he might die en route. Joe needed to be there with him. He had to go!

But he was a law enforcement officer, and the best thing he

could do for Hick, whether he survived or not, was to catch the son of a bitch who'd done this.

By now NOPD patrol cars had the street blocked. Others were running hot up and down intersecting streets searching for the assailant. Patrol officers on foot were doing the same. Two homicide detectives in plainclothes isolated Joe and began asking questions.

He produced his ID and described the situation.

"You ran from the garage to look for Agent Hickam?" one asked.

"He was late, which signaled me that something was wrong."

"And you found him inside the car?"

"Yes," Joe replied. "We—"

Joe broke off suddenly and looked around. First responders were doing their specific tasks. Uniformed policemen were holding back the crowd of curiosity seekers who had already gathered behind a temporary barricade. Gwen and the other two marshals were being questioned collectively by plainclothes detectives.

Shaw Kinnard and Jordie Bennett were nowhere to be seen.

Chapter 32

"Where are we going?"

"Just keep walking."

Shaw propelled Jordie across Canal Street. He was walking fast and with purpose, but they were swimming upstream of the pedestrians who'd been lured toward the apparent emergency behind the hotel, the destination of speeding vehicles with flashing lights and sirens.

She and Shaw crossed the streetcar tracks in the median and then had to wait for the traffic light to change before they could cross the lanes of oncoming traffic. Had he not been pushing her along, she couldn't have kept up with his brisk clip.

Without slowing his pace, he pulled off the hoodie and dropped it wrong side out into the lap of a homeless man who was semireclined in the recessed doorway of an abandoned building. The man didn't even look up.

Once on the other side of the busy boulevard, they entered the French Quarter. Even on a Monday night, it was thronged. The busy vendor of a souvenir kiosk didn't notice when Shaw yanked a t-shirt off a rack. It was a flashy purple-gold-and-green-striped thing with a sequin fleur de lis on the chest.

He thrust it at her. "Put this on over your shirt."

He also lifted an LSU baseball cap from off the head of a stuffed alligator and snatched several strands of Mardi Gras beads hanging from a peg. He put on the cap and draped the beads around her neck.

Beneath her shirt, the bulletproof vest was heavy and hot. Another layer would make it worse, but when Shaw ordered her again to put on the t-shirt, she pulled the gaudy thing over her head without missing a beat.

"How bad was Hickam?"

"Bad."

"Do you think he'll die?"

"Probably."

Her breath caught. "We should go back."

"And let Panella get you, too?"

"You can't be sure it was Panella."

"Keep telling yourself that if it makes you feel better."

"We left a crime scene. Joe Wiley will be beside himself."

"I'm doing him a favor."

"How's that?"

"You're one less thing he'll have to deal with tonight."

"I don't think he'll see it that way."

"Me either."

"You could always tell him that you placed me under arrest."

He threw his arm across her shoulders like an affectionate lover, pulled her close to his side, and nuzzled her hair away from her ear. "I have."

Astonished, she tilted her head back and looked at him. The upper half of his face was shadowed by the bill of the baseball cap, but there was no mistaking the set of his jaw. He wasn't kidding. She tried to shake him off, but he held firm, even though he grunted with pain as they struggled.

"You can't arrest me."

"Hell I can't, and if you don't stop that I'll cuff you for resist-ing."

"What are you arresting me for?"

"Lying to federal agents. The others didn't know you were, but I did."

"When did I lie? About what?"

"Your phone conversation with Josh."

"No one would even have known he'd called me if I hadn't told. Everything I said was the truth."

"Maybe, but what did you leave unsaid?"

She remained silent.

"Um-huh. It's that missing stuff that I want to hear, Jordie. Until further notice, consider yourself under arrest." And then he Mirandized her, whispering her constitutional rights into her ear as though they were sweet nothings.

Even though by now they were blocks away from the hotel, he didn't relax his vigilance. While playacting that they were an af-fectionate couple out for an evening of fun, he remained alert and watchful. He jammed his bloodstained hand into his jeans pocket to avoid it being noticed. When a police helicopter flew in low and hovered, he pulled her into a carryout daiquiri place where they stood in line like other customers until the chopper moved on.

Once he stopped abruptly in the middle of the narrow side-walk and let a pack of rowdy, inebriated young men eddy around them and then engaged one of the stragglers in conversation as though they were buddies.

After separating from the group and moving on, she asked, "Do we have a destination? Where are you taking me?"

Shaw didn't answer; she didn't bother to ask again.

She was well acquainted with the city and the Quarter, so she knew that in addition to quickly crossing streets in the middle of the block and ducking into and out of crowded shops, they were going in circles and doubling back frequently.

Finally she asked, "Are you afraid we're being followed?"

"Wishful, actually. I'd love nothing better than for Panella to be on our tail."

"Why?"

"I could take him out and not have to justify my means."

He wasn't kidding about that, either.

They walked for another half hour. Either he grew too weak to continue, or he became convinced that no one was following them. He slowed their pace, and, after taking a final look behind them, rounded a corner.

Different from the noisy, commercial streets, this one was dark and quiet. An elderly couple were walking an ancient-looking dog on a leash. Otherwise the street was deserted.

They had almost reached the next corner when Shaw stopped at an iron gate that led into a narrow alley between two brick buildings, both of which were shuttered and dark. Tiny ferns sprouted from cracks in the crumbling mortar.

He worked the combination to open the padlock on the gate, then pushed it open. The hinges squealed. Jordie wondered if perhaps that noise passed for a security system.

Once they were through the gate, Shaw reached between the pickets and replaced the padlock, then took her hand and led her down the alley, which wasn't much wider than his shoulders. The stepping-stones were loose and uneven, slippery with moss.

The alley opened into a walled courtyard dominated by a live oak tree that formed a canopy over the area. What at one time must have been a lovely garden was now derelict. The vines clinging to the enclosing walls were either overgrown or dead. The cherub in the center of the concrete fountain was missing an arm, and she seemed to be looking forlornly into the stagnant water in the basin at her feet.

Shaw climbed a metal staircase affixed to the building's exterior wall, pulling Jordie behind him. At the top, he worked loose a brick from the adjacent wall, took out a key and unlocked the door, then guided her into the enveloping darkness inside. He closed the door before switching on the light.

He tossed the key onto the top of a bookshelf then crossed to a window-mounted AC unit and turned it on. "I haven't been here in a few days, so it'll take a while to cool down."

Jordie looked around in wonder. The living area in which they stood shared an open space with a compact kitchen, an eating bar separating the two. A door on her left led into what was obviously a bedroom. The apartment was inexpensively but comfortably furnished, the pieces arranged to maximize the limited floor space.

After taking a long look around, she came back to him. "You live here?"

"No. An apartment in Atlanta is my permanent residence. If you can call it that. I'm rarely there."

"Then...?" She raised her hands to her sides and looked at him inquiringly.

"This belonged to my folks. They bought it cheap years ago. We stayed here whenever we came down to visit my grandparents. Mom liked the French Quarter."

"Does anyone live downstairs?"

"Not anymore. A bachelor leased it from my parents for a while, but when he moved away, they—" He shut down as though a switch had been flipped. "Doesn't matter."

"I think it does. If it didn't matter you wouldn't have kept the place all this time."

———◦———

Shaw turned away before she detected just how accurate she was. "I'll be back." At the bedroom door, he paused. "Don't even think about skipping out."

He went through the bedroom into the bathroom. Using liquid soap and the hottest water he could stand, he scrubbed

Hickam's blood off his hands, trying not to dwell on the amount of it he'd seen pumping out of him.

When the water in the sink ran clear, he dried his hands, peeled back the bandage to check his incision, then returned to the living room. Jordie had removed the t-shirt, beads, and bulletproof vest and piled them in a chair. Otherwise, she was standing precisely where she'd been, looking around in bewilderment.

"What?" he said.

"You're full of surprises. That's all."

He headed for the kitchen. "The place comes in handy. I camped out here when I was investigating Panella. I came by here last Thursday before hooking up with Mickey Bolden. Stocked some food and water in case I needed a place to stay out of sight for a while, dependant on what went down in Tobias. Little did I know." He took two bottles of water from the refrigerator and carried one to her.

They both drank, then she asked, "Instead of taking me to that filthy garage, why didn't you bring me here?"

"Too comfy. Too many people nearby. Too many avenues of escape. I needed an isolated and uncomfortable spot."

"In which to frighten and torture me."

"I didn't torture you. But hold the thought. It may come down to that later."

He took the burner phone from his shirt pocket and called Wiley, who took several rings to answer, and when he did he sounded physically beat down and emotionally hammered.

"It's me," Shaw said.

"She with you?"

"I'm looking at her."

Jordie motioned for him to put the phone on speaker so she could hear. Fearing the worst, Shaw said, "Hickam?"

"Alive. Critical condition."

Looking stricken, Jordie sat down on the padded arm of the

easy chair where she'd placed the articles she'd taken off. She'd said she didn't want anyone else to die because of her. That was before Royce Sherman. Now Hickam was another casualty. "Are you at the hospital?" Shaw asked Wiley.

"Just got here. Detectives released me so I could come. Hick's in surgery now. They've had to raid the blood bank. May take a miracle to pull him through."

Shaw ran his fingers through his hair. "I'm sorry, man."

"Thanks." Wiley cleared his throat and took a moment, then he said, "Why'd you run off?"

"Jordie's safety."

"That's a laugh. You and safety don't mix."

"I've also placed her under arrest and read her her rights."

"Really? Why now?"

Looking directly into her eyes, Shaw said, "I've come to believe like you do that she hasn't been entirely truthful with us. She knows more than she's telling. She's sure as hell got Panella worried or he wouldn't be sending her warnings. He hit Royce Sherman for shooting off his mouth. Now the attempt on Hickam—"

"—wasn't Panella."

Shaw twitched as though he'd been jabbed with that propeller again. "What?"

"A security camera caught the suspect walking fast down the sidewalk in the direction of Hick's car. This was just a minute or two ahead of the motorcycle cops who held back traffic. Some gangbanger."

"He's been arrested?"

"No."

"IDed?"

"No. No clear view of his face. He was wearing a hoodie."

"A *hoodie*?"

"Dark color like yours. Detectives surmise Hick thought it was you and lowered the window for him."

Shaw's mind went into a tailspin, but it always came back to how many coincidences it would require for a gangbanger in a hoodie like his to come along during that narrow window of time.

He remembered seeing Hickam's dangling left hand, his expensive wristwatch drenched in blood still strapped to his wrist. "Was anything taken? Wallet? Weapon?"

"No."

"Then I'm not buying it." He knew Wiley wasn't up to a debate right now, but precious time could be wasted on NOPD's erroneous conclusion. "It was Panella," he said.

"Told them that. Repeatedly. The detectives are leery."

"Did you see the security camera video?"

"One of the investigators played it back for me on his iPad." Wiley hesitated. "In the dark, jacked on adrenaline, having just given you that hoodie to put on, it's conceivable that Hick could've mistaken the guy on the sidewalk for you."

"But?"

"Wrong body type. Not nearly as tall as you."

"It was Panella."

"But he *was* favoring his left side. Walking fast but with a limp."

Jordie made a small but startled sound.

Shaw homed in on her. He said to Wiley, "I'll call you back."

Joe sat on the waiting room sofa, elbows on his knees, head bowed, staring at the ugly carpet between his shoes, praying. Sort of. Because he knew that's what Hick would be doing if their situations were reversed and he was the one whose life was hanging by a thread.

"Joe?"

He looked up and saw Marsha, and was furious enough to

want to yell at her, but too glad to see her to do anything except stand up and open his arms. She walked into them, and for long moments they just held each other. He soaked her up, thinking how vital she was to him. Everything about her. Her sassy humor. Her soft, familiar body. Right now, her strength.

When they finally pulled apart, he wiped his eyes, but assumed a put-out tone. "You're supposed to be locked in and under guard."

Although Kinnard had hung up abruptly and without explanation, his insistence that Panella was their culprit worried Joe enough to order police protection for his family. If it was Panella, he'd made the fight personal, and he fought dirty. Joe was taking no chances with the security of his wife and children.

Marsha said, "I had to see you. There's a policewoman inside the house. The kids are asleep and don't know I'm gone. One of the officers drove me. He gave me fifteen minutes." She kissed his face several times. "How's Hick?"

He guided her to the sofa and they sat down. She pressed against his side, fortifying him. "At the last second, Hick must've seen it coming and tried to avert. The shooter missed his head, but got him in the neck. Staff here waited on a vascular specialist to do the surgery. Hick's lost a lot of blood. Officers from every agency have shown up to donate. Even Morrow—the deputy I told you about?—drove up with some personnel from his department."

"On TV they said they were looking for a suspect caught on security camera."

"They're trying to get an ID on him but—"

"You think it was Billy Panella."

"The girl in Tobias said Royce Sherman's killer spoke through a voice enhancer. Nobody had mentioned that to her. How could she have made up a detail like that? And Hick's shooter was wearing a hoodie similar to the one Hick gave Kinnard. Like that was his little inside joke with us."

"How would he know where you had sequestered Jordie Bennett? Or about Kinnard and the hoodie?"

"I've been asking myself that. Only thing I can figure, he returned to the scene of the crime in Tobias. To snicker. Gloat. Maybe he marked us while we were there. Followed us back to the hotel. My decoy caravan didn't fool him. All he had to do was keep an eye on Hick's car."

He thumped his knee with his fist. "He's nervy as hell, and he's outsmarted me again, goddammit. Six months ago, he sensed that Hick and I were coming for him, and split in the nick of time. Am I ever gonna catch this fucker?"

She rubbed his spine. "Joe, don't do this to yourself now. You don't even know for sure it was Panella."

"There's no arguing it with Kinnard. He's certain."

"Where is he?"

"That's another story." He told her about Kinnard's disappearance from the crime scene. "He claims to have placed Jordie Bennett under arrest."

Marsha arched her eyebrow.

"Right." He told her what Hick had said about the steam escaping the hotel bedroom. Her only response was a thoughtful *hmmm.* He knew that sound.

"What?"

"All these people—men—in her life, pushing her around, pulling her this way and that. I feel sorry for her."

"Don't. Not yet. Kinnard may be in lust, but he also thinks she knows more than she's telling."

"What do you think?"

"Same. She's not coming clean about something."

"Panella? Herself?"

"Possibly, although she says no. But she's mama bear when it comes to Josh. You heard what I said to him this morning." Marsha had been in bed with him when Josh had called before dawn. "I intentionally tried to scare him into turning himself in.

That was before Royce Sherman's body was discovered. According to Ms. Bennett, that freaked him out. Now Hick? If we get confirmation that it's Panella—"

That instant, his phone rang. He answered and Kinnard said, "It was Panella."

———

"He had juvenile arthritis." Shaw held the phone out nearer to Jordie. "Tell him."

"He basically grew out of it," she said into the phone, "but it flares up when he's fatigued or sick, even with something minor like a sore throat, any malady that weakens his immune system. When that happens, his joints become inflamed, especially his left knee. It causes him to limp."

"I didn't know this," Wiley said.

"Neither did I," Shaw said. "Neither did anybody."

"Except Ms. Bennett."

"Yeah," Shaw said. "Except her."

Her face turned rosy with anger over his tone.

"She says Panella is self-conscious of the limp," Shaw said. "He's good at hiding it."

"Unless he's on his way to a murder."

"I guess." Shaw paused then asked Wiley how he was holding up.

"I'm okay. My wife's here." He told Shaw about the guards he'd ordered for his family.

"Good call," Shaw said. "Might be even better to get them out of town."

"I'll look into it as soon as I know more about Hick's condition."

"He still in surgery?"

"Far as I know." His voice went shaky. He switched to another topic. "You going to tell me where you are?"

"My own safe house. Panella won't find us."

Wiley sighed but let it drop, probably because he didn't have the energy to pursue it. "I don't suppose Ms. Bennett's heard from her brother."

"No. And she hasn't been out of my sight. Nothing on your end?"

"No," Wiley said. "I figured he'd call in a panic when he heard about Hick."

Jordie must've figured that as well. Shaw could tell by her expression that she was unsettled by her brother's silence.

"How are you doing?" Wiley asked. "Side hurt?"

"It's felt better. I need to lie down. But let me know when you get an update on Hickam, no matter what time."

"I will."

"My money's riding on him making it."

"Paramedics said you probably saved his life by curbing the bleeding."

"Let's hope."

"Yeah." Wiley's voice had turned gravelly with emotion again. He cleared his throat. "He still won't like you, though."

"Nobody does."

Shaw disconnected and replaced the phone in his shirt pocket. "Jordie."

For the entirety of his conversation with Joe Wiley, he hadn't taken his eyes off her. Now he walked toward her with a deliberateness that set off a tremor of apprehension. She had to will herself not to angle away from him as he came to a stop directly in front of her where she sat on the arm of the chair.

"From this moment forward, you tell me the truth. *All* of it."

"Or what? You threatened to kill me, and you didn't. What will you threaten me with this time?"

"Jail."

She hadn't even considered that. It took her aback and left her momentarily speechless.

"Where you'll have no chance of helping your precious shithead of a brother because you'll be fighting your own legal battles."

She swallowed drily. "I haven't been charged with a crime."

"Not yet. That could change. It'll take a while for state and federal prosecutors to sift through everything and determine if you're indictable. Meanwhile, you stay behind bars."

"You couldn't do that."

"You want to test me? Or simply tell me the truth here and now?"

"I have told the truth."

"Not all of it. You failed to mention your vacation with Panella. Three days. Lavish accommodations. Limos. Surely you remember. How could you have forgotten?"

"I haven't."

"Then why didn't you mention it when I asked you about your personal relationship with him?"

"Because there's no such thing!"

"Was there ever?"

"No."

"Never?"

"No!"

"Then explain why you went to Central America with him for three days. To move money?"

"No."

"Why did you go, Jordie?"

"It isn't relevant."

"The federal government thinks it is. *I* think it is."

"*Why?*"

"Because, dammit, I've got to know." He moved closer to her, radiating an angry heat. "Did you ever fuck Billy Panella?"

Chapter 33

———◆———

Jordie's shoulders slumped as she looked into his face. "No, Shaw. No."

He took half a step back, then turned away from her and walked over to another chair, where he sat down, leaned back against the thick cushion, and momentarily covered his eyes with his hand.

Concerned, she asked, "Are you about to pass out?"

"No."

"You should be lying down and resting."

"Later." He lowered his hand. "First I want to hear about that damn trip. If you weren't sleeping with Panella, why'd you go?"

"Josh insisted."

He gave a short laugh. "Josh insisted?"

"You have to understand—"

"Well, I don't."

"I'm trying to tell you," she snapped back.

He said nothing else. However, his steely gaze was unnerving. She left the arm of the chair and moved to a window that overlooked the courtyard. She opened the closed shutters just enough to see between the louvers and looked down on the woeful cherub in the fountain.

"Do you know about Josh's scars?" she asked.

"Scars? No."

"Wiley and Hickam know. I thought maybe during your investigation—"

"The target of my investigation was Panella for crimes other than his scam with Josh. Different division. I wasn't in on theirs."

She turned to him. "It's true, then, that you'd never seen me before last Friday?"

"No. I never had."

"When Josh turned informant, I made the news, too."

"I must've been busy. Or watching pay-per-view. I didn't know about you until I got here and Mickey told me that Josh Bennett's sister was our target."

"In the bar, you decided there on the spot to take me, to use me to catch them?"

"Yes." She was about to turn back to the window when he added, "But if I hadn't had that excuse, I'd have come up with something else. I started wanting you then, and it hasn't stopped." The way he was looking at her left no room to doubt him.

Her heart swelled with a mix of emotions, but she couldn't indulge them. There was too much left to explain. With reluctance, she turned to the window again, looked down at the cherub, and began.

"From the nape of Josh's neck all the way down to his ankles, his back is horribly scarred. Ugly, awful scars."

"What happened?"

"He fell into the fireplace and his pajamas caught fire. He was seven years old. I was nine. It was Christmas morning."

Shaw murmured something unintelligible, but it conveyed a lament.

She said, "You really should repair that cherub in the fountain. She looks so sad."

"Never mind the cherub. Get on with your story. What happened?"

She took a breath, continued. "The morning started out a happy holiday. Josh and I had woken up early and raced downstairs, excited, as kids are on Christmas. We drank hot chocolate while we opened our presents. Mother cautioned Josh not to drink it too fast or he would burn his tongue. After a catastrophe, you remember ironies like that.

"Anyway, after all the presents had been opened, Daddy went outside to check on his hunting dogs. Mother went into the kitchen to make waffles. Josh and I stayed in the living room to play with our new toys.

"One of mine was a Barbie. Josh was being a little brother, pestering me by flipping up her dress, messing with her hair, making fun of her boobs. I yelled at him to stop. Mom heard the quarreling and, like Moms do, called from the kitchen for us to quit fighting, that it was Christmas, that we didn't want to spoil the day by bickering. But Josh kept it up. He grabbed my doll. We got into a tussle over it."

She felt the familiar thickening in her throat and for a moment was unable to continue. She rather hoped that Shaw would grant her a reprieve and tell her that she didn't have to talk about it. But he didn't.

"It happened very fast," she said. "One moment Josh was jeering at me, holding my Barbie behind his back, taunting me, and in the next, his pajamas were on fire. I actually screamed before he did. Mother came running in. She hollered for Daddy, but she also had the presence of mind to push Josh to the floor and throw a rug over him. Daddy ran in, fell on top of Josh, and pounded his back until the flames were out. By then, Josh was screaming, too."

She noticed that drops of water were trickling down the

cherub's cheeks. It appeared she was crying. "It's started to rain."

Shaw didn't acknowledge her weather report. He said, "All these years, you've been atoning for an accident."

"It wasn't an accident. I pushed him."

"You were kids, Jordie. In a tussle over a toy."

She came around. "If I hadn't been fighting with him—"

"He holds that sword over your neck, doesn't he? He never lets you forget it."

Because he was so right, her burst of anger was quickly spent. "No. He never does. What you sensed that I omitted from our phone conversation today? He said that I wanted him dead, out of my life, that when Panella put a bullet in his head, I'd finally be getting what I want, rid of him."

He rubbed his eyes again and when he lowered his hand, he said, "Your parents?"

"To their dying days, they didn't let me forget it, either. Not maliciously. Just—"

"—just subtle but constant reminders that you were responsible for your little brother's tragedy."

"Something like that," she admitted quietly.

"While they were piling guilt on you, they made allowances for Josh. Every rotten thing he did was overlooked, tolerated, forgiven. He—"

"Shaw." The earnest plea in her voice stopped him. "Everything you're saying, I've said to myself ten thousand times. Therapists have repeated it to me ten thousand times. In here," she said, pointing to her head, "I know it wasn't my fault that our family was never the same. Daddy sought consolation in the beds of other women. Not my fault. Mother subsisted on tranquilizers and vodka. Not my fault.

"How they parented Josh after that wasn't up to me, either. Their indulgence turned him into a petulant tyrant. He loves nothing or no one. He thinks only of himself, and believes that he's entitled to a free pass because of the pain he suffered. I *know* all that.

"But I wasn't the one who spent months in agony. He was in the hospital for over a year. He had to endure skin grafts, life-threatening infections, and that was just the physical effects. His psyche was damaged more severely than his body. He didn't respond to child psychologists, clergymen, counselors of any kind. My parents allowed him to be abusive to the people who were earnestly trying to help him, and they undid what little progress had been made by spoiling him.

"Josh behaved like a monster, because that's how he saw himself. When he was well enough to return to school, he was subjected to curiosity and cruelty. You know how mean kids can be."

"Big sis to the rescue."

"Almost daily."

"He came to count on you to fight his battles."

"Yes, and there was no letup. The more I or anyone did for him, the more he demanded. He didn't take personal responsibility for anything. No matter what the transgression or failure was, it wasn't his fault. His life became one huge 'if only.' If only he weren't scarred, he could play sports, make more friends, girls would like him."

Feeling the weight of that unceasing burden to keep Josh happy and on an even keel, she propped herself on the windowsill. "I started out wanting to protect my little brother from further harm and ridicule. Then, I don't know, making up for that Christmas morning became a pattern."

"Until no matter what you do, even to this day, it's never enough. "

A reply was unnecessary. Shaw said, "But you've enabled him to abuse you like that."

"I'm well aware."

"Then why don't you tell him to fuck off?" Immediately he

dismissed his question with a wave of his hand. "Never mind. I understand why you don't. Not even when he insisted you go away for the weekend with his boss."

"Back to that," she sighed.

"Comes around like a bad penny."

His sharp gaze stripped away her defenses until she actually felt exposed and raw. She covered her face with her hands and drew such deep breaths to bolster herself that Shaw spoke her name with concern. When at last she lowered her hands, she still couldn't bring herself to look at him directly.

"I lied to Joe Wiley and Agent Hickam. I've lied to you," she said softly. "I went to Costa Rica to help Panella and Josh swindle several hundred thousand dollars. I don't know the total, but the amount isn't as significant as the fact that I participated in the . . . the con, I guess you'd call it."

Exhaling deeply, he sat forward, planted his elbows on his knees, and pressed his thumbs against his temples.

Quietly, she said, "You were right, you see, to place me under arrest."

He dropped his hands between his knees and looked over at her. "What'd you do?"

"What I'm good at. I hosted parties. Two dinners, one brunch. Served by white-coated waiters in the private courtyard of the villa I shared with Panella. I ordered the food, liquor, the floral arrangements, boxes of Cuban cigars for the gentlemen guests, Hermès scarves for the ladies.

"During the events themselves, small affairs actually, I played gracious hostess while Panella handed out colorful brochures featuring a place that didn't exist. At least not where he said it did. He pitched it as a retirement paradise for the well-heeled and discriminating. He encouraged the couples to buy partnerships in it while the getting was good. Of course, as partial owners they'd get first choice of the homesites overlooking either the sugar beach or the Emerald Golf Course."

"Did you know at the time that it was fictitious? Or were you duped along with the potential investors?"

"That's hard to say."

"No it isn't. Yes. No. Both easy to say."

"I didn't ask whether or not it was real because I didn't want to know. But that makes me no less culpable. I *believed* it was all a fraud, yet I stood by and watched nice people sign their money over to Panella."

"How much was your take?"

"Zero. Nothing. I'm not a thief."

He shook his head in perplexity. "Then what was your inducement?"

"Josh was the first to broach the idea. I was a professional party giver. I knew how to put people at ease, show them a good time, get them to relax. I would give Panella a classy veneer. I'd look good on his arm. Josh actually used those phrases, although I'm sure Panella coached him on what to say. I refused even to hear him out. I told him not only no, but hell no.

"But Josh didn't let it go. He said that his job, ergo his life, hinged on my doing him this one tiny favor. Was it too much to ask? Could I be so selfish as to refuse? And he used the old standby: Didn't I owe it to him?"

Shaw expressed his disgust with a terse vulgarity. She gave him a weak smile. "I'm giving you the abridged version. Josh kept after me for months. I continued to refuse. Then one evening as I was leaving Extravaganza, Panella ambushed me. He said it would be much healthier for Josh's career if I helped with this project.

"I actually laughed and told him that it would suit me fine if he fired Josh, that I'd rather my brother never work another day for him. Then I told him to go to hell, got in my car, drove home."

She paused and stared blankly for a moment before focusing on Shaw. "That was the night I learned that Panella doesn't take no for an answer. He texted me in the wee hours. After seeing the text, I texted back agreeing to make the trip and act as his hostess."

"What'd he say in the text?" Shaw asked darkly.

"Nothing. Not a single word."

"He must have threatened you with something."

"A cell phone video. He had rigged this effigy of Josh and dressed it in a pair of pajamas. He doused it with gasoline, held a cigarette lighter to it, it burst into flames."

Shaw closed his eyes briefly. "Jesus Christ."

"Josh is terrified of fire, you see. Of being burned. I...well..." She scooped her hair off her nape and rubbed it as she tiredly arched her back to stretch. "Effective inducement, wouldn't you say?"

"The sadistic son of a bitch."

"Yes. But it worked. I went to Coast Rica and did my part. On the flight home, Panella reached across the armrest and patted my hand, complimented me on the terrific job I'd done, and said he had some other ideas where I could be useful.

"I thought I was going to suffocate before that flight landed, because I realized that neither Josh nor I would ever be out from under his thumb. Josh was already his puppet, and after seeing that ghastly video, I would always be afraid to call Panella's bluff. If he could terrify me into giving a few parties, what else would he demand of me?"

"To sleep with him."

She leaned forward from the waist.

"He did, didn't he? When you were on that trip?"

"Shaw, I swear to you that's where I drew the line. I told him that if he touched me, he'd have to kill me. And wouldn't that be a mess? If I wound up dead in the villa where we'd hosted parties together, he'd be opening himself up to a criminal investigation."

She gave a small shrug. "I suppose he recognized the logic

in that. In any case, he left me alone. It wasn't about sex, anyway. He'd never exhibited the least bit of interest. It was control he desired, not me. But he never forgot that I said no to him. I believe that's one reason why he hired Bolden to kill me."

Shaw sat for so long a time just looking at her, that she feared he still didn't believe her. Finally he asked, "That was the only time you did anything for him?"

"Yes. Within a month of that trip Joe Wiley approached Josh, and I began my campaign for him to testify against Panella. But if there hadn't been a legal case in the making, if there had been no Joe Wiley or Agent Hickam, I would have done something to get him out of our lives. I returned from those three days in Costa Rica with the resolve to do that."

"What about your fiancé? Jackson?"

"In regard to the trip, you mean? I told him that I was attending an event planning convention that weekend."

"When he called you—"

"He didn't."

"For three days?"

"He had no reason to call."

Shaw looked at her with dismay. "'Honey, how are you? Did you have a good flight? How's the hotel? I miss you. Let's have phone sex and make it dirty.'"

Getting testy, she said, "He didn't see the need to call."

"If you ask me, Jackson didn't keep very good track of his woman."

"Well, I didn't ask you, and Jackson had no reason to doubt me."

"No? Then why did he call it quits at the first sign of trouble? He didn't stick around to see how involved you were, or not. He didn't vow to slay dragons for you or even to stand in the background and lend moral support. No, he left skid marks getting outta there and on to his debutante. In fact, what did Jackson ever do to inspire your love and admiration?" He ended by grumbling, "I don't like him."

She laughed softly. "He wouldn't like you, either."

"Nobody does."

"I do."

Chapter 34

———◆———

Following Jordie's hushed proclamation, neither she nor Shaw moved or said anything. For several moments, the only sound was that of rain pattering against the window glass.

Then he placed his hands—large, strong, beautifully shaped hands—on the arms of the easy chair and pushed himself out of it. He walked toward her in the slow, measured tread that she remembered from when they were in the garage. Except that this time as he got closer, she didn't tremble with apprehension but tingled with anticipation.

Standing in front of her, he took up her whole field of vision. Not that she wanted to look at anything except him.

He said, "Why?"

"Why do I like you?" How best to explain it? After consideration, she said, "Because you don't make excuses for yourself. You don't apologize for who you are."

He reached for her hand and pulled her up. As before, he cradled her face between his hands and tilted her head back. His eyes roved over her features, perhaps looking for a more comprehensive explanation for what she'd said, or for a protest when he nudged her feet apart so he could stand between them.

He bumped her once, then again, testing her willingness. She tilted against him invitingly, and when he paired the notch of her thighs with the erection inside his jeans, the warmth of desire spread through her middle like the finest of liqueurs.

She closed her eyes and let her neck go limp, relying solely on his hands to hold her head up. She whispered, "I don't want to fight you anymore, Shaw. Or fight this."

He dabbed the corner of her mouth with the tip of his tongue, then moved his mouth to her neck and gently sucked the spot just beneath her ear.

"Whatever this is," she said on a waft breath. "What is this?"

Lowering his hands from her face, he reached behind her, up under her shirt, and unhooked her bra. "This is further notice."

"What?"

"I said you'd be under arrest until further notice."

"I confessed to a crime."

"I'm about to commit one."

He slid his hands around her rib cage and into the cups of her bra. He made a sound of satisfaction as his fingertips played lightly over her tight nipples, then he ground them gently against his wide palms before his fingers closed around her breasts, tenderly but possessively.

Want, need, and surrender unfurled in her. Her mouth sought his, and when they connected, each was as greedy as the other. Even though they never broke the kiss, he managed to wrangle her out of her shirt and slid off her bra, and then his mouth was at her breast, sweetly tugging or teasing with his tongue. She slid her fingers into his hair and, for a time, their panting moans of increasing appetite were heard above the sound of the rain.

He lowered his head, resting the crown of it between her breasts so he could see to undo his fly. His rapid, hot exhales fanned her skin as he grappled with stubborn buttons. When all were free, he raised his head and looked at her. "I may be able to make it to the bed. If we hurry."

He took her hand and towed her into the bedroom. Not bothering to turn on the light, he flipped open the louvers of one panel of shutters to let in light from a lamppost down below. They formed stripes of light and shadow across the bed.

His boots hit the floor in two solid thuds, then he unsnapped the buttons of his shirt and pulled it off. From their time in the garage, Jordie remembered the hair-dusted pecs, corrugated rib cage, and enticing line of sleek hair that had directed her eyes to his waistband. But now the goodie trail widened into his open jeans, and the sight of his fully aroused sex stopped her breathing.

He pushed his jeans to the floor and stepped out of them. Then, noticing that she was arrested in motion, he asked raggedly, "You need help?"

"No." Quickly, she kicked off her shoes, unfastened her pants, and pulled them off.

He lifted her by the waist and set her in the middle of the bed, then followed her as she lay down. Even as their mouths met, he pushed her panties only as far as he could reach, then came up on his knees and finished removing them.

His hands skimmed over her breasts, pressing them briefly before moving past her ribs to bracket her hips. He bent down and nuzzled the V of hair, then slid his tongue between the lips of her sex and continued down with it until, by the time he'd parted her thighs and got between them, it was making sweeping love strokes around and inside her.

She gasped his name and reached for him.

He rose above her, entirely male, physically dominant, intent, but his expression was vulnerable with longing. The broad head of his penis probed her, found her tight but yielding. He made a low sound and, in one thrust, buried himself completely. His shuddering sigh became an echo of hers as he settled on her heavily.

"All I've thought about," he said, breathing the words against her neck, "being like this...inside you."

Her response was to clench.

"Ah, dammit, Jordie, don't. I don't want to rush it."

"Neither do I."

"But I can't help moving."

"Neither can I." She arched her hips up and rocked against him.

He groaned, planted his hands above her shoulders, and levered himself up. Then, as he'd promised her, he told her straight out: "I'm gonna fuck you now."

———

After several minutes of lying replete, he left the bed and went into the bathroom. By feel, he found fresh washcloths in the cupboard, waited for the tap water to turn warm, washed himself, and then carried another cloth to the bed where he washed her.

Meeting her gaze as he moved the cloth across her stomach, he said, "Pulling out. Hardest thing I've ever had to do."

"You didn't have to."

"I hadn't asked your permission."

"You never ask permission for anything."

"This is the one exception."

"You're mama raised you better?"

He couldn't hide his wistful smile.

She reached up and touched his cheek. "I'm sorry. I shouldn't have mentioned her."

"It's okay," he said, setting the washcloth on the nightstand. "She did raise me better."

As he was lying back down, Jordie sat upright and gave a

soft cry of alarm. She touched the bandage on his side. "You're bleeding."

A few spots had seeped through the gauze of the bandage and showed through the outer layer. "The incision leaked a little when Wiley and I were running after Hickam."

"Let me check it."

"I already did. It's fine. And even if it was a hemorrhage, you're not going anywhere." He pulled her down beside him, took her hand, and placed it over his resting penis.

"Good," she said. "I like it here."

He grunted with pleasure at the squeeze she gave him. "I noticed you looking before."

"How could I miss it?"

He shot her a crocodile grin. "In my dreams, you couldn't keep your hands off it."

"You dreamed about me?"

"When I was coming out of anesthesia. Really dirty stuff."

"Dare I ask?"

"Not unless you want to be embarrassed."

She laughed and rubbed her nose in his chest hair before resting her head on him. "That night in the bar, I wanted him to be you."

"Him who?"

"The man who called me there."

"It was me."

"Yes, but I didn't know that then. I saw you walking toward me. My heart rate kicked up. But you went past, didn't stop, didn't acknowledge me. I was disappointed."

"That is such bullshit," he said. "You didn't give me a second's notice."

"Oh, I noticed."

"Really?"

"Hmm. I thought, 'Bad boy alert.'"

"What's that mean exactly?"

"Dangerously sexy."

"Keep talking."

She laughed and raised her head, propping her chin on his sternum. "I've said enough. You get the idea."

"I couldn't get enough of looking at your ass. On that bar stool? Oh man. And I smelled your perfume. Made me want to bury my face in your neck. And in your cleavage." Turning his voice smoky, he said, "I think you can guess where else."

She ducked her head shyly then came up and looked into his face, outlining the C on his chin. "Are you ever going to tell me how you got this?"

"One of Panella's guys."

"One you had to—"

"Yeah. He was a knife man. I defended myself with a nine-millimeter, but not before he got in one good swipe."

"My God, Shaw. How can you be so blasé about it? He could have disfigured you."

"He did."

She kissed the scar, then whispered against his lips. "How little you know."

Keeping their lips together, he said, "One thing I know...your thumb is the second best thing that's ever happened to my cock."

"Please. I'm blushing."

"And you blush in all the best places. Come here."

He motioned her up until he could reach her nipple with his mouth. Under the brush of his lips, it hardened instantly, but he worried it with his tongue until he felt her belly quickening against his. He moved to the other breast. God, they were perfect.

So was her ass, which his hands lightly stroked, then firmly gripped when that thumb of hers discovered a tear of semen leaking from his slit and spread it over the tip. "Jesus, Jordie." His head fell back onto the pillow. He didn't believe he could possibly be more aroused, until he noticed her nipples, erect and glossed from his mouth. "Wet looks good on you."

"How does it look on you?"

A tidal wave of lust surged through him as she began inching down his front. She pecked kisses across the center of his chest, ruffled his chest hair by blowing through it softly, brought his hips up off the bed when her tongue delicately flicked his nipple.

Her hair slid across his belly like a veil of silk. When she got even with the wound she'd inflicted, she looked up at him with remorse and tenderly kissed the bandage.

She moved lower and nuzzled his navel, whisked her lips back and forth across the line of hair that tapered down from it. Then her face hovered above him for an eternity. He could feel her breath; he held his.

First the damp velvet touch of her lips, then glancing caresses of her tongue, and, at last, she took him into her mouth.

His erotic hallucinations had been nothing compared to the real thing. Unlike the porn star Jordie of his dreams, the real one was more giving, less expert, and all the sweeter for it.

His hands fisted in the sheets, but after a time, he couldn't help but grip one handful of her hair. Sweat broke from every pore. He growled her name in appeal. For what, he wasn't sure.

But Jordie seemed to know.

When it was over, he pulled her up beside him, eased her onto her back and rolled onto her, kissing her mouth long and deep, tasting himself. Finally coming up for air, he whispered, "I take it back."

"What?"

"Your thumb is the third best thing."

Chapter 35

———◆———

"Mr. Panella?"

"Speaking."

"I know it's terribly late where you are, but you left a message for me to call you an hour before the bank closes for the day."

"I did, and the time doesn't matter. I just got in, actually." Flicking sweat off his brow, he looked over at the hoodie, now lying on the floor just inside the door. It had spatters of the FBI agent's blood on it and would have to be burned.

The banker was saying, "Prior to calling, I took the liberty of checking to see that everything is in order. I noticed that you never requested the two-million-dollar wire transfer which we discussed a few days go."

No, he hadn't needed the two million because Mickey Bolden's recruit had turned out to be a cop!

Shaw Kinnard hadn't kidnapped Jordie from that bar. He'd *saved* her. All that bargaining and squeezing him for more money? Bullshit. Kinnard wounded, captured, and in custody? More bullshit.

"Mr. Panella? About the wire transfer...?"

347

"Yes, right, sorry, I was distracted."

He'd been hoodwinked. By Shaw Kinnard, who'd finagled a new deal for a hit he never intended to carry out. By FBI Agent Joe Wiley, who'd told him that Kinnard had been arrested.

He hated being had.

If he hadn't been in Tobias today, he might not have discovered the ruse. But he'd been drawn back to the town to enjoy firsthand the chaotic aftermath of Royce Sherman's murder. Of course, he hadn't gone near the side road where he'd shut up that redneck loudmouth for good, but he'd picked a spot in which he could remain out of sight while observing the comings and goings at the busy sheriff's office annex.

He'd recognized the girl when she arrived. She was wearing the same clothing she'd had on the night before while being pawed by Sherman. Today she had looked a wreck, crying her heart out, needing the supporting arm of a friend as she stumbled into the building.

No doubt she was grateful to be alive and equally fearful that he would decide he shouldn't have left a witness and would come after her. He couldn't be bothered. She would never be able to identify him. The electrolarynx could be implicating, he supposed, but since anybody could get one, that would never hold up in court.

Not that he would be caught or brought to trial.

He hadn't been all that surprised when Agents Wiley and Hickam joined the party. Like good lawmen everywhere they would have connected dot A to dot B and concluded that there were coincidences, and then there were *bizarre* coincidences, and that the murder of Royce Sherman qualified as the latter.

What had come as a shock—and more of one than he was willing to admit—was seeing Kinnard climb out of the backseat of their unmarked sedan. Anyone giving him only a passing glance might have missed the sharp cheekbones beneath the silly sunglasses.

However, if one was looking closely, Kinnard was recognizable from his mug shot, which had been shown on TV. He was accused of being the abductor from whom Jordie Bennett had been rescued. He was the alleged slayer of Mickey Bolden.

But he hadn't been shuffling along in an orange jumpsuit and leg irons, a prisoner. No, he'd been wearing cowboy boots and a hoodie. Despite the outfit, he was obviously very much a part of the law enforcement team.

Well, fuck me.

The group had stayed inside the annex for approximately an hour. When they piled into the sedan and left Tobias, he'd followed them back to the city, figuring they would eventually lead him to Jordie. Because trickery or no trickery, he still had every intention of killing her. The fact that he'd been made a chump only heightened his resolve.

The feds' car pulled into the parking garage of a multistoried hotel. The Panella Investments Group had once hosted a seminar in one of its conference rooms, so he knew its general layout. Recognizing both the unique challenges and opportunities that a busy hotel presented, he drove past the entrance to the garage and parked in another lot several blocks over.

Returning on foot, he took an idea from the FBI and bought a hoodie at a souvenir walk-up. He kept his head down and melded with the ebb and flow of foot traffic on the sidewalks surrounding the hotel while monitoring the maw of the parking garage.

At dusk, three official-looking SUVs caravanned into it. Soon after that, the police presence increased around the hotel—men in uniform as well as undercover officers. (Did they really think they would fool him?)

Something was about to happen. He'd considered retrieving his car. If they transported Jordie in one of the SUVs, he would need his car in order to follow them. But if he were gone even for a few minutes, he might miss the big event.

While still debating, he spotted the handsome black agent emerging from the hotel's parking garage on foot, carrying a pair of duffel bags. The agent crossed the street then turned and struck off down the sidewalk toward a waiting car. Not the one they'd taken to Tobias.

It was like a gift! Only a coward or a fool wouldn't have acted on it. Why not seize an opportunity to underscore that if you messed with Billy Panella, you did so at great personal risk?

He slipped from his hiding place between two buildings and moved along the sidewalk. As he approached the car, the agent was deceived by the hoodie. He'd actually lowered the car window. Last thing he said was, "Kinnard, what the hell are you—"

Phfft!

Smiling into the phone now, he wondered what the Asian banker would think of the coup he'd pulled off tonight. Who needed hired help? "I didn't request the wire transfer because I didn't need the funds after all."

"I see."

He didn't see, of course. He didn't have an effing clue.

"I hope you're not unhappy with our service."

He reveled in the man's deferential tone. Everyone wanted to keep Billy Panella pacified. "I contracted men to do a job. They turned out to be incompetent and untrustworthy. The job wasn't completed, but your bank's service wasn't an issue."

"Splendid. I'm glad to hear that." He paused. "What service may I perform for you today?"

What was this guy, a whore? Well, in a manner of speaking, he was. Which was why it was going to crush him to hear this.

"I want you to close all my accounts."

"I'm sorry?"

He adjusted the electrolarynx. "I want you to close all my accounts. Subtract whatever service charges apply, then withdraw every last cent."

"I don't understand."

"I'm moving these funds to another financial institution. Is that clarifying enough?"

The guy seemed to have swallowed his golden tongue. Seconds passed.

"Are you still there?"

"Yes, Mr. Panella. I'm just—"

"Can you handle this request, or do I need to speak with your superior?"

"No, I'll handle it."

"Thank you."

Obviously flustered, the banker asked for the details of where the funds were to be transferred. In the background, his computer keys were clicking. "And your password, please?"

He gave it.

More keyboard clicking. "Thank you, Mr. Panella."

"You're welcome." It had been such a successful twenty-four hours, he felt like being expansive. "Let me say, this isn't a reflection on you. It's been a pleasure doing business with you. I like your accent. Very classy, very—"

"Excuse me. I need the second password."

"What?"

"Jordan Bennett's password?"

Jordan Bennett's password? Had he heard right? "What are you talking about?"

"After opening the account where the lion's share of your funds were deposited, you contacted me a few days later and stipulated that two passwords be required to access that particular account. Yours and Jordan Bennett's."

He had done no such thing!

"Had you forgotten making that stipulation, Mr. Panella?"

Bloody fucking shit!

Chapter 36

The phone on the nightstand vibrated, waking them. Shaw disentangled from Jordie, reached for his cell, and answered.

She could hear Joe Wiley through the speaker. "Hick survived the surgery. He's in ICU. Holding his own, but, you know...it could still go either way."

"Good so far, though," Shaw said. "How are you?"

"Cross-eyed tired, but I'm gonna hang around."

"Keep me posted."

Shaw was about to click off when Wiley said, "Ms. Bennett still hasn't been out of your sight?"

Shaw placed his hand on her hip which was snug up against his groin. "No."

"Hmm."

"What?"

Wiley brought up the concern he'd expressed earlier. "The attempt on Hick has been on the news. I expected we'd hear from Josh in full freak-out mode."

"No way he can reach Jordie without our knowing," Shaw reminded him.

"True, but he hasn't even tried. And he knows he can call me."

"He's scared is all. Don't borrow trouble."

Jordie got the impression that Shaw was saying that as much for her benefit as for Joe Wiley's.

"Maybe he'd be spurred to call if we leaked to the media that she's under arrest."

Shaw didn't comment on that.

Wiley cursed. "You've breached ethics, haven't you?"

"Let me know if Hickam takes a turn. Either way."

Again Shaw started to hang up, and again Wiley stopped him. "Kinnard?"

"What?"

"I want Panella—"

"Me too."

"—dead."

Shaw's lips thinned into a grim line. "Even if I breach ethics?"

Wiley's response was to disconnect.

After replacing the phone on the nightstand, Shaw lay on his back, placed his left hand over his bandage, and gazed thoughtfully at the ceiling.

Jordie reached across him and stroked his hand resting on the bandage. "Does it hurt?"

"No."

"Liar."

He gave her a crooked smile. "I might've busted some stitches during that last go-round. All that back bowing. It was still worth it."

She smiled and laid her cheek on his chest. "You've never said, but I hope you're not married."

"A little late to be asking, but no."

"Ever?"

"It lasted less than two years. She liked me okay, I think, but she hated my job. I came home from an assignment, and she had moved out."

"Did you go after her?"

"She made the better choice. For both of us."

"Children?"

"No."

"All of that's true?"

"Scout's honor."

She gently plucked strands of his chest hair. "Of all the lies you've told me—"

"Part of the job."

"I know. But what I want most to be untrue is what you told me about your parents and how they died."

His body tensed, but he didn't say anything.

"You told me that you'd followed in your dad's footsteps."

"I don't want to talk about this, Jordie."

"I didn't want to talk about Josh."

He hesitated, then said, "All right. Fair enough. About following in Dad's footsteps, that's true. He wore a badge and carried a gun. Tough when he had to be. Bad guys hated to see him coming. Good guys looked up to him."

"FBI?"

"Local police department."

"Where?"

"If I tell you, I'll have to kill you."

She let that pass. "Your mother wasn't happy when you chose the same career path."

"No. After forty years, Dad retired without a scratch. Which made her think the odds were against me. She was afraid I'd get hurt, or worse."

She raised her head high enough to look into his eyes. "Did they die the way you told me?"

He stroked her hair, ran his thumb across her cheekbone. "You're hot, you know that? Smokin'."

Her look let him know he wouldn't get by with that.

He sighed in resignation. "They retired down here. When their renter left, they gave over the use of this apartment to me and moved into the larger one downstairs. Mom treated it like a dollhouse. Fixed it up. She loved it."

He continued combing his fingers through her hair but was staring blankly at the ceiling. "I could spin it a thousand ways, Jordie, but the short version is that Dad placed all his retirement money with Panella. He and your brother stole it. Forty years of savings, gone. By Panella's standards, it wasn't a huge amount. He never would have missed it. But to my folks it represented the reward for a lifetime of hard work and sacrifice. It evaporated.

"And he stole more than their retirement. He robbed Dad of his pride. He felt like a fool for being scammed. Broke him in every way a man can be broken. He was going to have to sell this place to get out from under the mortgage. When he called to tell me, he was crying, and said the worst of it was having to tell Mom that she would have to abandon her dollhouse. He said he didn't see how he could do it."

He paused, took a breath. "I guess he couldn't. She was asleep, never knew it, but I don't see how he could've done that, either."

"Shaw. I'm so sorry."

"Thanks."

"Don't dismiss my apology with a thanks." She took him by the chin and forced him to look at her. "I'm truly sorry that my brother played a key role in the deaths of your parents."

"Josh is as twisted a person as anybody I've ever heard of. I hate like hell the hold he has on you. But he was only Panella's facilitator. You said so yourself. A brainy one, granted, but would Josh have ever committed a crime if he hadn't been corrupted by Panella? He's the destructive one, Jordie. He's evil."

She returned her cheek to his chest. "I can't argue with that. But regarding your parents, I feel guilty by association with Josh and Panella. I don't know how you can be here with me like this."

"Then let me explain it." He eased her onto her back and loomed above her. "I saw you, wanted you, and didn't give a damn who you were related to. I still don't."

The first kiss left her breathless. All those that came after left her boneless. His lips and tongue were everywhere, a gentle suction combined with a fluid swirl—on the undersides of her arms, the insides of her thighs, behind her knees, the arches of her feet. They mapped her throat, breasts, nipples, navel, and the shallow channels that funneled from her hip bones to her sex. Where they lingered.

Murmuring endearments in the syntax of both sinners and saints, he lavished her with caresses. But before she came, he turned her onto her stomach, straddled her legs, and kissed his way down her spine.

Sliding his hand between her legs, he pushed his fingers into where he'd left her achy and melting, then in graphic detail, talked her through what he was doing to her. It was erotic and exciting and uniquely *Shaw*.

But what finally broke her control was the way in which he described, in ragged whispers, how good she felt to him. With his voice and touch leaving her no choice, she ground herself against his hand, undulating between his chest and the bed until she collapsed.

Before she had fully recovered, he turned her onto her back and pressed open her thighs. Then he was inside her, hard and full and vital, a male mating. He pulled her hands above her head and held them there, but not as securely as his gaze held hers.

His intensity wasn't entirely self-gratifying. He was sensitive to her responses, accommodating each slight shift of her body, interpreting every sound, anticipating what she wanted before she knew it herself.

She wasn't as satiated as she'd believed, because when he adjusted his angle so that each thrust, some slow, others quick, stroked her where she was most susceptible, she arched involuntarily, asking for more.

At the perfect time, he went deep and grafted his body to hers. The rotating motion of his hips was slight, but the pleasure immense. At that spot where they were fused, it collected, concentrated, and then burst, overwhelming her again.

He let himself come, his forehead against hers, his hands linked with hers above her head, his breath uneven and hot against her face.

They rested for long moments before he raised his head and looked into her face. He brushed aside a strand of her hair that had become ensnared in his scruff. She didn't realize her eyes had leaked tears until he sipped them off her cheeks. "I made you cry."

Worse, she thought. *You made me care.*

Neither addressed that he hadn't taken the precaution he had the first time, but as they pulled apart, they exchanged a look that acknowledged their awareness of it.

They spooned again. He placed his arm around her. She hugged it to her breasts. "Am I under arrest again?"

"I'm thinking."

"You'll let me know when you reach a decision?"

"You'll know."

"You'll put me in handcuffs? Tie my feet with a bandana?"

"No need to. You can't go anywhere."

"Fine. I told you, I like it here."

"Good." He pulled her closer and slid his thighs up beneath hers. "And, anyway, you don't know the combination to the gate lock."

Morning came.

By the time Shaw finished showering, wrapped a towel around his waist, and went into the living area, Jordie had the coffee made. "You didn't have to do that," he said as he took the mug she extended him.

"I didn't do it for you, I did it for me. I was in desperate need."

The cleavage above her own towel wrap was a distraction he couldn't resist. He kissed it, then they touched lips, clinked mugs, and sipped, but Jordie almost sloshed hot coffee over her hand when she recoiled at the sound of the buzzer.

"What in heaven's name is that?"

"Someone's at the gate." He set down his coffee and hurried into the bedroom where he whipped off the towel, jerked on his jeans, and retrieved his nine-millimeter. On his way out, he said to Jordie, "Lock the door behind me, and if anybody except me comes back, call 911."

He jogged down the stairs until his incision protested, then took the rest of the treads more slowly. As he approached the corner of the building, he stopped and peeked around it toward the street.

Joe Wiley said, "Don't shoot. But hurry up, let me in."

Shaw relaxed his gun hand and started down the path toward the gate, buttoning his fly as he went. "Hickam?"

"Holding his own. His aunt's voodoo must've worked. Everybody's cautiously optimistic."

"Voodoo?"

"At my request she took the pins out of your dolls."

"Thanks. I owe you." Dropping the drollness, he added, "Glad to hear about Hickam. I mean that."

"I know you do." Wiley motioned toward the bandage. "How's it feeling this morning?"

"Okay. But you don't look so good."

"Tired as hell. Marsha's furious. Said I should be home sleeping."

"This must be important then." Shaw reached through the iron pickets and dialed the combination, then unlatched the lock. He let Wiley through, then locked it back. "What's up?"

"She inside?"

"Yes."

"Under arrest?"

"No. I got her to come clean about Costa Rica." In three or four concise sentences, he told Wiley about Jordie's limited participation in the scam. "Panella coerced and threatened her. She didn't solicit or make a sales pitch. Took nothing from it. The guiltiest aspect of it is her conscience."

"Okay. I'm willing to shelve that for now and address it later."

"I figured. What's going on?"

"I'll tell you together. It's Josh."

Shaw stopped in his tracks and shot a worried glance up the exterior staircase before turning to Wiley. "Dead?"

"We don't know." Wiley chinned him up. "In any case, you've got to put some clothes on."

They climbed the stairs and Shaw tapped on the door. Jordie pulled it open. While he'd been outside, she'd replaced the bath towel with her clothing. Her hair was still damp, though, and Wiley noticed.

He also didn't miss the twisted sheets on the unmade bed, which he could see through the open bedroom door when Shaw went in to grab his boots, shirt, and the ball cap he'd shoplifted from the souvenir stand.

Wiley declined when Jordie offered him coffee. "No thanks. No time."

"Josh?"

Sensing her apprehension, he dispelled her worst fear. "We

have no reason to think he's been harmed. But we have a possible sighting."

"Where?" Shaw asked as he snapped the buttons of his shirt.

"Bayou Gauche. It's between—"

"Been there," Shaw said. "You have to wade through it."

"It's in the wetlands, which will make the search a challenge," Wiley said. "We'll drop Jordie at the FBI office. Gwen will stay with her while you and I go down there and check it out."

"Sounds like a plan." Shaw tugged on his boots. "Here's your vest back." He passed Wiley the bulletproof vest Jordie had used the night before. "We're ready."

They trooped down the stairs and along the narrow path, walking as fast as the loose stepping-stones would allow. Shaw went through the routine of unlocking and relocking the gate padlock.

As they crossed the street to yet another no-frills sedan, Shaw asked Wiley how he had learned about his apartment.

"Your man in Atlanta. Emergency contact info. I told him you wouldn't mind."

"I do mind."

"I'll take the secret of your French Quarter hideout to my grave."

"You could've just phoned me, you know."

"You have a car handy?"

Shaw didn't answer. The less people knew about him and his life, the better. For him. For them. He'd opened up to Jordie more than he had to anyone in recent memory.

He held the backseat door for her now, then said to Wiley, "Let me drive," and held out his hand for the keys. Wiley hesitated. Shaw said irritably, "You'll be making calls and doing all that Bureau shit. Let me drive."

Wiley tossed him the keys and got in on the passenger side. "Gwen said she'd meet us at the main entrance."

The streets of the Quarter were still asleep, virtually free of traffic except for delivery trucks. But inside the car, the three of them were keyed up and anxious. Especially Jordie. "When and where did this sighting of Josh take place?"

"*If* it was Josh," Wiley said. "But it sounds like him. It was Saturday afternoon at a parcel service drop-off box."

"Where he sent the package with the cell phone inside?" Shaw guessed.

Wiley nodded. "Agents tracked it back to that box, situated on the parking lot of a strip center. They canvassed the business owners. One of them knocks off early on Saturdays. As he was leaving last week, he remembers a guy walking away from the drop box. He called out to him that he got lucky, made it in the nick of time before the last pickup. Something like that.

"The guy didn't turn around, but he waved his hand in acknowledgment. The shopkeeper was shown a picture of Josh taken off the security camera in the convenience store. He said he couldn't be certain, but it looked like the same guy."

"What time did he knock off?"

"Three thirty. Fifteen minutes before the last pickup."

"And three and a half hours after Josh learned about Jordie's kidnapping on the noon news," Shaw said. Musing out loud, he added, "But he sent the package to Extravaganza anyway."

"In desperation, I guess," Wiley said. "He was hedging his bet that you'd already iced her. Like he did when he called me later that night and bargained with me for her safe return."

"I guess." The explanation didn't quite gel, but Shaw said, "At least this gives us a place to start searching for his haven."

"Haven?" Jordie asked.

"He's bound to have one," Wiley said and explained to her why he, Hickam, and Shaw thought so. "A place stockpiled with necessities where he could stay indefinitely. Someplace close to you." Noticing Shaw's frown, he said, "What? You disagree now?"

"No, Jordie's definitely his security blanket. But maybe we're being shortsighted. Maybe he didn't come back to this area only because it represents home. Maybe he has unfinished business in the neighborhood."

"The money?" Wiley ventured.

"That's my theory," Shaw said. "Because if Panella had it—"

"—he'd be lighting cigars with hundred-dollar bills," Jordie said quietly.

"Right." Shaw looked across at Wiley. "She's quoting me."

"Ah. Well, we won't know who has what until we find either him or Panella."

"Any leads on him?" Shaw said.

"NOPD is still convinced Hickam was shot by a gangbanger. They're only halfheartedly circulating the BOLO for Panella."

"Even after what Linda Meeker said about the weird voice?"

"They said that Linda Meeker was a hysterical preacher's kid caught doing a naughty, so anything she said is unreliable, and, anyway, those devices are easily obtainable off the Internet.

"Said a guy like Royce Sherman would have made scores of enemies among his white trash acquaintances, which is no doubt true. Bottom line, they think Royce Sherman and Hick are unrelated cases and remain skeptical that Panella is within ten thousand miles of the Pelican State."

"Skeptical my ass," Shaw scoffed. "Probably some were on Panella's payroll. Still are."

"Come now," Wiley said. "Are you suggesting there's corruption in the NOPD?"

Shaw gave him a wry smile. "You've got locals searching in and around Bayou Gauche for Josh?"

"Plus a squad of U.S. marshals and state troopers. Wish we had Morrow, but it's not his parish. Anyway, I told them to leave no stone unturned."

Shaw pulled in as close as he could get to the main entrance of the FBI building. "Keep the motor running," he said to Wiley. "I'll walk Jordie in."

"I'm not going in."

Shaw and Wiley turned in unison toward the backseat. Jordie's expression was as resolute as her tone. Further evidence that she meant business was the pistol she was holding on them.

Chapter 37

——◄●►——

Shaw lifted his gaze from the palm pistol to Jordie's face. "That looks like my Bobcat."

"I was afraid you'd miss it inside your boot when you put them on."

"I was in a hurry."

"I took it to protect myself in case it wasn't you who came back from the gate."

"Smart move. But why are you pointing it at Wiley and me?"

"Keep your hands where I can see them, please."

Shaw complied, actually raising his hands in surrender, which was vaguely mocking.

"I was about to give you the pistol back," she said, "but then Agent Wiley said I was being dropped off with Gwen while the two of you hunt down my brother. I decided to keep the pistol and use it to persuade you that I should go along."

Wiley looked over at Shaw. "This is what comes from sleeping with a suspect."

"She's not going to shoot me."

"She stabbed you."

"But she didn't know then that I'm a federal agent. She knows better than to shoot a federal agent, or even to brandish a weapon at one, especially when she's within full view of the fucking FBI building." As he reached the end of all that, he was shouting.

"Please stop referring to me in the third person."

"You're holding two federal officers at gunpoint, and that's what you're worried about? Third person?"

"I'm worried about the well-being of my brother."

He looked over at Wiley and said as an aside, "Lifetime pattern."

"Enough, Shaw! Put the car in gear and drive."

"I can't do that and keep my hands where you can see them."

"Stop being cute. I'm serious."

"You're really going to do this? Face criminal charges?"

"If I have to."

"The chances of succeeding here are nil, Jordie. Wiley and I are both armed. Raised hands or not, between the two of us we can—"

"You're not going to hurt me."

"Right, I'm not. Because you're going to come to your senses and give me the pistol. Now." He pushed his right hand between the front seats.

She yanked the small handgun out of his reach.

"Give me the friggin' pistol."

"Or what?"

"I'll take it from you if I have to," he warned softly. "I don't want to hurt you, but if it comes to that, I will."

"No you won't."

"What makes you think so? You and me last night? That was a time-out. We're back to business now."

That smarted, but she stayed focused. "You won't do anything—"

"Don't count on that."

"—because I know where Josh is."

She could tell he hadn't expected that. He looked over at Wiley, and, when he came back to her, his eyes were as razor-sharp as they'd been the first time she'd seen him in the bar. But now they were also glinting with anger.

"You've known all this time?" Then, shouting again, *"All this time?"*

"No." She shook her head. "I swear on my soul. Not until Agent Wiley mentioned Bayou Gauche. Then I knew."

She couldn't tell whether he believed her or not. His gaze was still hard and demanding. "All right, where is he?"

"Drive."

"We're not budging an inch till you tell us where to find Josh."

"I'll direct you to where I believe he might be, but only after we get to Bayou Gauche. Not before."

"This standoff is wasting time, Jordie."

"I'm aware of that."

"You're willing to give Panella time to find Josh first?"

"No, *you* are by sitting here!"

"Shit!"

With the expletive reverberating, Shaw faced forward, dropped the gear stick into Drive, and steered the car into a hard turn. "Feel free to read her her rights," he said to Wiley. "Or are you scared of her?"

Wiley frowned at the rebuke, but turned to Jordie. "Okay, you've got our attention. Start talking."

"You've seen Josh in what you referred to as freak-out mode."

"He comes apart at the seams. Easily."

"Correct. If he's cornered by U.S. marshals and state troopers, who do you think he'll best respond to? Armed officers? Or me?"

Wiley looked over at Shaw. "She has a point. She convinced him to take the prosecutor's deal when neither Hick, nor I, nor his own lawyer made a dent. If anybody can persuade him to give himself up now, it's her."

Shaw didn't comment, but his body language came through loud and clear. He was chewing his inner cheek, driving fast, his fingers clutching the steering wheel so tightly, they'd turned white. For letting his pistol get lifted, he was probably madder at himself than he was at her.

Wiley asked her, "So where do we find your brother?"

"I don't know that we'll find him, but I know where to look. You know the Christmas festival and boat parade they have on Bayou Gauche?"

"I know about it. Never been. Marsha says we should take the kids one year."

"I'm glad you brought this up," Shaw said. "Remind me to book my reservation."

She ignored him. "After the...accident, our family no longer celebrated Christmas at home, so we went the first year they held the boat parade. My dad's elderly aunt lived in Bayou Gauche. We picked her up at her house and took her to the waterfront with us.

"Josh worked at spoiling every family outing. That night he was particularly sullen. Bent on ruining everyone's time. He said he'd have rather stayed away from the crowd. Why hadn't we just left him at the aunt's house? He could've watched the parade from there."

She paused, studying first Shaw's and then Wiley's expressions. Both were skeptical, but neither spoke.

She plowed on. "To me her house seemed isolated. No neighbors to speak of. On the edge of a swamp. Its distance from town was deceptive, however, because the road to it winds around town. As the crow flies, it was much closer.

"When Josh said he should have been left behind, he pointed out to me that from the banks of the bayou where we were watching the parade, you could see the light poles from Great-

Aunt's boat dock. Just barely. But every once in a while you could catch the light from them twinkling through the trees."

"Twinkling?" Shaw's penetrating gaze was fixed on her in the rearview mirror. She avoided his scornful remark and stayed on Wiley.

He asked, "Is the old lady still alive?"

"She died not long after that. I hadn't thought of her or that occasion in years, not until you mentioned Bayou Gauche."

"What became of her house?"

"I have no idea. Dad wasn't an heir, if that's what you're thinking. We never went there again."

Wiley frowned. "What I'm thinking is that it's—"

"A crock of crap," Shaw said.

"—very incidental," Wiley finished.

"Ordinarily, I would agree with you," she said, addressing Wiley's comment, not Shaw's. "But Josh isn't ordinary. He fixates on things. Never forgets anything. If he remarked on her house, even incidentally, when he was a boy, it's still in his mind. Besides, he has no other connection to that town. What else would draw him back there even long enough to send a package?"

Shaw said, "It's so farfetched, it's—"

"It's *something!*" she snapped. "Do you have anything better?"

Wiley raised a hand, signaling for a truce, and asked her if she had an address or any portion of one for the house.

"No."

"That true, or are you just not sharing?"

"It's true, but I wouldn't share if I knew. You'd inform the marshals and everyone else, and they'd get there ahead of us. I want a chance to talk with Josh first." She raised the pistol slightly. "I demand it."

His annoyance plain, Wiley looked across at Shaw, who seemed to have run out of sardonic commentaries. Wiley came back to her. "Do you remember how to get to the house?"

"I was a child and didn't pay attention to directions, things like that. But once we hit town, I think I can follow my nose."

Wiley studied her for a moment, then said sternly, "You had better not be jerking us around, Ms. Bennett."

"I'm not."

"She's not." Shaw steered the car off the road so swiftly, Jordie and Wiley were slung aside in their seats. She managed to keep hold of the pistol as the car skidded to a sudden halt on the shoulder.

Shaw turned to her. "Don't you think I'd notice that the pistol in my boot was missing?" Then he turned to Wiley, who was looking at him agape. "I just wanted to see what she'd do with it. Since she didn't shoot us, I think she's told us the truth."

———◆———

Josh didn't know how Panella had learned about the house formerly owned by his great-aunt. After she died, it had stayed uninhabited for years and had become known by locals as the "haunted house."

When he'd inquired about it, the realtor had been glad to finally unload it. He'd bought it under a fake name and had been scrupulous not to leave a paper trail leading back to his ownership. He had thought it was a refuge known only to him.

He supposed it no longer mattered, though, how Panella had discovered it. He had.

He'd come in the early-morning hours, not at night, when Josh would have expected him. He'd been sitting at the kitchen table fiddling with the box of toothpicks as he was wont to do when contemplating a problem, like what his next move should be, when suddenly the back door was thrust open and Panella had stormed in.

Josh had nearly wet himself.

"You double-crossing motherfucker. Did you really think you'd get away with this?"

It was a rhetorical question. Panella had hauled him out of his chair with such force, his teeth snapped together, catching his tongue between them. He tasted his own blood. Panella threw him against the wall and held him there, his left hand pressing Josh's Adam's apple, vowing that if Josh didn't tell him what he needed to know, he would suffer hours of medieval-caliber torture before being allowed to die.

Now Josh's gaze moved from the man's unblinking eyes, to the pinkie ring that glittered from his left hand, and finally to the pistol held in his right.

Josh needed to pee, wanted to cry, wanted to tear out his hair in outrage, pitch a fit to end all fits. He'd been so close...so *close* to getting away. Now things weren't looking too good for his future, immediate, or long range.

"That banker must be mistaken," he said. "A password for Jordan Bennett? For *Jordie?* Why would she have a password to your account?"

Panella just stared. His expression never changed.

"Maybe it's her company name. Extravaganza. That could be it. No, that's probably too long. And passwords often require a combination of numerals and letters, don't they? They're usually case sensitive, too. Upper. Lower. Maybe her birthday? Her birthday backward? Our mother's maiden name?"

Realizing that he was babbling, he stopped, huffed several breaths to stave off hyperventilation, and tried to stop the pending onslaught of crippling anxiety. But he looked into Panella's face, and the panic attack roared toward him like an unstoppable freight train.

He had to produce that password.

Chapter 38

———◦⟨◉⟩◦———

With only a few miles remaining until they reached Bayou Gauche, Shaw, Wiley, and Jordie discussed terms.

The two men agreed to hold off notifying the law enforcement teams already conducting a search for Josh for the reason specified—that Jordie held more sway over her brother than anyone.

"The less pressure he feels, the better our chances that he'll see reason and surrender," she told them.

Addressing Wiley, Shaw backed her. "Besides, if we get a bunch of eager beaver lawmen hopped up before we even know that there *is* a house and that Josh is *there*, then my cover's blown for no good reason, and you look like an idiot for believing in a tale about twinkling lights spun by the fugitive's sister."

"I'll go along," Wiley said, speaking over his shoulder to Jordie. "And you'll get your chance to talk sense to him. But if he doesn't surrender within a few minutes, or does something the least bit nutso, I'm calling for backup. And I mean it. And I don't care if you do shoot me. Got that?"

"Goes double for me," Shaw said.

"Give me five minutes with him."

"Three," Shaw said.

She could tell by his stubborn tone that he wasn't giving on that.

"All right, three. And promise me that Josh won't be harmed."

"Can't promise that, Jordie," Shaw said with all sincerity, "because we can't predict what he will do."

He was right, of course. She wished for a peaceful, casualty-free outcome, but neither Shaw, nor anyone, could guarantee it. The denouement depended largely upon her brother's emotional stability, and that wasn't a reassuring prospect.

"Something else to consider," Wiley said. "We might run into Panella."

"Nothing to consider," Shaw said. "We run into Panella, he gets no more time to surrender than *instantly* before I blow him to kingdom come."

After that, the three of them lapsed into a somber silence like soldiers mentally gearing up for a dangerous mission.

Another grim possibility had occurred to Jordie: Before they reached Josh, he might be located by another law officer. If he tried to get away, he could be wounded or killed in the attempt. She felt that time was running out for her brother and willed Shaw to drive as fast as he could.

But as they entered the town of Bayou Gauche, she was seized by dread and uncertainty as to how the day would play out.

"Okay, which way?" Shaw asked from the driver's seat.

"If I'm remembering correctly, the house was on this side of town and off in that direction." She pointed. "Take a left at the first stoplight."

Just as they made the turn, Wiley's cell phone beeped. He checked the readout. "Hickam's mom."

"Take it." Shaw pulled into a filling station parking lot. "I have some rules of engagement to talk over with Jordie."

Wiley got out and answered his phone as he stepped away from the car.

Jordie, unhappy over the delay, said, "Rules of engagement?"

"Nonnegotiable rules. First." Shaw extended his hand through the space between the front seats.

She hesitated, then laid the pistol in his open palm. "It was a rash move, I'll admit. But would you have brought me along otherwise?"

"No way in hell. Would you have shot me?"

"I seriously considered it when you called last night only a time-out."

"I said that to test you, see what you'd do."

"I realize that now."

They shared a meaningful look, then he gave his head a small shake as though to pull him back into the here and now. "The threat of being shot didn't convert me to your way of thinking. You made sense. If we find Josh, you could be a valuable asset."

"Thank you."

"Hold off on that thanks, because there's something else." His serious tone arrested her attention. "I told Wiley about Costa Rica."

She had expected him to, of course, but the implications were daunting. "Does he see me as an accomplice?"

"He's thinking it over. Reason I'm telling you now is in case you're planning to bamboozle us, help Josh get away, something like that. It would make you look really bad in the eyes of the law."

"I won't."

"Okay."

"I swear to you."

"Okay." He held her gaze for several seconds, then said, "Now...the other rules."

A few minutes later, Wiley opened the passenger door and got in. "Sorry that took a while longer than it should have. The lady is so relieved she couldn't stop talking. Hick's regained consciousness. He's alert. Responds correctly to the questions put to him."

Jordie exclaimed her relief.

"That's good news," Shaw said.

"Not for you," Wiley said. "He woke up mad as hell. Remembered the hoodie, thought it was you who'd shot him."

"I hope somebody told him different."

"He still doesn't like you. But nobody does, right?"

Shaw looked in the rearview mirror and shot Jordie a look. She smiled back, but then her features returned to being taut with anxiety.

Following the directions she gave him, Shaw angled off the main road onto one whose bends were dictated by the winding bayou which it ran alongside. The swampy landscape on either side was a panoply of sameness, one perspective exactly like every other. With no signposts, either natural or man-made, one could get easily lost. He began to doubt Jordie's recollection.

But then she said, "There. On the right."

The turnoff was marked only by a rusty and dented metal mailbox. It sat atop a steeply leaning wooden post that seemed to be relying on the surrounding weeds to keep it from toppling. A quarter of a mile farther along the narrow gravel road, a house came into view.

"That it?" Shaw asked.

"Yes. I'm positive."

It didn't look at all hospitable or even habitable. There wasn't a sign of life about the place, not a blade of living grass or green shrubbery. Even the surrounding trees had been suffocated by the Spanish moss that hung from their bare branches.

"Looks like a haunted house," Wiley said.

"That would appeal to Josh," she said. "He likes video games with supernatural and horror themes."

Shaw stopped the car about fifty yards away from the house, but he kept the engine running as they assessed it. It was built in a typical Acadian style, supported on stout cypress beams, with a deep porch on three sides, shaded by the overhang. The exterior might once have been white, but the elements had stripped so much of the paint that the structure had been left a mournful gray that matched the monochromatic setting. Rust had taken over most of the tin roof. Snaggletoothed hurricane shutters hung crookedly from the windows.

"I don't believe in ghosts," Shaw said. "Which is why I hate that there are so many windows. We're sitting ducks for anybody who might be inside looking out."

"Josh wouldn't shoot anybody," Jordie said.

"Wasn't referring to Josh."

"Panella?" Without waiting for an answer, Wiley drew his weapon just as Shaw did. "No car here."

"I noticed that," Shaw said. "Not sure what it means."

"Maybe it means that I was wrong," Jordie said. "That no one's been here in ages."

"I don't think so." Shaw couldn't explain why he felt that. It was a gut thing.

"I should call for backup," Wiley said.

"No!" Jordie said. "Let's at least determine that Josh isn't here."

"Or that he is," Shaw said. "Sink down." He took his foot off the brake and drove slowly toward the house, then stopped about ten yards short of the steps leading up to the porch. He opened the driver's door and got out but remained crouched behind the door. Wiley did the same on the passenger side. Shaw looked across the car's interior and said, "This is your show."

Wiley called out Josh's name and identified himself. "I brought your sister with me. She wants to talk to you."

They waited in breathless anticipation, but there was nothing forthcoming from the house. Wiley tried again, putting more force behind his voice. "Josh? It's time to surrender. You keep up this nonsense, you lose your bargaining position for leniency."

The clock in the dashboard was a retro analog model. Shaw listened to it tick off another sixty seconds, and when still nothing happened, he opened the backseat door and motioned Jordie out.

"Take my place behind the wheel."

One of his rules of engagement had been that if she came along, she was to do what he said, when he said it. She slid out of the back and into the front without question or argument.

He placed his hand on the top of her head and pushed her down. "Stay low. I'd leave Wiley here with you, but we need to go in from two different directions. Any sign of Josh, the rustle of one leaf, a bug fart, you lay down on the horn."

"If Josh is in there, I'm praying he'll come out with his hands up."

"Me too. But in case another scenario plays out—"

"Like Panella?"

"Like anything. Hit the horn, and then floorboard the gas pedal."

"What about you?"

"Don't wait on us. You get clear. Understood?"

With obvious reluctance, she nodded.

Then he took the palm pistol from his boot and passed it to her. "If it really goes south, this is ready to fire. You've got seven shots. Don't hesitate. Point and pull the trigger. You understand?"

"Yes."

"Will you do it?"

She swallowed. "I don't know."

"Great. You choose now to turn perfectly honest. I'm used to you mouthing back."

She gave him a tremulous smile. "Be careful."

He kissed her hard and quick. "Count on it."

Hunkered behind the driver's door, he looked across at Wiley, who signaled that he would take the front. Shaw nodded and indicated that he'd cover the back. Each took a deep breath, then came out from behind his cover and ran toward the house.

Wiley clumped up the steps onto the porch. Before Shaw lost sight of him, he flattened himself against the exterior wall between two tall windows. Nothing happened. So far, so good.

Shaw dodged windows as he ran along the side of the house, staying close to the wall. He knelt once to look beneath the house, but the crawl space was clear.

When he reached the far corner at the back, he paused and looked behind him toward the car. Because of the glare on the windshield, he could barely make out the top of Jordie's head. It passed through his mind that he would kill anybody who harmed a hair on it. No matter who it was.

He slipped around the corner of the house.

The backyard was a patchwork of bare ground and weeds. A set of tire tracks led back toward the front of the house and presumably the driveway. There was a shed, a detached garage, both derelict, nearly falling down. A rickety wooden pier standing on rotten pilings extended over the bayou, two rusty light poles flanking the end of it.

He registered all this in the seconds it took him to reach the back door. It was unlocked and opened directly into the kitchen. He swept it with his pistol. It was a pig sty. Garbage and empty food containers were everywhere. The sink was filled with grease-filmed, opaque water. On the dining table, in addition to several empty TV dinner trays on which a cockroach was feeding, were a box of wooden toothpicks, a pair of eyeglasses, and a wadded-up lottery ticket.

Wiley came in through the door that connected to the front of the house and shook his head. "Clear." But Shaw pointed out the items on the table. The lottery ticket was a giveaway. Josh had bought one in the convenience store.

Shaw motioned for Wiley to stay where he was to cover both the front and back doors and tipped his head toward a hallway leading off the kitchen, pointing to himself. Wiley nodded. Shaw crept along the hall till he came to a doorway standing ajar. He nudged it open with the barrel of his pistol then rushed in swiftly but silently.

The window shades were pulled, making the room dim. It was minimally furnished. A twin bed with dingy sheets had been left unmade. An oscillating fan sat still on the nightstand, although the room could have used an airing. Dirty clothing was piled on the floor in one corner. Army khakis were among the other articles.

Shaw backed out without disturbing anything. Farther along the hall was another bedroom. It was vacant. There were no footprints in the thick layer of dirt on the floor. The bathroom between the two bedrooms was tiny. The shower stall was black with mold. The stained toilet stank of backed-up sewage. But the sink had been recently used. The bottom of it still had drops of water in it, and a damp towel had been folded over the rim.

He returned to the kitchen and reported to Wiley what he'd noted in the bathroom. "We can't be too far behind him. Or someone."

Not that he thought Wiley had overlooked either of the fugitives, but he wanted to see the front rooms for himself, and going through them was also the shortest route back to check on Jordie.

The kitchen doorway led into a formal dining area, empty except for a light fixture that was dangling from the ceiling by a cord. The living room beyond was also unfurnished, in total disrepair, and provided no hiding place. Planks in the hardwood floor were missing, but none of the gaps was large enough for a man to fit through. Besides, he'd just checked beneath the house. No one was hiding there.

He went through the front door and stepped onto the porch. Looking anxious, Jordie scrambled out of the car. He motioned her back. "This is his lair, all right. He's definitely been here, but there's no sign of him now." *Living*, he thought. He was afraid of what he and Wiley might find in one of the outbuildings. "Stay here."

"I want to see."

He shook his head. "It's a mess. Nasty. Holes in the floor. Unsafe."

"Where are you going?"

"To check the shed and garage around back. Same rules apply. Lay down on the horn."

Jordie waited until they disappeared around the back corner of the house, then came out from behind the car door and started for the house. She told herself that they might have missed a clue as to where Josh could be now, but her real reason for wanting to inspect the place herself was Shaw's evasiveness. What hadn't he wanted her to see?

She pushed open the front door, then paused on the threshold and surveyed the front rooms with dismay. She walked through them quickly and went into the kitchen where she remembered her great-aunt serving her and Josh Christmas cookies and punch.

She was appalled by what she saw now. Had her brother's mental state deteriorated to complete and total madness? How could he possibly live in this filth? Did he even recognize it as squalor?

Realizing that investigators would soon be summoned to collect evidence, she didn't touch anything, not that she would have. The bathroom was more sickening than the kitchen.

The sight of the disordered bedroom filled her with despair. When Josh had finally been released from his year's stay in the hospital, he was welcomed home with a newly decorated bedroom. Their mother had hoped that the surprise would boost his spirits. It hadn't, of course.

The comparison between that bright, newly outfitted bedroom to this sad chamber was an allegory of Josh's tragic and inexorable decline.

She returned to the kitchen. Through the window, she saw Wiley emerging from what appeared to be a work shed, while Shaw was bent down looking beneath a ramshackle pier. He would be upset with her for not obeying the rules.

She returned to the front porch and went down the steps. There she paused to look back at the house's façade and wondered why it had fascinated Josh. What about it had intrigued him enough to make him want to return? It wasn't pretty. It wasn't that large. The design was—

Suddenly she was struck by an incongruity.

Two gabled windows, symmetrically placed, jutted from the sloped roofline above the porch, but the house didn't have a second story. Or did it? Had she missed the stairs?

Puzzled, she went back inside, but it was as she'd thought. There wasn't a staircase where normally one would ascend from the living area to the second floor. She knew there wasn't one in the back of the house, or off the kitchen, because she would have seen it.

Standing in the center of the floor between the living room and dining area, she made a slow pivot. Taking in architectural details she hadn't paid attention to before, she noticed a narrow doorway in the corner of the dining room, concealed by its fit into the paneling and wainscoting.

The hair on the back of her neck stood on end.

She should alert Shaw.

Instead, she went over to the door and pushed it inward.

The smell hit her. Hard.

She covered her nose and mouth, as much to stifle her sob as to keep her from breathing the odor. Swallowing fear and dread, she gave the door a firmer push. It opened wider to reveal a steep staircase. "Josh?" Breathing swiftly through her mouth, she called again, "Josh? If you're up there, please come down."

There wasn't a sound except for the beating of her heart.

Above her, sunlight shone in through the two windows so she could see to climb the stairs. The higher she got, the brighter the light became. It filled the attic at the top of the stairs with inappropriately cheery light, because the only thing in the space was a black body bag, zipped closed, lying on the floor.

"Oh, Jesus. Oh no!" She slumped against the doorjamb, covered her mouth again to stifle her keening sounds, and stared at the bag. She squeezed her eyes shut, hoping against hope that when she opened them, it would be gone.

It wasn't, of course.

She should alert Shaw.

But she owed Josh this one final penitence.

On rubbery legs she walked to the bag and knelt down beside it. Her hand shook as she took hold of the metal tab and unzipped the bag all the way down, then spread it open.

She screamed. Or would have.

Except that a hand was clamped hard over her mouth from behind and an eerie, overamplified, horribly distorted voice said, "Guess who?"

Chapter 39

———◆———

As Shaw and Wiley walked from the pier back toward the house, Wiley mopped sweat off his forehead with his sleeve. "I was afraid we'd find his body or a grave in one of those buildings."

"Crossed my mind."

"Your side hurt?"

"Yeah."

"There's blood on your shirt."

Shaw seemed not have heard that. He was distracted, his brow creased with concentration. "You called this in?"

"They're on their way. We gotta keep them from trampling those tire tracks. If we get a cast, maybe we can type Josh's car."

Without breaking stride, Shaw looked toward the house. "See that it's done quickly, then let's get everybody out of sight. We should lay an ambush. Didn't look like he cleared out for good, did it? He left clothes behind. His glasses."

"Maybe he didn't leave of his own volition," Wiley said. "Maybe he was removed."

"By Panella, you mean?"

"Exactly."

"Maybe," Shaw said thoughtfully. "But nothing indicates that a fight took place."

"Hard to tell. The place is a shambles."

"I know, but..."

"What?" Wiley prodded.

"I don't know. Something keeps bothering me."

"Heat's bothering me," Wiley mumbled, blotting his forehead again. "What's bothering you?"

"I can't quite pull it up." He slowed. Wiley paused with him. Shaw said, "The first time I talked to Panella was on Saturday afternoon. Called him on Mickey's phone to begin the negotiation of a new deal. That was around two o'clock."

"Okay."

"That same afternoon around three thirty, Josh shipped Jordie a cell phone."

He turned to stare hard at Wiley, but Wiley got the impression that Shaw wasn't seeing him at all, but rather a puzzle with one vital piece missing.

Suddenly Shaw said, "Those devices are easily obtainable off the Internet."

"Pardon?"

"That's what you said. Earlier today." He whipped his gaze back to the house, then his long strides started eating up the distance back to it. By the time Wiley caught up to him, he was pushing through the back door.

"What are you thinking?" Wiley asked as he followed him through the kitchen and into the dining room.

"Josh wasn't hedging his bet when he mailed that phone. He *knew* Jordie was alive. An hour and a half earlier, he'd heard her shout through the speaker of the phone."

By now they'd reached the porch. Shaw drew up short and, in the instant that Wiley saw the empty driver's seat, Shaw said, "Oh, fuck me." He drew his pistol. "Search the house," he shouted as he leaped over the steps, landed hard on the ground below, and took off running.

Wiley spun around and ran back into the house. The first thing he noticed was the opening in the corner of the dining room. He ran toward it, saw the staircase and bolted up it.

Nearly gagging on the smell, he topped the stairs and saw the open body bag on the attic floor.

Inside was a badly decomposed corpse. The eyelids were held open with toothpicks. The skeletal right hand was holding a pistol. On the left, a diamond ring glittered from the pinkie.

It was Billy Panella.

Chapter 40

Josh had clouted her over the head with the butt of his pistol. Close to losing consciousness, she'd been unable to protect herself when he pulled her hands together in front of her and secured them with flexcuffs. She'd barely swallowed the nausea rising in her throat before he stuffed a handkerchief into her mouth to prevent her from shouting for Shaw and Wiley.

He had dragged her down the staircase with such haste she'd almost stumbled over him. She wished she had. Of course, he might have shot her right then, ending her life before Shaw even knew she was in trouble.

Shaw.

The blow had left her dazed, her vision blurred. When they reached the bottom of the staircase, Josh grasped her bound hands, pulled her through the living room, down the steps, and across the clearing in front of the house. He then plunged into the thicket.

They'd been thrashing through it for several minutes now. Dizzy and disoriented, Jordie had glanced over her shoulder as she lurched along behind her brother, but already her view of the house was blocked. It was as though the hostile terrain had swallowed them. Shaw had warned her of the swamp's hazards the night he'd taken her.

Shaw.

It was as though she wasn't gagged and had spoken his name out loud, because Josh said, "That numbskull Mickey Bolden sure could choose his sidekicks, couldn't he? He picked a *cop*? Or is this Shaw Kinnard character FBI? Treasury?"

When and how had Josh discovered that Shaw wasn't a hit man and kidnapper?

"Doesn't matter what kind of cop he is," he continued. "He ruined everything on Friday night. What really hacks me, I never got my advance back from big fat Bolden."

Her mind was beginning to clear, but nothing Josh was saying made sense.

"Hurry, Jordie." He picked up his pace, roughly tugging her behind him. "No time to waste. Soon, he and Wiley will discover Panella's rotten corpse. Won't that be a surprise? Sure as hell came as a shock to you, didn't it?"

He stopped and turned suddenly. "Using an electrolarnyx was a stroke of genius if I do say so myself." He removed it from his rear pocket and held it up to his throat as he said, "Even Mickey Bolden was fooled into thinking I was Panella, and you know what bosom buddies they were."

Jordie recoiled.

"What's the matter? Don't like the sound of it?" Laughing, he replaced the instrument in his pocket. "I'll keep it as a souvenir of my stint playing Panella. It wasn't easy, you know, keeping the cell phones straight, which to answer as Panella, which to use when I was myself. Talk crude and tough like Panella would. 'Kill her, already!' Then 'fraidy cat Josh." He changed his voice into a falsetto. "'I'm so scared. Is Jordie okay? Please save my sister.'"

The last of the fog was lifting from her brain, and things were becoming horrifyingly clear. Josh, not Panella, had plotted her death. He was the one who'd bargained with Shaw to end her life.

He rambled about Panella somehow discovering that he planned to turn informant. "I had no idea he knew about the house, but he barged in early one morning. He got rough and threatened me with the most disgusting methods of torture. You wouldn't believe what he threatened to do to me if I didn't tell him everything I'd already told the feds about our fraud.

"But I didn't feel the least bit bad about betraying him. Why should I? I'd done all the brain work. When it boiled down to it, he was nothing but a smarmy front man with capped teeth."

This wasn't the Josh who pitched fits, had panic attacks, and blubbered when frightened. This Josh was calmly detached, and he was terrifying. Frantically she looked behind her again, but the thicket through which they'd just come appeared undisturbed except for a cloud of microscopic insects.

"Anyway, back to that morning six months and thirteen days ago, there he was, holding me against the wall, choking me, growling and snarling, being Panella. He didn't expect cringing, hysterical me to shoot him in the belly. I'm not that good a shot. I went for mass. You should have seen the look on his face."

He turned his head and showed her a gross imitation of it before continuing on.

Shaw and Joe Wiley would discover her gone and come looking for her. She just had to live long enough for them to get to her, because she knew with certainty that Josh's intention was to kill her. He wouldn't be confessing all this if he planned to let her live.

How much time did she have? How long would it take for Shaw to find her? Would she ever see his face again? His scarred, severe, beautiful face.

Josh was telling her that he hadn't had time to dispose of Panella's body before he was due to tender himself to Uncle

Sam. "I had no choice except to bag him up and leave him here, and actually, since I got back, he and I have had some interesting conversations." He giggled. "Of course I did most of the talking. He just laid there, staring up at me. For a change he was forced to listen while I ranted. I loved it. He really stunk up the place, though."

She scanned the surroundings for something she could use to defend herself. Even if the ground were strewn with potential weapons, her hands were bound and Josh was giving her no time to stop. Each time she stumbled or slowed down, he nearly pulled her shoulders from their sockets, jerking her along.

He was still talking. "After I killed him, I went to his house and made it look like he'd left in a hurry. Everyone jumped to the conclusion that I knew they would, that he'd successfully skipped the country. All I had to do was cool my heels for a while, let things settle down, gradually alter my appearance for the day I would escape.

"I took a risk by coming back here, but I didn't want to miss all the fun. The fallout from your getting whacked, that is. I planned on hiding out here to enjoy the hubbub, the media coverage. But, thanks to Bolden's humongous screwup, things took a turn and put me behind schedule on disappearing for good.

"I've perfected becoming invisible, you know," he said, continuing in that frightfully normal, conversational tone. "Nobody sees me because I don't want them to. Which is how I was able to go to the redneck bar unnoticed. I nearly came unglued last Friday when Bolden called and told me you'd walked into the very bar where he and Kinnard were having a drink. That is not your kind of place, Jordie. How'd you happen to be there?"

He looked back as though expecting her to reply. She made pleading sounds against the gag.

He resumed walking and talking. "Never mind. It doesn't make any difference now. I went there Sunday night to check the place out. The loudmouth put me in such a foul mood. That was also the night when Wiley informed me of your rescue. Your *second* rescue. Foiled again. I decided Panella needed to surface, scare the shit out of everybody. *'He's out there. I know it! He's gonna kill me!'* " he screeched, mimicking his own hysteria.

"The black guy? Hickam? He was dropped in my lap, so to speak. I acted on impulse, but it was brilliant. How about this?" He began limping. "I knew that would jog your memory, and you'd tell them that it had to be Panella."

Then he *tsk*ed with regret. "But Hickam didn't die. I should have gone for mass then, too, but I'd done so well with that redneck, I thought a head shot would work. Oh, well, one can't have everything one wants."

He was insane. How could she defend herself against someone who'd lost all touch with reality? And she was running out of time to think of a way. Just ahead of them was the bayou. On the bank was a small fishing boat, apparently his destination.

He pulled her over to it and yanked the handkerchief from her mouth. "Josh," she gasped. "Please? Let me help you."

"Help me? That's a laugh."

"What is it you want?"

Cautiously he took a step back, but was still within a foot of her as he raised the pistol. "To disappear and never have to worry again about people gaping at me."

"Nobody gapes at you."

"Yes they do. You made sure they do. You pushed me into the fireplace and made me a freak show."

Stall, stall, stall. She tipped her head toward the boat. "You intend to escape in that?"

"No, silly. My car is parked just around the next bend. I can make it that far in this boat. You'll be dead, and I'll be long gone before they can catch me. But in order to disappear, I need my money."

He waggled the pistol as though to remind her of it and that it was still aimed at her. "You're the only thing standing between my fortune and me. What's the password?"

"Password?"

He rolled his eyes. "We don't have time for you to play dumb. Give me the password. The second password. The one required to access the main account. 'Jordan Bennett's password,'" he said in a ridiculously tony British accent.

"Josh, I swear to you, I have no idea what you're talking about." She raised her bound hands in appeal. "How could I have a password into an account I know nothing about?"

"You cracked my security codes."

"That's absurd. I wouldn't know how, or even where to start."

He screwed up his face mistrustfully, then seemed to come to a conclusion. "You wouldn't, would you? Even if you'd had access to my computers, which you didn't, you're not smart enough to know how to do something that complicated."

"That's right," she said, grasping at that and hoping to appeal to his pride. "You're the genius, not me. I've never been as smart as you."

"Not even close."

"Because you're so intelligent, you must realize that you can't escape."

He resumed his chatter as though she hadn't said anything. "What I'm thinking now is that if Panella was on to my betrayal, and he knew about this house, he must've gone in behind me and added that second password. He put it in your name, knowing how badly that would irritate me. Yes, that must be what happened."

"No doubt you're right. But that's history, Josh. They'll find his body. The police will come and—"

"Not your worry. You'll be dead."

"You don't want to kill me, Josh."

"But I do, Jordie," he said with exaggerated sincerity. "You made me a monster. You destroyed my entire life."

She knew that to continue arguing with him would be pointless and probably would only provoke him into killing her immediately. "I know I made mistakes," she said with contrition.

"Yes, you did. The biggest one being when you said, 'I'm done.' Remember? There I am, manacled, being hauled away like a common criminal, and there you are, hugging me goodbye, tears in your eyes. Oh such a sweet, supportive, loyal sister. Aren't you wonderful?"

He sneered. "But wait. What's that you're whispering in my ear? 'I'm done, Josh.'" He jabbed the pistol toward her. "You don't get to say 'I'm done.' Not when it was you who ruined me. You'll never be *done*. Never!"

His voice had gone maniacally shrill. Realizing it, he composed himself and said with chilling nonchalance, "In a way, I'm actually glad Bolden botched it. I have the pleasure of killing you myself."

"You're not killing anybody."

Chapter 41

———◦((◦))◦———

Shaw had followed the scrambled footprints into the thicket.

He was no longer under the delusion that Panella was responsible for the murder and mayhem of the past week. Once he had connected all the disjointed pieces, the picture had become startlingly clear. Elements to the case that had seemed not quite to fit before had suddenly fallen into place.

Josh had impersonated Panella, deliberately turning everyone's focus on the meanie, while the stool pigeon duped them all. Shaw would kick himself later over not seeing it before, but when he'd started into that thicket, his focus had been on protecting Jordie from her deranged brother.

Josh was brilliant enough to have pulled off this elaborate charade, but he was also as crazy as a shit house rat. Like all rats, he got even crazier when trapped. Shaw hoped to God Wiley would have the presence of mind to caution every law officer on their way not to blare their arrival. He'd thought about stopping his pursuit long enough to text Wiley a message to that effect, but that would have cost precious time. He'd kept moving.

It was insufferably hot and sultry. Sweat had begun to sting his eyes. It had plastered his shirt to his torso. But he'd kept up a steady pace until he'd caught snatches of conversation up ahead, which meant that he was gaining on them. Ordinarily he would have been worried that his crashing progress through the brush would alert Josh that he was closing in.

But he'd doubted Josh was aware of his encroachment. Josh had been making more noise than he, snapping twigs, rustling foliage, and he'd kept up a running dialogue at full volume. The guy was completely psychotic.

Which had driven Shaw near crazy himself. He hadn't heard anything from Jordie. Was she seriously wounded or unconscious? Josh might have already killed her and was only carrying her body somewhere for disposal.

That thought had chilled Shaw even as it had caused him to sweat more profusely. He muttered a blasphemous stream, followed by a prayerful chant, rage and worry twisting his gut where he'd felt stitches giving way to tension and exertion.

When he realized Josh had stopped somewhere ahead of him, he'd slowed down and had gone the remaining distance as noiselessly as possible. He'd taken a position behind a tree trunk and peered around it.

Jordie was alive! Thank God. She was standing on her own two feet. But her hands were bound in front of her. She had dozens of bleeding scratches on her arms. Blood had run down the side of her face from her scalp and now dripped off her chin.

Her expression was a tortured mix of compassion, revulsion, and terror, perhaps fully realizing for the first time that not even her selfless, sacrificial love was sufficient to penetrate her brother's madness.

As Josh aimed the pistol at her, her face had remained stark with fear, but she looked him straight in the eye and didn't cower.

Shaw had battled a primitive impulse to drop Josh immediately, but that would have traumatized Jordie. He wouldn't do that to her. Besides, the government didn't want Josh dead. It needed him in order to recover the stolen millions.

So he'd blinked sweat from his eyes and, as an officer of the law, assessed the situation with as much professional detachment as he could muster.

Nevertheless, he vowed that if that crazy son of a bitch killed Jordie he was going to cut his fucking heart out.

Now, not too loudly, but with authority, he said, "You're not killing anybody."

Jordie's head snapped around toward the sound of his voice. She gave a sob of relief.

Josh didn't even flinch. "Who's that skulking behind the tree?"

"FBI Special Agent Shaw Kinnard. Drop. The. Gun."

"No."

"If you don't, you're a dead man."

Jordie said, "He means it, Josh."

He yelled at her to shut up.

In his peripheral vision, Shaw noticed motion among the trees and undergrowth on the far side of the bayou. Other officers had arrived and were taking positions. He hoped to hell that if this came down to a shoot-out, they were all good marksmen. Jordie was standing too damn close to Josh.

Josh said, "You really spoiled my plan last Friday, Kinnard. But you can't save my dear sister this time."

"I can kill you. And I will unless you drop the gun."

"Josh, please."

"Better listen to her, Josh. She watched me pop Mickey Bolden without a blink. Last chance. Drop the pistol and back away from her."

"Do as he says. Please." She raised her hands and placed them beneath her chin in a begging motion, then dropped them back to waist level. "Put the pistol down, Josh. Surrender. I'll help you."

"Like you've helped me before?" he screamed. "I don't need your help anymore."

"Please, Josh." Her wrists were straining against the flexcuffs. "Please. I implore you."

"Shut up, Jordie! Just shut up."

"Josh, please don't make—"

"You ruin everything! I hate you!"

Shaw saw Josh's trigger finger tense, then several weapons fired almost simultaneously.

Chapter 42

J oe Wiley was curious. "When did you put the vest back on?"

"When you left the car to take your call from Hickam's mother," Jordie said.

"One of Kinnard's rules of engagement?"

"He insisted." While they were alone in the car, Shaw had made her take off her shirt and put the vest on underneath it. "I thought it was an unnecessary precaution, but if I hadn't been wearing it, I would be dead." She brushed away a tear.

Wiley, standing at the foot of her hospital bed, cleared his throat and shuffled his feet, clearly uncomfortable with the situation. "Josh...uh...none of you had a choice."

"I know."

She had slipped Shaw's palm pistol into her pants pocket when she'd gone inside the house to see for herself what was in there. During her face-off with Josh, realizing that his psychotic determination was to end her life, she'd distracted him with a begging gesture. When she lowered her hands from her chin, she'd managed to ease the pistol out of her pocket.

The shot she'd fired had been one of the barrage that had cut him down.

"The ME says any one of the shots could've been fatal, so unless you really want to know—"

"No."

"I didn't think so. If it's any comfort to you, he died instantly."

She'd missed seeing the worst of it. She'd been flat on her back, thrust backward onto the ground by the impact of the bullet her brother had fired at her.

"I hear you have a heck of a bruise," Wiley said.

"Larger than my fist. The X-ray revealed a hairline fracture." She touched her breastbone. "Which is why they've kept me here for another night. They're giving me pain meds, and I'm still under observation."

She'd been transported to the ER by ambulance, although she barely remembered that. It was probably for the best that her recollection of those hours immediately following the crisis were fuzzy.

In addition to the fracture and bruise on her chest, the scratches on her arms had been treated with topical antibiotics. Two stitches had been required to close the cut on her scalp due to the blow. She also had a slight concussion from it.

Added to these physical injuries were the emotional ones. She suffered bouts of uncontrollable weeping followed by periods of depression that left her nearly catatonic. The medical staff concluded that she needed a few days to recover from the ordeal.

"What's one more night? Better to err on the side of caution," Wiley said for something to say.

She didn't bother to add anything.

It was an obligatory conversation between two people who had survived a catastrophe. They had matters to discuss, but the issues were delicate, and each was as reluctant as the other to broach them right now.

After a lengthy, awkward silence, she said, "Gwen Saunders called. That was thoughtful of her, wasn't it? And Deputy Morrow came by this morning."

"In an official capacity?"

"Royce Sherman's murder was his case. Josh's confession closed it. But he didn't make the visit seem official. He expressed his condolences."

"My wife sends hers, too."

"Please thank her for the calla lilies." She motioned toward the windowsill where now several flower arrangements were lined up.

"They're from both of us," he said, "but Marsha picked them out."

"She must be terribly relieved that you weren't injured yesterday."

"Pissed off, if you want the truth. She said a glorified accountant had no business chasing around the countryside with a loaded weapon."

Jordie gave him a weak smile. "She sounds like a sensible woman." A beat, then, "You told Agent Hickam how it ended?"

"He's on the floor just above you here. Still in ICU, but, yes, I filled him in. He couldn't believe . . . well, none of it."

"My brother tried to kill him."

"He doesn't hold that against you, Ms. Bennett. Josh is the only one accountable for the crimes he committed."

She picked at the edge of the cotton blanket covering her. "He played all the roles well. The spoiled man-child with acute anxiety. The downtrodden employee corrupted by his overbearing boss. But a cold-blooded murderer? I never would have guessed Josh capable of that."

"Or of hating you bad enough to want you dead."

"No," she murmured. "I never would have guessed that, either."

Wiley sensed her rising emotion and didn't say anything until she'd used a tissue to blot her eyes. He then told her about a banker in Malaysia who'd called to inquire if Mr. Panella had remembered that second password that had caused him so much consternation.

"The call came in on one of the many cell phones we found in Josh's house. I asked the banker if he'd ever spoken to Jordan Bennett personally. No, he said. He'd never had the pleasure of dealing directly with that gentleman. He'd assumed Jordan Bennett was male."

"Does that let me off the hook, then? You no longer suspect me of collaborating with Josh and Panella?"

"Your participation in the Costa Rican scam will be reviewed, but I don't believe you'll face charges, especially if you agree to assist us."

"Assist you?"

"This case has been a multilayered tangle and will continue to be. We still don't know everything Josh and Panella did jointly and separately to try and screw not only their clients but each other. Things like those Malaysian accounts could come to light off and on for years."

"Years?"

That was a dismal thought. Had she been so naïve as to think that with the discovery of Panella's body and Josh's death, the case would be over, sealed, and forgotten? When she was released from the hospital, the media would be all over her. She intended to ask Adrian Dover to be her spokesperson and release a public statement that hopefully would satisfy them, but she doubted it would.

She also faced the grim duty of seeing that Josh's ashes were interred. He should be placed with their parents, she supposed, although she had no idea whether or not that would have been his wish.

And, it seemed, she would be cooperating with and even contributing to the government's ongoing investigation. It was little enough for her to do in recompense for her brother's crimes. Civic duty demanded it. She also felt a moral obligation. "Possibly I can help restore some of the losses to Josh's victims." Unfortunately, she couldn't restore what she most wished she could: Shaw's parents.

Wiley nodded, but uncomfortably shifted his stance again. "As to your personal loss, Ms. Bennett, I'm sorry it ended the way it did."

"I'm not." Seeing his surprise, she smiled wistfully. "Before you start thinking what a wretched person I am, let me explain. I mourn my brother's *life* far more than I do his death. What other outcome would have been better or more merciful?

"The indignity of a trial where he would be on constant display, gaped at? Years spent in prison where he would be subjected to God knows what kind of cruelty? No, Agent Wiley, that would have been torture of the worst sort. When I pulled that trigger, I wasn't saving myself. I was saving Josh. I can't mourn that his torment has ended."

"The torment he caused you is over, too. You must feel freed."

"I do. Actually what grieves me most," she said, her voice cracking, "is that I don't grieve him. That makes me truly sorrowful. For both of us."

His look of compassion and understanding touched her deeply and brought tears to her eyes.

Discomfitted by them, he coughed. "Well, I'll leave you to get some rest. You've got my number if you need anything." He turned and headed for the door.

"Agent Wiley?"

He stopped and turned but had trouble meeting her gaze. When he finally did and saw the unspoken question there, he heaved a sigh and shook his head. "I don't know, Jordie," he said, using her given name for the first time. "He pulled a lot of stitches and was brought here to be stitched up again, then came to the office last night and filled out all the required paperwork. I stepped out to grab a coffee. When I came back, he was gone. Nobody's seen him since."

She pressed her head into the pillow and closed her eyes. "Nobody will."

Epilogue

Three months later

Jordie and her Extravaganza staff celebrated the transfer of ownership.

The party commenced at four o'clock when they presented her with a crystal-studded Mardi Gras mask as a going-away gift. They ate canapes. They raised toasts. They said their collective and individual good-byes and swapped promises to stay in close touch.

At five o'clock, she called an end to the farewell party before it became maudlin. "My last official act as boss—former boss—is to send you all home. I'll turn out the lights and lock the door when I leave."

They must have sensed that she wanted to spend a few moments alone in the space in which she'd built her business. One by one, they hugged her and left. Her personal assistant was the last to go. As she swiped at her tearful eyes, she said, "As we were uncorking the champagne, a package was delivered to you. Probably from a grateful client. I left it on your desk."

When Jordie was alone, she went into her private office. All her personal things had been packed and removed already, but the space was still so familiar. She listened to the whistle in the AC vent and noted that the crack in the floor tile was the same length it had been the day she moved in. The window blind had never hung straight, no matter how often she'd tried to balance it. She would look back on these imperfections with fondness.

For the last time, she sat in her desk chair. She reached for the FedEx envelope, opened it, and dumped out the contents.

A heap of camouflage-print bandanas landed on her desktop.

"They come twelve to a pack."

He was standing in the open doorway, one shoulder propped against the jamb, dressed very much as she'd seen him the first time. The pearl snaps on his shirt winked in the late-afternoon sunlight coming through the window with the crooked blind.

She found her breath, her voice. She'd lost her heart three months earlier. "Wasn't it I who owed you a twelve-pack?"

"Was it?" He shrugged. "Who's keeping count?"

Afraid he would see the emotion threatening her eyes, she looked down at the bandanas, picked up one and rubbed the fabric between her fingers. "This supply should last me awhile."

"Depends on what you use them for."

"They have lots of uses."

In a voice husky with suggestiveness, he said, "I can think of several right off."

She stood up and rounded the desk, but that was as far as she got before her knees went too weak to go farther. He pushed away from the doorjamb and walked toward her until only a few feet separated them. For the next few moments they just took each other in. His scar stood out against his scruff. His hair was uncombed and needed cutting. He looked completely disreputable and altogether desirable.

"How did you get past the guard in the lobby?" she asked.

"I'm a fed, remember?"

"Oh, right. You're carrying an ID now?"

"No. I just got past the guard in the lobby."

Naturally he had. She wanted to laugh and cry at the same time. She motioned toward his left side. "How is it?"

"Good. Only pinches every now and then."

She took a swift breath. "I'm so sorry for that."

"I had it coming." His eyes were as incisive as ever as they scaled down her and remained. "First time I've ever seen you in a skirt."

"Shaw?"

"Damn. Those legs."

"Shaw?"

"Hmm?" His eyes tracked back up to hers.

"I...I..." She stopped, then said on a gust of air, "I'm surprised to see you."

"Your sign is gone."

"What?"

"The one on the freeway. Extravaganza. Glitter letters. Fireworks. I came down to get some work done on the cherub. As I was driving in from the airport, I noticed your sign had been replaced by one with a bucket of fried chicken."

"The billboard rental came up for renewal. I declined because the advertising budget is no longer up to me. My former employees pooled their resources and bought me out."

"You sold your house, too."

"Joe Wiley told you?"

"I called him from the car. He said y'all have been tying up all the loose ends."

"I think—hope—that my part in the Panella-Bennett case will soon be over. But for a while yet I may be needed to verify this or that."

"Wiley said Hickam's able to put in half days now."

"He's thinner."

"His happy tailor will get backlogged."

She smiled. "Hickam does credit you with saving his life."

"He'd've done the same for me." He paused, then said, "So you're leaving?"

"After everything . . ." She made a small gesture with her hands. "I have to make a change. Start fresh."

"I get that." He looked around the empty office before coming back to her. "Where are you going?"

"I haven't decided." Then she blurted, "You had work done on the cherub?"

"Oh. Yeah. It would've been cheaper to buy another one. But Mom put her there, and she loved the thing, so I had the missing arm replaced. Also had a landscaping service come in and clean up the courtyard, paint the staircase. It looks almost respectable."

To cover the catch in her throat, she asked if he was going to make the townhouse in the Quarter his permanent address.

"No. It'll still be a place I come back to."

"When you need somewhere to lay low."

He slid his hands into the rear pockets of his jeans. "Actually, I'm not working undercover these days."

That goosed her. "What?"

"You remember the girl in Mexico?"

"Who would die bloody without better training?"

"I said that so many times to so many people that it finally made it to the wrong ears. Or the right ears, I guess. The right ears said if I didn't want people dying bloody, why didn't *I* start training them better? Piqued my interest. But I laid down some conditions."

"Such as?"

"No relocation to Quantico. I'd get final say on accepting or rejecting a candidate, and I'd be a hard-ass because I'd be teaching them stuff that's not in the handbook."

"And?"

"No bureaucrat looking over my shoulder and harping about

policy or proper procedure. I won't have my methods second-guessed by someone who's never wallowed in the gutter with the Panellas of the world."

"And?"

"No necktie or haircut like Wiley's. That would have been the real deal breaker."

"What did they say?"

He raised a shoulder. "They said, 'You got it.'"

"They must value what you have to offer."

"Galled Hickam no end. Anyhow, I'm working out of a facility near Atlanta, the location of which is classified. Of course most of the training takes place outside the classroom."

"That sounds exciting. Will you be—"

"Jordie?"

"What?"

"Enough of this shit."

He was on her in an instant, his hands clasped around her head, his mouth on hers. They kissed with such heat and hunger that she was surprised when he ended it way too soon. "Jordie, when it all went down, I had to walk away. I—"

"I know."

"I was still undercover. It was about to become a zoo."

"I understand that. I do."

"You weren't seriously injured. I made Wiley swear to that on the heads of his children. So after completing all the official BS, I split."

"And stayed away," she said in a voice that was unexpectedly husky with emotion.

His regret plain, he sighed. "Yeah, I did."

"Why?"

He looked away, took a breath, came back to her. "Because I didn't know how you felt about Josh and the way it ended. My bullet took him out."

"They don't know which—"

"I do. He didn't feel it or any that came after. I couldn't stand to see you hating me for that."

"I don't."

He clasped her head tighter between his hands. "You need to know this. You need to *accept* it. If I had it to do over again, I still wouldn't hesitate. I would do—"

She laid her fingers vertically against his lips. "I would do it over again, too. It ended the way it had to. Josh was liberated, and so was I."

"Wiley told me that was your feeling."

"To the bottom of my soul."

"Years from now you won't—"

"No."

He searched her face and seemed satisfied that she was speaking honestly. Then his expression turned wry. "Then Wiley—who's like an old woman busybody—said that as long as I was in the neighborhood, I might want to touch base with you."

She looped her arms around his neck. "Remind me to send him a bottle of wine. *Fine* wine."

"I want to touch base, all right. Especially third." He slid his hands to her bottom and brought her up against him. They kissed again and when he at last raised his head, the sharp eyes she loved speared into hers. "They throw fancy parties in Atlanta. I've never been to one, but that's my understanding."

"That sounds like a promising market. Certainly worth exploring."

"I've been giving thought to upgrading my accommodations. You know, buy some furniture. A kitchen stove."

She laughed.

He smiled, but then turned serious. "Jordie. I was lousy at this before, and I may still be lousy at it. But I don't want to spend the rest of my days wondering about what might have been with you. With us. I for damn sure don't want to spend another night without you. I already formed the habit of you. I want you in my bed and under me every night. Even if it means tying you up with those hankies and hauling you off like I did before."

She kissed the C-shaped scar on his chin. "What if I want *you* under *me*?"

He grinned, swept his thumb across her lower lip, and just before kissing it, whispered, "Still mouthy."